BLOOD
ROSES

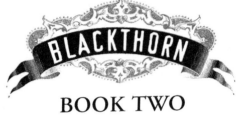

BOOK TWO

LINDSAY J. PRYOR

Bookouture

Published by Bookouture

An imprint of StoryFire Ltd.
Carmelite House
50 Victoria Embankment
London EC4Y 0DZ

www.bookouture.com

ISBN: 978-1-909490-03-1

BLOOD
ROSES

For Moth

With very special thanks to:

Anita and Christine
For keeping your faith in this story ever since New Voices.

Lesley and Rhyannon
For helping me believe I could do this.

My amazing team of supporters, especially:
Tracey, Fiona C, Kelly, Aimee, Fiona W, Jane, Linzi, Tima and Incy.

And not forgetting Oliver/Bookouture for continuing to believe in this
series and making this such a fantastic journey.

Chapter One

It was the last place on earth Leila should have been. The thought of what she was about to do sickened her to her soul. She was supposed to kill vampires, not save them. Those were the rules. That was the lore.

But then again, the lore never accounted for wayward younger sisters.

Leila stepped out of the car and into the darkness of the dank alleyway. The breeze swept her hair from her shoulders, wafted the hem of her dress against her thighs. If she'd had time to go home and change, she would have put something more suitable on – something that may have at least made her feel a fraction less vulnerable.

Clutching the straps of her rucksack, she scanned the several storeys looming above, rain trickling down the dreary walls. Yells echoed down from the road, suppressed by the low monotonous beat of trance music vibrating through the open fire-exit doors ahead. The air in Blackthorn felt alien in its density, its toxicity. Her head buzzed as if she'd just taken off on the runway but hadn't yet reached that comfortable height. She couldn't just see the darkness – she could feel it.

It was the final confirmation that she was making the worst mistake of her life.

A mistake she'd had no choice in making.

Alisha had been missing for days but, based on her track record, it still wasn't long enough for the authorities to act.

Sleep-deprived, sick with worry and brimming with fury at the possibility of her youngest sister's ongoing nonchalance towards her feelings, Leila had stayed behind for another late night at work rather than face the flat alone. But as soon as darkness had arrived in Summerton, so had the call.

'Lei, it's me.'

Despite the flood of relief, irritation had won out. 'Alisha? Where the hell are you? I've been going out of my mind! Four days! Four days and not a single call! You know how it's been. Have you any idea—'

'Leila, just shut up for a minute. Please. I need you to listen to me.'

In that instant she'd known something was horribly wrong. Whether it had been the uncharacteristic strain in Alisha's tone or that gravel effect she only got after crying, one thing was for certain – this was not like the other times.

'I need your help,' Alisha had said, seemingly biting back the tears – tears of desperation that had been verging on panic. And Alisha never panicked. Ever.

'Okay,' she'd said, softening her tone. 'Take it easy, Alisha. What is it? What's wrong? Are you hurt?'

'No. No, I'm okay.'

Leila had held her breath at her sister's hesitation.

'But I need you to do something for me,' Alisha had added. 'You know the purification book – the one Grandfather gave you?'

Tendrils of unease had squeezed. 'What about it?'

'I need it.'

'What do you mean you need it? For what?'

'I'm in serious trouble, Lei.'

Something heavy had formed in the pit of her stomach. Every tiny hair on the back of her neck had stood on end. Already two steps ahead of what her sister was about to say, she'd backed out of earshot into the depths of the library's storeroom. 'Where are you?'

'I'm in Blackthorn.'

Hearing it slip from Alisha's lips had been the equivalent to a punch in the chest. The same feeling of sickness had encompassed her as when she'd been told the search for Sophie had been abandoned – that their sister had been gone too long.

She'd instinctively switched to a tense whisper. 'What the *hell* are you doing there?'

'I'll explain later, but I need you to come here and bring the book with you.'

In the dense silence of the storeroom, Leila had slumped into a nearby chair before her legs had given way.

'Leila? Lei, are you there?'

'What on earth have you got yourself into this time, Alisha?'

'Tell me you're coming. Please.'

'I want to know what's going on.'

There had been an excruciating moment of silence. 'Someone needs a purification.'

Leila had already known the answer, but still she'd asked the question. 'Someone?'

'A consang. He's drunk dead blood.'

Consangs, short for the consanguineous, was a new political term adopted by vampires who'd resolved that the representation of a kinship, an affinity by blood, would create a more positive image than the negative images of well-established clichés. But a simple superficial change in terminology didn't alter what they were: they'd always be vampires – every last parasitic, deceitful, devious and manipulative one of them.

And her little sister was amongst them.

'How do they know about the book, Alisha?'

'I can't explain over the phone. You have to come here. Now.'

'But you know I can't bring the book there. If that book—'

'Please! If you don't, they'll kill me!'

Her stomach had flipped. 'I'm going to call the Intervention Unit—'

'No! No, if you do that you'll never see me again. Leila, listen, you have to get to the top border of Lowtown and wait at the café on the corner. Someone will meet you there in a couple of hours.'

'A couple of hours? Alisha, I've got to get across three districts, through two border offices—'

'There isn't much time. When you get there someone called Hade will meet you. He'll escort you through Lowtown, get you across the border and bring you into Blackthorn.'

'Who the hell is Hade?'

'Please, Lei. Please tell me you'll do it?'

Leila had tried to convince herself that it wasn't happening. That it couldn't be happening. But it was. Her worst nightmare had finally beckoned, just as she'd dreaded all her life. The vampire-infested Blackthorn district wasn't safe for any human. For Leila, it was deadly.

'Promise me they haven't hurt you.'

'They haven't. Not yet. They said I'll be fine if you bring the book. Leila, please, you've got to help me.'

Leila had closed her eyes. Swallowed hard. 'Just do as they say until I get there. I'm on my way.'

They'd been waiting when she'd arrived at the café a little over two hours later. She'd assumed the one who'd greeted her to be Hade – a tall, blond twenty-something with piercing grey eyes and a crew cut that was as harsh as his chiselled and stubbly face. Two silent bulks had accompanied him. All three, to her relief, were human. None of them would answer any of her questions, refraining even from eye contact with her. Their orders had clearly been to collect her with maximum speed and minimal explanation. Minimal explanation being a flash of wallet-sized, photographic evidence to confirm they had Alisha.

It had been a reality made even more painful by the fact it was Alisha's favourite snapshot. It was six years old now and Alisha had been just nineteen back then. She was hugging her two big sisters like there was no tomorrow, each of them grinning inanely at the camera. Sophie was doing her best cross-eyed look, irreverent Alisha had her tongue poking out and Leila, the eldest and standing out from her fairer sisters with her russet hair, was laughing at them both.

They'd driven to the border of Blackthorn. A far cry from the sophisticated and flawless high-security control of Summerton into Midtown and the lesser but still effective security from Midtown into Lowtown, Lowtown to Blackthorn had been a law unto itself.

The border office into the notorious vampire district had resembled a cattle market – people busily sweeping through the barriers, no one recording the movements, security officers marking the perimeter more as a deterrent against trouble rather than active involvement.

The mass of milling bodies had been overwhelming, the air dense with the alien scents of everything from smoke to sweat. Leila had tried to hold her breath, desperate not to let any of the intoxicating substances into her lungs as Hade and the bulks had escorted her through the crowds, their presence ironically reassuring amidst the swarms of both humans and vampires.

A black Mercedes had been waiting for them out on the street on the other side of the turnstiles.

Removing her rucksack and clutching it to her chest, Leila gazed out of the back-seat window as she was driven even further from all she'd ever known.

Blackthorn was everything she'd imagined it to be and worse. Her beloved vibrant-green spaces and sporadically spaced houses had been replaced with a sprawling mass of compacted, characterless buildings on dark, dismal streets. Noise boomed out from neon-lit basements and shopfronts. Pollution merged with the stagnant smell of street-sold food. The overfilled streets were chaotic with people milling and partying. People laughed, tussled and argued as noise poured from every open window, alley and recess.

She'd tried not to stare at the people lingering in doorways and on corners, something she never witnessed in Summerton. People back there had pleasant homes to go to, purposes. Now the sanctuary of home felt a million miles away and the phone call from Alisha like a dissipating nightmare.

The minute the Mercedes had slowed outside a nightclub, the crowds having parted to reveal an alleyway, fear had consumed her.

As she'd stepped out, Hade at least having the manners to open the door for her, her legs had nearly given way. Pulling her rucksack back on, she'd taken a deep steadying breath, a cold spray of rain hitting her upturned face as she'd told herself for the fiftieth time that she could do this.

Now her attention switched from the dreary storeys above back to Hade.

He cocked his head towards the open fire-exit doors and she followed him inside.

They stepped into a dimly lit corridor, the bulks behind keeping so close that she was virtually frogmarched along the concrete tunnel.

She followed Hade down one corridor then another, through double doors after double doors, Hade only stopping to key in security codes. Keeping a firm grip on her rucksack straps, the weight of the book and her Kit Box to assist the spell starting to tug, her five-foot-six-inch strides were no match for the swift and purposeful march of the six-footers escorting her.

The music gradually evaporated into the distance, the density of the corridors making her ears thrum. As Hade led her into a stone stairwell, they finally hit a wall of silence. He nodded to the bulks, both of whom promptly turned back the way they came, leaving Leila and him alone.

She glanced anxiously into the darkness above before following Hade up the steps, the low square heels of her boots scuffing against stone as they climbed three floors.

Passing through a final door and stepping out into another dim corridor, Hade stopped outside the lone elevator and keyed in a code.

Entering first, Leila backed up and clutched the handrail behind her. Despite taking slow, steady breaths as they ascended, her breathing involuntarily became shallow again as the doors slid open.

'Is this it?' she asked, still clutching the handrail as Hade stepped out into a broad hallway.

'Sure is.'

'And my sister's here?'

He gave her a single nod.

'I'll want to see her before I do anything,' she said.

'That's up to Caleb.'

'Is that who I'm meeting – Caleb? Is he the one who has my sister?'

'He's also the one who doesn't like to be kept waiting. And tonight less than ever, so I suggest you move.'

Reluctantly, she uncoiled her damp palms and stepped out.

The hallway was surprisingly luxurious. The richness of the dark cream walls was deepened by the soft glow of the elegant, cast-iron wall lights. The dark floorboards were highly polished, the blue-and-gold runners plump and soft under foot.

Hade stopped at the ornate mahogany double doors at the end and keyed in another code. As the doors clicked open, her tension surged as she followed him inside.

The extensive open-plan room was immaculate. Four broad oak steps led down to three black leather sofas positioned in a horseshoe central to the expanse. A low glass coffee table segregated the sofas, a large flat-screen television marking the opening. Midway on each wall to her left and right were hallways that mirrored each other – seemingly wings to opposite sides of the building. Dominating the top right-hand corner of the room was a highly polished mahogany bar. Straight ahead, glass doors opened out onto a generous stone terrace, the late-night breeze inciting the voile to momentarily mask the otherwise unspoiled view across the district.

Hade led the way down the steps. 'Wait here,' he said before taking the hallway to the left, marching down to the door at the end.

Leila wrapped her cardigan and jacket tight around herself. Folding her arms, she took a couple of steps forward. She glanced down the silent corridor where Hade had disappeared, peered out onto the terrace before turning to the hallway to her right as she searched for any sign of her sister.

She felt him before she saw him, the physical presence behind striking her sixth sense. The sudden chill was encapsulating, the tension excruciating. She had to turn around – like a tiny mammal knowing the bird of prey was looming above, Leila had to look.

From the way her hackles had risen, she would have pitched him at over seven foot tall with the physique of a heavyweight wrestler, but the male that stood behind her was maybe just short of six foot. Absent of bulk, his lithe body was nonetheless clearly honed and powerful beneath his fitted, short-sleeved grey shirt.

Her attention was immediately drawn to his perfectly toned forearms and biceps by the black tattoo scrolling out from beneath his left sleeve, another coiling up around the right side of his neck. His handsome face was framed by dark hair cut close around his neck and ears. Loose bangs scraped his low straight eyebrows and emphasised his intoxicating dark-framed eyes. If he was human she would have guessed him to be in his mid-thirties.

Leila caught her breath, a warm flush engulfing her as his vibrant green eyes fixed pointedly on hers – eyes encased by thick, dark lashes that only exacerbated their intensity – eyes that were sharp, intelligent, astute and merciless.

The eyes of a vampire.

She could feel it as clearly as if she were holding a white-hot coal.

As those vampire eyes assessed her slowly and purposefully, she instinctively took a step back and clutched the straps of her rucksack tighter.

Pinned her to the spot by his sullen gaze, a flush of trepidation and excitement flooded her. Amidst the dim surroundings, the breeze from the open doors stirring his hair, he looked utterly preternatural to the point of being hypnotic. He was every inch the vampire and every inch the last thing that she should be considering remotely appealing.

Leila forcibly snapped herself from her daze, berating herself as she reminded herself where she was and why she was there. More to the point, of what he was and that it was he who was clearly holding Alisha for ransom. This, undoubtedly, was Caleb. 'Where's my sister?'

'Show me the book,' Caleb said, a sexy rasp exacerbating his surly tone.

'Tell me she's all right.'

'Alisha's fine.'

'Prove it.'

'The book first.'

Leila tightened her grip on her bag. 'If you want it, you let me see her.'

The tension in the room nearly squeezed the life-breath out of her as Caleb narrowed his eyes. She took another wary step back, dropping her hands from her rucksack ready to defend herself.

He held his penetrating gaze on her for an uncomfortable second longer than was necessary before he looked across at Hade and cocked his head towards the hallway behind.

Hade nodded then disappeared from sight, reappearing seconds later with a small figure.

She looked tired, worn and tearful, with no characteristic mischievous bounce in her brown eyes. Alisha stayed perfectly still a few feet away, her gaze on Leila hesitant.

Leila heaved with relief but as she stepped forward to greet her, Caleb caught her by the upper arm with a powerful, commanding grip. Electricity pulsated through her, the impact of his touch startling her to stillness.

'Do what you came here to do,' he said. 'Reunion later.'

Leila's gaze snapped to his as she instinctively tried to pull her arm free. 'And then what?'

Alisha broke the silence. 'Just do as he says, Leila. Please.'

Leila glanced across to her.

'Please,' Alisha pleaded more quietly, her wide eyes reddened from crying.

Leila wavered for only a moment longer before pulling away from Caleb. She slipped her rucksack from her shoulders and unzipped the main compartment. She slid out the book and grudgingly held it out for him.

Caleb flicked through the pages then looked back at her. 'You can read this, right?'

She didn't dare tell him she was a little out of practice nor that she had never, technically, carried out any of the spells at all. But she nodded. 'Yes.'

Handing the book to Hade, he stepped up to her.

Leila instinctively backed up against the sofa, her heel catching the base as she grasped the soft leather. Warily holding his gaze, she knew she'd strike back if she had to, but she wasn't stupid enough to instigate it. And she wasn't stupid enough to jeopardise Alisha. A little bit of humility had to be the order of the day; the rest she'd work out from there.

'And you can perform the spell?' he asked.

'Yes.'

He grabbed her wrist, held her hand up to expose her protest rings — one gracing her thumb, the other her little finger — engraved silver bands that danced in the artificial light. They were the ultimate sign of defiance against the social acceptance of his kind, worn by those who stood against the so-called consangs' steps towards political acceptance. Vampires *could* never and *would* never play a role in any decisions that affected humans, and she unequivocally and unashamedly believed *every* human being had a responsibility to see to that.

He barely looked at them as his eyes narrowed on hers. 'Your sister assures me you're smart, but you coming here wearing these makes me think otherwise.'

Leila tried to pull her wrist away but he held it fast, his closeness intensifying the subtle scent of alcohol and smoke that mingled intoxicatingly with the musky woody undertones of his aftershave. 'I'm not going to hide how I feel just because I'm here.'

There was a hint of an amusement in his eyes, but it never reached his lips. 'I hear you're not our biggest fan.'

Her unease escalated as he searched her eyes. A light perspiration swept over her. He *couldn't* know what she was – not just by looking.

She held her breath, her heart throbbing painfully. The flutter of excitement she felt in her chest disturbed her. But she forced herself with every iota of willpower not to look away from those intimidating green eyes. Worse still, behind the aesthetics there was something more than the emptiness she expected – something beyond soulless, heartless windows. Within those eyes that should have looked dead, there was something deep, poignant and entrancing.

She swallowed harder than she would have liked, hating the way her body responded immediately to his. She knew it was wrong – deeply and horribly wrong on too many levels. But she still found her gaze wandering down to the top two unfastened buttons of his shirt, a gap that revealed a tantalising glimpse of smooth, honed chest. She lingered on his full but masculine lips, his strong jaw, before sliding back up over his perfectly formed nose to his eyes. Beautiful eyes that lingered coaxingly on hers for another uncomfortable couple of seconds before he finally pulled away.

'Let's do this,' he said, retrieving the book from Hade before leading the way back down the hallway.

Chapter Two

Leila tentatively entered the bedroom alone with Caleb.

The vampire she'd been summoned to save lay on his back on the king-sized bed directly ahead. Clearly unconscious, a worrying sheen of perspiration engulfed him despite his subtle shiver. His body was frighteningly pale, exacerbated by the dark sheets that covered him to mid-chest, his arms exposed by his sides.

She glanced nervously at Caleb. The anxiety was as evident in his eyes as she was sure it was in her own. 'He looks really sick,' she said quietly.

'He is.'

'How long has he been like this?'

'Sixteen hours.'

She gripped the book tighter against her chest. 'What if this doesn't work?'

His gaze snapped to hers, eyes menacing at the prospect she might fail. 'You said you can do this.'

'He might be too far gone.'

'If my brother dies tonight, your sister dies – slowly and painfully.'

Leila narrowed her eyes at the injustice of his threat. 'Have you any idea how hard it is to bring a vampire back from this?'

'Your sister gave me her word that this would not be a problem for you.'

'Under duress.'

'Are you telling me she lied?'

Leila stared back down at the dying vampire. 'What's his name?'

'Jacob. Jake.'

She took a wary step closer.

Jake was almost as handsome as his brother, but his closer-cropped dark hair gave him a harsher edge. His lips were narrower, his lashes and eyebrows finer. His toned body was bulkier – too bulky for her taste, unlike the athletic litheness of Caleb.

Leila stopped at the side of the bed and placed her book and rucksack on the covers. She took out her Kit Box and glanced back over her shoulder at Caleb. 'I won't be able to concentrate with you watching me.'

'I'm not leaving you alone with him.' Caleb strolled around the opposite side of the bed and pulled up a chair. Turning it the wrong way, he straddled it, his arms resting on the back as he watched her every move.

Leila knelt by the bed. It had been eighteen months since their grandfather's death. And, until that night, eighteen months since she'd run her fingers over the hard but worn blue canvas cover. Eighteen months since she'd traced her fingers over the gilded title: *Purification*.

If it hadn't been for her grandfather, she would never have known about her talent. A talent he'd helped her hone as she'd read and interpreted the words contained within his archaic texts. Texts he emphasised the importance of again and again alongside her need to protect herself and her sisters from *them*.

He called them vampires too, and he knew the truth about them. Truths he had learned from his descendants and from the prophecy books he'd held in his charge. Books he then left to her. Books for her to safeguard and keep from all but her own eyes. Books useless to anyone without an interpreter to impart the words.

And somehow they'd tracked her down.

She turned the heavy cream pages and read the small cursive handwriting. None of the books were reproduced. They couldn't be because their power was in their uniqueness. A power that could only be evoked by a speaker endowed with the talent.

Fingers numb, hands trembling, the pages seemed to blur as she tried to remember where she had found the section earlier. It had seemed so much easier to locate without a virtually dead vampire in front of her and his uncompromising brother, less than six feet away, clearly not in the mood for failure.

Fumbling through the pages, she finally stumbled on it. She traced the text with her fingers, struggling to focus as she interpreted each word and symbol. Thumbnail to her teeth, she scanned the diagrams.

If her grandfather could see her now, preparing to save a vampire's life – the ultimate sacrilege for her kind – she had no doubt he'd be horrified.

Rubbing her hair back from her forehead, she detected light perspiration equally dampening her palm. She reached for her wooden Kit Box and turned the brass key. As it opened, the various sections spread out. Tiny drawers and compartments revealed a variety of objects as a rich aroma of herbs and spices filled the air. She took out a small white ceramic bowl and clutched it in her hand whilst she continued to trace her fingers along the text. Reaching back into her box, she took out three tiny jars and emptied a small amount of powder from each into the bowl.

'Do you have a match?' she asked.

Caleb took his lighter out of his pocket and strolled around the bed to give it to her.

She accepted it and tried flicking it into action but the damned thing eluded her, worsened by her trembling hands.

He took it back and flicked it into operation with ease.

She held the bowl up to him. 'Light what's in the dish, will you?'

He did as he was asked. The contents quickly burned, a sweet and woody odour filling the air. Seeming to sense that his close proximity had broken her concentration again, he handed her the bowl and stepped away, resuming his seat opposite.

'I take it he drained the victim from the neck?' she asked, keeping her attention on the book.

'Yes.'

'Right side or left?'

'Left.'

She ran her finger along a few more lines then reached into the box for three sprigs of herbs and a small pewter charm. After laying them on the bed beside the book, she closed the box and put it on the floor out of the way. She stood and bent to unzip her boots. She pulled them off along with her jacket and cardigan. Picking up the dish in one hand and the sprigs and charm in the other, she climbed onto the bed.

Hesitation and apprehension swamped her as she uneasily and cautiously sat astride Jake's hips. Her gut churned at the proximity, let alone the intimacy of the act. Sitting back on her haunches, thighs pressed against his, she kept her back straight as she gazed warily down at the dying vampire. Laying the sprigs and charm on the bed beside him, she placed her fingers in the dish.

Caleb caught her wrist in an instant, startling her. 'Take them off,' he commanded.

She glanced down at the silver rings. 'Silver may harm you, in your vampiric state, but Jake is beyond that now.'

Caleb tightened his grasp. 'I said, take them off.'

Leila frowned in defiance as their gazes locked. But, as he let her wrist go, she reluctantly relented and slid the rings off, putting them on the bedside table next to him.

Forcing herself to refocus, she placed the tips of her fingers back in the dish. She rubbed the contents across the left side of Jake's neck, down his chest, and ended the unbroken line in a hook beneath his heart.

She reached across to pull the book closer, frowning deeply as she struggled to recall some of the inflections as she read. Placing a sprig above his head, one upon his heart and another beneath his feet, she put the charm on his forehead. Exhaling unsteadily, she held the flat of her palms an inch above his chest.

Jake flinched, seemingly scowling as if he sensed something.

'You might want to grab something he can throw up in,' she said. 'His body should expel the bad blood if this works as it says it will.'

Caleb reached for the black bin beside the bedside table and placed it next to the bed.

Leila tensed her spread fingers as she lowered her palms an inch closer to his heart. Feeling the heat emanating from within her, heat that would flow down into his body, she braced herself. Not betraying a word, she silently recited the incantation. She closed her eyes and pressed her hands flat against his skin, skin that felt like cold clay, as she recited the confirmation three more times.

She stopped. Withdrew her hands. And opened her eyes.

There was silence.

Nothing happened.

She glanced anxiously at Caleb, her pulse picking up a notch. But his attention was firmly on his brother. She took a breath to steady herself before spreading her fingers over Jake's heart again. This time she applied more pressure as she recited the words with more conviction – a hushed whisper that would be nonsense to anyone but her. With every iota of energy in her, she willed it to work, her eyes tightly shut as she kept her focus on letting the energy flow through her.

She repeated the incantation again, and again, ending with a resounding draw of breath before she opened her eyes.

Jake lay perfectly still.

Too still.

He stopped trembling.

Stopped shivering.

She frowned. He was too far gone. Or she had read the inflections wrong. Or the herbs had been too old. Or her positioning was out. Her gaze snatched to Caleb as she tried to contain her panic.

But Caleb's gaze didn't flinch from his brother as the seconds ticked away, the atmosphere thick enough to be static.

'I did what—' she began, but suddenly Jake flinched.

His chest expanded as if in a desperate grasp for air. He started trembling beneath her again then convulsed.

Leila flinched and recoiled off him. Backing off the bed, she retreated against the wall as Caleb grabbed hold of his flaying brother.

Straddling him, pinning his hands to the bed either side of his head, his legs to the mattress, Caleb held Jake down with impressive strength as he glared across at her. 'What the fuck is happening?'

She shook her head, her pulse racing. 'I don't know. I've never done this before. I followed the instructions—'

'You've never done it?' Caleb momentarily turned his attention back on his brother, who was convulsing more violently now, before glaring back at her. 'Exactly what spells have you performed?'

She shrugged, struggling for an explanation.

Despite the force of Jake's spasms, Caleb continued to hold him down with ease, held him until he gradually calmed, the convulsions easing.

Jake wrenched free of his brother, stretched over the side of the bed and vomited thick, black blood into the bin. Gasping, he fell onto his back, scanned the room as if confirming his bearings then frowned at Caleb now sitting on his haunches. Closing his eyes again, he smiled. 'Hey, Caleb.'

Caleb smiled in return, just briefly, his lips parting to reveal a glimpse of perfectly aligned neat white teeth, a hint of elongated incisors. 'For fuck's sake, Jake.'

Jake languidly turned his head to look at Leila and frowned. 'Who's she?'

'She saved your life.'

Jake stared up at the ceiling. 'I feel like shit.'

'You're lucky you feel anything at all. How many times have I told you to pull back, huh? You've always got to push it that one step further, haven't you?'

Jake grinned. 'What do you expect? *No* just wasn't in her vocabulary.' He eased himself onto his elbows to examine Leila more closely as Caleb pulled off the bed.

'Then a little self-control wouldn't go amiss, Jake.'

'Easing up on the lecture wouldn't go amiss either.' He narrowed his eyes questioningly. 'Leila?'

Leila frowned in confusion.

The door burst open.

'Jake!' Alisha lunged through the doorway and threw herself onto the bed on top of him, flattening him, despite her small frame. Her fair hair covered her face as she eagerly kissed him on his lips, his forehead and his cheek.

Perplexed, Leila watched her sister until realisation, disbelief and then horror slammed into her.

'Easy, tiger,' he said softly, brushing back Alisha's hair. 'I haven't been gone *that* long.' He glanced at Caleb. 'Have I?'

'Over sixteen hours. Like I said, you're lucky to feel anything at all.'

'I can't believe you're okay,' Alisha declared, her eyes glossing. 'I told you she could do it,' she said to Caleb. 'I told you she'd make him better.' She smiled up at Leila. 'Thank you.'

Chapter Three

If the betrayal had stabbed her any harder or faster, Leila would have bled. She knew the answer, but the question still fell out as the facts unfolded before her. 'What is this?'

Alisha suddenly stilled. She bit into her bottom lip as she looked at her sister sheepishly. 'Listen, Lei, I can explain.'

Taken over by more rage than she was sure was healthy for a human being, Leila spun on her heels. She pushed past Hade now marking the doorway, her bare feet slamming against the floorboards as she stormed back into the living room.

Alisha hurried after her. 'Lei, I'm sorry.'

Leila spun to face her. 'I don't want to hear sorry. I want you to tell me I've got this wrong.'

Alisha lowered her gaze.

'How long has this been going on?' Leila demanded quietly.

'A while.'

'A while?'

Alisha shrugged. 'Two months. Nearly.'

'Two months? You've been involved with a vampire for two months? You?' Leila could barely say it as she lowered her voice. 'And you involved me?'

'I had to. I had no choice.'

'No choice?'

'You saw the state he was in. I panicked. But then I remembered about the book and what you could do. I couldn't just let him die. I had to say something.'

A kick in the gut would have been preferable. 'It was you? *You* told them about the book?' Leila marched up to her, her voice hushed. 'You told them about *me?*'

'I had to.'

'You betrayed us? Our family? For *him*? Have you any idea how dangerous this is? Have you any idea what I've been through to-night? I thought they were going to kill you. How could you lie to me like that?'

'I didn't lie to you. I just made it sound different to how it was. Lei, I wouldn't have brought you here if you were in danger.'

Leila stared at her, unable to believe her sister's nonchalance. 'I'm an interpreter, Alisha. Nothing but a witch to them. Or have you forgotten?' She shook her head as she stepped away. 'I can't believe you've done this.'

'Even if I got the book here, it's not as if I can read from it, is it? And time was short – too short for me to come and get you and explain it. Besides, I knew you wouldn't come if I told you the truth. I knew you wouldn't let me back here if I came to see you myself, especially if I tried to take the book with me.'

'So you tricked me?'

'It was the only way.'

'You chose him over me.'

'It's not like that, Lei.'

'What if I couldn't have read it? What if it hadn't worked? What if it had gone wrong?'

'But I knew you could.'

'Get my things. We're leaving.'

Alisha backed away. 'No.'

'No?'

'You don't understand what he means to me.'

'He's a vampire, Alisha.'

'He's a consang. And I love him.'

Leila widened her eyes before laughing curtly in despair. 'What, like you loved Carl and Martin and Toby? Oh, and like you loved Phillip? Those three weeks were the best ever, right?'

'This is different.'

'Because they were actually your own species? The only thing that's different is that for some godforsaken reason you have decided to...' she hesitated. 'Alisha, I'm not going to argue with you. Get my stuff. And get anything of yours. We'll finish this conversation when we're home.'

Alisha took another step back. She crossed her arms defiantly across her chest, her brown eyes locked defiantly on Leila's. 'You can't make me.'

Leila turned away for a moment. She closed her eyes and bit into her bottom lip. It was all she could do to stop herself screaming at her sister. She tuned into the sounds of the district travelling with the breeze through the open terrace doors. Alien sounds that only exacerbated her unease as they defined the danger they were both in, even if Alisha couldn't see it yet. But Alisha didn't see danger in anything or, if she did, she treated it like a fairground ride –especially when Leila was the one pointing it out to her.

'I didn't go out looking for this, all right?' Alisha said. 'I didn't plan to fall for a consang.'

'Vampire.'

'I didn't even realise what he was at first. I was in Lowtown, he approached me in a club, and we started talking.'

Leila turned to face her again. 'You know they're everywhere there at night. You should never have been there in the first place. You know the risks.'

'I wasn't at risk. Not after I met him.'

'You're a human in Blackthorn.'

Alisha tugged down the collar of her shirt, revealing the nook of her neck, the small tattoo there. 'He marked me, all right? No consang will touch me. Caleb, Jake, they have standing around here. No one messes with them.'

Leila shrivelled up her nose in distaste. 'You let him mark you?' Unease clenched her chest. 'How the hell are we going to explain that when we try to get back across the border?'

'He did it to protect me.'

'If you were at home you wouldn't need protecting.'

'Because all humans are such upstanding citizens?' Alisha released her collar. 'Lei,' she said. 'This isn't a fling. I really care about him.'

'And does he feel the same way?' Leila glanced towards the hallway as Hade emerged.

He sent them both a fleeting glance before striding across to the steps and up and out of the front door.

'Yes,' Alisha said.

'Which is why he was with another woman.'

'He likes to feed.'

'But he doesn't have to. Isn't that what they tried telling us all – that they had other ways of sustaining themselves? That feeding on humans was legend, myths of old, primitive? That simple medication now provides them with what they need?'

'It gives him a buzz. Not that you'd understand any of that.'

'He was with another woman, Alisha. He bled her to death. Doesn't that tell you anything?'

'You really don't understand, do you?'

'I understand exactly what I need to understand. I came here because I thought I was saving your life. And now not only do they have their hands on grandfather's book, they know what I can do, too. Do you really think they're going to let us go?'

'Jake gave me his word.'

'Well, that's all right then.'

'There's no need to be sarcastic.'

'Don't you dare tell me how I need to be.'

'Caleb promised me he'd escort you back to the border of Midtown once this was all over. That was part of the deal. You saved his brother's life, Lei. He owes you. He owes both of us.'

'Well, something tells me he's not the kind too keen on being indebted to someone like me, Alisha.'

'He gave me his word.'

'Then get our stuff and tell him we're ready to leave.'

'I told you, I'm staying.'

'You're leaving. And you're leaving now.'

Alisha hesitantly held her sister's glare. 'You know, there are a lot of girls down in that club who would give anything to spend time up here with these two.'

Leila shook her head in disgust. 'Is that what it is, Alisha? Is that what you see in him?'

'I love him.'

'Sounds like infatuation to me.'

'At least I know how to have a good time. At least I don't spend my life in a stuffy library with my head in century-old books. At least I go out there and have fun. I'm making the most of being alive. You criticise the consangs, but you might as well be the undead for all the excitement you get in your life.'

Leila stared at her, momentarily stunned to silence before grabbing her sister by the arm. She marched Alisha out onto the terrace and spun her to face her. 'We have a duty, Alisha,' she whispered sternly. 'Grandfather taught us that stuff for a reason.'

'No, he taught you. You're the one who has the talent, not me. And I'm glad it's not me who's got it. I wouldn't be you for anything. I like my freedom. And that's what Jake gives me. But for as long as you stay tucked up all safe and sound in Summerton, you'll never understand. You're too indoctrinated to ever understand.'

'I'm not indoctrinated.'

'You soaked up everything grandfather taught us. You've never even met a consang before tonight, so how can you possibly pass judgement on them?'

No matter how tempted she was to blurt out the truth, this was not the time for revelations. Instead she shook her head in bitter disappointment. 'I think the only one who's indoctrinated around here is you. He's really got to you, hasn't he?'

'I'm with him because I want to be. Because I choose to be. This is the twenty-first century we're in, not the eighteenth. Read the head-lines. They're not preying on us, attacking us in dark alleys and taking us against our will. People are getting involved with them volun-tarily.'

'So that makes it acceptable?'

'Drag your head out of your archives and take a good look around, Lei. Move on and accept that maybe grandfather was wrong.'

'If he could hear you now—'

'But he can't, can he? He's dead. Gone. Just like Mum. Just like Dad. And just like Sophie might be if we don't find her.'

Leila's heart skipped a beat. 'Tell me that's not what this is about?'

'She could still be alive. And if she is and if she's here, Jake will find her.'

'Is that what he's promised you?'

'He can find her. I know he can.'

'In exchange for what?'

Alisha glowered at her. 'At least I'm doing something. At least I haven't given up.'

'Given up?' Leila glared at her, her fury escalating as indignation hit her hard. 'Ten months I looked for her. Ten months! While you were out getting drunk, taking comfort in whoever would listen to you, I was the one phoning the authorities, knocking on doors and putting up pictures. It was me who paid for the private investigators, the ads in the newspapers…' She shook her head and marched past the large, round marble table that looked more suitable for sacrifices than al fresco dining. She stopped at the barrier and clutched the cold steel rail as she stared down the hundred-foot drop to where people swarmed the streets. If Sophie was amongst them, she was a grain of sand in a cove. 'Alisha, I'm not discussing this with you anymore.'

'Lei, just spend a couple of hours here. You'll see they're no different to us. You'll learn more by spending one evening with them than another minute with your head in those stupid books.'

'One of those stupid books saved your so-called boyfriend's life tonight.'

'And I am grateful to you, Lei. More than you can understand.' She stepped alongside her. 'So is Caleb. So is Jake.' Alisha caught her by the hand. 'It doesn't matter that you're a witch.'

Leila snatched her hand away. 'Interpreter.'

'Whatever. They're not going to hurt you.'

Leila held her gaze. 'Then prove it. Because from what I can see, the longer we stay here the more at risk we are. So I'm telling you – either you get us out of here now or your new friends won't know what's hit them. And neither will you.'

❋ ❋ ❋

'I ache all over,' Jake said as he eased himself up against the headboard.

Caleb withdrew his attention from the doorway where Alisha had run after her sister. The shock in the witch's eyes had been convincingly real, supporting Alisha's claims that Leila had no idea she was a frequenter to Blackthorn. The relief in Alisha's eyes on seeing Jake was equally convincing.

He leaned back against the chest of drawers facing the foot of the bed and folded his arms as he turned his attention back to his brother. 'If it's sympathy you're looking for, you've got a better chance of persuading me to install a glass roof. You're a fucking idiot, Jake.'

Jake managed a hint of a goading smile despite his brother's disapproving glare. 'Survived though, didn't I?'

Caleb didn't reciprocate. 'Hade, go and show your face down in the bar. If there are any awkward questions, spread the word that it was all just a rumour. Jake's fine and no one died. As far as anyone's concerned, we're in business negotiations.'

Hade nodded. 'Sure thing, Caleb.' He glanced across at Jake. 'Good to have you back, Jake.'

Jake smiled at him and rested his head back against the wall as their employee, their friend, exited the room and closed the door. 'You missed me, right?'

Caleb took a cigarette from his top pocket and placed it between his lips to avoid giving his little brother the verbal and physical retaliation he deserved. He needed to stay calm and focused. It wasn't over yet. 'You are one more stupid move away from me putting a leash around your neck,' he declared, igniting the tip.

'Come on, Caleb. Don't be mad. I got caught up in the moment, that's all. She couldn't do enough for me.'

'Sex and a feed do *not* happen together. And you only feed on the approved. You know the rules.'

'Yeah, your rules.'

'My rules to protect you from this very thing happening. Maybe now you'll finally see you're not invincible.'

'It was just a fun time that got out of hand, that's all. It won't happen again.'

He exhaled a terse stream of smoke. 'Good, because you repeat a trick like that and I'll kill you myself, understand?'

Jake tried to sit up further but failed. Instead he slumped back against the pillows again. 'So what happened? Alisha just confessed to her sister being a witch?'

'Basically. I take it you didn't know?'

'I think I would have remembered to mention it. What about the book?'

'Theirs. The witch came fully prepared.' Caleb strolled over to sit on the bed at his brother's feet. Pulling the purification book closer, he flicked through the pages. 'It seems we have quite the librarian in our midst.'

Jake handed him the ashtray from his bedside table. 'She's cute, too, huh?' he remarked with a conspiratorial smile.

Caleb didn't smile back. 'What do you know about her?'

'Leila? Not a lot. She lives in Summerton. She works in some kind of library and archive department. She doesn't approve of vampires and drives Alisha crazy trying to tell her how to live her life apparently. How the hell did you get her here?'

'Alisha inferred she was being held hostage.'

Jake raised his eyebrows slightly. 'A hostage? Well, that explains the reaction.'

'What about the girl you wasted, Jake? What did you know about her?'

'What's that got to do with anything?'

'You hook up with a girl who just so happens to have a very powerful witch as a sister. A sister who just so happens to have a very precious and rare book of spells that we've only ever heard of in folklore. And one of those spells just so happens to be the only known cure for the dead blood you just happen to consume from a complete stranger seemingly willing to dance that close to the edge with you. A fact which your girlfriend, incidentally, seems absolutely fine about.'

'You make it sound like some kind of set-up.' He frowned at his brother's unflinching gaze. 'You think that girl tried to kill me? For Leila to save me? And that makes sense because...?'

'It's all just a little convenient, don't you think?'

'Caleb, even if any of that did make sense, Alisha would have to have been a part of it. She would have been playing me for weeks.

Sorry, but I know when a girl's faking. And I was the one who approached her, remember? We got lucky, that's all.'

'Not necessarily.'

'What do you mean?'

'We can't rule out that the witch has only used a holding spell – a nice temporary measure. She leaves, dawn comes and you go right back to the state you were in.'

'No way. She's three districts from home and surrounded by vampires, with no chance of getting herself or her sister out of here in one piece without help from one of us. It would be a suicide mission.' Jake frowned. 'What's really going on here, Caleb? What are you not telling me?'

Caleb exhaled a slow pensive stream of smoke. 'No ordinary witch has the power to do what she did tonight. Certainly not one as apparently inexperienced as her.'

'So her talent's strong. That's good, right?'

'So talented that she performed nothing short of a miracle? Not just any witch can purify a vampire's blood, Jake, especially not when they're as near the Brink as you were.'

'So what are you saying?'

'There's only one breed of witch powerful enough to do what she did tonight.'

Silence encapsulated the room as Jake held his brother's gaze. He frowned then smiled with unease – a smile that quickly faded. 'You're kidding me, right? This is some kind of wind-up for me fucking up tonight.'

'You think I'd joke about that?'

'But they're extinct.' His eyes flashed with uncertainty. 'They've been extinct for decades – six at least. Haven't they?'

'Maybe not ones savvy enough to lay low. Ones who are savvy enough to stay away from areas like this. Ones who now have that luxury because of the protection of boundary laws.'

Jake forced himself into a seated position. 'A serryn? Here? Her?' He shook his head. 'No way. If she was, Alisha would have to be insane to bring her here.'

'If Alisha's not a part of it, she either loves you enough to risk bringing Leila here or she's clueless about her.'

'Is that even possible?'

'Serryns are devious, lying little sluts, Jake. Even to their own families when they need to be.'

Jake frowned. 'But if the strength of talent was the giveaway, you must have had your suspicions even before you brought her here.'

'I didn't have much choice, did I? I had to take whatever chance I could or you were dead anyway. But I know serryns don't save vampires, Jake. Not that easily.'

Jake's eyes flashed with concern. 'And you needed to know if there was one still on the loose.'

Caleb closed the book and pushed it away.

'What are you going to do?' Jake asked.

'What do you think I'm going to do? I'm going to find out for sure.'

He frowned. 'But Leila must be assuming you don't know. I mean they're undetectable to the untrained eye, right? What if she was just planning on slipping in here and then slipping back out again? Is it really a good idea to make it obvious you know? And what if she is? It's not like you can do anything about it.'

'Can't I?'

Unease ignited in Jake's eyes. 'I know how you feel about them, but this is Alisha's sister we're talking about. Alisha who helped save my life. I owe them. We both do.'

'And at dawn we'll know, won't we?'

'You're going to keep her here? All night? Are you insane?'

'Because letting her go *wouldn't* be insane?'

'Keeping a living, breathing serryn under this roof is not the way to handle this, Caleb.'

'Neither is letting one back out onto the street. You know I can't do that.'

'No, what you can't do is go down that path again.' He leaned towards his brother. 'Caleb, you're making a mistake. She's just a witch. A witch that can get us prosecuted for blackmail and kidnap if you go ahead with this. You hold on to her tonight, you have to hold on to her forever. That means Alisha too. You're not just potentially fucking things up for you; you're fucking things up for me. It's not worth it on a hunch.'

'Seventy years' experience of hunting them is telling me this is more than a hunch.'

'Even if it is, someone is bound to know she's here. They'll come looking for her.'

'You know how many people go missing in Blackthorn every night. Besides, Alisha made sure she didn't tell anyone. Apparently the witch doesn't have anyone *to* tell. She's quite a loner by all accounts.'

'Okay, you want to give it until dawn then do that. Make some excuse that it's safer for them to travel in daylight. They won't dispute that. And letting them leave together will soften the blow. Then at dawn, when you see I'm right, you can let her walk away – no testing, no proof, no questions asked. Don't search for answers you don't need to find. If you're right about her, the less she suspects, the better.'

'And if this is a set-up? What if that's what she wants – to get in here, to get on the inside and lower our guards?'

'You're being paranoid.'

'How many of them have you had to deal with, Jake? We need to know what we're up against and there's only one way to be sure.'

'And if she *is* what you think she is, and you prove it?' He frowned at his brother's fleeting glance as Caleb stood from the bed. 'Tell me you're not going to kill her. Caleb, we need to talk about this. You act on impulse and you're going to regret this.'

Caleb placed the ashtray back on the bedside table and exhaled his last stream of smoke. 'When do I ever act on impulse, little brother?' he replied as he met Jake's troubled gaze.

'And what am I supposed to say to Alisha?'

'That dawn's the safer time to go, just like you suggested. You tell her you need to get down to the club for a couple of hours to show your face and stop any awkward questions about how we saved your life – any of which could put her talented sister at risk. Tell her you want her company. Tell her whatever you need to, but I want her out of this apartment for the rest of the night.'

'If Leila is a serryn, you shouldn't be alone with her.'

He smiled. 'I think I'm more than capable of handling her, Jake.' He glanced down at her two small silver protest rings as he stubbed out his cigarette. 'It's time me and that little fledgling out there got to know each other better.'

Chapter Four

Alisha all but stomped back down to Jake's room. It was an over-reaction on Leila's part – just a stupid overreaction that was so typical of her. And now she had the embarrassment of telling Jake that they had to leave, because she knew the look in Leila's eyes – a look that told her she meant every word of it.

It was going to be so humiliating.

She'd known it had been a risk getting Leila there. She knew that as soon as Leila discovered the truth, she'd be furious. She knew it was too much to expect Leila to be quietly escorted back off the premises without protest, willingly leaving her little sister behind in the evil domain. She would have argued more, but she knew Leila was better off left out on the terrace before any more of the routine spiel started coming out – especially in front of Caleb. Jake would probably find it amusing but from the little she knew about Caleb, he'd find it anything but.

She sighed with impatience as she stopped at Jake's door. Caleb had been nowhere in sight so she guessed he was probably still inside too. She felt her nerves give way, her heart pounding.

She knocked on the door before turning the handle, and stepped inside.

Caleb's gaze met hers from the far side of the bed. Her stomach flipped. Two months of occasional glances in her direction and it still made her feel like an inadequate teenager on every rare occasion they made eye contact.

From the first moment she'd seen him across the club, before she'd even known he was Jake's brother, her pulse had raced – a rate that had become painful when Jake had introduced them. Her heart had sunk as Caleb had only responded with a swift dismissive glance before taking his brother aside to discuss club business.

But that was Caleb's way. She'd learned that much. Caleb needed neither people's time nor approval, which only added to his appeal. Jake and he were so different in that respect. Jake thrived on the attention that Caleb ignored, attention instantly brought by being Caleb's brother. And females who weren't impressed by Caleb's aloofness were quickly placated and enamoured by Jake's flirty and more accessible manner. But Caleb was always the ultimate goal and everyone knew it.

The brothers were co-owners of the club as well as other various ventures around the south side, but Alisha knew that, beneath Jake's bravado, it was Caleb's determination and resilience that had made it all the success it was. It was Caleb's focus that kept the businesses thriving. It was Caleb's reputation that kept away the competitors. Jake's charm and party attitude kept the drinks flowing and the females flocking, but it was Caleb who held it all together.

Just as he'd somehow held it together when he'd found her clutching the unconscious Jake down in the VIP area of the club.

She'd agonised over telling Caleb about Leila, not least knowing she would be furious when the truth was finally out about where her little sister had been spending her nights away from home. And then there was that stirring of uncertainty about Caleb. His business acumen and zero tolerance weren't the only things he was reputed for.

But when there seemed to be no other hope, when she'd seen for the first time panic in Caleb's eyes, she had to speak up. She spoke up or she lost Jake. She could deal with Leila's wrath if that meant saving Jake's life.

And save him they had.

And despite what Leila believed, Caleb wouldn't forget that. Caleb was true to his word. Caleb loved Jake more than he loved anyone and, from what she'd seen, was the only one he was capable of loving. He would be indebted to them both. And part of her hoped it would be enough to win a little bit of his approval.

Jake smiled from the bed. 'Hey, gorgeous. Stop looking so worried – I'm fine.'

'Leila's not. She's really angry with me, Jake.'

'I'm not surprised.'

'She's told me to come and get her stuff. She wants me to go with her. Now.'

'What's her hurry?' Caleb interjected.

She glanced at him still casually leaning back against the wall, hands resting behind his back, his unsmiling gaze fixed on her.

'Aside from being in the last place on the planet she ever wanted to be?' she replied. 'I did warn you she wouldn't be happy.'

'Where is she now?' Caleb asked.

'Out on the terrace. Getting plenty of much-needed air. How long have we got?'

His green eyes narrowed slightly. She wasn't sure if there was a glimmer of coaxing behind them but they made her as uneasy as the question that followed. 'For what?'

'Until someone can take us to the border.' She glanced anxiously at Jake then back at Caleb. 'You promised us an escort.'

'You need to go and keep Jake company down in the bar first.'

Her heart beat a little faster. She glanced nervously at Jake. 'Should you really be going down there?'

'We've got to make sure no one believes this happened tonight. There's only one way to do that.'

'But you don't need me. I mean, you know I'd like to but...'

'But what?' Caleb asked.

She looked back at him, not liking the edge of confrontation in his tone. She knew only too well he wasn't used to people questioning him. 'Do you want to be the one to go and tell Leila we're staying a bit longer?' she asked, a little too curtly.

He pulled himself away from the wall with a hint of a smirk that did little to reassure her.

She stepped toward the foot of the bed in a pathetic attempt to block his way. 'I was kidding,' she said, unable to contain the panic in her voice. Caleb versus Leila was one face-off they could all do without.

Caleb folded his arms. 'Why so anxious, Alisha? What do you think I'm going to do to her?'

She looked to Jake for reassurance again. The look in his eyes provided anything but. She reverted her attention to Caleb, her inability to read what was going on adding to her unease. 'I didn't say you were going to do anything. I just need to think of a way to explain why she needs to stick around.'

'Then I'll talk to her. You don't have to leave right away, do you?'

'No, but…' There was no *but*. No *but* except the fact her sister despised vampires more than anything else, and the longer she was there the more likely her views were going to spill into Caleb's unappreciative lap.

'So you get ready to go down to the bar with Jake and I'll keep Leila company.'

She broke from the intense pull of his gaze to look back at Jake.

'Come on, sweetheart,' Jake said. 'Another hour or so won't hurt. I thought you wanted her to spend a bit of time in Blackthorn?'

'I do, but…'

'What are you really worried about, Alisha?' Caleb asked, snatching her attention too easily back to him.

She struggled for the right way to say it. 'She has some strong views. I don't want any friction.'

'I saw the rings. What *is* her problem with us?'

The right thing to do was to end the conversation there or at least try to divert away from it, but Caleb's unrelenting gaze remained fixed on hers. 'It's not all her fault. Our grandfather filled her head with some bad crap. Not that I didn't love him,' she hurriedly added as guilt gripped her chest. 'I mean he brought us up, looking after Mum after Dad left her just before I was born, and then looking after us when Mum died. I know it wasn't easy for him. But with them it was always about the books and the prophecies because of Leila's talent.'

'What prophecies?'

'I don't know,' she said with a shrug. She really didn't – not the full extent. She'd never wanted to take any notice. It had always sounded so dull when they were growing up. 'Vampires taking over the world and all that kind of stuff. I never believed any of it.'

'But Leila believes it?'

'He taught it to her from like the age of five or something, when she started interpreting. I guess it's ingrained. It made her a bit para-noid, you know?'

'You talk about your grandfather in the past tense.'

'He died eighteen months ago. That's how she got all his books and stuff. He left everything to her.'

He narrowed his eyes pensively. 'And what happened to your mother?'

She lowered her gaze to the floor. She still felt uncomfortable saying it – a reminder of the treachery of what she was doing.

'She was killed by a vampire,' Jake cut in. 'Attacked in an alley.'

She looked back up at Caleb. 'It was in Midtown,' she explained. 'So we know it must have been someone of importance though we never found out who. Sophie stumbled on it a few years ago. She found it in some newspaper article. Grandfather never told us the whole truth. I guess we were too young. I was no more than two at the time. Sophie was only six. I guess there was never a right time to bring it up. I guess Leila has never got over it. But you can't all be judged the same, can you? Or where would the whole human race be?'

'No wonder this is the last place she wants to be,' Caleb remarked.

'She's not been the same since losing our grandfather. Since losing Sophie. Now she's stuck in that library even more than she ever was. She can't help the way she is. I know she's a bit narrow-minded but she's a good person. And she's not as tough as she makes out. I just want you to understand why she's the way she is in case she says anything stupid. I don't want you to take things personally. I was hoping that being here would help soften her views but I guess there's not much chance of that now and the longer she stays here, the worse it'll probably get.'

Caleb looked across at Jake, something unspoken and unreadable passing between them. She'd seen them do it countless times – some kind of shared understanding. Usually she found it a sexy characteristic of their tight bond; now it just made her uneasy. But she didn't dare question Caleb as he stepped past her, leaving her alone in the room with Jake.

She looked back at him, her pulse racing. 'I'm not comfortable with this, Jake.'

Jake eased off the bed. 'Don't look so panicked. He's just going to talk to her.'

'Exactly. She's going to end up saying the wrong thing to him, or he's going to say the wrong thing to her—'

'Alisha, relax,' he said, pulling level, clipping her chin. 'We're supposed to be celebrating. Get yourself changed and we'll head down to the club.'

'Jake, this is serious. She has a habit of speaking before she thinks, particularly when it comes to your kind. I'm warning you, there's going to be trouble.'

'Leila saved my life tonight. Do you think Caleb's going to forget that? That I will? Trust me – Caleb will sort it.'

'So he's not planning to keep her here?'

'For what?'

'I don't know. Her spells and stuff?'

'If Caleb wanted a witch, he'd get himself a witch.' He brushed her hair back from her face. 'Why did you never mention her talent before?'

Alisha shrugged. 'I didn't know how you'd take it. I didn't know if it would affect things.'

He caught her wrist and pulled her closer, his blue eyes sparkling. 'Is that your only secret?'

Right then being playful was her last thing on her mind. 'Promise me Caleb won't hurt her.'

'Why would he?'

She shrugged. 'I saw the way he was with her before you woke up. He didn't like her wearing the protest rings.'

He frowned. 'You really are worried, aren't you? I've never seen you so uptight.'

'You're not the one who's got to live with the aftermath of this.'

'It'll be fine,' he said, brushing her hair back from her neck.

But as he leaned in, she pushed him away. 'You'd better not.'

He pulled back, stared deep into her eyes. 'What's the problem?'

'Leila's mad enough. I don't want her to know about you feeding on me too.'

He widened his eyes slightly. 'Are you serious?'

'It's bad enough I'm dating you. If she knows I'm feeding you as well, she'll flip.'

'Maybe you should tell her about some of the other things I've done to you,' he said with a playful smirk as he leaned into her neck again.

'Jake, I mean it,' she said, her free hand to his chest. 'I need to be careful.'

'It's no fun if we're careful,' he whispered in her ear before raking his incisors down to her pulse point.

'No,' she snapped, wrenching free. 'Wait until we get down into the club.'

'So you are coming then?'

'You think I'm going to let all those stray females fawn over you?'

He wrapped his arms around her waist. 'You know how this works – it's only you I bring up here.'

She gazed into his eyes. 'I know.'

'Then ease up,' he said, catching hold of her hips to ease her back against the door. 'Anyway, you're hardly one to criticise.'

'What's that supposed to mean?'

'Do you think I don't see the way you look at Caleb?' He leaned closer, a taunting gleam in his eyes. 'Maybe it's me who should be jealous.'

Alisha broke a smile. 'Maybe you should be.'

Jake slid his hands over her shoulders to her behind, tugging her closer. 'I wouldn't go there if I were you.'

Alisha raised her eyebrows coaxingly. 'No? Don't you think I could handle him?'

'He'd eat you alive.'

'Sounds like fun.'

'You keep thinking that.' He entwined his fingers in her hair to gently ease her head aside, kissing her lightly up her neck.

She'd never asked him if he cared. It had never seemed important until then. 'You promise you'll look after us?'

'I'll take care of you every step of the way,' he said with a smile.

'I was so scared I'd lost you, Jake. Watching you like that. It was horrible.'

'So show me how glad you are to have me back,' he suggested, lowering his incisors to her neck again.

'Not there,' she said breathily. 'Do it somewhere Leila won't see. I mean it. She'll freak. And I just don't want to deal with it tonight, not after everything else.'

Jake smirked as he lowered to his knees, dragging his kisses down her cleavage, her stomach, his eyes gazing playfully up at her as he lifted her dress to expose her thighs. 'What about down here?'

Alisha nodded. She slid her hands over the back of his neck, up through his closely cut hair. 'Just take it easy this time, all right?'

She tried to relax, her head pressed back against the door, her breathing terse. His tongue felt cold, wet against her inner thigh as he licked her as if she was coated in sugar. Then, as he bit, she flinched, involuntarily gasped, and grasped his shoulders. She could feel him smile as he started to suck, one hand gripping her thigh so as to keep it steady, his other hand pressing against her hip, keeping her pinned to the door.

Closing her eyes, she relaxed into the discomfort, the sensation, the knowledge that, for those few moments, he was completely lost in her and her alone; not the multitude of others that swooned and crooned after him, scrabbling for his attention. In those few moments he was hers. In those few moments she was the one he wanted. The only one he wanted.

This is what Leila could never understand. Any more than Leila understood why she'd had to risk so much to save him.

❊ ❊ ❊

Leila seemingly remained oblivious to his presence as she sat perched on the edge of the round table, her gaze lost in the distance. Her bare toes rested on the bench, her knuckles pale as she hugged herself. Her fine, shoulder-length hair was caressed by the breeze, a breeze that swept the subtle aroma of strawberries and white lily towards him – a scent as fresh, delicate and enticing as the witch herself.

She looked so unguarded that Caleb almost doubted his suspicions, but he couldn't doubt the spark in his defence mechanisms the moment their eyes had met. He'd hunted enough to know one when he saw one, whatever clever façade they hid behind. And the deadly female on his terrace was going to learn, if she didn't already know, that not even the most adept of her kind fooled him.

Catching a glimpse of him in her blind spot, Leila flinched, her startled gaze meeting his.

'Not quite Summerton, is it?' he said, stepping across the threshold to join her.

She reverted her gaze to the view, but he knew she was remaining diligently aware of his approach in the corner of her eye.

'And very different to what you're used to, I'm sure,' he added, strolling across to the barrier. Facing the view, he braced his arms on the rail as he surveyed the sector he'd built up from nothing but ruins. 'It's a very different view from up here,' he said. 'On the ground you see ruin, deprivation, neglect. Up here, looking over the expanse, you see a community. One that, despite its impoverished state, has found a way to work together, or at least maintain peace by staying apart. A community that knows it'll take nothing for it to implode so abides by its own rules, its own laws, its own survival mechanisms.'

'A community run by crime, by bullies, by intimidation, by a select few who have taken it upon themselves to be in charge. A community run by fear.'

He couldn't help but smile at her ignorance. 'Believe it or not, this used to be nothing but fields when I was a child. I spent my youth climbing trees and swimming in lakes around here under clear starry nights.' He turned to face her, folding his arms as he leaned back against the barrier. 'Long before the Regulations obviously.'

She squeezed her clenched hands in her lap. 'Regulations that allowed our kind to be protected.'

'Protection that brought with it all the privileges, despite the fact it was your kind who ruined the landscape in the first place.'

'I'm not here to talk politics, Caleb.'

'I thought you'd love the opportunity, what with those special little rings of yours.'

'I'm entitled to an opinion.'

'I never said you weren't. I'm merely pointing out that at least we understand limitations whereas your kind's selfishness knows no bounds.'

Her hazel eyes narrowed. 'And where would your kind be without ours to sustain you? We die, you die. You die, we survive. I think there's a pecking order in that, don't you?' The glare was brief before she reverted her attention back to the view, her pretty eyes brimming with a defiance and indignation that both irritated and aroused him.

'Your vehemence is admirable, fledgling, even if the ignorance that gives it its foundation is laughable.'

'I know more than you think.'

'As if I would dare to underestimate someone so experienced and worldly. Someone with such textbook knowledge.'

Leila frowned at his mocking as her eyes snapped back to his. 'Textbook knowledge that saved your brother's life.'

But serryns didn't save vampires. Not even if their last breath, the final beat of their heart, depended on it. Serryns existed for one purpose and one purpose only: to kill as many vampires as possible – male, female, even youths – in as cruel and vicious a way as they could.

And under any other circumstances, this witch's – or if his instincts were right, this serryn's – entertainment value would have taken some surpassing. And he would have already been breaking her down, stripping her of everything she was until she was nothing but a shell.

Yet something about this one was already niggling him. Beneath her flattering knee-length tea dress, her feminine, slender body was toned but most definitely not honed from training or combat. There were no bruises, no marks and not a single scar that he could detect. Every inch of her skin was pale, smooth and unblemished. Even her long, delicate fingers ended with flawless nails.

He looked back at her pretty eyes, her sensual mouth, not a hint of make-up to emphasise either. But it wasn't that her appearance was void of purposeful seduction, it was that her whole demeanour was. Because although he knew only too well from experience that a serryn's facade didn't have to mean a thing, her nervous tension in his presence most certainly did. He was either looking at his first latent or she was one hell of an actress.

'And you did good tonight,' he said in response. 'You and your textbook.'

'I did what I had to,' she said, maintaining her avoidance of the intimacy of eye contact.

Strolling over to join her, he eased up onto the table beside her, purposefully an inch too close so that their thighs were almost touching. 'I know it wasn't easy for you.'

Leila tensed, her breath quickening, but she didn't move, her eyes saturated with unwavering tenacity.

He leaned back on one arm, bracing it just behind her, not close enough to touch, but close enough for her to feel the threat of its proximity. Her cheeks flushed and she clenched her hands until her knuckles were pale, holding her breath for longer than he was sure was comfortable. But still the wilful little witch remained rooted to the spot. 'In fact, it must have really stung, considering how you feel about us.'

When she refused to respond, he couldn't help but smile.

'I make you uneasy, don't I?'

She met his gaze, albeit fleetingly again. 'You don't.'

He raked his gaze slowly and purposely intrusively from her dainty feet, up over her shapely legs, her pert chest to then linger on her eyes. 'So, is all this nervous tension because you've never been alone with a vampire before? Or is it that you're not good with males of either species?'

She frowned. 'You're a vampire and I'm, as you like to put it, a witch. Our kinds have never exactly got along have they?'

'Which makes you coming here tonight all the more brave. Alisha tells me this is your first time out of Summerton.'

'I've been to Midtown before.'

'But never Blackthorn.'

'I have no reason to come here.'

'I bet you're itching to get home, aren't you? It must be very un-comfortable for someone like you here, with nothing but vampires for miles.'

She glanced at him, the wariness clear in her eyes. He could hear her heart pound and predicted what was to follow.

He caught her wrist as soon as her feet touched the floor. 'Something wrong?'

She could barely look at him. 'I'm going to check on Alisha.'

'Alisha's fine. She'll be down in the club with Jake by now.'

Her eyes flared in panic. 'But I told her to get our things together.'

'I told her there was no hurry.'

Scowling, she moved to step away, but Caleb caught her by the hip and tugged her between his thighs. Pushing the wrist he held behind her back, the static surge surprised him as their eyes met again. He'd known too many of them. Too many to justify what she inexplicably roused in him. And he knew her kind too well to know she shouldn't be looking at him the way she was.

She slammed her hand to his chest in protest. 'What are you doing?'

Panic. Genuine panic. She was becoming more intriguing by the minute and those ragged, shallow breaths were almost as enticing as the soft, warm body he contained between his legs. He tauntingly appraised her throat and cleavage. 'You're not as confident as you like to portray, are you?'

'Let me go,' she warned.

Peeling her hand from his chest, interlacing his fingers with hers, he gently pushed it behind her back to join the other, holding them securely with one of his. 'Something tells me you've been in that cosy little nest of yours too long, fledgling.'

She tried to tug free, her erratic breaths caressing his lips. 'Maybe I just don't like being this close to you.'

'Flatterer,' he said, gently brushing her hair back from her neck. He traced his lips up her smooth warm skin, her scent powerful, pure and dangerously compelling.

She flinched and futilely tried to pull back, panic flaring in her eyes. 'Don't,' she warned. 'You don't know what you're doing.'

'Oh, I know exactly what I'm doing,' he whispered against her ear. He reached into his back pocket and flicked the lid off a syringe. 'As you're about to discover. *Serryn.*'

Chapter Five

Leila woke lying on her back on a cold, stone floor. Sensing her constraints, she gasped against her gag. Her arms were manacled either side of her head, and her legs, spread a foot or so apart, were also bound.

The room spun and pulsated from her heavy sedation as she scanned the bare, moonlit chamber. At first she thought it was her giddiness, but realised the floor had a subtle decline –a decline towards some kind of drain below. More manacles hung on the wall behind her and further manacles to her right, dark stains marring the stone beneath them. A breeze channelled through the high, barred window to her left, adding to dankness of the thirty-foot-square enclosure. She strained her neck to look behind her left shoulder towards the sound of male voices distant beyond the open steel door.

Serryn.

It was the last thing he'd said to her as he'd held her arms behind her back – as he'd held her against him with a strength that had sent a surge of simultaneous panic and arousal through her body. He'd brushed his lips against her neck as a cruel taunt, causing goosebumps to ripple over her skin. She'd been convinced he was going to bite – believing that serryns were indeed powerful enough to wipe out any vampire's notorious self-preservation. Even inept, latent serryns like her.

Caleb knew.

Somehow he knew what she was.

She shivered. Still delirious and disorientated, she wriggled her wrists and ankles, trying to see if there was any give in her binds. She coughed with the effort, her throat arid.

And heard footsteps.

She stared back over at the door, her heart pounding, her breath held.

The second Caleb appeared, her stomach vaulted. She stared at the sword in his right hand, its blade glinting in the moonlight.

Jake followed close behind him. Metal grinded against stone as he dragged someone strapped to a chair along with him, slamming him to a halt under the window.

The man in the chair was maybe in his late twenties, trim but muscular, his floppy fair hair almost masking his eyes. Another vampire. She could sense it. There were grazes on his face and both his lips, and one eye was swollen. He sent a wary glance in Leila's direction as he watched Caleb approach her.

She kept perfectly still, her breaths curt and erratic behind her gag as Caleb stepped astride her hips. His eyes, darkened by the moonlight, were as hostile as the room he was intending to either slaughter or imprison her in. Eyes she didn't dare break from as he placed the tip of his sword against the base of her throat with an unnervingly steady precision.

'Leila, meet Tay. Tay, meet Leila.'

She shot a nervous glance at Tay, who anxiously glanced back at her.

'You two might have a lot in common,' Caleb said as he slid the sword slowly down her cleavage and over her knotted stomach, before stepping away again. 'Tay's been a very bad vampire, even if he does insist on denying it.'

Tay's nervous gaze locked on Caleb as he approached, his wrists straining under the pressure of the ropes that bound his arms to the armrests.

'Tay made the unforgivable mistake of thinking he could double-cross me and Jake. Swindle us. Unfortunately he made the fatal error of overlooking the loyalty of our nearest and dearest work associates – associates whose loyalty can't be bought at *any* price.' He pressed the tip of the sword against Tay's throat.

Tay's eyes bulged in fear. His hands clenched, his wrists and legs straining against the restraints, the veins in his neck and his temple throbbing.

'Even more unfortunately, I have a complete intolerance for anyone who thinks they can deceive me.' Caleb pushed the tip of the sword into his flesh, just a little, but enough to make him bleed. Tay squealed behind his gag, his eyes wide and pleading as they stared up into Caleb's. 'Which Tay should know only too well,' he added. He lowered the sword again and stepped away, twirling the heavy weaponry as if wielding a child's toy.

As he sauntered back over towards her, she knew it would be the easiest thing in the world for him to drive the blade through her right there and then. But she guessed that wasn't his intent.

Not yet.

Caleb crouched beside her, on the far side from Tay. She flinched as he brushed a few loose strands from her eyes and cheek.

'I've been mulling over what to do with you, Tay,' he said, addressing the bound vampire despite looking at Leila. 'Whether to make an example of you or make you disappear like you never even existed.' He slid the back of his cool hand gently down over Leila's throat, the tension thickening in the already dense room. 'Then along comes the perfect solution.'

Leila's pulse raced as Caleb lay the sword beside her. He pulled a roll of leather from his back pocket and unravelled it to reveal an array of syringes. Her heart leapt.

Hell, no, this wasn't happening. He couldn't drug her again. Whatever he was planning, she couldn't be unconscious. She stared up at him and shook her head, her eyes wide with panic.

'What's the saying?' Caleb removed one of the empty syringes, flicking off the lid. 'Killing two birds with one stone?' He met her gaze. 'Don't worry, sweetheart, this will only hurt a little.'

Caleb wrapped his cool hand around her forearm and pressed the tip of the needle against a vein in the crook of her arm. Leila pleaded behind her gag, cried out in protest, but still he slid the needle inside.

She flinched, closed her eyes and twisted her head away, wincing as he extracted her blood.

Withdrawing the needle, he left Leila palpitating as he stood and strolled back over to Tay, the loaded syringe in his hand.

And then she knew.

The horror struck her hard, fast and painfully.

She knew exactly what was coming next.

❋ ❋ ❋

Caleb stood in front of Tay, the vampire's cold blue eyes glowering up at him in fear. It was a necessity like so many necessities in Blackthorn. It was about survival and survival was about reputation. Not just anybody became somebody in Blackthorn, and it was even harder becoming a somebody when you were a nobody. Caleb had the fortune of his reputation – his history of being one of the few intrepid serryn hunters – but he still had to stay ahead, and staying ahead meant never letting his guard down. Ever. It meant no mercy and no second chances. Any sign of pity could be fatal. He had to maintain his reputation for being guarded, disciplined and brutal, especially in his line of work. Running a club was hard. It was the core of their culture. And holding on to the most successful club in Blackthorn was no easy feat, not when there was always someone waiting to step into those shoes.

Tay had worked with him long enough to know better than to try. He needed to be an example for any others who might think the same way.

The same was true for the serryn behind him. If he was right, if there was a ploy involved in her coming there, she needed to know exactly what she was up against. She needed to know that when it came to her kind, Caleb had no compassion or mercy at all.

'Do you know what this is, Tay?' Caleb asked, holding the syringe up. 'This is a vampire's worst nightmare. A stake through the heart, burnt to ashes, being beheaded – they're all child's play compared to this. Merciful even. This here is a little tube of agony like you can't comprehend. A few droplets of this blood will weaken you more than a month without feeding. Half of the contents will leave you delusional, delirious and sweating blood. It'll send pins and needles so excruciating through your body that you can't walk, you can't see, you can't even think. A couple more syringes will make you lose control of every limb, every function. It'll saturate your brain so your skull expands with the pressure of the swelling. It's all you'll know for days, weeks even. One extra little dose on top of that will make every single one of your veins explode, every internal organ implode, an agony you'll feel right until the last moment. This little tube of terror, Tay, is pure serryn blood – fresh, warm and straight from the source. I should know – I hunted them for long enough.'

Tay stared warily back at Leila before glancing back at the syringe. He shook his head and mumbled something behind the gag.

Caleb reached for it and tugged it down. 'What was that?'

'There ain't no serryns anymore,' Tay said, his eyes brimming with fear, spittle trickling down his chin. He slid his tongue tersely over his bottom lip. 'They're extinct. Everybody knows that.'

Caleb exhaled a curt laugh. He looked at Jake, and Jake smiled back. 'He doesn't believe me.'

Jake folded his arms. 'Oh dear, I think he's calling you a liar, Caleb.'

Caleb shrugged. 'Maybe I *am* wrong. It's been a long time since I've run into a serryn. No, sorry, strike that – it's been a long time since I've tracked one down, tortured her, slaughtered her and burnt every toxic part of her. So, maybe this time I have made a mistake. Maybe I'm losing my infamous touch. Maybe you're right, Tay, buddy. Maybe that girl over there is just a regular little witch.' He held up the syringe, his thumb on the plunger. 'Shall we see?'

Tay recoiled into his seat, his eyes wide. 'Wait!'

'What? Not so sure now?' Caleb asked, strolling around the back of him.

'You've had your fun, Caleb. I fucked up, okay? I admit it. You let me go, and we'll work this out. I'll do whatever you want.'

'I've got plenty who will do whatever I want, ones who know better than to step over the line. But thanks for the confession.' Caleb yanked Tay's head back by his hair. Exposing his neck, he slammed the syringe into his artery and pressed down the plunger.

Tay eyes bulged. His fingers flexed. His whole body went into spasm. He thrust his chin upwards, exposing his neck, his veins distending.

Caleb sauntered away, twirling the syringe in his fingers before crouching by Leila again. He reached across her, tucked the syringe back in the leather roll, glanced back over his shoulder at Tay before looking back down at her. 'Potent little thing, aren't you?'

Leila turned her head away, the look in her eyes one of genuine horror.

He caught her by the jaw. 'What? Don't you want to watch? I thought this was the best bit for you?'

But Leila defiantly slammed her eyes shut.

Caleb glanced over his shoulder again as Tay jerked more violently. Blood started to splutter from his mouth and trickle from his eyes as he cried out in pain.

Jake took a step back. 'Unbelievable,' he said. 'From one syringe?'

'I told you she was powerful,' Caleb said, standing. He strolled back towards his brother as he twirled his sword again, comfortable and lax in his hand.

'How long's this going to go on for?' Jake asked.

'Could be hours. Could be days.'

Tay flayed as he gurgled in agony.

'Could be weeks.' Caleb stopped in front of Tay and watched him for a few moments.

He snatched a glance at his brother, at the distress and discomfort in his eyes. Seeing serryn effects for the first time wasn't easy. But he needed him to know; he needed him to understand why he had to keep Leila there. He needed him to understand what her kind was capable of. And he needed to be sure his brother kept a safe distance. Just one mouthful of her blood in his system and no amount of spells or potions were going to bring him back this time – temporarily or not.

He returned his full attention to Tay. He might have been a thief and a liar, but no vampire deserved that level of suffering. And Caleb refused to be *that* much of a bastard. He'd done what was necessary. He'd made his point.

He drew back his sword-wielding arm and thrust the blade with swift and fatal precision direct into Tay's heart.

And there was silence.

❄ ❄ ❄

Lying frozen and shuddering on the dungeon floor, Leila kept her head turned away from the worse macabre nightmare she had witnessed since that one night.

As the rain pounded outside the dungeon window, gushing down from the drainpipes, lashing against the walls beyond, her drug-induced state re-evoked the long-suppressed childhood memories.

She was back in the alley, sickness rising at the back of her throat, her small frail legs leaden as she stared down at her mother's limp body discarded to the ground. Then she was turning to run, just like her mother had screamed at her to do.

She was pounding through overfilled puddles, the cold murky water saturating her plimsolls and jeans. Squeezing through the gap in the broken door, she was entering the dark, abandoned building. She was running through and under crates, scrabbling, leaping, falling and picking herself up again as she heard him tearing the door off its hinges. All the time she could hear him closing in on her – the flap of his coat, his terrifying laughter.

He grabbed the scruff of her neck and lifted her off the ground, letting her dangle as he stared into her eyes. He laughed as she swiped futilely at his face and kicked at his chest.

He tore her coat, her jumper, exposing her neck. His incisors extended through his sneer and he bit. Hard. Mercilessly.

She had jerked at the excruciating pain, her breaths curt, tears filling her eyes.

And she'd fallen hard to the floor as he'd released her.

She hadn't understood the gurgling sound he'd made. Hadn't been able to work out why he stared at her the way he did when he stumbled back, his hands clutching his throat.

She hadn't understood why he'd fallen to his knees as he coughed up blood, his nails tearing the stone floor.

And she hadn't wanted to understand.

She'd run back the way she'd come – back through the torn-off door and back up the alley towards her mother. She'd grabbed her arm and tried to pull her towards the road, pleading with her to wake up, pleading with her to run with her. But her mother hadn't moved. Her mother had been silent, staring up at her with glazed, dead eyes, blood still pumping from the artery in her neck.

And Leila had collapsed to the ground beside her, her face buried in her dead mother's clothes as the clouds released their own tears.

She was nine years old when it had happened, four years after her grandfather first discovered her talent for reading the archaic languages. He told her the whole truth the night after he'd brought her back from the alley.

His words echoed through her mind like it was only yesterday. 'You're more than just an interpreter, Leila.'

She had been sat at his desk, surrounded by his books and papers. The fire had been flickering in the hearth, the wind billowing against the window. She'd known he was about to say something that was going to change everything. She'd seen it in his tired, wrinkled eyes and the tense and uneasy way he'd sat.

'We never know which generation it will strike. It skipped your grandmother and mother but it rests with you. The rarity of what you hold is more powerful than you can imagine. It is a gift for humanity and the most lethal curse to the vampires. You're a serryn, Leila.'

She'd read about them before in the texts from his collection. She didn't understand most of the explanations, but she knew the gist. Serryns were special. Rare and special. They could kill vampires. 'But I don't understand,' she had said. 'I've tried to, but I don't.'

'In time you will.' He'd placed his large, warm hand over hers. 'And when you are ready, I will tell you everything you need to know to keep you safe.'

'From them?'

'From them and all their enemies. The vampires will want to destroy you because they hate what you are. They will want to protect themselves and to protect their own kind from you and from others who will use you to get to them. That is why this must stay our secret. Without your mother and father to protect you, it is down to me to keep you safe. That is why we can't tell the authorities what happened tonight, why they must never know you were there. That's why I had to dispose of that vampire's body. If they knew what you were, they would want you too.' He squeezed her hand tighter. 'This must be our secret, Leila. You must never tell Sophie and Alisha you were there. You must never tell them that you saw what happened or they will be at risk too. No one must ever know.'

No one should ever have known. That was what she had always intended. That was why she should never have stepped foot in Blackthorn.

She warily glanced over to see Caleb wiping his sword off on Tay's trousers before strolling over towards her, spatters of Tay's blood on his jeans, his shirt and face.

This was it. She and Alisha were as good as dead. Killed by a vampire, just like their mother.

She braced herself as he stepped astride her hips again, as he held the tip of the blade against the bare flesh beneath her collarbone. She glazed over, still weakened by the sedative, cold perspiration sweeping over her.

'Now. What to do with you,' he said, tilting his head to the side as he tauntingly traced his gaze down over her. He pressed the flat of his sword to her outer thigh and slid the cold metal upwards, taking the hem of her dress with it to her hip. With expert precision he slipped the very tip of the sword under the thin hip-band of her underwear.

Leila held her breath, only too aware that the blade could slice through the delicate fabric with no effort at all.

'Don't worry, that would be too easy,' he said, lifting the sword back to her collarbone. 'I prefer a fair fight.' He paused. 'So, does Alisha know what you are?'

She glanced anxiously at Jake as he stepped alongside his brother, his arms folded, his brow furrowed.

Caleb slid the sword to her cheek, forcing her to look back at him. 'I asked you a question,' he said, his green eyes narrowing. 'Does she know?'

Tentatively holding his glare, she shook her head.

'Did you tell anyone else where you were coming?'

Reluctantly, she shook her head again.

He raked her slowly. 'I've known some brazen serryns in my time, but never one who's walked so seemingly unprepared into a vampire's lair.' Retracting his sword, he crouched down over her. 'That either makes you reckless or just plain stupid.' He kept his gaze locked on hers for a few uncomfortable seconds longer before he stood again and stepped away.

Caleb dragged the chair containing Tay's dead body back towards the door. Jake followed behind and slammed the steel door shut, leaving her alone in the moonlight.

Leila dropped her head back against the floor. Trying to catch her breath, she scanned the room again. The place had been built to be impenetrable. The walls were solid, the window too high, the bars too close together.

Was this how others of her kind had felt when they were trapped?

No, others of her kind wouldn't have got themselves into this situation in the first place. Others of her kind would have undergone their training, not just their studies. Others of her kind would have slain the dying vampire then taken out his brother before marching out of that club with their sister right beside them. More to the point, others of her kind wouldn't have been stupid enough to go there in the first place.

Leila took a deep, shaky breath and stared up at the stone ceiling. The room contracted and expanded as she teetered on the edge of consciousness. The breeze washed over her as the dankness of the chamber filled her lungs, the rain still pounding outside the window, the wind howling.

Locked in a vampire's torture chamber with no way out and not the first clue of what she was going to do about it.

She closed her eyes. All she could see was Tay writhing in agony – writhing in agony from *her* blood. Blood that Caleb injected in him knowing exactly what it would do.

Caleb who had killed one of his own with such cruel ease.

He was a monster. And now she was at his mercy.

Chapter Six

Jake closed the dungeon door. He stepped around Tay's lifeless body, Caleb having abandoned it still strapped to the chair in the tiny interrogation room that sat between the dungeon and their office.

Caleb was already at the drinks cabinet, his back to him as he poured them both a whisky.

Tay had it coming. He had no doubts about that. But even for Caleb, the serryn venom was a cruel tack. Necessary, Caleb had told him before they'd gone in there – the perfect solution to both problems. Because Caleb always was methodical.

But this was not good – not only having seen just how terrifyingly accurate Caleb had been in his descriptions of a serryn's potential, but because Jake knew, remembered, just how vicious Caleb could be when it came to them.

They always did it to him – triggered something: a darkness that Caleb found difficult enough to contain anyway since suffering at the hands of one at such a young age. He'd survived, was an extremely rare and fortunate one who had, but the unspoken trauma had changed something inside of him – something that wouldn't heal. Jake had never needed to know the details of what had actually happened to Caleb that night to see that.

And the loss of their eldest brother, Seth, thirty years later had only fuelled Caleb's darkness. Seth who had been killed breaking up a brawl – a brawl he would never have been on the streets to be a part of if he hadn't been wrongfully dismissed with disgrace from his duties with the Higher Order.

Caleb would never forgive the Higher Order for that – not least Jarin, the high-ranking, lying vampire who had accused his loyal bodyguard of cowardice in order to cover his own back. Jarin, who had betrayed and humiliated Seth even further by unjustly placing him on the dishonoured list.

They had both idolised their older brother – but for Caleb, Seth had been the father figure they'd never known. And Seth had been the only one capable of tempering Caleb.

Caleb had slipped into an even darker place after that – immersed in resentment, restrained from enacting revenge only by knowing the repercussions for Jake and anyone else he had left to care about.

Then along came Feinith – the beautiful, sensual, Higher Order vampire with an offer Caleb couldn't refuse: a chance to appease some of that pent-up frustration and turmoil by hunting serryns.

But it had only done the opposite.

For the decades during his hunting, there had been too many dawns of Caleb returning home blood-splattered, wounded and darkly unrepentant. Worse, he'd seen his brother thrive on the depravity and cruelty he had engaged in. There were times when he'd lost his brother to it and not only physically. Emotionally the serryns created an impenetrable barrier in him. Seventy years of hunting serryns had turned him into something almost unrecognisable from the brother he had grown up with.

He knew Feinith had a lot to do with that and he'd never forgive her for it. Feinith had fed that side of Caleb. Caleb's tumultuous on-and-off furtive relationship with her during his hunting days, let alone the years that had followed, had done nothing to abate the darkness that had almost consumed him.

Sixty years since Caleb's last kill, he'd hoped it had been the last of it. The ban on the hunting of serryns, let alone them seemingly becoming extinct, had since let Caleb rebuild his life. And Jake had enjoyed having his brother back – the real Caleb: a Caleb not weighed down with the need and desire to wipe every single serryn off the planet. Tension and energy he had instead ploughed into building the businesses.

But having seen how Caleb had looked at Leila, the way he'd dragged that blade slowly and coaxingly down her defenceless body, told him how close his brother still lingered to the edge. And more than ever, he knew why he needed to get her out of there. Not just for Leila's sake, but for his brother's sake too. He couldn't have that brother back – the uncompromising, bloodthirsty, depraved Caleb. Not for anything.

'Caleb, we've got to get her out of here,' he said, joining his brother at the arc of CCTV monitors that bowed against the wall directly ahead.

Caleb's attention was fixed on the image of Leila lying on the dungeon floor. 'Not now we've got more reason than ever to wait until dawn, we don't.'

'And then what?' He watched Caleb knock back a mouthful of drink in silence. 'Caleb?'

'How old do you think she is? Twenty-five, twenty-six?'

'Alisha's twenty-five and I know Leila's a few years older than that. Why?'

'She should have been active years ago.'

'Active?'

'Hunting. Did you see that look in her eyes when I killed Tay?'

He had. He'd seen the fear. He'd seen the horror and disgust at what her blood had done. A look that was a far cry from the serryn warriors Caleb had spoken of. 'It wasn't exactly a pretty sight.'

'It's what they're made for, little brother. It's what they live for. I've seen looks in those cold bitches' eyes that would chill you to your core.'

'Which is all the more reason why we should get her out of here quick.'

Caleb ran the rim of the glass across his lower lip as he stared pensively at the screen. 'She can't be a latent. They're teenagers, not women in their twenties.'

'Maybe she's the exception to the rule.'

'There is no exception to the rule when it comes to them. And there never will be. Besides, she may not have liked what she saw in there but she knew what was coming, so someone's taken a bite out of her before. That in itself should have been enough to trigger her, so what's holding her back?'

'Maybe she only found out recently.'

Caleb looked back at the screen as Leila gently arched her back from the floor in a vain attempt to stretch. 'A serryn with cause on top of instinct, from what Alisha told us. Recent or not, there's something more to this.'

'I don't like the look in your eyes, Caleb. I know that look. Think about what you're doing. What if she has saved my life?'

'Her kind owes us thousands of lives. Do you think if it wasn't for Alisha, she would have had any intention of helping you?'

Jake frowned. 'You saw it yourself in there. She's not like them.'

'Or she's exceptionally good at what she does.'

Caleb wiped his thumb repeatedly over the control panel, drawing the image closer. She shuddered, no doubt cold and exhausted. And judging from her pained attempt at stretching again, the discomfort at being on the hard floor had well and truly set in. Her eyes were reddened, her pale cheeks flushed. Caleb drew in closer still on her face, on those pretty hazel eyes. And when he did so, there was something in Caleb's eyes too – something dark, something deadly, something Jake had hoped never to see again.

'You made a deal with Alisha,' Jake reminded him. 'You made a deal with them both. You never go back on your word.'

'If I let her walk out of here, I'm putting every one of us beneath this roof under threat.'

'Caleb, you can't do this.'

Caleb's eyes flashed darkly as he looked across at him. 'And I can't let her go. Not now. She's not going to walk away and pretend this never happened. She's either going to come back here fully fledged and without Alisha to worry about, or she's going to bring the whole Vampire Control Unit down on us – and that's attention we could do without. Let alone if word gets out I let her go. That'll be our reputation gone, and we will be finished here in Blackthorn. You know what the fallout of this could be.'

'And if the Higher Order hears about it our lives aren't going to be worth living anyway. You know how much Jarin is itching to get at you. It's bad enough he's suspicious of your relationship with Feinith– '

'*Ex*-relationship,' Caleb interjected. 'She walked away from me for good the minute she betrothed herself to that lying bastard.'

'Caleb, finding out you've concealed a serryn will give him the perfect excuse to prosecute you.'

'Then we need to make sure nobody *does* find out. Which is why I need you back at front of house keeping an eye on things while I deal with this.'

There was no way he could leave his brother alone with her. Not knowing there were worse things than death that Caleb could inflict. Much worse things. 'By doing what?'

'Nothing for you to worry about.' He knocked back a mouthful, ice clinking against glass.

'I'm not leaving you alone with her.'

'Need I remind you I'm not the one with the self-control issues, little brother?'

'No, but I know you like to play dangerous, and that's just a little too close to the edge. Whether she's active or not, that blood flowing through her veins is still poisonous. She needs to be kept out of the way. We could get Hade to take her somewhere. Hand her over to someone until dawn. Keep it underground. You've got enough loyalty to keep this hushed.'

Caleb glanced back across at his brother. 'And what's the fun in that?'

'I knew it. I knew you wouldn't be able to resist. Caleb, I can't let you do this. Not for your sake. Not for hers. If you're right, if she has done a holding spell, you need her alive, right? She dies, I die with her.'

'I'm not going to kill her.'

'You can promise me that, can you?'

Caleb looked across at his brother. 'Until dawn, yes.'

'When was the last time you fed, Caleb? A proper feed.'

'I'm fine.'

'I'll line a couple of girls up for you. Get yourself sated. You need to tackle her with a clear head.'

'My head is perfectly clear.'

'Like an alcoholic says to a full bottle of Vodka. Caleb, I'm not happy about this.'

'There's only one way I can make a decision, Jake. If that façade is real, she won't be able to keep it up all night. If I want to see what she is, I've got to lower those defences first.'

Jake's grip tightened on his glass. He knew exactly what that meant. 'If you're to justify whatever it is you're planning to do to her, you need that façade to slip, you mean. You want her to prove herself to be like the others. That's the main reason you're keeping her here. You're insane. I am not going to let you do this – this crazy power game you're starting up is going to stop right here.'

'Is that my brother actually stressing about something?'

'Look me in the eye and tell me you're not daring her to do something.'

'I am making sure we're prepared.'

'Making sure she knows who's in charge, more like. But this is too dangerous, even for you. And don't forget Alisha's in the equation.'

'Is she still in the club?'

'Hade's keeping an eye on her. I told her there were a couple of things I had to sort. But she's going to start getting twitchy in another hour or so.'

'Then ply her with plenty of drinks. Use one of the spare apartments tonight. I don't want her around until tomorrow. I don't want you around either. As soon as those sedatives wear off properly, reality is going to sink in and I don't want you in the firing line.'

'And what about you? What if you take a bite? What if she's that one serryn too many? Like you said, what if she is exceptionally good at what she does? It's been a long time for you, Caleb.'

'Not long enough for me to forget how to handle them,' he said, staring back at the screen.

Jake needed to get back in the dungeon and warn her. He needed to tell Leila to keep calm. He needed to tell her that if she kept her head down, he would work on Caleb to let her go.

But this was his brother. His brother whom he loved and trusted. Caleb was no fool when it came to them. He'd always told him how devious they were and how manipulative – luring vampires in, making them see whatever they needed them to see. He didn't know if she was any different, not really. He only had Alisha's word for it. But he did know his brother. And his brother knew how to handle serryns better than anyone else ever had.

Jake indicated towards Tay's abandoned body out of sight in the room behind them. 'What about him?'

'I'll incinerate him. We don't want any traces of her blood found. And give that photo we've got of the sisters back to Hade. Tell him I want the other sister found.'

'Why?'

'She could prove useful.'

'How?'

'Just trust me, Jake.'

Jake hovered then ran his hands back through his cropped hair before exhaling a reluctant, terse sigh. 'You'd better know what you're doing.'

'When don't I?'

Jake tongued his teeth as he shook his head slightly, hands falling to his hips. 'I'll sort Alisha but I'm checking on you in a couple of hours. No arguments,' he said as he stepped over to the door.

He looked back over his shoulder at his brother, but Caleb's attention was back on the screen.

Closing the office door behind him, Jake stood in the corridor, the music vibrating up from his right.

He had to give Caleb more credence. He never lost it. Ever. He got carried away but the hunt was always perfection, from the tales he'd heard. Every serryn execution was controlled. It was what made him so damn good. It was what made him the most successful hunter of serryns back all those decades ago. Caleb bit only when he wanted to bite. And no serryn had ever succeeded in convincing him otherwise. That was what made him so proficient. That was what had made him the best. And he'd been up against the best and won.

This would be no different.

And Leila wouldn't act. Leila would think only of getting her and Alisha out safely. And he had to trust in that. She'd be smart enough to know. And his brother, if he really believed she had done a holding spell, loved him too much to do anything to put him in jeopardy before dawn.

He had no choice but to leave them to it for now.

Leila had to get through this one on her own.

Chapter Seven

The wind whipped against the side of the building, whistling through the gaps in the window, the chilled air taunting Leila's skin. Laughter and voices echoed from far beyond, reminding her of a world that carried on without a care of what was going on in the shadows.

A metallic clunk resounded as the door was unlocked. She looked over her shoulder to see Caleb entering the room, only this time he was alone and armed with two empty chairs.

Caleb – the self-proclaimed serryn hunter.

She'd heard of them, read about them. She knew they were as rare as serryns themselves. She also knew how revered they were. Only the select intrepid few even dared to take on serryns. Serryn hunters were brutal, cruel and merciless. They were also the strongest of their kind, both physically and mentally. They had to be. Serryns were renowned for breaking any vampire they chose. But even the most powerful of her kind were known to waver under the prospect of coming up against a true hunter.

And she wasn't surprised if they were all like him. Caleb was lethal for more reasons than his proclaimed skills.

He locked the dungeon door, crossed the room towards her and planted the chairs a couple of feet away.

Leila braced herself and clenched her hands in their constraints as he stood astride her hips.

'I'm going to untie you,' he said, his stern eyes burning into hers. 'But if you try anything stupid, including attempting to utter one nasty little spell, even a hint of an incantation, I will strap you back down and go and rip your sister's heart out. Do you understand me?'

She had no doubt he meant every word. She begrudgingly nodded.

He took the key from his back pocket and crouched at her feet. He released her ankles first and then her wrists.

As he took a step back, Leila pulled down her gag and took a deep intake of breath. She sat up too quickly, the blood rushing to her head, tilting her off balance, forcing her to lean back on her arms.

'Take it easy,' he said. 'The sedative will be in your system for a little while longer yet.'

She looked up at him, his green eyes darkened in the shadows as he held out his hand to help her up – a hand that was as steady as his uncompromising gaze.

Ignoring his offer of assistance, she got to her knees. She waited a moment, realised she didn't have enough balance, and sank back onto her haunches again. She clutched her icy-cold feet and squeezed to try and evoke some circulation as she warily watched him ease into the nearest chair side-on to her.

Having one more go at getting to her feet, she succeeded, relieved both to be standing and off the hard floor. She wrapped her arms around herself in an attempt at some much-needed warmth – another luxury her constraints hadn't allowed.

He kicked the free chair towards her. 'Sit down.'

She felt her indignation soar, but she knew the sensible thing right then was to comply. She perched on the edge, her hands clutching either side of the seat as she fought against her shivering, at the indignation of her situation, the fear.

Reaching forward, he placed his hand between her knees and dragged her seat towards him. He leaned back again as he rested his foot on the left rung of her chair. 'Not exactly dungeon material, are you?'

She released her right hand's grip on the side of the chair so as not to risk brushing his thigh and instead wrapped her arm protectively across her stomach. She squeezed her knees together so their legs wouldn't touch. He'd taunted her with his proximity on the terrace, but she wasn't going to give him the satisfaction again.

She glanced over his shoulder at the open door. Everything in her screamed to make a break for it, but there was no telling where she was or her chances of finding Alisha. Wherever they were it still had to be Blackthorn, and that meant far more vampires than Caleb out there baying for her blood.

Besides, she didn't stand a hope in hell of outrunning him – and he knew it. Something told her the unlocked door was his way of daring her to try. She lowered her gaze to the floor.

'Look at me,' he said.

She closed her eyes for a moment, resentment tearing through her.

'Look at me or you'll learn the hard way that I know like asking twice.'

She tore her gaze from the floor to glower up into his green eyes.

He smirked. 'Well, if that isn't a "fuck you" glare, I don't know what is.'

He couldn't have been more right, but she ignored the coax. Instead she averted her gaze to the stains beneath the manacles. Stains she had already worked out were blood. Her stomach tightened in contemplation of how recent they were.

It took all her restraint not to demand where Alisha was, if she was okay, but she guessed it was pointless asking him anything.

'You didn't seriously think you'd get away with it, did you?' he asked. 'Saunter in here and saunter back out again unnoticed?'

She turned her head away and kept her lips closed.

'I'm talking to you,' he said.

She sighed with defiant resentment.

In the corner of her eye, she saw him lean forward, hands loose between his thighs, his head tilted towards her. 'Just to make it clear, I can *make* you talk. It's a method I'm all too happy to adopt. It just depends how much of your dignity you'd like to retain.'

Begrudgingly, she met his gaze. And as he looked at her as though he could tear her apart without cause, it wasn't just fear that overwhelmed her – the injustice of his judgement infuriated her.

But for now she was alive. This time he had come in unarmed. A conversation was required and one she had to participate in whether she liked it or not. 'Where's my sister?'

He leaned back again. 'With Jake. Probably intoxicated by now but happily oblivious to any of this. He's keeping a watchful eye. And there are a couple keeping a watchful eye on him – just in case.'

'In case of what?'

'Let's neither of us be naïve. You're a serryn. Jake's a vampire. Isn't there some kind of serryn lore against what you did tonight?'

She hated the word coming from his lips. She hated the way he made it sound real. 'I came here as an interpreter, not a serryn.'

'Is that right?'

'I did what you asked.'

'But so far I've only got your word for that, haven't I?'

She frowned. 'You saw me do it.'

'You seemed to do it. But I also know how very effectively holding spells can be used to get you witches out of tight spots.'

Her heart leapt. It hadn't even crossed her mind. 'You think I did some kind of trick?'

'At dawn, we'll know, won't we?'

Dawn. Dawn was hours away. It was out of the question. He had to be insane if he planned to hold her there that long. It was unthinkable. 'You can't keep me here.'

'You'll find I can do whatever I want. You're in *my* territory now.'

As those dark green eyes glinted, she knew that was only too true. Just as she now knew why she was still alive – if she had done a holding spell and he killed her, Jake died with her.

Ironically his suspicion appeared to be her current salvation and she wasn't stupid enough to argue to the contrary. 'How did you know what I am?'

'I've met enough. And the fact it takes something a hell of a lot more powerful than a regular witch to do what you did tonight.'

'So you had your suspicions even before I came. But you still brought me here?'

'I had no choice.'

'And you accuse *me* of being stupid or reckless?'

She could tell from the narrowing of his eyes that he didn't appreciate the jibe. She glanced at his blood-smattered shirt from Tay's execution – reminder enough to stay smart. She warily looked back into glossy green eyes assessing her pensively, attentively reading her every reaction, her every expression. And she begrudgingly struggled under the intimidation of those beautiful eyes so dark in the shadowy room, his black hair untamed over his thick, straight eyebrows. She was back where she was the first time she saw him – that instinctive, deep sense of desire washing over her again, consuming her; something innately, intensely sexual awakening despite her fear.

She clenched her hands, irritated and bewildered by her attraction to him. It was impossible for a serryn to find a vampire attractive. They were inherently immune to their charms. But more than that, he stood for everything she despised. Everything she had learned since a child to despise. But equally she knew she would have to be dead on the inside not to see his appeal.

She stared at the floor. It was pointless arguing with him. And argue with him she would if death or torture were imminent. But seemingly they weren't. As her teeth chattered from more than the cold, she clenched her jaw.

'So,' he said, 'how can Alisha not know what you are? Because unless she's a remarkable actress, she really is clueless about you.'

Her gaze snapped back to his. 'You said something to her? You said she was oblivious.'

'She is. For now.'

Her heart pounded. 'Your problem is with me, not her. Let her go.'

'In case you haven't noticed, our siblings are somewhat enraptured by each other. I don't think she's planning to go anywhere.'

Leila narrowed her eyes. 'If you hurt her…'

'You're hardly in a position to be making threats, are you, serryn?'

'You have no right to do this to us. I came here to help.'

'Which, of course, you would have done willingly if your sister hadn't been in the equation.'

'Just as I'd be dead or sold already if your brother wasn't in the equation?'

His eyes glimmered in the moonlight. 'So how does she not know?'

'Because there's no need for her to know,' she said. 'And you owe me not to tell her.'

'I thought we'd established I might not owe you anything yet.'

This time she wouldn't break away. This time she stared right back into those penetrating green eyes. 'Believe what you want. At dawn, you'll see.'

After a couple of seconds, Caleb stood. He forced a knee between hers, kicking her thighs apart as he stepped between them.

Leila recoiled, clutching either side of the seat. She leaned back to break the intimacy as he gently caught her jaw, forcing her to meet his stony gaze.

'You'd better hope so,' he said. 'Because I've got you exactly where I want you. You and your little sister. Just you remember that.'

He held her gaze for a moment longer before stepping away.

Leila caught her breath, still clutching the chair as she watched him saunter across to the door.

She expected him to slam and lock it behind him, but instead he left it wide open – an invitation, an instruction, for her to follow.

Chapter Eight

Leila couldn't move at first. The door that should have been a symbol of open arms suddenly became a looming threat, the dungeon paradoxically morphing into her security net. But as silence beckoned from beyond, she pulled herself from the chair and stepped warily over the threshold.

Clutching the architrave, she scanned the tiny, windowless room. It was bare aside from a single chair secured to the floor. Directly opposite was another open door. She crossed the concrete floor, her bare feet too numb to detect the change from stone to wood.

The office was generous in size but enticingly snug with its mahogany floor and furniture, complemented by dark green leather sofas in the middle of the room. An impressive desk sat at an angle in the top right-hand corner ahead. Above it, secured to the wall, was a sword, unmistakably the one Caleb had been wielding.

Central to the wall ahead, an arc of monitors, five screens high and at least twenty across, was a dominating feature. A broad black leather chair rested off-angle where the workstation bowed inwards.

As she stepped further into the room, she was instantly drawn to Caleb stood in the open doorway to her left, shoulder against the doorframe.

She could hear the distant monotonous beat of bass music beyond, a clear indication they were still in the same four walls of the club. Hopefully Alisha was too.

She stepped past the sofas, scanning the arc of monitors as she passed – monitors that showed every angle and recess of the club.

Images rebounded back at her in all their colourful but silent glory: the dance floor, the bar, the entrance, booths, further rooms, corridors, stairwells. Some people were dancing, some talking, some entwined within each other, some in small clustered groups, some wandering alone.

As she approached, Caleb stood upright and backed into the corridor.

He could be leading her back to Alisha, or leading her to somewhere even less pleasant than the dungeon. Whatever his plans, she knew she had no choice but to follow.

He led her along the stone corridor and through the first set of double doors. The now sealed fire exit to her right showed her exactly where they were, and, more than likely, where they were going. Only this time, instead of being accompanied by Hade and his sidekicks, she was being escorted by Caleb himself.

Padding silently alongside him, the circulation returning painfully to her feet, she tried to not be unsettled by the easy nonchalance of his strides. Alone with a loose serryn by his side, he should have at least shown some anxiety, should have at least felt a little unnerved by her, but she knew his composure was no act. It was the exact same composure he'd had when he'd pumped a syringe full of her blood into one of his own. She wondered just how many serryns he'd killed and how he'd managed to survive. More so, how the hell she'd been so unlucky to collide with him in the first place. Blackthorn was crawling with vampires. Her sister had to choose one whose brother hunted her kind for money. And sport.

Caleb pulled open the next door and let her through first again, doing the same with the second and then the third set of doors. She tried to focus on the way ahead and not the broadness of his shoulders or the perfection of that lean, clearly athletic body.

Pushing through the last set of doors, he opened the single one at the end of the corridor and held it for Leila to enter the stairwell.

The chasm suddenly felt colder, darker and even more threatening than it had a few hours before – a time when she was sure she must have been too numbed by worry for Alisha to register her own fear fully. She stared into the darkness above before looking across at Caleb.

'After you,' he said, indicating towards the steps.

The act of chivalry unnerved her and she hovered awkwardly in the deathly silence. 'My eyes haven't adjusted. I'll follow you.'

'They'll adjust soon enough,' he said, cocking his head towards the steps as instruction for her to move.

It could have been deemed a trivial concern, but every instinct screamed that having a vampire follow her up a dark stairwell wasn't exactly the most self-defensive move. But with no option but to concede, she clutched the metal handrail and climbed the concrete stairs. Every step felt laborious, her legs heavy. She knew it had a lot to do with the sedative, but more so it was the knowledge Caleb's eyes were scorching into her from behind. She wondered how much of it had been done to purposefully taunt her, or whether it had merely been a strategic move in case she lost her balance and fell.

Arriving at the top, Caleb reached past her to pull open the door. As his cold hand touched hers for a split second, Leila withdrew hers immediately from the momentary intimacy.

She stepped into the hallway and followed him into the open elevator to the left.

She leaned back against the wall as the elevator doors slid shut. Clutching the handrail behind her, she lowered her head.

The ascension made her realise just how ill she felt, the subtle movement curdling her stomach. She had stopped shivering but the light-headedness took over and her legs started to tremble.

She glanced up at Caleb from beneath her eyelashes only to see him gazing blatantly back at her. The directness made her falter and lower her gaze to the floor again.

The elevator doors opened and Caleb indicated for her to step out first before leading the way down the familiar hallway back towards the penthouse.

Leila took his cue to step inside first and was relieved to find the lounge empty – empty of any other vampires at least. But her chest clenched with disappointment at not seeing Alisha.

As Caleb sauntered down the three broad steps, the reality of her situation hit her hard and fast – maybe because the initial shock was wearing off, or maybe because the suppressive effect of the sedative was finally evaporating from her system. Whatever the reason, as she hovered on the top step and looked out at the terrace, she remembered exactly what had led to her waking up strapped to the dungeon floor.

He could have done anything to her in the interim. Anything could have happened in the time she'd lost. Anything at all. And she wouldn't have a clue. He could have already lined up potential buyers if it was his intent to make a profit rather than kill her. She could have been surrounded by them bartering over her unconscious body. For all she knew he had already taken her blood once and tested it, the incident with Tay in fact just for her benefit.

Queasiness engulfed her. 'I need the bathroom,' she declared with more urgency than she'd intended.

'First door on the right,' he said, indicating to the hallway which she now knew led to Jake's room.

She didn't look back as she hurried down the steps. Shoving open the bathroom door, she burst inside and slammed it behind her. She scanned the expansive room. It was bigger than both their kitchen and lounge together at home, clinical with its black marble floors and tiled walls. She hurried across to the toilet directly opposite. She reached it just in time, the sudden pain in her stomach, the acid in her throat, the cold perspiration sweeping over her only just giving her enough warning she was going to be sick.

Tears accompanied her vomit until she had nothing left to extract. Reaching for some tissue, she wiped her mouth, flushed the toilet and leaned back against the wall. She pulled her legs to her chest and wrapped her arms around them, the heated floor a small comfort in the passing minutes.

She should have just told him in the dungeon that he was wrong. She should have looked him in the eye and assured him that she hadn't done a holding spell, but his doubt over her word was the only thing keeping her alive. Her and Alisha. If she surrendered that information, she surrendered her leverage. Caleb would be free to do what he wanted and she couldn't afford him that power.

But there was that chance, a small chance that Alisha was right – that he would stand true to his word.

And let go of the species that he clearly despised? The species he had no pity or remorse for?

And how was she to explain and then prove she was a serryn in blood and in name but nothing else?

And admit how dangerously unprepared she was? Something she had never had reason to regret before. Something she never thought she'd regret.

It had been two days after her seventeenth birthday when her grandfather had introduced her to Beatrice. There were questions he couldn't answer that she could – answers he felt more befitting from her.

They'd traipsed into the centre of Midtown and up to the third floor of what would have once been the attic of the Victorian house. It was dim and dusty, the walls concealed behind stacks of books and papers.

'You're not what I expected,' Beatrice had said, her dark wrinkled eyes furrowed on Leila. She'd poured a cup of tea and handed it to Leila in a fine china cup and saucer. 'But you won't be what they expect either – and therein lies your greatest advantage.'

Leila had accepted the cup though she'd never drunk tea in her life. Beatrice was an acquaintance of her grandfather, an elderly woman, and for both of these reasons Leila would treat her hospitality with gracious gratitude despite her reluctance to be there.

Beatrice was eighty-four. She was the only known surviving sibling of a serryn. Her sister had died over thirty years before at the age of forty-three – an extremely impressive age for a serryn, by all accounts. If Beatrice was anything to go by, her sister had been an attractive woman. Tall, curvaceous and elegant, her taut black skin was flawless other than the wrinkles that gathered around her eyes and mouth. Her large brown eyes were intelligent, quick, enquiring.

'You have a lot of books,' Leila had remarked for want of something, anything to say other than what she had been taken there to discuss.

'Do you like reading, Leila?'

'I love it. I'd like to own a bookstore one day.'

An awkward silence had filled the air, one she could still feel now just remembering it.

'Carmen had dreams of becoming an architect,' Beatrice had said. 'Buildings were her passion. But free choice is not an option for those of the heritage, Leila.'

Leila had looked up into her dark brown eyes. The urge to challenge her had been overwhelming, but she'd forced herself to remember her manners. She was there to listen, not to talk.

'It sits uncomfortably with you, does it not?' Beatrice had added. 'What you are?'

'How can it not?'

'Your grandfather has spoken to me of your internal struggles. I empathise. It took my sister years to come to terms with what she was.'

Leila had said nothing as she took another sip of tea.

'None of you choose this, Leila. I know it's hard. No prospect of marriage, children an impossibility, as is a normal job. It's a difficult future to accept when you are so young. Some of you embrace it more readily than others. But with fight integral to your very nature, having your destiny chosen for you doesn't sit easily with any of you, I know.'

'Well, destiny can do whatever she wants. I have my own plans.'

Beatrice smiled. 'A fighter indeed.' Her smile had waned. 'And I have no doubt that the tragedy you have suffered has made you stronger.'

Her grandfather had told her not to speak to anyone of that night. Clearly that hadn't included Beatrice. But if Beatrice had wanted expulsion of Leila's inner turmoil, she was going to be bitterly disappointed. 'Things happen.'

'Indeed,' was all she had said before they'd fallen to silence again. 'I know it may not feel like it now, but it will help you when the time comes.'

'What will?'

'The rage. Especially as it is so well suppressed.'

Leila had narrowed her eyes. 'If you're about to tell me everything happens for a purpose, Miss Charn, then I fervently request you don't.'

She had almost smiled as she'd taken a steady intake of breath. 'That's what I'm talking about.' She'd leaned forward to place her cup on the table, her eyes not moving from Leila's the whole time. 'And those eyes. I've never seen such depth. You may be even more powerful than your grandfather believes.'

Leila had stood up and placed her cup on the table. She'd stepped away, folding her arms as she stopped in front of a glass cabinet of books.

'Leila,' Beatrice had said softly, as she'd stepped up alongside her.

But as she'd reached out to touch her arm, Leila had pulled away. 'I don't want to be having this conversation, Miss Charn. I didn't even want to come here, but I did because it is what my grandfather wanted. I will read my books and I will study hard. I will know everything that needs to be known for me to be a good and effective interpreter. I will learn those prophecies inside out. But I am never, ever, pursuing the serryn part of me. I am never going anywhere near one of those things, and I will never let one of those things anywhere near me. I'm sorry, but that's the way it's going to be. And nothing is going to persuade me otherwise.'

Now as Leila sat enclosed in the vampires' bathroom, the declaration seemed sheer idiocy.

She should have known she wasn't going to be able to hide from it. Not forever.

She pulled herself to her feet, a little too quickly, and pressed her hand to the wall to steady herself. She stepped over to one of the two basins.

She might be untrained, but that didn't mean she couldn't play it smart. And that meant no outbursts, no being argumentative and no proclaiming her beliefs. She had to stay unthreatening, calm and compliant. At least until she came up with a plan.

For a while at least, he needed her alive. She had until dawn. It was a temporary reprieve. It would give her time – time to think, time to work out what the hell she was going to do. Her and Alisha were okay for now. That was the main thing.

She washed her hands thoroughly. Scooping mouthfuls of water to rinse her arid mouth, she rid herself of the acidic aftertaste. She opened the cupboard beside the sink and searched for some toothpaste to freshen her mouth. She found it at the same time as finding the toiletry bag on the middle shelf. She reached for it and took it out.

It was Alisha's – vibrant pink and emblazoned with a picture of a diamante-encrusted kitten. It was a few years old. She and Sophie had bought it for her one Christmas as a joke against her appallingly girly taste. She'd never thought Alisha had kept it. And there, in the vampires' apartment, she'd kept a little piece of them. She'd kept a little piece of home.

Leila's throat constricted and she fought to swallow. All the sleepless nights she'd had in the previous three months when Alisha hadn't come home and this was where she had been – sleeping soundly in a vampire's bed in the centre of Blackthorn.

Where had their lives gone wrong? Grandfather long gone. Sophie missing. Alisha sleeping with a vampire. It was her responsibility to keep Alisha safe, to keep both her sisters safe, and she had failed. If she hadn't, Alisha wouldn't have turned to a vampire for what she was missing. She would never have been there now – neither of them would, the hours ticking towards their undecided fate.

She would get Alisha out of there somehow. Back to Summerton. Back home. No one messed with her family. And certainly not a vampire.

She opened the bag and rummaged inside. It was all standard Alisha stuff, brimming with make-up and creams. But she did find a toothbrush.

Leila thoroughly brushed her teeth. Filling the sink with warm water, she washed her face and neck and wiped any traces of the dungeon off her arms, legs and feet. The heat of the water made her skin tingle painfully at first until the blood flow started to catch up, at which point the act became soothing.

She put the bag away and glanced at her watch. Less than eight hours until dawn. Less than eight hours to think of a way out. Eight hours up close and personal with Caleb. Her survival would be a miracle.

But she could handle this. She could do this. Somehow she would beat this.

Leila stepped back over to the door. After a couple more seconds of hesitation, she took a deep breath and pulled it open.

The living room suddenly seemed darker, the voile over the terrace doors wafting languidly with the passing of the storm.

There was no sign of Caleb, but the aroma of fresh coffee in the air told her he either wasn't far away or was intending to come back.

Wrapping her arms around herself, the gentle breeze ruffling her dress, she hovered awkwardly before heading over to the terrace.

There was no sign of him out there either.

She headed back inside and perched on the sofa, only to stand again as he appeared down the hallway that mirrored Jake's.

With only a swift glance in her direction, he stepped behind the bar. He emerged moments later with a glass tumbler of amber liquid in one hand and a mug in the other. Stepping up to her, he handed her the coffee. 'You look like you need this.'

She looked distrustfully at the contents then back into his sullen green eyes.

'Don't worry, I haven't drugged it,' he said. 'As you've seen, I'm not that subtle.'

She accepted it, the heat making her hands tingle.

'Come with me,' he said, and turned back the way he had come.

Chapter Nine

Leila remained warily rooted to the spot for a moment. But reminding herself to be acquiescent, she followed him down the hall.

Reaching the end and opening the only door on the right-hand side, Caleb indicated for her to enter first.

Leila snapped back a breath as she stepped inside. The room had to be at least thirty-by-fifty foot. Three out of the four walls were masked floor to ceiling with bookcases, housing the largest collection of books she had ever seen outside of the library.

Void of any artificial light, the expanse was ignited by an amber blush from the roaring fire set in the bookless wall to her right; a warm glow that mingled with moonlight from the two tall segregated sash windows ahead. Facing the window directly in front of her was a winged-back armchair, its forest green and gold fabric complementing the heavily embossed drapes that pooled in excess on the polished dark-wood floor.

Another winged-back chair sat beside the fire, facing a double sofa with its back to Leila. Central to that wall and beside the fireplace was an ajar door, darkness looming from within, another bookcase on the far side of it. A lengthy mahogany table, accompanied by two chairs, sat in the distance to her left.

She looked up at the ceiling, spellbound for a moment by the intricacy of what was clearly the original plaster coving of the building, two ceiling roses encircling the black chandeliers. The musty scent of books and leather mingled with the aroma of burning wood filled the room.

Leila glanced nervously over her shoulder as Caleb closed the door behind them, stepped over to the fire and placed his drink on the ornate mahogany mantelpiece.

'Take a seat,' he said, the fire clearly for her benefit and doubtlessly the primary reason he'd led her to the room.

As he disappeared through the dark doorway, she hesitated for a moment before perching central on the sofa. She leaned forward and craned her neck so as to peer into the room now ignited by a faint, distant glow. A heavy drawn-back curtain hung over the solitary sash window to the left, partially covering the window seat. Beside the window was a large, broad chest of drawers. A black metal bed seemed to sit against the wall directly ahead of the door, an ornate brass orb marking the corner. Aside from that, all she could see were the bedcovers, the same rich navy as the curtains.

She pressed her knees together, grateful for the tingling heat already encompassing her feet and shins as she tucked her slightly in-turned feet into the warm tufts of the deep-pile rug. She took a sip of her hot drink, grateful for the added warmth sliding down her throat. The coffee was sweet, the kind of sweetness that was given to assist someone after shock.

Caleb emerged minutes later, his blood-smattered grey shirt removed. In its place he wore a black one which he'd left unfastened, displaying every honed, hardened muscle of his bare chest. She could now see the tattoo that coiled around his neck was the aggressive upward curl of the tail of a scorpion that covered his right pec. On his flat stomach, slightly to the left, something Celtic spiralled down out of sight into his jeans. Jeans that sat low on his slender hips and revealed an inch of the black hip band of his underwear.

The rush was exhilarating, the instant tension in her body making her short of breath. Feeling herself blush, she was grateful for the darkness.

Feet now bare, he silently stepped over to the fireside chair and collected something from the mantelpiece before he sat down.

Removing a cigarette, he returned the packet to the mantelpiece, his biceps flexing with the motion. He ignited the tip with the lighter he had used back in Jake's room, before discarding that alongside the packet. The whole process was smooth and well-rehearsed – enigmatically captivating.

Smoking was prohibited in Summerton along with every other pollution source, let alone because of the irrevocable damage it did to the smoker's body as well as those nearby. It just wasn't tolerated. But that didn't matter to vampires. It had been proven that it had no effect on them. She remembered it was a clever argument used by anti-vampiric protesters to add weight to their argument that vampires were perfectly able to survive in pollution-riddled Blackthorn.

She'd always thought it a detestable habit, but there was something mesmerising about the way Caleb had ignited the tip with easy precision, drawing attention to his strong hands and competent fingers. And when he exhaled a steady stream of smoke through those entrancing lips, she felt an uncomfortable rush that sickened her.

She glanced back at the tattoo on his pec and wondered how many others he had marking that perfect, honed body. She silently berated herself but not more so than when he looped an arm around the wing of the chair, emphasising the strength in his biceps and forearms, his shirt gaping to reveal more of his smooth, sculpted chest.

His hint of a smirk told her he'd noticed and she instantly averted her focus to the flames.

'You're very quiet,' he said after a few painful moments.

She kept her eyes on the fire, refusing to meet his gaze, the heat only exacerbating the sense of claustrophobia. 'What's there to say? I know you're not going to let me go. Not now you know what I am.'

'Then look me in the eye and swear you haven't done a holding spell.'

She glared back at him. 'Look me in the eye and swear you'll let my sister and me go.'

It was only a slight smile but it was enough to make her stomach flip. 'Whatever each of us claims, the other isn't going to believe. I guess we both need to wait until dawn for the truth. And in the interim, we both know this is best kept pleasant.'

She couldn't help but glower at the hypocrisy of his rebuke. 'As pleasant as charming my sister into deceiving me, forcing me into saving your brother, sticking needles in me and locking me in a freezing dungeon?'

'I'm sure you'll excuse my lack of hospitality under the circumstances.'

'There's no excuse for what you're doing.' She lifted the mug to her lips and took a steady-as-she-could sip as she stared back into the flames.

In the corner of her eye, she saw him exhale another stream of smoke, his gaze, she could feel, still fixed on her as the fire crackled through the silence.

She feigned an itch behind her ear, using the motion to pull her hair over her cheek as a barrier against his scrutiny. She shouldn't have cared how she looked. It should have been the last thing that mattered, but she still found herself wondering what state she was in – not just from the ordeal but from days of sleepless nights and overworking, let alone the poor diet and worry of the last few weeks.

She knew she should have been reassured by her unappealing appearance, not ashamed. But she knew it made no difference. It wasn't the physicality of serryns that attracted their vampire victims, though the attractive ones were clearly the most successful. It was the temptation in a serryn's eyes, the chemical balance that exuded from their blood that drew vampires in against their will. Once the charm was turned on, the vampire was helpless, whatever the serryn's physical attributes.

But she was not one of them. Never had been one of them. Never would be one of them.

'Alisha tells me you work in a library,' he said.

'I collect, repair and restore old books.'

'Very glamorous.'

'I happen to like it.'

'Not quite slaying vampires for a living though, is it?'

'I told you – I have no interest in that.'

'You're a serryn – it's all you have interest in.'

'I'm an interpreter, that's all.'

'An interpreter with very bad blood.'

'Which you gladly used against one of your own knowing the effect. Whatever Tay had done, he didn't deserve that.'

'That's what intrigues me about you. You really didn't like what you saw, did you – what your blood did to him? You should have enjoyed it. It's what you're about. It's why you exist.'

'You don't know anything about me.'

'I know how to get you to talk though, don't I?' he said, exhaling another stream of smoke, a playful glimmer in his eyes.

She blushed at the directness of his gaze. She instantly broke from it, despite loathing the fact she had faltered. She lifted the mug to her lips and stared back into the flames in frustration, reluctantly absorbing the intensity of the silence.

'How many vampires *have* you killed?' he asked.

'I haven't killed any.'

'Except Tay.'

She glanced at him. '*You* killed him. Not me.'

'There have been others though. You turned away as soon as I gave Tay your blood which meant you knew what was coming.'

'Of course I knew what was coming.'

'But if it was the first time, curiosity would have made you watch.'

She looked back into his eyes – those darkly framed, stunning green eyes. 'Why, how many serryns have you killed?'

'Not enough.' His eyes lingered coaxingly on hers. 'Clearly.' He exhaled another stream of smoke. 'Never a latent though. I've yet to have that pleasure.'

She frowned. 'Makes you feel good, does it – torturing and murdering women who are victims of their blood type, stereotyped by your kind just because we're a threat to you?'

'Because you're all just innocent victims to your nature, right?' His vibrant green eyes emanated something between amusement and displeasure. 'Remind you of anything?'

She stared back into the flames, his perceptiveness doing little to help abate her tension. Just sitting there, the draw to him was compelling. Whatever it was about him, it was intensifying, only adding to her annoyance and unease.

'An anti-vampiric protestor but an inactive serryn,' he said. 'How does that work exactly?'

'Just because I don't approve of you doesn't mean I have to kill to make my point.'

'And what point is that?'

'What you really are – when you're not hiding behind superfluous terminology.'

'And what are we really?'

She defiantly stared back into his penetrating gaze. 'You're the one who's keeping us prisoners here even after we saved your brother's life. Why don't you tell me?'

He almost smiled again. 'No – *you* tell me.'

'You want to rule us,' she remarked. 'That's all you want. You've slipped down the power chain and you don't like it.'

'Is that what your magic books tell you? The propaganda of your forerunners?'

'I don't need to have read about you to see what's right in front of my eyes.'

'And what's that?'

'Proof of why the regulations are in place.'

He frowned. 'Dogmatic little thing, aren't you?'

She knew she'd already said too much. She looked back into the flames, trying to block out the intensity of his presence.

'So do those books also tell you you've got to be the monster to chase your monsters?' he asked. 'How, to carry out your cause, you strip yourself of every iota of humanity whilst hypocritically hiding behind its mask?'

She glanced back at him, but she wasn't going to engage in the debate.

'It doesn't matter who the vampire is, what they've done, where they're from,' he added. 'Male, female or child, your kind has only one objective – make us suffer for what we are. Because suffering is what it's all about, isn't it? Luring vampires to their deaths, tempting them to bite. You feed us your poison then sit back and watch our incurable agony, revelling in it and boasting of our torture. Because that's what it is – hours, maybe even days of torture, depending on the dosage your kind has chosen. So don't you look at me with that sanctimoniousness in your eyes.'

Leila forced herself with every iota of willpower not to retreat. 'How can you judge me when you just tortured and murdered one of your own? What kind of cold-hearted monster does that make you?'

'A cold-hearted monster would have left him to suffer. A cold-hearted monster would have already brutalised and violated you in ways you can't possibly conceive.'

Her stomach flipped. 'And what are you planning to do with me instead, Caleb? Kill me like the others? Use me as some kind of weapon against anyone who displeases you? Or are you just going to sell me to the highest bidder?'

'Maybe I could just rent you out as my serryn whore – the ultimate vampire risk-ride.'

She glared at him as indignation and fear fought each other for supremacy. 'If I'm half as dangerous as you claim, why are you even in here talking to me?'

The glimmer of amusement in his eyes irritated her, his self-assurance annoyingly alluring. 'Don't fret. I've never been tempted to take a bite out of one of your kind yet.'

'And what about Jake? The reason I'm here in the first place is seemingly because of his lack of self-control.'

'Don't you concern yourself with Jake.'

'But I will concern myself with my sister.'

'I know you're struggling to get your head around this, but Jake's not doing anything against Alisha's will.'

'I'll be the judge of that.'

'Know every part of her, do you, Leila? Just like you knew she was here? Alisha knows what she's got herself into, and my brother has made her no false promises. What they choose to do is up to them.'

'I'm here because he was with another woman,' she reminded him.

'Another woman he fed on with Alisha's full knowledge.'

'And she just nods and agrees because she's too infatuated with him to see him for what he is.'

'He likes variety in his feeding and he sleeps around, but Alisha's the only one who gets through the door. She can walk away any time she wants.'

'We both know that's not true. Not anymore. And that's why I don't want Alisha to know about me.'

Not that Alisha would even know what he meant if he told her that her sister was a serryn. Sophie would. They'd had an awkward conversation about it a few years before. After Sophie came home with news that she'd found out a vampire was responsible for what had happened to their mother, it was all she'd talked about for months. She was convinced the killer was still on the loose. The Vampire

Intervention Unit had never found out who was responsible and the case had been closed. It had been the first of its kind in Midtown and had raised a lot of questions that the authorities wanted brushed under the carpet. Fortunately so had her grandfather. No witnesses had ever come forward. They couldn't – she was the only one. She and her grandfather, who had turned up in less than half an hour when she'd used her mother's phone to call him. A half an hour in the darkness having dragged her mother beside the dumpster, huddling into her lifeless body as she waited.

From the moment she was old enough, Sophie had been determined to track down who was responsible. She wanted to know every way possible to kill vampires. And, inevitably, during her research, she'd come across references to serryns.

How she'd kept her mouth shut when Sophie had probed her for information, Leila wasn't sure, but she had. She remembered even now her pulse racing, her palms turning clammy as she'd been on the verge of confessing all. But she'd had to remind herself what her grandfather had said – it would put both of her sisters in danger. One mention of what she was outside of the four walls, and they would all be at threat.

And here they were – Sophie no doubt on her vampire vengeance mission and Alisha embroiled with one of the things. If she'd told them both, maybe neither of them would have been at risk. Instead, her aim to protect them had ironically evoked the very opposite.

'Worried about how she might react?' Caleb asked.

'It'll only create conflict and it's a complication that isn't needed before dawn. If she finds out what I am, and she works out you knew, she's going to be on you for answers. It's best if we keep it to ourselves. The simpler this is, then the better all round.'

'I'm not going to argue with that.'

'Good,' she said, a little taken aback by his acquiescence.

'Fine,' he responded.

Her toes gripped the rug as she studied his eyes, trying to work out what was going on behind them; trying to work out what to say next whilst he purposely left her faltering.

Unable to handle the proximity anymore, she placed her coffee on the floor and stood. She needed to get away from him, where she could breathe again and forge some safe distance. She expected him to tell her to resume her seat, but he didn't. She strolled to the periphery of the room, starting at the books nearest the door. 'And I suppose I'm in here to keep Alisha and me apart?'

'That and the unhealthy shade of blue you were turning. Like I said, you're not exactly dungeon material.'

She glanced back at him. 'Used it enough to know, have you? I thought your kind had moved on from all that torture and pain.'

'You can't believe everything you read.'

She broke from the coaxing in his eyes and focused on the seventeenth-, eighteenth- and nineteenth-century literature that she passed: history, politics, military, legends. There was everything, from calligraphy to identifying trees, to philosophy. She ran her fingers over the leather, canvas and paper bindings, thriving on the energy of knowledge contained within. 'Where did you get all of these?'

'This place was a library before it became a club.'

She glanced back at him too soon, she realised, not to mask the disapproval in her eyes. 'You closed it down?'

'It had shut down long before then. A fire had taken out the whole rear and left wing of the building. This is the only original part to remain.'

'So the rest of the books were destroyed?'

'A lot were. Some were stolen. Some were binned. Some got bought by collectors. I saved all the ones that remained when I bought the place. The rest are my own collection from over the years, particularly the first editions.' He stood and cast his cigarette into the fire before taking his glass off the mantelpiece. He stepped in front of the fire, the amber glow of the backdrop darkening his outline, making him look even more intimidating.

She lifted one of the small, leather-bound books from the shelf. She opened the first page to check out the publication date. 1898. She looked back across at him. 'How old are you?' she asked, surprising herself with her directness.

'A lot older than you.'

'I'm thirty-two,' Leila declared, quickly realising she had said it with more pride than was warranted.

'Like I said,' he replied, lifting the glass to his lips, the remains of the ice clinking against the glass, 'a lot older than you.'

She stopped at the far side of the table. Scanning the shelves, she reached out to take out another title. She searched the front of the book for the publication date. 1917. Another first edition. She felt a shudder of elation and tenderly turned through the first few almost-transparent pages before placing it carefully back on the shelf and reaching for another. The weighty botanical reference book felt phenomenal in her hands. After a quick scan, she placed it back on the shelf and reached for another. The value of the scarce books, far more than just in monetary terms, overwhelmed her as she stumbled upon title after title that her archive records had dictated were lost.

But even in her absorption she sensed him approach behind her. She slotted the book back into place with clumsy hands and turned to face him just as he reached her side of the table. Bare feet silent on the wooden floor, his stealth only added to his sexiness, that predatory ease such a natural part of him.

She tried so hard not to look back down at his chest as he stood leaning against the table, one hand loosely holding the edge. His candour as he stood almost half-naked in front of her was as intoxicating as the rest of him. To be that relaxed, to be that confident, to be that, quite frankly, territorial. And even from where he stood, almost six feet away, she could still pick up hints of the enticing, musky scent of his aftershave.

'So is this your plan – to keep me in here until dawn?' she asked.

'You're free to wander the penthouse.'

'And see Alisha?'

'Like you said, this is best kept simple.'

She stepped backwards a little further along the bookcase – anything to create some distance, but not daring to turn her back on him.

'Were you telling the truth when you said no one knows you're here?' he asked, lifting the glass to his lips.

She frowned, feeling her defensiveness kick in. 'Considering I was warned against telling the authorities, yes.'

Not that she had anyone but the authorities *to* tell. The truth of her own isolation scraped through her. If she lost Alisha, she was totally and utterly alone. That was why she had acted so impulsively that night – that was the truth of why she had just gone straight there without a strategic plan. Like a parent diving in an icy river after their swept-away child, she had thought only to do what she could as quick as she could. But Caleb didn't need to know how negligently impulsive she had been.

'No backup plan? No telling anyone where you were going? Nothing?'

She glanced across at him. 'I'm not the one who has problems sticking to their side of the deal.'

He smiled briefly, revealing a flash of his additional incisors – much narrower and sharper than his neighbouring canines – amidst his even, white teeth. If, *if*, he had been human, if they were a million miles away from there, where none of this was happening, the beat that her heart skipped there and then, the shiver of excitement she felt, would have flagged the instant undeniable truth that Caleb was more than just handsome – he had the potential to be irresistible.

She slotted the book back in place and backed up a little further.

'Your mother was killed by a vampire, right?' he asked.

Her stomach knotted. There was only one way he knew that. She felt a surge of anger at Alisha for allowing the intrusion.

'A serryn with the perfect excuse for vengeance on top of an insuppressible instinct to slay my kind,' he continued, 'and instead of fulfilling your duties, you tuck yourself away in a library repairing books. Fascinating.'

'Instead of speculating, you should be grateful.'

'Grateful?'

'That I choose not to act on it.'

He raked the length of her body with his gaze in a way that made the hairs on the back of her neck involuntarily spike. 'Don't hold back on my account.'

Her breath caught in her throat. The playfulness in his eyes was intoxicating, stunning her for a moment. He was flirting with her. Or challenging her. More likely the latter. This was *not* how it was supposed to be – a vampire taunting a serryn, coaxing her to action.

A cool breeze swept through the open window, causing the curtains to breathe. Smatters of rain hit the pain, exacerbating the silence.

'And is that what you're hoping?' she asked. 'That I'll prove myself to be what you believe I am, so you have the perfect excuse to go back on your word and slaughter me?'

'If I want to slaughter you, I'll slaughter you. I already have excuse enough.'

'So the fact I've made a choice to abstain counts for nothing?'

'That's just it, isn't it? A serryn with enough courage to come into vampire-infested Blackthorn, but is afraid of her own existence.' He placed his glass on the table and strolled towards her. 'You're quite the enigma, aren't you?'

She braced herself as he stepped in front of her, flattened herself against the bookcase when he placed a hand beside her shoulder.

'And if you're telling me the truth,' he said, 'I have myself an exceptionally talented serryn grappling with what she is. And I'm intrigued as to why.'

'I'm not grappling with anything. I told you, I just came here as an interpreter.'

'Interpreter. Witch. Poisonous temptress. Makes no difference.'

A cold panic consumed her at her body's instinctive sparking to his close proximity. She pressed herself tighter against the bookcase to break the intimacy – to create some distance between her and the stunning but deadly vampire who was staring her down, all five foot eleven inches of perfection in one lethal package. 'You need to back off, Caleb.'

'You need me to back off, you mean. Is that latent serryn in you calling for me to bite?'

'I think I'd be putting a little more effort in if I was trying to seduce you, don't you?'

'You don't have to be offering it on a platter to be tempting, fledgling. Quite the opposite, if you know what makes a vampire tick. Thrill of the chase, the oldest thrill in the book. Because my kind are, after all, hunters by nature.' He ran the back of his cool hand gently across her collarbone. 'Just as your kind were put on this earth to debase and degrade yourself with us for the good of the human race.'

She struggled to swallow against her arid throat, her heart jolting at the feel of his skin against hers – the surprisingly delicate caress a stark contrast to the callousness of his raw words. She flinched, but refused to move. 'And like I said: if that's what you're hoping for between now and dawn, you are going to be bitterly disappointed.'

'I admire your self-proclaimed resolve, but you can only fight what you are for so long. Eventually the hand that nature has dealt you will make you become what you were meant to be. You have no control over it.'

A light perspiration encompassed her as panic consumed her not only at what he would do, but the thought of what she wanted him to do. She bit back shallow breaths. A hot flush ignited her cheeks, every muscle in her body tensing, heat rushing between her legs. And as he gazed deep into her eyes, she couldn't move. Didn't want to move. And it took all her strength not to respond to the overwhelming draw of those enticingly masculine lips.

'I know what I'm capable of,' she said. 'And you being in here alone with me is putting us all at risk. This is all about your ego taking a battering because a serryn saved your brother's life, and now you've got to prove, by having me wander around the place, that you're still the one in charge – that you're in control.'

His gaze lingered on hers until she felt he wasn't going to look away again. But she needed to show him she wasn't afraid of him, for the sake of her dignity if nothing else. Serryns weren't afraid of vampires. It was the other way around. That was the way it was supposed to be. He was revelling in her nervousness and she was only helping fuel his arrogance.

'How long have you known what you are?' he asked.

The question took her aback. 'What does that matter?'

'You were nine when your mother was killed, right? Alisha was telling me Sophie looked into it a few years ago. That she was the one who found out a vampire was responsible. You must have been in your mid-twenties then. I'm surprised you'd never looked into it yourself. Unless you already knew. Knew and still did nothing about it. So I'll ask you again, how did you find out what you are?'

She stared at him but remained silent, her grip tightening on the shelf at the small of her back.

'Was it on purpose? Or by accident?' he persisted. 'Because we've already established there was at least one before Tay. And taken from your fear responses down in that dungeon, it wasn't a pleasant first time. It was certainly distressing enough that, if you're telling me the truth, you couldn't bear to face it again. An experience so bad as to repress those urges and instincts. We're talking real deep-rooted trauma here.'

Unease wrenched at her stomach at his perceptive line of thought.

'What was your mother doing down some dark alley anyway?' he asked.

She rubbed her fingers over her clammy palms before clutching the shelf again.

'Only I'm wondering if maybe it wasn't entirely his fault,' he added.

'Not his fault that he chose to tear her throat out, you mean?'

'I'm just saying if she was playing in dark places she shouldn't have been—'

Resentment soared through her – a need to defend her mother. 'She was on her way back from a school play.'

'Really?'

'Really.'

His gaze lingered on hers. 'Whose?'

Discomfort stirred in the pit of her stomach. 'Does it matter?'

'Was she a teacher?'

'No.'

'Then a doting parent. Whose play was it? Yours? Alisha was only two at the time so it wouldn't have been hers. Or Sophie's? Because if she was on her way home, I'm guessing one of you had to be with her. And as Sophie had to look into what happened, I'm guessing it wasn't her. Which means it had to be you.' His gaze was intensely unrelenting. 'Something tells me that your mother being killed and you finding out you were a serryn might have coincided. Maybe rather than you picking on some poor bastard as your first victim, some poor bastard picked on you. He took a chunk out of your mother then came for you and got far more than he bargained for.'

She glowered at him. 'Victim? He ripped my mother's throat out after leading her down a dark alley with the faked cry of a child.'

'Which you would have had to have been there to know, right?'

The pause was painful. Her escalating heartbeat thrummed in her ears as she broke from his intrusive gaze to stare down at the floorboards.

'Your sisters didn't even know you were there when she died, otherwise Sophie wouldn't have had to research it herself,' he added. 'You covered it up. Just as you covered up that you're a serryn. Quite the closed book, aren't you, fledgling?'

She snatched a glance back at him, the triumph in his eyes calling her to retaliate. Instead she tightened her grip on the shelf, her toes curling against the wood.

He leaned slightly closer, his lips only inches from hers, causing every nerve ending in her to spark. 'Only not quite as closed as you'd like to be. You haven't opted out of being a serryn by some moral choice; you're just too scared to face up to it, which is probably the real truth why you don't want your sisters to know. You're ashamed. You don't want them to know how you've abandoned all the potential to avenge your mother because you're scared.' He almost smiled again. 'It must be tough knowing if you'd told your sisters the truth about killing that vampire the same night, Sophie would most likely still be safe at home. I see more and more why you don't want Alisha to find out, especially as she's all you've got left.'

She should have pushed him away, but she couldn't – not only because she knew it would be futile, but because something else was stirring inside her. That same alien something that had stirred the first time she'd laid eyes on him. Something unsettling. Something she knew, for her and her sister's sake, she had to suppress.

'I think I've got about as up close and personal with you as I want to for one night,' she said, hating the hint of a tremor in her voice.

'I'm right, aren't I? That was your first experience of a vampire. Nine years old, down a dark alley with him slaughtering your mother right in front of you.'

She inhaled sharply in an attempt to calm herself as her gaze remained locked on his.

'You're scared of me,' he said, the goading clear in his eyes. 'A serryn scared of a vampire. Have you any idea how pathetic that is?'

The distaste in his eyes made her stomach clench. He almost hated her more for not acting on what she was than acting upon it. It was cruel. Unfair. Damned if she did and damned if she didn't. But as he stood there in judgement of her, her indignation simmered to barely tempered rates.

Refusing to be intimidated, she forced herself with every iota of willpower to look him squarely in the eyes. 'Have you any idea how pathetic it is punishing someone for something they haven't done, just because of their DNA?'

'I'm not punishing you.'

'No?'

'No. You'd know if I was. Trust me.'

Her stomach flipped at something that seemed to be somewhere between a promise and a threat. 'I don't know what's evoked this inherent hatred of my kind, but you need to learn to deal with it for the time I'm here because I will not be threatened. Do you understand me?'

He leaned closer again, his lips less than a couple of inches from hers. 'Now try saying it without trembling,' he coaxed, his smirk infuriating her further.

'I'm trembling because I'm angry.'

'And insuppressibly turned on, right? Your resolve isn't quite so cut and dry when you're up against the real thing, is it? Not quite so easy to maintain when you're not safely tucked away in vampire-free Summerton.'

'You see me as nothing more than something to be tortured, slain or sold off as a commodity. That's hardly the most seductive of traits.'

'Tell your eyes that.'

'Don't flatter yourself.'

'I'm not. I just know that serryn inside of you is just scratching to get out.'

'And if you bite, I'm not getting out of here. So I'd rather you not be this close to me.'

'Now who's flattering themselves?' His gaze didn't flinch. 'Do you know this is what they used to do with you rare reluctants? Your own kind used to lock you in a room with one of mine to battle it out until only one survived. How long do you think you're going to last, fledgling, with all that suppression simmering inside?'

Leila held her breath as she lingered too long in those penetrating green eyes. 'You want to keep this civilised, so do I. All four of us can get out of this alive and unscathed but that is only going to happen by us co-operating with each other. Mistakes happen. For all our sakes you need to back off because if you bite me, it will kill you. You've seen it for yourself, what I'm capable of.'

'I'm not going to bite you, fledgling. But I should warn you how intoxicating the mingled scents of fear and arousal are to us. And they are both coming hard and fast from you whether you want to admit it or not.'

'Or maybe it's all part of my lure,' she said, her petulance hard to suppress. 'So I'd be careful if I were you.'

His lips curved into a hint of a smile, disarming her and knocking her confidence even more. 'Very clever,' he said softly.

'Just a civilised warning.'

The seconds that passed felt like agonising minutes as Caleb appeared to be cruelly making the most of her fear. His mouth lingered within touching distance of hers, their breathing intermingling in the passing moments – hers slightly erratic, his noticeably less frequent, calm and controlled.

Her heart pounded at the thought of kissing him and how easy it would be. That was the darkness that terrified her. The darkness she fought to suppress for fear of it taking over. She would prove that she was in control, if not of anything else, at least of her own actions. She was not a serryn in anything but name. She was not going to be a serryn. She could control it, just like she'd always controlled it – something that had always been so easy, so straightforward. *Until* she was face-to-face with him.

The closer she got to him, the more she felt it. But she wouldn't let it be triggered. She wouldn't let the slippery slope take her.

Someone had to care for Alisha. Someone had to find Sophie. Someone had to protect her grandfather's books. Someone had to stop the facts falling into the vampires' hands. They were her responsibility. It was all her responsibility.

'You do know I can make you fledge, don't you?' he said. 'I don't even need your consent. In fact, you're more likely to spread those wings without it.'

A cold panic consumed her, but *something else* was underlying it – something that curbed outright fear. 'Force yourself on all your serryn victims, do you? How disappointing.'

'Oh, they were all willing. And far from disappointed.'

The rain beat heavily against the windowpane, tapping like tiny frantic fingernails in warning. A gust of wind smashed another collection against the glass.

Her heart pounded uncomfortably. 'And is that before or after you kill them?'

He almost smiled. 'Now don't go giving me those thoughts.'

'Like you haven't already planned what you're going to do with me.'

'I don't think that far ahead.'

'You strike me as someone who plans everything that far ahead.'

'I'm flattered you've paid that much attention.'

'What have I ever done except save the most precious thing to you?'

'*If* you saved him. Remember the jury is still out on that one. But by dawn it will be irrelevant anyway. I'm going to initiate you by then,' he said. 'I want you to know that. Because I will not and cannot let you go.'

She glowered back at him. She could tell by the look in his eyes that he didn't like it, but she refused to break first despite the ache in her gut. Her pride compelled her to double bluff him, despite her instincts telling her to the contrary.

'Then do it,' she said, more calmly than she could believe she was capable of in spite of the tension accumulating in the back of her throat. 'Do whatever you're going to do and unleash the serryn. And I'll watch you choke on my blood. Because you will. I can guarantee it.' She stunned herself with her boldness, a shot of pride sweeping through her despite the pounding behind her ribs that told her she'd just made a huge mistake.

Her heart leapt, her stomach flipped, as he brushed her hair back from her neck, glanced at the exposed flesh before looking back into her eyes – his surprisingly and terrifyingly composed.

'The trick, fledgling, when you want to tempt a vampire to bite, is to mean it in your eyes, not just in angry words,' he said. 'Better luck next time.'

He pulled away, picked up his glass from the table and crossed the room.

She watched him open the door and disappear out into the hallway, Leila staring into the void he left behind, her nails leaving grooves in her palms.

❊ ❊ ❊

Caleb slammed his empty glass down on the bar and braced his arms across the surface.

The temptation to prove the sanctimonious witch wrong had been overwhelming, something deep inside urging him to overpower her. He should have made the most of the opportunity. He should have got it over with and proved his point – pinned her down and taken her to the brink of her survival instincts until the serryn in her had no option but to be unearthed.

And he might have if it hadn't been for those telling dilated pupils staring back at him as he'd trapped her against the bookcase. A serryn's pupils always *constricted* when they were cornered. And she could only hold his gaze in anger or fear; any other time it was just too intimate for her – another trait he'd never come across in a serryn. The seduction of their gaze was one of their most powerful tools. But this one had no idea how to use it and certainly took no pleasure in it. In fact, the closer he got to her, the more intimate the questioning, the more she shied away.

More intriguingly, it wasn't out of repulsion – not by the way she had responded to him. She had actually blushed at his advance. He'd seen the appreciation in her eyes. He'd heard the subtle increase in her breath as she tried to avert from temptation. Because she had been tempted.

He'd been right when he'd sat next to her on the terrace, when he'd pulled her close between his legs just before he stuck the needle in her. Just as he'd seen when she looked up at him from the dungeon floor in fear masking a suppressed attraction – something she was clearly fighting.

And it wasn't only *her* attraction to *him* that troubled him. The serryn most definitely had an allure all of her own – a deadly allure. Even more deadly after her reticence had almost made him explode.

He thought back to the hues of the flames bringing out the subtle copper in her hair and the paleness of her flawless skin; the inward curve of her waist that eventuated the subtle feminine sway of her hips as she'd padded silently around the library. And he hated how he throbbed and ached with the frustration of her reticence. An ache in his groin that had only intensified as he'd gazed into resilient hazel eyes far more toxic than her body. There *was* something different about her – something transfixing about her, drawing him in more than she should have.

He unscrewed the cap off the nearest bottle and poured himself a shot, knocking it back in one before he poured himself another.

Her willpower was immense. Her self-control was proving impressive; her ability to suppress her instincts remarkable. Either that or her terror of vampires was entrenched too paralysingly deep for anything but denial.

It only added weight to his theory about what had happened in that alley. Whether she knew she was a serryn before then or not, it was a hell of an experience for a nine-year-old kid. And a hell of an experience for the son of a bitch who thought it acceptable to attack a mother and her little girl. He hoped it had been excruciating for the gutless bastard.

But he couldn't allow himself to believe the mirage he was seeing, no matter how plausible. Too many decades of experience told him it was just one manipulative game after another. He felt the irritation tightening its hold on his chest. Because if she kept her resilience up, if she proved herself to have saved Jake come dawn, he was going to have to let her go despite it going against everything he believed in, every instinct.

And he wouldn't let that happen. *Couldn't* let that happen.

He had to get her to unleash her true nature. She was there for the breaking, and breaking her he clearly was because he *was* a temptation to her. He pulled at her resolve. He made her doubt herself.

He poured himself another shot and knocked it back.

If she was inactive – *if* – he *would* initiate her, because all he needed was one sign of her true nature to do what was necessary. He just needed to be damned sure, if she was already powerful enough to be inciting him that much as a latent, that he could contain both himself and her in the aftermath if he unleashed her fully.

And then, come dawn, she'd be his to do with as he wanted.

Chapter Ten

Leila stared into the burning embers, in the same position she'd sat for the past couple of hours, the same thoughts running through her head over and over again.

Like the predator he was, Caleb had sensed her fear and he'd thrived on it. He'd been toying with her, the glimmer in his eyes making it clear he'd liked the way he'd made her suffer under the intensity.

But more disturbing than the sadistic game-player he'd revealed himself to be was *her* arousal from his enjoyment.

She shouldn't have felt like that – the superficiality of her attraction to him splintering her integrity. Butterflies flitted in her stomach at the thought of how much she had wanted those vampire lips against hers; how she'd wanted him to push that one step further.

She couldn't lie to herself and excuse it as merely a moment of weakness, a response to a stressful and exhausting night. She knew what she had felt amidst her fear was excitement – excitement at how lethal he was, how shameless, how self-assured. He evoked something in her – something alien, something liberating.

She needed to get a grip and fast.

Caleb was used to dancing near the edge. He'd been there and survived with a hell of a lot more proficient and experienced serryns than her. And he was openly and unashamedly planning to bring the serryn out of her, his blatancy in his intentions adding to the insult.

And because of that, instead of adhering to the warning signals, she was incited to challenge him, to ignore the sensible option in keeping her mouth shut and her head down. If it hadn't been for the embarrassment, the prospect of him laughing in her face, she would have just come out with the truth of *just* how latent she was, if only to wipe the condemnatory look off his face.

She stood from the sofa. Hiding in that room any longer, despite it being the sensible thing to do, grated on her pride too much.

His walking away had been all the evidence she'd needed that he'd equally had to temper himself. That in itself had proven he really did believe in the possibility of the holding spell or, as every instinct told her, she wouldn't have been standing after challenging him the way she had.

She may have been at risk, but so was he and she had to remember that. The fact he was playing for dominance was proof that part of him had to be intimidated by her. In his territory he wanted her to know who was in charge. And using his sexual self-assurance was one far too obvious way.

But her thighs still trembled as she stepped out into the hallway. Her heart still pounded painfully as she headed down to the lounge to follow the sound of the TV. And her pulse raced as she saw him.

On the sofa nearest the terrace, Caleb sat with his back to her, facing the TV. Legs stretched out along the length of the sofa, he held a glass in the hand of the arm that rested on the back of it whilst he flicked through a book with the other.

She stepped closer, all the hairs on her arms standing on end. But she knew it was from more than the temperature of the late-night breeze drifting through the open doors.

He didn't look up from her purification book as she sat on the sofa opposite him.

It sickened her to see her grandfather's precious book in a vampire's hands – all the secrets it contained, secrets that should never fall to the attention of one of his kind.

She tucked her hands under her thighs as she furtively watched him. But he didn't flinch other than to take a mouthful of amber liquid.

She lingered on his strong jaw, his masculine lips, the pensive look in his beautiful green eyes. She'd go as far as to say perfect if it hadn't been for the darkness inside of him. If it hadn't been for him being a vampire.

On the TV, the voice-over drowned out the heated background discussion outside the Global Council office. The well-dressed woman stood with authority and composure amidst the crowds, the microphone curled discreetly around her ear. 'Speculation as to whether Nathaniel Amilek will indeed run for a political place has sparked debate across the globe tonight. Of course, this isn't the first we have heard of these rumours but, though as yet unconfirmed, the reluctance of Amilek's representation to substantiate to the contrary when queried directly tonight has evoked discussion as to whether they may be on the brink of an emerging political statement. If this is the case, we could see an unprecedented campaign dominating the globe within days.'

The shot switched to Amilek nodding politely at the cameras, his head bowed, his mass of grey hair flopping over his aged face as he faced the interviewer. The poster-boy for the consang movement towards political equality made her skin crawl with resentment.

'You've been told you cannot possibly be considered for a seat on the Global Council due to regulations in the Fourteenth Constitution, which clearly states that those of shadow origin cannot be selected to preside over the laws of humankind,' the interviewer declared.

'We've come so far in so many ways,' Amilek responded. 'We just want to have the same rights – for housing, for education, for jobs.

This old constitutional law only proves how much of a division there still is. Progression is needed. Either we contribute or we don't.'

Leila glanced back at Caleb to see that even this statement hadn't averted his attention from her book.

The news broadcast switched to one that had become familiar territory over the past two weeks. The Vampire Control Unit had been brought into disrepute by revelations of corruption at the top of the establishment. Both the head of the VCU and the head of the entire Third Species Control Division had been brought into custody and charged along with another counterpart who had left the VCU some years before. One of their own had come to the witness stand, the stepdaughter of the boss of the VCU and one of their best agents – Caitlin Parish. She hadn't been seen since appearing in court and many suspected she had gone into hiding until things settled down.

The speculation was that she'd gone into hiding with Kane Malloy – the very vampire whose sister had been murdered by those who had been prosecuted. It was claimed she had been having an illicit affair with him, evoking the scorn of her colleagues more than her whistle-blowing on corruption in the agency.

Whatever her motivation, Leila didn't doubt it took guts to do what Caitlin did. She had proven that not all agents were corrupt – even if she had got embroiled with Kane Malloy. She'd at least managed some damage control following the outcry in Blackthorn when the news had emerged. Others claimed her statement had been part of the TSCD covering their tracks for that very reason, so fearful were they of the news leaking out another way.

Whether she was involved with Kane was still clouded with a huge question mark.

Leila's grandfather had spoken a lot of Kane Malloy. He was a law unto himself – anti-establishment and even anti his own Higher Order. Rumour was he was one of the rare master vampires. She didn't care what his status was – Kane had been the stuff of night-mares for her growing up, and more than enough reason to stay as far away from Blackthorn as possible.

The image of the handsome vampire flashed up on the screen – because handsome he was, not even she could deny that. And un-fortunately, so was the one laid out in front of her. Only no one had warned her about Caleb. No one had warned her there were vampires as bad as, if not potentially worse than, the notorious Kane Malloy.

'Do you know him?' she asked, needing to break Caleb's silence, to at least get him to acknowledge her – to do something to distract him from her book. 'Kane Malloy.'

'We've never met,' Caleb said, his attention unflinching from the page he was reading.

'He practically rules this district, doesn't he?'

'Not every patch.'

'Not yours, you mean.'

'He stays out of my business, I stay out of his,' he said, turning the page. 'That way there's no need for complications.'

'So is he as bad as they say?'

He glanced across at her, before looking back down at her book. 'As who says?'

'Everyone.'

'Reputation goes a long way in this place.'

'Which is why that scandal isn't going to do the TSCD much good. Do you think he made it up, as some people have said?'

'I doubt it. It's about time the TSCD had what's coming.'

'Needless to say you don't approve of them.'

'That's the polite way to put it.'

'And what about the Higher Order? Do you have much to do with them?'

He turned over another page. 'You suddenly have a lot of questions.'

'Alisha always tells me I should try to understand more.'

'The Higher Order only ever grace this district with their presence when they want something or have some punishment to inflict that they think will earn them points with the Global Council – anything that will maintain their luxury and privileges in Midtown. They can go fuck themselves as far as most of this district is concerned.'

'Not quite the unified front they like to display then?'

'If you're talking about Amilek, he's a waste of space. He's just a puppet whose strings are being pulled.'

'So you're not backing him?'

Finally he looked across at her. '*Now* you want to talk politics?'

'It's just a question.'

He held her gaze for a moment before turning a couple more pages.

'You must be supporting his fight for equal rights,' she added. 'Isn't that what you all want?'

'We're not equal to you. We're superior to you.' He glanced across at her again, a glimmer of playful challenge in his eyes. 'Whatever pecking order you prefer to believe in.'

'If you're so superior, why aren't you already in charge? How come you're still confined?'

'Humans have let the Third Species down big time. One day that'll be rectified.'

'You think so?'

'I know so. There's only one way we're getting into power and it sure as hell isn't through him and his policies.' He closed her book and placed it next to him before turning to face her square-on. 'But you already know that, if you're anywhere near as knowledgeable as your sister makes out. And she makes you out to be a very smart little librarian indeed.' He leaned back, rested his feet on the table, his legs slightly bent, one arm draped across the back of the sofa. 'And it's going to be lethal for you again if the prophecies do come into fruition in your lifetime. You'll be in a very precarious position if vampires rule. You won't have the luxury of being able to hide in the safety of Summerton then, will you? You'll be forced out of that shell whether you like it or not.'

'That's not going to happen.'

'Why – because the Global Council put all these borders in place to guarantee that? Hiding behind their claims of working towards equal rights when all they wanted to do was have contingencies in place to minimise risk if the chosen one ever *does* appear? Are you still going to stand by and hide in your library then, hoping it'll all go away?'

His mention of the chosen one knotted her stomach, a conversation she couldn't afford to develop. 'I have the right to choose what I do.'

'And why *are* you so against what you are? Why, when you could make quite a killing? Literally. A girl as pretty and sexy as you, you'd have no problem reeling us in.'

She felt a flutter in her chest at his compliment as much as the once-over he gave her with those seductive eyes. 'For what? To become something I'm not? I know how addictive it gets – how serryns who have done it for long enough forget who they are, lose all sense of themselves. I don't want that kind of life.'

'So it's the loss of control that scares you.'

'I just don't want to have my throat bitten into by vampires every night. Let alone everything else that comes with the job.'

'You're almost convincing.'

'Believe what you want. Just at least admit you have no intention of letting me go even when I do prove you wrong.'

'So if I did let you out of here, then what? You'll walk away and forget about all of this?'

'I'm more than capable of pretending none of this ever happened,' she said, her pulse racing in hope.

'But what if I don't want to let you go? What if I want to keep you here for my own amusement? For my own pleasure.'

Her heart skipped a beat. 'You know that would be a mistake.'

'Maybe I think it's worth the risk. Maybe I think you're worth the risk.'

She frowned at the remorseless self-assurance in his eyes. 'Are you just incapable of guilt?'

'For what? Getting to your kind before they get to mine?'

'At least I'm trying to understand you. But your mind is already made up. The truth is you *want* me to be like the others. You need me to be like them. You can't handle the fact that I'm different. I think that says more about you than me.'

He finished the remains of his drink. 'Is that what you keep telling yourself, to ease those feelings of inadequacy?'

'I have nothing to feel inadequate about.'

'You can't even look me in the eye for any sustained time.'

'I know what I'm capable of. *That's* why I don't look you in the eye.'

'So you do accept that this is out of your control? That the serryn will out whether you choose it to or not.'

'That's not what I'm saying.'

'Sounds like it to me.'

'Don't put words in my mouth.'

'So you're no threat to me or my brother or any other vampire for that matter.'

She frowned. 'I'm telling you, you don't know me.'

'I know exactly what you are and what you're capable of. I knew everything about your kind even before your grandparents were born. You're all the same. Deceit and manipulation become second nature until they're your only truths as you revel in your debasement, itching for your next conquest. You reel us in and then you spit us out, and that's all there is to it. It's what you were created for. And there's no exception.'

'Which has justified every single slaughter, right? Have you never felt remorse?'

'For protecting my own?'

'But you did it for money. For bounty. You were a hired assassin. For the Higher Order, right? It sounds to me like you don't think much of them, yet they paid your wages. Principles don't matter much when it comes to money, I assume?'

'*Paid* being the operative word. I used to work for them. Not anymore.'

'Because you thought we were no more.'

'Exactly.'

'And how much would they be willing to pay you now if you handed me over?'

'Oh, they'd expect you for free – loyalty to our leaders and all that. But I'd probably be able to barter a very lucrative sum I should imagine.'

'And is that the real reason you want me alive at dawn? Because I'm worth more breathing than dead?'

'I have all I need. I don't need to sell you. The Higher Order don't need to know my business, just as I'm not interested in theirs. What goes on here is between me and you.'

'Me, you and the people we love.'

'And you've just got to remember that.'

'And if I am proved innocent?'

'That's not going to happen.'

'Because you're going to see to it, right? I'm going to be here until you've turned me into what you want me to be.' Despite her resolution, she stood up and glowered down at him. 'You can go to hell, Caleb,' she said, and stepped away.

'Sit down,' he said curtly.

She froze to the spot. With all the courage she could muster, she glared back across her shoulder at him.

His stunning green eyes narrowed sternly on hers. 'I said, *sit down*.'

She shouldn't have hesitated. She should have resumed her seat. But beneath the accumulating fear was a rush of excitement. Of intoxicating anticipation of what he'd do if she continued to defy him.

She didn't know where it came from. Even felt angry for going back on her promise to herself that she wouldn't provoke him. But the fact she remained standing there, as they stared each other down, told her that this was the power her kind felt when faced with them. She didn't have to be afraid. Not afraid enough to do whatever he demanded.

If she was going to walk away, she knew the sensible option was to turn towards the bathroom and lock herself in until every sinew of her body stopped sparking under the intensity of those captivating eyes.

But she didn't opt for the sensible option.

Whether it was pride, indignation or plain rebelliousness that governed her decision, or whether the serryn in her was starting to surface, she turned back down towards his room –the ultimate defiance, entering his most personal territory uninvited. And her body shuddered with the excitement of the challenge, at what he'd do next.

Each step felt laborious as she marched back down the hallway, her legs quaking, her mind not engaging fully with what her body was doing, the latter coming against her will.

She stepped back into the library, the only light in the room from the remains of the burning embers. She marched across the room to the winged-back armchair and slid the sash window up, desperate for air despite the late-night chill. Her skin prickled as she looked out over the district, bright lights igniting the dense darkness, the intoxicating smells and sounds once again a reminder of how far she was away from the silence and sanctuary of home. The rain had ceased again momentarily, but the air was still thick with the threat of an ongoing storm.

He wasn't going to let her defiance go that easily, she knew that much. And now she'd taken that bite, she had to chew and swallow what was to come, however bitter the taste.

Taking a few deep, steadying breaths, she sat in the chair, needing to before her legs gave way.

Her heart leapt as she heard the quiet closing of the door behind her, but she wouldn't look over her shoulder. Her stomach clenched and, to her loathing, it was from more than just fear. Sat in the darkness muted only by the distant amber glow of the starving fire, she braced herself.

Stepping in front of her, Caleb leaned against the spare strip of wall beside the window.

After a few painful seconds, she built up enough courage to look up at him. Her heart pounded erratically as their eyes met.

But he didn't say anything. She wished he would. She wished he'd say anything to break the density of the two-foot gap between them. His silence only infuriated her further, his demonstration of control sparking every urge for her to claim it back.

And as he calmly lowered to the floor, it only unnerved her more. He placed one foot possessively on the leg of her chair, forming a barrier to the easiest of her escape routes.

'You're a belligerent little madam, do you know that?' he said, his eyes glinting.

'Because I won't roll over and play dead? It's not going to happen.'

'I've worked that out for myself.'

'Then why haven't you also worked out how insane all of this is?'

'This is all part of it, fledgling. Not losing your nerve already, are you?'

'If I was losing my nerve, I would have sat back down out there.'

'So this isn't you running away?'

'You're too used to everyone doing as they're told.'

'That's because other people learn faster.'

She exhaled curtly. 'Is this the best you've got? I defy you so I get a pep talk?'

'We both know you're going to get more than a pep talk.'

Her stomach flipped. Eyes that were composed stared back at her with uncompromising intent.

She moved to stand but he slid his bare foot up to the arm of the chair, closing her in. She clutched the arms of the chair, and froze on the edge of the seat.

'You run away a lot, don't you?' he said.

'I'm not running away; I just don't like being around you.'

'If you're so confident in your convictions, why does it make you so uncomfortable having me this close?'

She moved her lowered gaze to his groin. She could slam her foot into it so easily.

'You wound me and I'll be forced to check everything still works,' he warned.

Her gaze snapped to his and she was met with dark, coaxing eyes.

'Unless a tussle will make all this easier for you?' he added. 'Reduce the guilt.'

She frowned. 'You're twisted, you know that?'

She instantly recoiled a few inches as he eased onto his knees in front of her.

She clutched the arms of the chair as he closed the gap between them. Despite her racing pulse, she didn't attempt to fend him off as he reached behind her knees and parted her legs, pulled them around his thighs. Her grip on the chair tightened as he slid her towards him in one swift move, his jeans soft against her inner thighs.

'I'm more than twisted,' he said, his lips dangerously close to hers. 'I'm the worst kind of vampire your grandfather warned you about. But you're the one who's craving me, so what does that make you?'

She stared into his dark green eyes, his constricted pupils. She'd never noticed how his irises were subtly rimmed in black before, how they were flecked with hints of brown, a sharp contrast to the darkness of his thick lashes.

She didn't struggle. She wouldn't give him the satisfaction. Maybe it was because she knew it was futile. More likely because she knew, abhorrent as it felt acknowledging it, she didn't want to.

'I don't crave you,' she said, despising the way her body responded instinctively to his, her flight defences inactive. Even in her fear, something felt so right, so natural. Whether it was because of her infuriating attraction to him, or because her serryn nature was pushing to the surface, she couldn't be sure. But every muscle in her body tensed, heat rushing between her legs, her resilience weakening.

Her heart jolted as he prized her left hand from the arm of the chair, pressed it gently into the crevice between the back of the chair and wing – an unyielding, purposeful act that had her heart pounding as she was forced to lean back. She glanced at the powerful hand encompassing her wrist, tiny and fragile in comparison, before looking back into his eyes. They weren't smiling anymore as he lifted her right hand to draw her inner elbow to his lips.

His tender kiss against her sensitive flesh made her stomach flip – a kiss that he brushed lingeringly down the length of her arm to her wrist. Her toes coiled against the wooden floor, one knee instinctively bending, her foot clamping the edge of the seat as he released her right hand again, pressed his hard body against hers.

Something in her, something dark and frightening, was responding to him, despite every ounce of common sense screaming at her that it was wrong.

He was goading her, letting her know he wasn't afraid, letting her know he was in control, wanting her to fall. He was inciting her to act within her nature and against her better judgement.

And she knew he could turn on her at any moment if she did just that.

In that moment she believed herself capable of making him bite. The thought of it made her stomach clench – but not with fear. It was an unforgivable thought; the excitement she felt stirring abhorrent.

The ache in her chest became painful, the subsequent guilt from her stirring arousal oppressive. As his lips lingered less than an inch away, she breathed in the intoxicating scent of alcohol. Shivers swamped her. At that moment she wanted him to kiss her. She needed him to kiss her. Those vampire lips so enticing despite the lethality they concealed.

But it was an intimate contact he denied her.

She breathed heavily in shame and resentment. This was not about intimacy. This was about dominance. This was about control. This was a lesson about defying him. And he wanted to see her panic. He wanted to see her squirm. He was expecting her to try and fight him off.

This was a battle of wills. A game of dares. He was willing to take the risk and he was clearly laying down the challenge for her to also. And maybe she would have thought twice – the sensible and controlled Leila – if her anger and indignation hadn't been so rife.

But, damn it, the feel of his cool skin against hers was dangerously alluring. The dark look in his eyes as he tempted her to fight him was enthralling. He clearly sensed her discomfort and the fact he liked it thrilled her again – all that dangerous potential he was holding back.

As he released the wrist that he had kissed to tuck her hair back behind her shoulder, expose her neck, she clenched her hands at the taunting glimpse of his incisors.

But she wouldn't break. Caleb was not like him – the one who had grabbed her so viciously by the nape of her coat as a child, letting her small frame dangle five feet off the ground.

And the feelings he evoked were nothing like the feelings she'd had back then.

But as she felt Caleb's soft lips against her vulnerable artery, she could barely breathe as she prepared herself for those hard, lethal incisors to pierce deep.

Instead, he licked her slowly and coaxingly up the length of her throat, his saliva cool against her heated skin. He ran his palm down her cleavage, running it along her ribs, directly beneath her breast, pulling the fabric down a little with the pressure as he lowered his mouth to the exposed mound of flesh.

Leila reluctantly arched into him, her free hand now gripping the arm of the chair as he unfastened the top buttons on her dress to tug the fabric down more, his mouth grazing her breast through the thin lace of her bra.

She gasped, hating herself for it. Hating the way her body betrayed her arousal to him so transparently.

He slid his tantalisingly lethal lips back to her neck, his hand coiling over hers on the arm of the chair, pinning it there. He shifted their positions, so as to get closer. Every muscle in her body tensed as she felt his hardness through his jeans, the pressure against the pulsations between her parted legs was almost too much to bear.

Letting him get that close was a mistake. Teetering at the pinnacle of the slippery slope, she needed to back away before momentum took her.

As the hardness of his incisors made contact with her flesh, memories hit her hard and fast – nothing but air beneath her feet; the vampire laughing before he bit; her mother's blood still staining his mouth.

And the pain. The excruciating pain as he bit into her tender flesh.

She closed her eyes, nails scraping against the arm of the chair as she tried to calm herself, feeling herself crumble the way she had back then: the first time she'd known what pain was; the first time she'd known what helplessness felt like, and just how vicious the world could be.

'Is that where he bit you?' he asked, swapping to the other side. 'Or was it here?' He lightly nipped over her artery, making her flinch, before kissing along her jaw line, his lips then hovering less than an inch from hers again.

She caught her breath and held it as he took her right hand in his again, pinned both wrists together, held them above her head against the top of the chair. Forced to arch herself into him, his hard chest pressed against hers, reminding her of the strength behind it.

'Did he restrain you while he bit you?' he whispered against her ear. 'Do you only associate it with bad things?'

Kissing her behind her ear, he bit her on the earlobe before easing her thighs further apart.

The rush was overwhelming, the need and desire to have him inside her overpowering. His body against hers no longer felt alien, the seductive coaxing in his eyes distracting her from her suppressed fear. The firmness of his hold, the feel of his hard, powerful body against hers, had her complying against her will. And she started to submit to him, not in words, but she knew her disloyal body was giving him all the right signals that she wasn't going to fight him.

He'd stop. He'd have to stop. He wasn't stupid enough to cross that line. He was expecting her to panic. He was expecting her to break first. He was expected her to plead with him to stop.

But despite the risk, there was no way she was backing down.

And as he reached between them to unfasten his jeans, her pulse almost flatlined with its intensity.

He'd pull back. He had to pull back. He couldn't be *that* arrogant, *that* self-assured.

That suicidal.

But he slid his hand between her legs and pushed her knickers aside, his cool fingers making her stomach jolt as they brushed the throbbing sensitivity between her legs.

He interlinked the fingers of one hand with hers, gazed deep into her eyes – eyes she knew were betraying every emotion she was battling. She knew he was looking for clues, looking for responses, the fact he was so attentive to her only adding to her arousal.

As the tip of his erection melded into her, she bit back a breath.

What she was considering doing wasn't only stupidly danger-ous; she was breaking every rule – her consent beyond justification, beyond redemption.

Giving in meant no going back. It was irresponsible. The conse-quences unforgivable.

Her body instantly tightened the way it always did – an instinc-tive reaction to the intimacy she had always and would always deny herself. And she despised it. She'd always despised it. Despised how her body's automatic resistance made her feel: frigid, useless, defunct.

But for once she was grateful for it. She wanted to see the look in his eyes when he realised how wrong he had been in his judgement of her – when he had the physical proof that she'd not yet liberated the serryn inside her.

Then come dawn, when she'd proven him wrong about the hold-ing spell too, he'd have to let her go.

And something inside her suppressed the warnings – something that wanted this more.

Something that wanted *him* more.

Immersed in the moment, captivated by eyes that filled her with calm in a way she wouldn't have thought possible, his self-assurance counterbalancing her uncertainty, it seemed worth the risk.

'Go ahead,' she said. 'Do it. And then bite. And when your brother comes up here to check on you, I'll have him too.'

As his eyes narrowed slightly at the threat, her heart thudded painfully. The intensity in them, the firmness of his touch pulsating through her skin making every nerve ending tingle.

As he eased inside her a little further, she involuntarily flinched.

The others had sensed it, and they had stopped. She'd always tried to hide it, tried to ignore it, but whenever it came to that inti-macy, she could never give herself enough to relax.

Because no matter how much she wanted to be like everyone else, she knew she never could be, so fearful was she of what it could potentially unleash. Sometimes she'd sob afterwards – resentful and frustrated at the curse she either controlled or instead controlled her. Sex meant only one thing – the slippery slope to a life she could neither advocate nor tolerate – the trigger to uncaging her serryn nature. Sex for her could never be about the pleasure of love, about a future. She could never have the future others had. And it was unfair to make anyone she came to care about think otherwise.

The others had sensed that tension and had withdrawn.

But seemingly Caleb had no concern about that.

Seemingly Caleb was going to persist no matter what. He was going to overcome her reluctance and conquer it. And maybe that's what made the difference. Maybe the others had been too kind, too compassionate, because the way her body was reacting to his insistence seemed terrifying confirmation enough that he was evoking something – something that stopped her caring of the consequences.

Consequences that could mean unleashing something as dark and dangerous and lethal as him.

But Caleb didn't seem to care about that, either.

And right then, neither did she.

She breathed heavily, intoxicated by the sensation of him breaking inside her inch by inch, quaking under the alien feel of him inside her. She gazed back at him, perfectly still, waiting to see if he'd know and what he would dare to do next.

And as his gaze snapped to hers, her pulse raced as those entrancing green eyes narrowed then flared slightly.

Eyes that told her he had sensed it.

She should have felt relief at his withdrawal, but instead she astounded herself as she ached in reluctant disappointment.

But she snapped back a breath when he withdrew only to push himself back inside her again – slow, controlled, but more forceful.

He pushed her thighs further apart, wrapped his arm around the small of her back to tilt her hips towards him.

She breathed steadily to calm herself, her hands clutching his. She cursed silently as he persisted until her body became more willing.

And it was the willing that stunned her – his perseverance intoxicating.

She shuddered, her escalating arousal finally allowing him to penetrate her more deeply, until, with a final thrust, he filled her to the hilt.

❋ ❋ ❋

It seemed Jake had been right to look at him the way he had down in the office – to fear losing him again to the darkness. He wasn't in his right mind when that took over. The acts he had committed proved that. Depravity, cruelty and brutality came hand in hand with who he once was. And it had been a battle to overcome it.

And in many ways he had. But clearly not enough. Because any iota of decency would have forced him to pull back when he'd felt it.

The witch had been telling the truth: she was inactive.

He should have pulled away. Especially when, instead of a look of hatred, those glossy eyes were laced with desire.

No serryn had looked at him like that. No serryn was ever capable of looking at a vampire like that.

But instead of tempering his actions, he had been fuelled by the need to consume her. Those enticing eyes, her parted lips, her ragged breaths had only incited him further.

She'd felt too good, her tightness becoming slicker as he'd persisted, the tension rippling through his own body. And as he'd felt her start to relax, her breathing finding its own rhythm, it had almost been too much.

Eyes that had stared back at him should have made the most of his moment of weakness, his approaching climax, and drawn him in to bite. Instead they'd remained uncharacteristically submissive as he'd pushed both her wrists together, restrained them above her head, her baited breath inciting a dormant rush in him as she'd trembled under his grasp. And he'd made the most of the moment – where her body was craving him too much for her mind to take hold.

He'd tried to release her wrists. He'd tried to force his hands to un-coil from them, but he'd involuntarily clung to her like static. It was as if somehow she'd been holding him there despite his instinct to retreat.

Something in him had stirred. Something that made him more than just uneasy. Something that tore at his pride, his self-assurance, his resolve. Something deep within, something dangerously unsettling, told him she was already challenging the very things that defined who he was.

By unleashing her darkness, he was unleashing his own. Only this was a more lethal darkness than he had ever encountered before.

It was supposed to have been about proving she was no different, but she *was* different.

This serryn, in the short few hours she had been there, was already evoking him to bite.

The warmth of her skin, the pulse beneath that tender flesh, the feel of her soft, pliable body…

She was a witch of the highest calibre; a serryn with phenomenal potential based on how quickly he'd responded to her. The way his heart beat too hard, the ache from his pending climax – one he knew was going to be more powerful and intense than he'd had in a long time.

He gripped her wrists tighter.

He needed to taste her.

And as he pressed his lips to her throat, felt his incisors extend in preparation, her soft, warm body, her relenting to him, only escalated his need.

❋ ❋ ❋

Terror flooded through her. If the serryn was going to surface, it was then.

She had to fight it. She had to fight it with all her will. Now was the time to beg him to stop. Now was the time to fight him as he nudged her head to the side, making access to the artery there as easy as it could be.

In that split second, if he chose to bite her, he would. And, more terrifying, in that split second, she wanted nothing more. To be that close to him – that intimate with him. As close as she could get.

As he thrust into her again, she clenched her fists, her climax awakening too quickly for her to control.

His last thrust was direct, powerful.

Leila cried out, arched her back, her voice echoing around the library. The sensations entwining through her body overwhelmed her, encapsulated her. She trembled as her climax consumed her, wiped her mind, every nerve, every sinew of muscle numbing from fingers to toes as she was trapped somewhere unknown for the passing moments, her whole body in pleasurable pain as she came.

She shuddered with her release, her climax offsetting his, Caleb coming inside her with a force that made him jolt and gasp.

He withdrew immediately, leaving her body cold with perspiration, her mind numb, so wrapped in her own orgasm that she forgot to be grateful they were both still alive.

Chapter Eleven

Leila remained on the edge of the seat, clutching the arms of the chair, the air prickling her skin.

It was nothing like she'd imagined. It had been so simple. So uncomplicated. So shockingly easy. It was as if something in her had snapped. Or something had shut down.

It was as if she'd been in a haze – a haze where she knew everything that was happening. It was as if all those mental blocks that had stopped her before, for some inexplicable reason, just didn't matter.

At the very least, she thought she'd feel different. She thought something would have been triggered – the darkness that had terrified her for so long. But there was nothing – nothing but a deep sense of satiation and completion. She may not have felt different, but she had to accept that something was clearly happening. It must be, for her to have consented like that. The transformation had to have begun simply by being in his presence, by being there in Blackthorn. Maybe the transformation was just slower than she thought.

The reality of how disastrous it could have been hit her hard and fast.

She looked up at Caleb as he stood a couple of feet away from her, side-on as he refastened his jeans.

Caleb who had taken her fear and anxiety and effortlessly overcome them within minutes – the very thing she believed impossible, not least with a vampire. Thoughts of how he'd made her feel still raced through her. The intoxicating thrill of his touch – a touch that still lingered pleasurably on her skin. An unfamiliar ache still throbbing within her.

She wondered if it was what all vampires were capable of – if that was the allure Alisha saw, that others saw. Or she wondered if it was just Caleb. If he was capable of making anyone feel like that.

But it was clearly something he was void of feeling in return, from the way he straightened himself out as if merely redressing after a shower. Never had it been clearer how good he was at what he did. This was his job – she was his job. And his detachment proved it. It had been nothing more than an act to show her he wasn't just in charge physically, but emotionally. He had set out to prove a point and he had done so.

And she was unforgivably gazing up at him like a schoolgirl with a crush on a rock star.

Anger she should have directed at Caleb, she directed at herself. Anger at letting him mark her in the most defiling way possible. Because that was how she felt – defiled. Used by a master craftsman for whom seduction was as easy and routine as dressing himself in the morning.

The only things she thought she was any good at – self-control and despising vampires – and she'd failed miserably and unforgivably at both.

She dropped her gaze to the floor, knowing any look of smug triumph on his face, in his eyes, would have broken her. Instead of redeeming herself, she had proved herself to be exactly what he accused her of being.

He had been right – she could only contain it for so long.

'There's no need to look so traumatised,' he said, breaking the silence.

She glanced up at him warily, embarrassment limiting her gaze. 'That shouldn't have happened.'

'It's a bit late for that kind of resolve.'

'I'm just saying.'

'The moon hasn't fallen out of the sky, there hasn't been an earthquake, bolts of fire aren't consuming the earth. It's hardly a global disaster.'

His nonchalance, whether intentional or not, struck her deep.

He turned away from her and strolled over to the fire. He threw a couple more logs onto the embers. He was mulling over something as he stared at the logs crackling and spitting on the reigniting fire. Something that kept his head lowered, his arms braced on the mantelpiece.

She wondered if he, too, realised how dangerously close they had been. Maybe he'd been as caught up in the moment as she had, and now reality was striking him, too.

As Caleb reached for his cigarettes on the mantelpiece and lit one, she stood from her seat and hovered awkwardly.

'This has to end now, Caleb. You have to let me go.' When he didn't acknowledge her, she took a few wary steps towards him. 'I mean it, Caleb. The longer you keep me here, the more at risk we all are. You have to see that now.'

'I must admit, I didn't expect you to give it up quite so easy.' He exhaled a curt stream of smoke as he looked across his shoulder at her. 'Not after all your proclamations.'

She felt a pang somewhere deep. 'Do you have to put it so coldly?'

'How else would you like me to put it?'

She could see the anger in his eyes, the resentment, and she hated to admit the fact that it hurt her as much as it frightened her. 'Trust me – you're not half as surprised as me.'

He inhaled before bracing both arms on the mantelpiece again.

Her throat tightened. 'You're angry with me. Why?'

He glanced across at her again, his eyes dark despite the resurging fire.

She took a step towards him. 'You instigated it. Not me.'

'I seem to remember you telling me to bite. I seem to remember you threatening my brother.'

'In the heat of the moment. I was angry.' She frowned and took another step towards him. 'Don't you dare blame me for this! Do not twist this to your own ends.'

'How? By saying it as it is?'

'That's *not* how it was.'

'No, because I'm covered with scratches and bruises from you trying to fend me off.'

She stared at him aghast, irritation coiling in her chest. 'So it *was* a test?'

'Like you didn't know.'

'And I failed, right? You set me up and now I'm to blame for the fallout? I can't win, can I? Damned if I do and damned if I don't.'

He turned to face her. He inhaled again before dropping his cigarette-holding hand to his side. 'Playing the martyr doesn't suit you, Leila.'

It was the first time he'd used her name. It disarmed her for a moment, falling too enticingly from his lips. 'Maybe not, but playing the complete and utter bastard clearly suits you.'

His smile was fleeting. 'Now that's the serryn fighting spirit I'm used to.'

'My anger is nothing to do with being a serryn! It's because I'm being held hostage in the middle of Blackthorn by a murderous vampire who is clearly void of any principles!'

His lips curling into a hint of a smile infuriated her further. 'Void of any principles?'

'Don't smirk at me,' she warned. 'I have proved myself to you. You know what I've been saying is true.'

'Because you spread your legs for the first vampire who showed you some attention?'

She exhaled in curt disbelief as she shook her head.

'Did you think I'd stop?' he asked. 'Usually I would have. Virgins really aren't my thing. They're right up there with my biggest turn-offs. But at least now you can see that proclaimed self-control isn't quite as tightly packaged as you like to think.'

'That's not how it was.'

'No? The evidence from our playtime begs to differ. You're not going to pretend you didn't enjoy it, are you? Only the outcome would make that lie somewhat transparent. You can't hide the obvious, fledgling – even behind such vehement words.'

She narrowed her eyes, fury simmering deep. 'You arrogant, conceited, smug…'

'For every hour you're here, you're going to come undone bit by bit. And it's already started. Sorry, sweetheart, but it's the way you're wired. It's what I've been telling you. Well done for being able to say no to all those nice human boys all these years, but the only males that will ever turn you on are the ones you're made to kill. Don't worry, it'll get easier now you've given yourself to me once – now you've seen how easy it is, how there's nothing to it.'

He eased back into his chair, smoke lingering in the air around him.

Something in her snapped. Never had she felt anger boil inside her so ferociously. She trembled, rooted to the spot. The tightness in her chest was painful, the clench at the back of her throat the only thing holding back furious tears.

'I did what I was asked to do,' she said, suppressing her fury with every bit of energy she had left. 'What I was told to do. I never wanted to come here. I never wanted to go anywhere near any one of your kind.'

'So what do you want? My sympathy?'

'Your sympathy's the last thing I want.'

'That's a dangerous thing to say to a vampire, fledgling.'

'As dangerous as you keeping me here? You could have bitten me tonight, do you not see that? Are you too arrogant to see that?'

She turned away, her arms folded, when a terrifying thought struck her. She spun to face him again, her hands falling loose to her sides.

'You *were* tempted, weren't you?' she said. 'That's why you're angry. You think this is down to me.' She took another step towards him. 'I warned you. And I will not be blamed for your weakness.

I will not be your scapegoat, do you understand me? This is your mistake, Caleb – keeping me here when you should have let me go.'

'Out onto the streets. Letting you loose in my territory. That's really responsible.'

She exhaled in frustration. 'I am not like them! I will not be like them! How many times have I got to say it before it sinks in? Why would I want to? Out there, trawling the streets, soliciting myself for a kill, letting vampires do whatever they want to me, not caring as long as it leads to their demise. Giving myself away night after night until there's nothing left – losing my heart, my soul, my conscience. Addicted and helpless to my base instincts: murderous, deviant, unashamed. I'm more than that. I have a life and an entitlement to life. To choices. To my family. To self-respect and dignity. Why would I want to lose all that to be trapped here, forced to reside in Blackthorn away from all I know and love, deemed a feeder, banned from crossing back into Summerton? What sense does any of that make? But there is nothing I can say or do to make you believe me, so there's no point even trying. You say I'm dogmatic but you're impossible! You can't see what's right in front of you. But I guess a closed mind negates the need for open eyes, doesn't it, Caleb? And everything about you is closed.'

She marched back over to the chair in front of the window before she was tempted to say anything more. Sitting down, she wrapped her arms around herself and lowered her head.

She expected him to leave her there in the silence, lost in her own emptiness, but he stepped in front of her, tilted her head up so she was forced to look at him.

He turned his head to the side slightly to exhale a steady stream of smoke away from her. 'Look me in the eye and tell me you haven't done a holding spell.'

She glowered at him in the silence.

'You can't, can you?' he said, his narrowed eyes further darkening his vibrant green irises.

'And give up my only leverage? The only thing keeping me and my sister alive? You wouldn't believe me even if I told you. You don't believe anything I say.'

'Do you blame me?'

'No. I understand, okay? I may have always lived in the safe confines of Summerton, but I know enough about this place. I know our worlds have different rules. I know only the strong and the brutal and the powerful survive in this territory. I understand that you rule your dominion tightly and mercilessly because it's the only way you can safeguard what you have. I understand that compassion doesn't last in Blackthorn and, as you have nowhere else to go, you have no choice. I understand you despise me. You have to protect what is yours, and there is no greater threat to that than a serryn loose in your territory. But all I want is out of here. All I want is to go home with my sister and never come back.'

As he frowned, studied her pensively, a small fragment of hope ignited.

'Keep me until dawn,' she said. 'If that's what you need to do. But put me back in the dungeon.'

'And give you time to breathe, you mean.'

'The whole situation is going to combust if you don't. We cannot be near each other. If you were tempted to bite, then we're in trouble. I'm clearly too powerful for you. I know it grates on your masculinity, but it's a fact.'

But Caleb's gaze snapped over his shoulder almost as if he sensed someone was there even before the door opened.

Jake flicked on the light, and stepped into the room. His arms were tense by his sides, anxiety rife in his face, his troubled eyes fixed on Caleb as something unspoken passed between them.

The male who stepped in behind Jake was tall and smartly dressed in a tieless black suit, his long hair combed neatly from his head. He stood to the right, opening the doorway.

Caleb's eyes narrowed coldly, his whole demeanour tensing.

Dread consumed Leila as a female stepped across the threshold, her cropped white-blonde hair shining in the artificial light – light that defined her stunning elfin features as her large icy-grey eyes locked directly on Caleb.

Chapter Twelve

Tugging Leila from the chair, Caleb stunned her by tucking her behind him, keeping what could have been mistaken for a protective grip on her wrist, his attention unflinching from the vampire who sauntered gracefully towards them.

She was tall, lithe, a toned slender leg appearing from behind the deep slit in her long, tight dress. The dark purple silk shimmered with the purposeful sway to her hips, the spiked heels of her silver sandals clicking rhythmically against the wooden floor.

'Caleb,' she crooned, her full pale lips smiling languidly. She sauntered past Jake, her height matching his.

Jake's frown was unflinching, his anxious gaze in Caleb's direction adding to Leila's unease as much as Caleb's tense grip.

'Feinith,' Caleb replied coolly.

If he hadn't seemed so surprised, and displeased, to see Feinith, Leila could have easily believed that he'd been stalling with her – that she was about to be handed over. But both the look in Jake's eyes and Caleb's protective stance demonstrated the contrary. And whoever Feinith was, the fact Caleb felt the need to shield Leila from the visitor only alarmed her more.

Feinith stopped square-on to him and tilted her head to the side, jealousy stabbing deep in Leila's gut as the vampire dragged a long painted nail teasingly down the buttons on his shirt. Her skin was tight, flawless, but something behind her large, preternaturally bright eyes betrayed her true age. She smiled more fully, revealing a hint of incisors. 'It's been a while. Too long.'

'For you maybe,' Caleb said.

Feinith smiled, a smile that didn't reflect in her eyes. She bit into her plump, pale bottom lip as she assessed him appreciatively. Slowly she slid her hand back up his chest, over his shoulder, her painted fingernails glistening. 'Still as perfect as ever,' she remarked, her palm exploring each of his toned curves. She slipped her hand up under his shirt at the waist, a hand that disappeared out of Leila's sight. 'Remember this,' she exclaimed softly as she moved closer. 'Such a pretty tattoo. Do you remember what you said when you had this done for me? When you promised me loyalty forever?' Her mouth met his, Feinith kissing him deeply, intimately.

Leila lowered her gaze to the floor. What she was feeling made no sense, the pain in her chest uncomfortable.

'So reluctant,' Feinith mused, pulling back slightly. 'Things have changed.'

'Betrothal does that.'

'Come now, Caleb. Don't sulk, my love. You know I have to stay true to my rank.'

Leila's gaze snapped warily to Feinith. Rank meant only one thing.

'Except when you're on your back under me,' Caleb remarked coldly.

Her mouth and throat turned arid. She didn't know what was worse – a Higher Order vampire stood less than a foot away or that Caleb had been with that vampire and, seemingly, it hadn't ended by his choice.

Feinith tutted playfully. 'Ouch. You are bitter.'

Wherever Feinith's hand had wandered, Caleb caught her wrist and pushed it away. 'No, you *wish* I was bitter. Sorry to disappoint. What do you want, Feinith?'

'I've come to find out what you've been getting up to.'

'That's none of your business.'

'You'll always be my business, you know that,' she said, gently easing her wrist from his grip but not relinquishing her gaze. 'Especially when you summon a witch to save your dying brother.'

Leila's heart skipped a beat.

Feinith smiled. 'Don't look surprised, Caleb. You can't seriously believe word like that wouldn't spread.' Turning gracefully on her heels, she sauntered over to Jake. She circled him, her hand sliding over his chest, around his back, her attention not leaving Caleb the whole time. 'One minute Jake's on the edge of second death and the next he's partying it up in the club again. There's only one way that can happen.' She strolled back towards him. 'So, either there was a nasty rumour going around, or you've been a very, very bad boy.'

'You know what rumours are like around here,' he said, his tone impressively unwavering.

Feinith smiled again, only this time the look in her eyes chilled Leila to the core. 'Who would have thought it – my precious Caleb harbouring a serryn? And protecting her from my presence, too. How sweet.' She leaned into his ear so Leila could hear her every word despite her whisper. 'You've tasted her. I can sense it on you. What else have you done with her, Caleb? Insatiable as ever I'm sure.' She licked her lips slowly and smiled. 'And did the little slut give herself to you willingly?'

She pulled away again, turning her back on him. 'Of course she did. They all do. That's why you were my best hunter.' She turned to face him again. 'Still, I'm flattered that you should go to such extremes to taunt me, Caleb. Of course, I may be feeling the remotest bit of jealousy, as I've no doubt you intended, if I hadn't been so impressed you found one. But then if it was going to be anyone, it would be you. And from the way she's clinging to you, I assume she knows nothing of your past? Of the depraved things you've done to her kind? Remember that serryn in Holliwell? Remember what you did to her? I thought she was going to bleed to death before you had time

to reach your pleasure. But you kept her going. For how long was it?'
She strolled back up to him. 'Eighteen? Twenty hours? That was quite
some night. That was our first joint venture, wasn't it, Caleb? Your way
to impress me. To prove your prowess.' She paused. 'Your devotion.'

Leila felt as if she'd been kicked in the stomach. She twisted her
wrist in his grasp, but his grip only tightened.

Feinith pushed her hips longingly against Caleb's as she slipped
her slender fingers around the back of his neck. 'I can still see it now.
I just have to close my eyes and it's there,' she purred, lowering her
long, elegant lashes, her lips parted. 'You thrusting yourself viciously
into her. Your hands cruel and coarse on her body. You used to love
to make them scream, didn't you, Caleb? The louder the better. And
wow, did some of them scream.'

Leila tried to yank her wrist free, but Caleb's vice-like hold
strengthened.

'Still,' Feinith said, stepping away to gracefully perch on the back
of the sofa before leaning back slightly with poise and balance, 'even
with your background, the Higher Order are going to be far from
impressed when they hear about this. You know the rules, Caleb.'

'Your rules, not mine.'

'Take her,' Feinith said, giving the bodyguard behind them the nod.

Leila's heart leapt, her stomach flipped.

'Don't touch her,' Caleb warned.

The bodyguard stilled. Whatever glare Caleb had thrown his way,
it had clearly worked from the bodyguard's hesitancy as he looked to
Feinith for further instruction.

'So defiant,' Feinith purred as she spread her arms. Crossing her
long legs, she twirled her foot playfully in the air.

'I found her. That makes her mine. They're the rules I live by.
Not yours. And not the Higher Order's.'

Feinith studied Caleb for a moment then cocked her head
towards the door as an instruction for the bodyguard to back off.

'Come here,' she said to Caleb.

Leila expected him to tell Feinith where to go. Instead, he released Leila's wrist and stepped up to the sofa as instructed.

Leila backed up against the bookcase, watching the showdown as they stood side-on to her, facing each other.

Feinith smiled, rubbed the toe of her sandal up and down the outside of Caleb's leg before sliding up to his crotch. When Caleb didn't flinch, her smile broadened. 'I shall, of course, be able to conceal this little...' she pondered playfully over her choice of word, 'reluctance. I will explain your lack of openness as merely a temporary disinclination. That may abate them. And I can always request your punishment be handed to me,' she added, pressing hard against his groin, causing him to wince.

Caleb pushed her ankle aside. 'You're not having her, Feinith.'

'Stubborn as ever. But don't delude yourself for one moment that I, any of us, will accept your defiance. Any witch that enters Blackthorn belongs to the Higher Order. Any serryn found is to be handed over with immediate effect. Alive. That is the law.'

'Any witch that enters my club, my territory, belongs to me – serryn or otherwise.'

She eased off the sofa, looked deep into his eyes, before pressing close to him, lips almost touching his. 'That little bitch belongs to the Higher Order.'

'That little bitch is mine,' he whispered back. 'I don't work for the Higher Order anymore, remember?'

After a few moments of silent, pensive contemplation, Feinith smiled. 'Okay. What do you want for her, Caleb?'

'You don't get it, do you?'

Feinith frowned. As her cold eyes locked on her, stabbing her with their icy glare, Leila looked away, her jaw clenched. 'My, my, she is a powerful one. The first serryn to control the infamous Caleb Dehain.'

She turned to step towards her, but Caleb cut in front to create a barrier. 'Stay away from her.'

The malice in the vampire's razor-grey eyes overshadowed her smile. 'Ironic. A vampire notorious for slaughtering serryns playing hero to one. Come on, Caleb, enough of the games. We both know what this is about.' She pressed close. 'I broke that infamous heart of yours and you want revenge. I understand. And I'm flattered, Caleb. Really I am.'

'Would you be so flattered if I told you to go fuck yourself?'

Feinith's eyes flared in indignation. She sidestepped him, forming a perfect triangle between him and Jake. Cruelty emanated from her eyes. 'And how does Jake feel about the serryn being here?' She glanced across at him then back at Caleb. 'With what happened to Seth…'

Jake's attention snapped to Caleb. 'What's that supposed to mean?'

'Don't,' Caleb warned her quietly, his gaze stony on hers.

Feinith smiled. 'He still doesn't know, does he?'

'Know what?' Jake asked.

'And I thought you boys told each other everything,' she remarked tauntingly, running her fingers back down his chest.

Caleb slammed her hand away with a viciousness that made Leila flinch. Even Feinith seemed momentarily taken aback.

She frowned. 'All these decades and you still haven't told him.'

'Caleb?' Jake asked, taking a couple of steps closer, his eyes narrowed.

'Jake, honey, your oldest brother wasn't killed in a brawl,' Feinith declared, taking a few sensible steps back. 'He was slaughtered by one of the sluts your brother's now protecting.'

Leila leaned back against the bookcase for support. Blood pumped in her ears, her legs feeling too weak to hold her.

'You vicious bitch,' Caleb hissed.

Feinith smiled maliciously.

Even amidst her fear, Leila's heart ached for him at Feinith's betrayal. But she couldn't allow it – she couldn't allow herself that weakness – not now she knew that his despising her wasn't just instinctive to his nature: it was personal.

Not now she knew exactly what he was capable of and just how lightly she had got off. For now.

'Caleb?' Jake took a step closer. 'What's she talking about?'

'I'm talking about your brother having to think very seriously about what he's got himself into here.'

'You had no right,' Caleb said quietly, his narrowed eyes locked on hers.

'And you have no right to keep an undeclared serryn under your roof. All the years you've spent building this place up, your reputation – could all be gone in one click of my fingers, Caleb. Without either, where would you be? I'll give you an hour to think it over. But I want that serryn bitch before I go or I'll burn this place down, rip Jake's heart out and force-feed it to you. Do we understand each other?' She tilted her head to the side slightly as she reached up to run her fingers over his lips, before kissing him lightly. 'We'll pick up where we left off somewhere more private. I'll be down in your office waiting. Don't take too long.' She turned and stepped away. 'Oh, and it goes without saying that my people are watching you. We'll know about every move you make. So make the right ones. For all your sakes.'

She sauntered back over to the door and shot him a glower across her shoulder before disappearing across the threshold, her bodyguard closing the door behind them.

Chapter Thirteen

The silence that descended on the room was excruciating. Leila's heart pounded painfully as her gaze flitted between the confusion and distress on Jake's face and the fury on Caleb's.

'Tell me Feinith's lying,' Jake said quietly, his narrowed eyes locked on his brother.

Caleb's attention remained fixed on the door.

'Caleb!' Jake snapped, the tremble in his voice reinforcing the anguish in his eyes. 'Tell me it's not true!'

'She shouldn't have done that,' Caleb said quietly. Too quietly.

Jake's eyes flared in horror. 'You told me he died breaking up a fight.' He paused. 'You lied to me.'

Caleb said nothing as his gaze snapped back to his brother.

'How do you know?' Jake demanded. 'How do you know it was one of them?'

The seconds ticked by as Caleb's gaze on Jake remained unwavering. 'I was the one who found him.'

'Dead?'

Caleb shook his head.

Jake's eyes widened. 'Like Tay?'

'I had to end it. I had no choice.'

'You?' Jake took a step back. 'You killed him?' Jake turned away, held his trembling hands to his head before spinning to face Caleb again. 'And you never thought to tell me any of this? Just how bad was it?'

Caleb looked to the floor again before meeting his brother's stunned gaze. 'I found her and I dealt with her.'

'How?'

'She suffered. That's all you need to know.'

Jake's frown deepened. 'You confided in Feinith. You told that cold-hearted, manipulative, power-hungry bitch, but kept it from me – for all these decades?'

'You found it hard enough to accept he was gone. What was I to do? Tell you the truth? Have you hunting down every single serryn you could find too? Do you think I wanted you ending up dead like Seth?'

'Tell me that's not the real reason why you took up the hunt. Tell me that wasn't how she hooked you into working for them. You know how Seth felt about it, so please tell me you didn't start it in his name.' He shook his head at his brother's silent confirmation. His frown deepened. 'Then at least tell me that's not the real reason why you kept Leila here. Tell me you're not that stupid.'

'I can't believe you're asking me that.'

'No? So this isn't giving you just a little sense of triumph? One small payback for Feinith coupling with Jarin?'

'This has nothing to do with Feinith.'

'I thought you were over her, Caleb. I believed you when you told me you were over her. A year, but she still strolls straight back in here like nothing has happened.'

'I *am* over her.'

'I've seen your twisted games with her first-hand too many times, remember? You must be loving being able to say no to her. You've had some fucked-up playoffs with her over the years, but this has got to be the ultimate. Only this time your warped power games could bring the wrath of the entire Higher Order down on us.'

'If she wanted the rest of the Higher Order involved, they'd be here.'

'Which tells me she's here for more than just that serryn. She's back for you, Caleb. She'll always come back for you.'

'Then she's going to be bitterly disappointed.'

'Is she?'

'I will sort this.'

'How?

'She's not coming in here demanding whatever she wants.'

'She's our only advocate in the Higher Order right now, unless you've forgotten. You play checkmate with that lethal bitch and we're in even deeper shit than we already are. You should have let Leila go when I told you to, then none of us would be in this mess.'

'I can handle Feinith.'

'No one can handle Feinith. Least of all you. She's not going to let this go. So considering you can't give her Leila, you'd better come up with something else quick.'

Despite Jake's curt exit, the slam of the door behind him, the room still felt oppressive.

Leila's attention snapped back to Caleb as he marched over to the table, kicked one of the chairs across the room. He paced the library like a caged predator, his eyes blackened with fury, his incisors protruding behind his sneer. With one hand, he yanked a bookcase from the wall opposite her, then another. They crashed to the floor in a thunderous roar, their contents spilling over the floor. Grabbing the table, he flipped it over with ease, a stream of expletives pouring out of his mouth.

Leila clutched the bookcase behind her, the devastation a stout reminder of the power of the creature in front of her. A temper, if turned on her, she wouldn't stand a chance of walking away from. The same temper he would have no doubt unleashed on the serryn who had murdered Seth. She had no doubt now what agony she had gone through.

He marched across to the hallway door, his eyes glazed, his demeanour lacking its characteristic composure.

As he too slammed it behind him then locked it, Leila's legs weakened enough that she had no option but to slide to the floor.

❄ ❄ ❄

Caleb stepped up to the bar. He snatched a glass from the counter and leaned over to reach for the whisky bottle. He filled the glass to a third of the way and knocked it all back in one before bracing his arms on the counter. He looked over his shoulder to see Jake was out on the terrace, staring out across the district.

He sighed heavily before pulling himself away from his drink, stepping out to join him.

'Stay away from me,' Jake warned, his grip tightening on the barrier.

'We need to talk.'

'Oh, *now* we do.' He glowered across at him as Caleb pulled level. 'Not a century and a half ago when you should have come to me instead of her.'

'And have you driven by the same hatred as me? Have you running into battle with them? You weren't equipped for it. You weren't skilled.'

'I had a right to know.'

'I was trying to protect you. I didn't want you consumed with it, like it consumed me.'

'You could have come to get me. You could have let me see him.'

'You wouldn't have wanted to.' Caleb braced his own arms on the barrier and gazed out over the district lights as he relished the night air.

Jake kept his head lowered.

Caleb knew he wasn't ready to deal with it yet – the full truth of what had happened to Seth that night. And Jake's silence about it told him *he* knew it, too. It would take time to sink in. Then there would be the questions. Then there would be the conversation they should have had years before then.

'I'm right, though, aren't I?' Jake said, his eyes sullen. 'Feinith used your festering hatred of that first serryn, renewed by the one that killed Seth, to reel you in.'

'It wasn't just down to her.'

'But she encouraged you.'

Caleb looked back ahead, his free hand tightening on the barrier. He could feel his brother's eyes burning into him.

'*Have* you slept with Leila?'

Caleb knew he didn't need to answer.

'Why, Caleb? Why go that extra step?'

Caleb knocked back a mouthful of drink. Because he'd needed to prove something to himself. Because he'd wanted her to unravel. Because he'd needed to prove himself right. Because, quite simply, he'd *wanted* to.

But he hadn't wanted to enjoy it. He hadn't wanted the buzz she had given him. He hadn't wanted the anger and frustration that had followed. He hadn't wanted to be left questioning himself.

'I saw the way Feinith looked at Leila, Caleb,' Jake added. 'She's only going to make this even more personal now. You know how possessive she is over you. Please, just tell me that's not why you slept with her. Please tell me you didn't use Leila for that.'

Jake was right – there was a time when this would have been the perfect opportunity to have Feinith right where he wanted her.

But not anymore.

'How many times do I have to say it, Jake? Feinith means nothing to me.'

'Then why sleep with Leila? What were you thinking? She's done nothing but save me.'

'You make it sound like a punishment.'

'Wasn't it?'

Caleb knocked back another mouthful. 'It just happened.'

'Oh, please – this is me you're talking to. It never "just happens" with you.' He paused. 'Are you attracted to her?'

Caleb glanced across at him and scowled. 'What's this – the night of stupid questions?'

'Things were looking intimate enough when I walked in. And that was quite the protective stance you gave her when you saw Feinith.'

He'd stunned himself with his reaction – the way he had shielded her had been instinctive even if he didn't comprehend it.

'I wasn't planning on letting her get close enough to see what Leila is.'

'And that's all there was to it?'

Caleb met his brother's narrowed gaze. 'I know what you're thinking.'

'So were you? Tempted?'

Caleb looked ahead again. 'No.'

'Caleb, I've just found out I've already lost one brother to a serryn. I can't lose another.'

He broke from Jake's troubled gaze. He couldn't tell him how close he'd been – how stupidly close. He couldn't put that weight on his brother's shoulders, not when he hadn't come to terms with it himself yet. 'You won't.'

'You're sure?'

'I'm perfectly sure.'

Jake looked far from convinced, his brow still furrowed with concern. 'All the same, maybe now more than ever it's time to put her somewhere else. Maybe put her in one of the apartments like we've done with Alisha. Hade can watch her. Humans are immune, right?'

There was no way he was letting Leila out of his sight now – not only because of the risk Feinith posed but because of his own need to prove to himself that it had been nothing more than a moment of weakness.

'I know what I'm doing,' Caleb said, sensing the impatience in his own tone, adding to the uncomfortable feeling of knowing Jake's accusation wasn't as empty as he was trying to get him to believe.

'Things go wrong, Caleb. Neither of you might intend it to, but it could. It already is.'

'I'll find a way to sort Feinith.'

'Then you'd better do it quick. Because if you say an outright no to her and she reports it to the Higher Order, we're over – us, the business, our reputation. We either get prosecuted or banished, and where will we go? I'll tell you – to The Pit with the rest of the vampire scum. And she'll do it, Caleb.'

'We have two things on our side – she wants Leila alive and she wants this kept quiet. I've just got to work out why.'

'And while you're working that out, Leila is also working out exactly what she's up against. She's not just going to sit back and do nothing. We're on borrowed time from every angle. You wanted the serryn in her unleashed, Caleb, you might have just done it. Face up to the fact you might finally be out of your depth this time or we're all going to sink.'

Chapter Fourteen

Caleb glared at the bodyguard who had the gall to block the door to his office.

The vampire skivvy may have been at Feinith's beck and call, but fortunately he still knew enough of Caleb's reputation to break eye contact and step aside.

Feinith was sat at his desk in the corner of the room, her legs elegantly stretched out on the surface amidst the papers she was riffling through. 'Well, well, this business truly is thriving, isn't it? Quite the little gold mine. But you always were the success.' She stood up from the chair and sauntered towards him. She smiled as she stopped in front of him, placed her palms on his chest. 'I see we're alone this time. How romantic.'

He slapped her hands aside. 'What the fuck do you think you were doing telling Jake?'

She widened her eyes slightly, took a step back. 'Come on, Caleb. You know better than to defy me.'

'You gave me your word that it would stay between us. Only us.'

'And you promised me loyalty but that still didn't stop you giving it to that little whore.'

'Like you're giving it to Jarin?'

She smirked. 'You *are* jealous.'

'No. I just despise your hypocrisy.' He pulled away and marched over to the window, yanking back the drapes.

'Okay, so I apologise. Is that what you want? It came out in a temper, but if you will tease me so…' She stepped closer to stroke his face, her slender fingers playing over his jaw. 'You know, you're still the best I've ever had, Caleb.' Pushing herself between him and the window, she ran her hand back down his chest towards his groin – a delicate hand that summoned death as easily as ordering a drink. 'The very best.'

He didn't flinch. 'I wish I could say the same.'

Feinith smiled. 'I understand why you want to protect yourself.' She licked her lips and leaned in to kiss him. 'Vulnerability doesn't sit easy with you, does it? And you hate how I make you feel.'

'You always think you can win me around, don't you?'

She smiled against his mouth. 'You've never wanted anyone like you want me. And we both know it.'

But not anymore. As he gazed into Feinith's eyes – eyes so cold and emotionless in every way that mattered – he'd never known it more. How numb he felt in her presence, unable to bear the touch of the female he once craved, who he once thought capable of fulfilling his every need.

She had excited him once, enthralled him as he'd immersed himself in carnality, revelling in the submersion into his primal instincts. Feinith had fulfilled so many of those darker needs, so much so that she'd become an addiction he couldn't be without. He had adored her. Thrived on the way they sparked. Before she'd torn him apart as she toyed with his feelings – feelings he'd believed were love.

She had relished in his darkness, his cruelty, his brutality, and had encouraged it. Now it sickened him, because he understood that all she had done was encourage him deeper into those depths for her own satiation. And hearing those descriptions of his past deeds dripping from her lips with such amusement made him feel a pang of shame – and not least, for some inexplicable reason, because of Leila's presence as she uttered them.

'Is that what you tell Jarin?' he asked.

Feinith paused, her lips hovering, but there was now a slight frown marring her flawless forehead. 'You know how it works. He's of good inheritance. An equal.'

'But we both know you don't get off on having an equal, Feinith. Tell me, does he truly know just how much you enjoyed your visits to me? What all those business trips really entailed, in every little detail?'

'I'm not accountable to anyone, Caleb. I do what I want to do. Betrothed or not.'

'Jarin will never satisfy you, Feinith. He won't even come near to what I can do. And you know it.'

'He won't need to. Because you're going to keep on satisfying me, Caleb. Just like you always have. This doesn't have to change anything.'

Caleb pulled away, turning his back on her as he strolled away. 'You take so much for granted.'

'We don't have to be of the same breeding to want each other, Caleb.'

'Only because the novelty would wear off if we were.' Caleb turned to meet her gaze. 'We both know I'd no longer have the same appeal if you couldn't sully yourself by being with me.'

Feinith stepped towards him. 'I want you for who you are, not what you are.' She stopped within inches of him. 'Betrothed to Jarin or not, you'll still be able to give me everything I want. And staying betrothed to him will only add to that.' She pressed her lean, hard body to his, a body he'd explored in every way possible. 'And I know how much you enjoy having what you shouldn't.'

She unzipped his trousers, sliding her hand inside his shorts. It was a hold that had once been enthralling and provocative. He'd loved her confidence, her sexual prowess and her want of him. And she had wanted him. Deeper than she'd ever admitted. Deeper than she ever would admit.

But instead of feeling that spark as she touched him, he felt numb. As she kissed down his neck before sliding her tongue up to his ear, images of what he'd done flashed in front of his eyes again. The depraved things they had both relished in now made his blood run cold.

'Though you might find it hard to believe, I do have other things on my mind beside you, Feinith.'

'But nothing more important than me. That's the only thing you should have on your mind right now.' She squeezed but then she released him, withdrew her hand from his shorts. She arched an eyebrow. 'You really are difficult to please tonight.'

He pulled away, fastened his jeans, and leaned back against the sofa, his arms folded. 'You made a big mistake telling Jake, let alone threatening him.'

She raised her pale eyebrows slightly. 'So is that what this little mood is about now? You know I wouldn't *really* hurt him.'

'You already have.'

'Then you shouldn't have been playing hard to get. I can't have you humiliating me like that. I won't. I'm only trying to help you. You know how much trouble you'll be in if the Higher Order find out about this. How much trouble I'd be in if anyone knew I was here. I wanted to give you a chance. I'm doing this for you.'

'Of course you are,' he said. 'As selfless as ever.'

'The Higher Order—'

'Fuck the Higher Order.'

'I know how you feel about them, Caleb. I know how much it frustrates you. I know you disagree with so much of what we are about, but it's about what is fitting.'

'About keeping us underlings in our place, right?'

'The mixing is not acceptable. You know the bloodline must be retained. Weaken our bloodline and we weaken our cause.'

He exhaled curtly. 'Don't hide behind that, Feinith. You despise some of the ways of the Order as much as I do. You're not worried about the bloodline; you're just worried about weakening your reputation – losing your place, your influence, your power. None of which you would be willing to give up for me.'

'I have given myself to you time and time again, like I have given myself to no other. Is that not enough?'

'No, Feinith, it isn't. But I'll think about what *is* enough.'

Feinith's eyes narrowed in irritation. She placed her hands on her hips, her temper beginning to seep out. 'Is that what this is, Caleb? Blackmail? Is that why you're holding her back?'

'Come on, Feinith. You clearly want her. *Really* want her. There has to be something more in it for me than just handing her over.'

'Don't make me take her from you.'

'I will kill her before you get within twenty feet of her. I assume you want her alive?' He saw the flare in her eyes. For the first time she was unsettled. Unsettled because she knew him well enough to know he meant every word and that he didn't bluff. She wanted Leila alive. The look in her eyes told him she *needed* her alive, an advantage he needed to hold on to. 'Tell me, Feinith, why did the Higher Order change the rules on the serryn slaying? There never was an explanation.'

She frowned. 'And as I've told you before, those issues don't concern you.'

'They do now. You playing this so cautiously tells me you must want her badly. Why is that?'

'Just give her to me, Caleb.'

He folded his arms. 'Always the stalemate, isn't it, Feinith?'

'You know her value. It's no great secret. There's money to be made for her blood – blood we cannot risk having black-marketed on the streets.'

'Control you can't risk having taken away from you, right?'

'There were those using them against us, Caleb. Human and vampire alike. We have to keep order. We have to keep control.'

'And that's the only reason you want her? To keep that little pot of poison off the street? To keep the peace.'

'Exactly.'

'So why not let me carry on killing them? Same outcome.'

She studied him warily for a moment, the uncharacteristic unease in her eyes even more rife.

He sauntered over to the drinks cabinet. 'It seems we have some serious negotiating to do,' he said, placing two glasses on the counter.

'You wouldn't kill her,' she said, her usual steady tone wavering a little. 'She's too convenient a bargaining tool for you.'

'And far too entertaining between the sheets to dispose of just yet.' His eyes lingered coaxingly on hers as he held out a glass to her.

'You are not invincible, Caleb,' Feinith warned, reaching for the drink. 'You dance too close to the edge with that one.'

'Is that what concerns you, Feinith – my welfare?'

'There is self-assurance, Caleb, and then there is stupidity. Now give me the serryn, or my patience will wear out.'

'I'd say her market value just went up a hundredfold, wouldn't you? Instead of selling her on the street, I sell her direct to the Higher Order. Just like old times.'

'Money? This is about money?'

'When has it ever been about money, Feinith?'

'Then what do you want?'

'I'm not sure yet. I'd like some time to think about it.'

'No.'

He shrugged. 'Then I'll deal with the serryn myself.'

She stepped up to him. 'You wouldn't dare.'

'I made a vow that I would not rest until every one of those bitches that slaughtered my brother is wiped off the face of the Earth, remember? And I've already got this one right where I want her. Why wouldn't I?'

'You truly think you can bargain with me over this?' Her eyes narrowed in fury. 'You think I can't have this place torn apart to find her if I wanted to?'

'So do it,' he said, his arms spread. 'Let them come in here. Let them search every corner. But you'll never find her. I promise you that. Then you'll be forced to admit to your lover and the whole Higher Order that you had a serryn in your grasp and you failed.'

She shook her head slightly. 'You wouldn't risk prosecution. For Jake's sake you wouldn't. You'd be finished here. Banished to The Pit. To nothing.'

'And you wouldn't risk exposing that you'd come here to collect a serryn non-legitimately. Because Jarin doesn't know, does he? Or he'd be here revelling in finally having a reason to see me go down. No, I think your actions so far could throw up a lot of awkward questions.'

He stepped up to her. 'I think it would be far more sensible for you to curb your impatience for a few more hours while I mull over how I'd like this to work to my advantage and how you're going to make up for what you did tonight. In fact, if you hadn't burst in here making your demands, if you'd had the good manners to call first and offer me something in exchange, we could be avoiding all of this. Do you really want to further your mistake and make this more complicated than it needs to be?'

'I am not walking out of here without her, Caleb.'

'Then make yourself at home. The sofa isn't as uncomfortable as it looks. But you already know that. You'll excuse me for not inviting you into my bed, but it's going to be occupied for a while.'

Feinith shook her head slowly, her eyes narrowed. It was clearly one jibe too many but she watched him with wary caution. 'Caleb. Always the game-player. But you know I'm not going to walk away from this until I get what I want.'

He knocked back the contents of his drink. 'So come back tomorrow night.'

He placed the glass back on the drinks cabinet, tension gripping him as he waited for her to take the bait.

'I'll be back at dusk,' she said. 'And you'd better have your demands.' She turned away with the appeal of a sulky child, slamming her glass on the workstation as she passed. 'Because after that,' she glowered across her shoulder, 'I won't feel like playing anymore.'

Chapter Fifteen

Leila clutched the edge of the sofa seat, her foot bouncing in agitation on the floor as she looked back over at the open sash window.

From the grey sky, dawn could have only been a couple of hours away at most – a dawn that had seemed terrifying enough, but now her and Alisha's freedom had never seemed more impossible.

Now that the Higher Order were involved, there was no way she was getting away.

She bent forward, rested her elbows on her knees and clutched her head as she tried to calm the terror that tore through her at the prospect of being prisoner in some Higher Order lab somewhere, her blood siphoned off for the rest of her life for them to use to maintain order in the ranks.

Or worse.

No – they couldn't know. It was a secret only ever passed on by word of mouth from the patrons to their serryn wards. A secret each of them guarded with their lives.

A secret the Higher Order could *never* know.

She had to get out of there. She had to get out of there now. Somehow.

She stood, wrapped her arms around her chest and turned to face the room. So many of his beautiful books lay limp and discarded on the floor. All she had as an indication of his civility, his humanity, lay damaged and torn – cast aside so easily in his fury.

That was the real Caleb she saw in those moments – the vampire who wasn't holding back to play her to his own ends. That was the true Caleb – not the vampire who had scrutinised her so curiously before they were interrupted, the ice in his eyes, for just a moment, melting, revealing more than just a cold killer. The reassuring grip of a vampire she thought was shielding her from the enemy until she heard the facts spill from Feinith's lips – the torture and depravity and cruelty they had shared. Worse, had enjoyed.

Caleb, whom she now knew had every reason to hate her kind with every fraction of his being.

A hatred she understood and reluctantly empathised with only too well.

She stepped amidst the chaos and fell to her knees on the floor. Closing the covers on the books nearest her, she realigned broken spines before putting the books in neat piles.

She sank back on her haunches.

Just as she'd sensed from the moment she got that call from Alisha, just as she'd sensed it the minute she'd arrived in Blackthorn, there was no going back. Even if they did stand a hope in hell of getting out of there, they'd both be checked and tested at the border back into Summerton. If they couldn't convince the authorities Alisha had been an unwilling feeder, she would be banned to Lowtown alone to fend for herself. They could discover Leila was a serryn and then that would be it – the authorities would own her, leaving Alisha truly alone.

Things were never going to be the same again.

And she had to accept that.

But she and Alisha *would* get out of Blackthorn, even if it was only as far as Lowtown. They would get out of there – away from Caleb and Jake, away from the Higher Order. They'd be together and they'd get through it.

She stood and scanned the room. He could be gone for a matter of minutes or another hour, but he would be back.

She needed something to fight with.

She looked towards his bedroom and strode across the threshold. The rain smattered against the sealed window, drawing her attention to the window seat tucked in the corner to her left before she tentatively scanned the room. The bed directly ahead looked dangerously soft, the pillows plumped up invitingly. To her right was an ajar door to what she could see was an en suite. Between that and a double wardrobe to the right was a chair – a chair on which she saw the shirt he had worn in the dungeon, and something poking out from beneath it.

Blood thrummed in her ears.

She strode over without registering the journey, her gaze locked on the corner of the partially exposed leather wrap. She pushed the shirt aside, unfolded one side of the leather and stared down at the syringes.

Her heart pounded.

The thought sickened her at what her blood would do to him, for more reasons than she felt comfortable allowing herself to acknowledge. But it was either that or the unthinkable alternative.

She didn't owe him anything. Anything at all.

She removed one of the clean syringes from the sleeve and stared down at the tip. She hated needles. Always had. Her first and only other encounter with needles before Caleb was after her mother's murder. The Serryn Union had to be sure. They'd assured her it was only for lab tests, where her blood would be mixed with a sample of vampire blood. She'd gone along with her grandfather's advice.

She remembered the look on his face the night he came to pick her up. They'd had the vampire's body removed and with it any evidence of what had happened. But they'd had to leave her mother there to be found. The official story she'd been told to give was that her mother had been called away by someone at the play so had asked her grandfather to come and pick Leila up, and that was the last they had heard of her.

Leila still didn't know what was harder – watching her mother die or leaving her still-warm body abandoned and alone in that dark alley.

And that's what she had to remember. What they were capable of. What Caleb was capable of. She wouldn't allow herself to be next. And she certainly wouldn't sit there helplessly waiting for them to decide her fate, let alone Alisha's.

Grasping the syringe, she tucked herself away in the bathroom where she would hopefully be able to clear away any evidence if Caleb did return.

Inside was plush and immaculate. A simple roll-top bath and glass shower cubical sat opposite the toilet. A basin and towel rail sat directly ahead, plump towels draped over each rung.

She leaned back against the roll-top bath but, with her legs too weak to sustain her, she lowered herself cross-legged to the floor.

Her hand trembled, her palms perspiring as she placed the needle against the crook of her left arm, relieved Caleb had opted for the right arm in the dungeon.

She immediately pulled it away again, the prospect of it piercing her skin turning her throat arid.

She rested her head back against the cold ceramic.

Taking a deep and steadying breath, she clenched and un-clenched her hand to encourage the blood to flow. Barely able to look, she placed the tip of the needle over one of the thicker veins. She breathed and exhaled deeply, and slid the needle in.

She leaned her head back again as she drew back the plunger, the pain making her bite into her lower lip, making her light-headed, a hot shiver flushing over her. The nausea was overwhelming. She couldn't even bear to look for the first few seconds but then forced herself to see if she had taken enough. Seeing the syringe a third filled with her blood, she pulled the needle out and lifted the crook of her arm quick-ly to her mouth. She sucked to try and curb the pain and stem the flow.

She needed to hide the syringe somewhere. She couldn't just go at him with it – he'd snatch it off her in an instant. She needed it to be somewhere where she could get her hand on it with ease.

Somewhere he wouldn't notice. Somewhere she could catch him unexpectedly.

She looked back down at the syringe.

And she also needed to have a backup in case she failed.

❄ ❄ ❄

Caleb descended the steps into the lounge and joined Jake at the bar.

Jake closed Leila's purification book and pushed it aside. 'What's happening?'

'I've bought us some time,' Caleb said, easing up onto the stool beside him as Jake poured him a drink. 'Only until tomorrow night, but it's something.'

'How did you manage that?'

'I told her I wanted to make it worth my while. It helped that she thinks I'm going to concede. You know Feinith.'

'But it's nearly dawn, Caleb. What if Leila proves you right? What if she has saved me? There's no way you can hand her over. What then?'

Caleb knocked back his drink, reached for the bottle and unscrewed the cap to pour himself another. 'Let's not get ahead of ourselves.' He glanced over his shoulder out at the pale grey sky through the sealed terrace doors, before looking back at his brother. 'How are you feeling?'

Jake knocked back a mouthful of whisky, his hand tense, his eyes lowered. He shrugged. 'Fine.'

He didn't look fine. But then he couldn't expect him to.

'Have you checked on Alisha lately?' Caleb asked.

'She's out of it. Probably will be for hours.' Jake knocked back the remains of his drink before pouring himself another. 'Not that that's a bad thing.'

'You really care about her, don't you?'

'We look after our own, Caleb, that's how it's always been. We show loyalty to those who show loyalty to us. She took a risk bringing Leila here. She took that risk for me.'

Jake took another large mouthful before staring down into his half-empty glass.

Caleb licked the remnants of alcohol from his own lips and stared ahead in the silence for a few moments. 'I'm sorry you had to find out that way about Seth.'

Jake kept his gaze lowered. Caleb could see the emotion brewing in his eyes. Emotion he clearly didn't want his big brother to see right then.

'But I'm not sorry I didn't tell you,' Caleb added. 'I did what I had to in order to protect you. I know you may not see it that way but it's—'

'I know why you did it.' He met Caleb's gaze. 'And I know how hard it must have been for you to bring Leila here. Why you've been having so much trouble getting your head around the fact she might have saved me. But she has. And any time now you're going to see it.'

The need to protect Jake was overwhelming. The need to reassure him, particularly in those final few minutes, wrenched at him. But Caleb couldn't reassure him. He couldn't agree with him. Because, as confident as Jake was that Leila had done purely what she'd been brought there to do, Caleb couldn't believe it. Not enough. Not when encompassed with the deep-rooted pain that at any moment he could be back on the cusp of losing the only one he had left to love.

And if that happened he would drag her up there and she *would* do what she'd been brought there to do. And she would see the Caleb that drove the reputation. She would see the Caleb even his brother dreaded. Because he couldn't lose another brother. He *wouldn't* lose another brother.

Caleb glanced back up at the clock, at the seconds scraping by.

'How did you know where to find him? Or was it just a fluke?'

Caleb took a slow steady swallow of his drink. 'I was due to meet him. When I got there, he wasn't around. I waited. And waited.

I asked around and found out he'd left with a woman. We both know that wasn't Seth's style.' Caleb glanced across at his brother again to see he had his full attention. Finding the distress in Jake's eyes too oppressive, he looked down at his glass before taking another mouthful. 'It took me about an hour to trace his steps but I got there. She'd taken him to a derelict building tucked out of the way so no one would hear his cries. He'd bitten and she'd left him. Alone.' Over a century later, it still made him sick to say it, the anger always there ready to surface. 'In the dark and in the cold, on some stained, dirt-ridden floor.'

Jake stared up at the ceiling then turned his head away so Caleb wouldn't see the anguish in his eyes that consumed the space between them. 'You ended it quickly?'

'As soon as I could bring myself to do it.'

'You held him until the last moment?'

'The very last moment. And a long time after that.' Caleb knocked back a mouthful of drink to curb his tears. 'But do you know what he told me? Even after that? Even knowing what that first serryn bitch did to me? "Let it go." He still wanted me to let it go.' He looked back ahead. 'I shouldn't have listened to him the first time. I should have started hunting all those decades before, then there wouldn't have been any serryns left *to* slaughter him.'

Jake looked back at him. 'He didn't want you to succumb to it, Caleb, just like you didn't want me to.' He hesitated. 'Just like he wouldn't want you to hurt Leila now.'

Caleb held his brother's probing gaze. 'I understand how you feel, but it's not just about what she is – it's about what she can become. Don't you see that?'

'You have no right to judge her. No right to predict her future.'

'There are no exceptions, Jake.'

'There's always an exception.'

Caleb continued to hold his gaze until the familiar grating of the day-shields lowering diverted his attention back over to the terrace doors. The grey sky gradually disappeared behind the darkened-glass barrier, dawn minutes away from igniting the horizon. He looked back at Jake. 'We'll know soon enough, won't we?'

'Whatever happens,' Jake said. 'Don't let Feinith use you, Caleb. Don't let her bring that part of you out again. Please. She'll destroy you, whether it's by her hand or making you think it's by your own volition. Don't let her.'

'I'm not going to.'

This time when Jake looked at him, he held his gaze. 'Promise me.'

'I promise you.'

They both looked up at the clock. The hands continued to scrape in silence. After ten minutes had passed, Jake looked back at Caleb.

'It's dawn,' he said. 'I'm still here, just like I said I would be. Just like Leila did.'

Caleb stared back into his glass.

The evidence was undeniable. Against all her better judgements, against her very nature, Leila had saved Jake's life.

He should have been celebrating; instead, despite his all-consuming relief, he struggled to swallow as he knocked back the remains of his drink, the bitter aftertaste coursing down his throat.

Chapter Sixteen

L eila stood abruptly from the sofa as she heard the scrape of the key in the door. She turned to face it, her back to the dead fire, her hands tense by her sides.

She hadn't known what to expect, but it wasn't for him to be alone, or enter with a mug of hot coffee and something to eat.

'Here,' he said, chucking her an apple, Leila surprising herself that she caught it. 'I wasn't sure what you'd like but you need to eat something. I'll get you some proper food later.'

Joining her at the sofa, Caleb placed the coffee on the floor beside her before turning his attention to the fire. Within moments the flames were flickering again, adding much-needed warmth. He sat back in the fireside chair, one leg outstretched casually as he cut sections off his own apple with a knife, taking each slice directly off the blade.

Leila clenched the apple in her hand, her heart pounding uncomfortably as the seconds grated past.

'Well?' she asked.

'Jake's fine.' He met her gaze. 'But you already know that.'

Her relief was fleeting until it was overshadowed by the reality of knowing he no longer needed her as anything but a pawn in whatever game he was playing with Feinith. 'Not that it makes a difference now, right?'

He took another slice of apple, but didn't say anything. She tried not to look at the knife he turned slowly and deftly between his fingers, the metal intermittently catching a glint of firelight.

'Where's Feinith?'

'She's gone for now.'

'For now?'

'She's coming back later.'

She didn't need to phrase it as a question. 'For me.'

Cutting off another slice of apple, Caleb met her gaze. 'Why does she want you, Leila?'

'As if you don't know.'

'I mean why does she want you alive?'

'I didn't realise she did. Is that what you've been discussing all this time? What did you negotiate for? What are you hoping to get out of this?'

He glanced at her before turning his attention back to his apple. 'You have a very low opinion of me.'

'And so unfounded, right?'

He cut off another chunk. 'We were banned from killing you but they never told us why. New orders were introduced that any serryn found alive was to be taken directly to the Higher Order. So I'll ask you again: Why?'

She looked down at her apple to break from the intensity of his gaze. Lifting the fruit to her lips, the first bite was surprisingly comforting, the sharpness refreshing to her dry mouth. She chewed the small piece slowly, the swallow uncomfortable. If it was a trap, she wasn't going to play ball. 'They're your Higher Order. You worked for them.' She met his gaze in the boldest move she could muster. 'You tell *me*.'

He assessed her gaze in the silence. A second longer she was sure she would break, but he averted his gaze back to his apple. 'If you don't tell me, I can't help you.'

She exhaled curtly. 'Help me? The only way you can help me is by getting Alisha out of here and away from all this.'

'No can do, fledgling. You heard Feinith. They'll be watching the place. She leaves here and she's going nowhere but straight into their hands.'

'Otherwise you'd let me go?' Despite him not answering, she had to cling on to the prospect that it was what he meant. 'There's got to be a way out of this place that they don't know about. Alisha certainly doesn't need to be here.'

He looked up at her, her heart skipping a beat in a way she wished it wouldn't as his green eyes rested on hers. 'Yes, she does.'

Frustration simmering, she frowned. 'Why? To make sure I do as I'm told still?'

'Ironic as it might seem, the safest place for you both is here with me. And as I'm the one who summoned you here, that makes you my responsibility.'

'I'm no one's responsibility, least of all yours. Use me as some convenient bargaining toy in your power games with your superiors if you have to, but don't drag my family into it too.'

'A bargaining toy? Is that what you think you are?'

'Me and Alisha are alive for a reason and it's obvious what it is.'

'And what's that?'

'Don't play games with me, Caleb. I saw enough. And from the way Feinith pushed you around, I think it's obvious she knows exactly what buttons to press.' She regretted it as soon as she said it – part in desperation, part in anger but mainly, and more alarmingly, in jealousy.

'And I'm the only thing between you and her, so watch your tone.'

Leila braced herself as his intense glare held hers. 'I'm the only thing between you and *her*, you mean. Clearly this is a private arrangement or the rest of the Higher Order would already be here.'

'Careful,' he said. 'That sounded like jealousy.'

'Far from it. But I can read between the lines. I saw the way she was with you. I saw the way you looked at her.'

'The way I looked at her?'

Anger wrenched her gut at the glimmer of amusement in his eyes, at the slight upward curve on those enticing lips.

'Was it painful, fledgling, watching her with me?' he asked, the coax clear in his tone.

'Jake was right, wasn't he? That was why you slept with me. You knew she'd come here.'

'I had sex with you because I wanted to.'

'To entrap me. But I'm not going to be a pawn in your twisted games anymore, Caleb. I should have been long gone. None of this should be happening. This is all your fault.'

'What do you want me to say?'

'I want you to admit you were wrong to keep me here.'

'We all act on what information we have at the time.'

'That's not good enough.'

'Not good enough?' His eyes narrowed. 'Who the fuck do you think you are?'

'I'm the woman whose life you're on the verge of ruining because I came here to do the right thing by *your* family.'

'We all have choices. You chose to put your sister above everything you've been taught. No decent serryn would do that. That's why the guidelines are in place. You fucked up just as much as I did.'

She felt something inside her snap. 'How can you say that?'

'We both went against our better judgement to save those we care about, despite the fact we knew it was wrong and we knew of the potential fallout. You had a choice, Leila. A choice to come here. A choice whether to reach your full potential. Take some responsibility.' He leaned forward and threw his apple core into the fire.

She should have bit her tongue but she couldn't. 'Don't you dare lecture me.'

'I'll admit you've proved me wrong. What you did for Jake, I never thought possible. But that doesn't change the situation now. Looks like we both ended up deeper than we intended.'

'Well, thanks for that,' she said tersely. 'I appreciate it. Even if it is several hours too late.'

'That's not an apology, Leila. You can't blame me for not trusting you.'

'No, I don't. Especially now I know what happened to Seth, which, believe it or not, I'm really sorry to hear. Just as I know Fein-ith's backed you into a corner. But whether you intended that to happen or not, and I don't know what I believe as far as that goes, but Alisha and I are both still stuck in the middle. And that's down to you. You have to get us out of here.'

'And what then, Leila? You're really going to walk away from all this and never come back? Never report it? Even if that's the truth, now that Feinith knows you exist, do you think she won't hunt you down? You might think you're safe in Summerton, but it's not inac-cessible, no matter what your politicians tell you to justify charging you your extortionate rates. It certainly isn't as impenetrable as they like you to think. The Higher Order, and those with connections to them, has ways and means. They know who to pay off. She'll find you. Only I won't be around to help you.'

'I told you – I don't need your help. I just need you to get me out of here and I'll sort the rest.'

'I don't know if your naivety is endearing or irritating. She may come across cool, but she was simmering when she saw the way I protected you. This has become personal.'

'Thanks to you.'

'I think we've laboured that point enough.'

'And I'll keep labouring it. You've used me from the outset. If it's not one thing it's another. So please excuse me for feeling slightly aggrieved.'

He stood.

She tucked her hand under the sofa seat, her fingers extending to check the syringe was still there.

She wrapped her hand around the shaft, uncertain how quickly she'd be able to extract it. She knew she'd have to wait until he was closer, until he wouldn't catch a glimpse in the corner of his eye. She had no doubt his reaction times were second to none and she knew she only had one shot at it.

But instead of approaching her, Caleb strolled past the sofa. Stepping amidst the mess his temper had left behind, he lifted the first bookcase off the floor and pushed it back against the wall, all the muscles in his back and arms tensing. He did the same to the one next to it before returning the books back to their rightful place a few at a time.

She needed him close. She needed him as close as she could get him.

She tucked the syringe behind her back as she stood and turned to face him. 'So what now? I'm to remain a prisoner here until you finally hand me over, is that it?'

'Unless I can find a way through this.'

'My hero,' she said.

He glanced across at her as he slotted more books back into place.

Aggravating him was not going to help. She needed to get him to lower his guard.

She watched him as he slotted more books onto the shelves, as she struggled with something more placating to say.

'Feinith shouldn't have announced about your brother like that to Jake. It was cruel.'

Busy reinserting pages into a split book, he didn't look at her. 'That's Feinith for you.'

'And that's quite a temper you've got,' she said, the battle between her head and her heart rife as she watched him tend to each battered book in turn. 'Remind me to stay on the right side of it.'

He glanced across at her again as he picked up another pile of books.

After a few more moments of hesitation, she stepped over to join him. She lowered to her haunches. The moment he turned his back on her, she slotted the syringe between the pages of one of the books.

As he looked back across his shoulder at her, her heart pounded, but he merely stood and placed a few more books on the shelf.

She reached for more books and added them to the pile, looked up to see him glancing in her direction again. She carried them over to the bookcase next to his. She slotted them amidst some others, lying down the syringe-contained one within easy reaching distance so she could tuck her fingers between the pages. She leaned back against the bookcase to cover her tracks.

'So was Jake right? Did what happened to Seth start it all? The hunting? Was she the first serryn you'd come across?'

He gathered up a few more books until enough time had lapsed for her to believe he wasn't going to answer. 'I came across my first thirty years before then, when I was seventeen.'

Clearly he'd been proficient, even at a young age. 'Which you survived.'

'Only because she decided against a quick death.'

'What did you do? Escape?'

'Seth and a few others found me. They'd been watching her and followed her back one night.'

'Did Seth kill her?'

'No. The others did.'

'Why not him?'

'He said once someone started, it was difficult to stop.'

'Then he was killed by one?'

She let her gaze linger on him in the silence, the distant pensiveness in his eyes making him seem almost human. But he wasn't human. And she had to remember that.

His silence said enough.

'For what it's worth, I'm sorry.' Her fingers played over the loaded book at the small of her back, guilt tapping at her heart more than she felt at ease with. 'What did she do to you?'

He glanced at her, raked her swiftly with his gaze. 'You look exhausted. You should get some sleep.'

'I have no intention of sleeping. Feinith got up here once; she could get back up here again.'

'She won't be back until dusk.'

'What did you say to her?'

He placed the few books he had in his hands on the shelf beside her, bringing him dangerously close. 'I told her I needed to think of something I wanted in return for you.'

'So you admit you're going to bargain?'

'I never said that.'

'At least have the courage to be honest with me, Caleb. Or are you scared of what I'm capable of if I believe I'm fighting for my life?'

He rested his arm on the shelf beside her shoulder, giving her his full attention. 'You don't believe that already?'

'I think it's obvious I do.'

His eyes sparkled in a way she found treacherously playful considering the circumstances. 'So do I need to tie you up again? Limit the threat?'

She couldn't let him toy with her. But she could play along now that she had his full attention, now that she had him that close. She took a steadying breath and hoped he hadn't noticed. 'Only if you feel you can't handle me. Can you handle me, Caleb?'

'Is that an open invitation?'

'Taken from our last encounter, it doesn't appear you deem invitations necessary.'

'Need I remind you that you were more than willing?'

'Are you saying it would have made a difference if I wasn't?'

'You have a lot to learn about me.'

'In such little time. What a shame.'

His smile in response to her sarcasm was fleeting. 'I *can* be nice, you know.'

Her heart pounded. Feinith's descriptions of what he was capable of trickled through her mind again and left an unwelcome burn. 'Like you were last time?'

'You think I wasn't?'

'Compared with what I've now learned, I think I got off very lightly.'

'You did.'

'Because you couldn't risk the potential coaxing of your mistress by damaging the goods, right? Let's not make that out to be anything more than it was.'

'None of this has anything to do with Feinith.'

'And I'm supposed to believe that?'

'If I was going to hand you over, I would have done.'

'If you didn't want to bargain – you said it yourself.'

'No, I said I bought us some time. Which you should be grateful for.' He braced his arms either side of her shoulders. 'So why don't you tell me the real reason why Feinith wants you alive?'

She looked deep into his eyes, her fingers brushing the edge of the book. 'I told you why.'

'She doesn't abide by the Higher Order laws. Not when it comes to what she wants. And certainly not when it comes to me. She has slain females I have merely looked at the wrong way, yet she agreed to leaving you here. This is about more than playing games with me.'

'I'm guessing you failed to get the answer out of her, so you expect to get it out of me?'

'I have more ways and means with you.'

'Easier, you mean.'

'No, just more interesting. More enjoyable.'

Her stomach flipped. 'So you enjoyed being with me,' she said, despite knowing she was only opening up to more precarious banter – banter that had got her into enough trouble last time.

His smile was brief. 'What is it that you're most scared of, fledgling – becoming one of them or *is* it the pain of the bite?'

'If I become one of them, the second is inevitable.'

'Both of which you forgot long enough to give yourself to me.'

She slid the back of her fingers along the pages of the book. 'So did you sleep with her too?' Leila asked, unable to contain herself. 'Before you came to try your luck with me?'

'Why would I have sex with her when I've got you up here?'

Her heart skipped a beat. 'That's one hell of an assumption on your part.'

'Is it?'

'Why would I have any intention of sleeping with you, with everything I now know?'

'Because it felt good.'

He leaned in, traced his kisses up her neck to behind her ear.

Kisses of a vampire dangerously in control.

Leila shivered, every tiny hair on the back of her neck and her arms prickling as he nipped her earlobe.

'I thought that talent of yours made you immune to our charms,' he whispered. 'Not a little chink in that conviction is there, serryn?'

'You seem to think so.'

Despite it wrenching at her stomach, she knew what she had to do. She had to get a grip and make the most of his distraction, his arrogance – the only chance she might get.

She turned her head further to the side to expose her neck, offering it to him.

She felt him pull back and their gazes locked.

She knew she was trembling but she couldn't help it, just as she couldn't help the surge of arousal that flooded through her. Making him hesitate, making him look at her with those deep, pensive eyes made her feel empowered.

He hadn't expected that response and she wondered for a moment if it had been a mistake. She slipped her fingers into the book in preparation but instead of retracting as she thought he might, he leaned in again and licked slowly up the length of her artery.

She caught her breath as he lowered his body slightly to press his hardness tight against her groin.

Just as she had coaxed him, he was upping the ante and coaxing her – daring her to tempt him. His confidence was infuriating but dangerously exciting.

'One bite, Caleb, that's all it will take.'

'Once more inside you could be all it takes,' he whispered in her ear, making her stomach flip. 'Right now, I'm willing to take the risk. Are you?'

❆ ❆ ❆

Both she and Feinith were hiding something, and being out in the cold was irritating. He needed to know what he was dealing with. He needed to know what he was up against. But forcing it out of her wasn't what he wanted. He wanted to make her tell him not through pain but by taking her to the point of not caring anymore, just like he had last time. He wanted to consume her that much. Right then and right there.

And he needed to get that close to her again. After the last time, he needed to prove he could enjoy her body without being tempted to bite. He needed to overcome the desire despite knowing that, if she was that powerful, he was contemplating suicide getting that close to her again.

But the rush was intense.

And never more so when she did the last thing he expected – when she turned her head to expose her neck to him.

He drew back slightly to study her eyes.

He couldn't tell if the clever little witch was double bluffing him or trying to make him think twice, but it wasn't going to work. If she wanted to play this way, he'd see what she had the confidence to do – what the serryn in her would compel her to do. How far she'd be willing to go before showing her true colours.

And as she reached out, slid her soft, warm hand down his neck and chest, he had the stirring feeling she might actually surprise him.

❊ ❊ ❊

She couldn't believe she was doing it – playing along. But she wasn't going to play the victim and she sure as hell wasn't going to allow him to see her that way.

And she needed to be sure he was distracted enough. He was still watching every move she made and she needed those defences down. She needed to draw him in.

She didn't have to be afraid. She had succeeded where many didn't in that she could control it. She *would* control it. And as she slid her hand down that hard chest, she knew it wasn't going to be unpleasurable. A part of her needed to do this. To touch him. To let that restrained part of her out. For just for a few moments she'd allow herself that.

Perilously moving her other hand from her concealed weapon, she used both hands to unfasten the buttons on his shirt, not daring to meet his gaze as he watched her in the silence. She could tell she had confused him and it spurned her on, button by button, until his shirt lay open.

He'd been right about the jealousy. Seeing Feinith run her hands over him had made her stomach clench in an alien and unpleasant way. She abhorred thoughts of what he'd done and abhorred the thought of him sleeping with that beautiful vampire just as much – the thought of Feinith doing what she didn't have the courage to do; taking Caleb as her own; sharing those things with him.

But a part of her couldn't deny wanted to claim that same ownership of Caleb.

She ran the flat of both her hands down that perfect, honed chest, her fingers playing hesitantly over every defined muscle, sliding them as low down his flat, hard stomach as she dared before slipping them back up over his pecs to his strong shoulders, his biceps that strained from his braced arms either side of her.

'You can get yourself in a lot of trouble touching a vampire like that.'

She looked into his eyes albeit fleetingly. 'I'm already in trouble, aren't I?'

'If you can't finish what you've started, yes.'

She let her fingers slide back down again, lingering over his taut waist, itching to slide lower but uncertain she had that much confidence yet.

She knew what to do. She knew exactly what to do. Without qualm, she'd learned a lot of ways to satisfy the males in her life, to compensate for not being able to go that extra step. But with Caleb it felt different. With the others, she had felt in control. She'd felt safe.

She lingered over the tattoo she guessed was the one Feinith lay claim to. 'Is this the one you had done for her?'

'I did a lot of things for her.'

'Were you together long?'

'A few decades. On and off.'

'While you were hunting? Is that how you and Feinith met?'

'Yes.'

'I thought the Higher Order are only supposed to mix with other Higher Order vampires.'

'Feinith doesn't care much for rules. Not if she's able to keep it under cover. And neither do I.'

'So your relationship was secret?' She looked back up at him as her fingers dared to brush along the top of his low-slung jeans.

But he didn't answer that one.

He was aroused. Glancing back down at his jeans was enough to tell her that. He almost looked distracted. Focused, lethal, perceptive Caleb seemed a little lost in the moment.

It was what she needed.

It was working.

She could do it. She had the power to get the control back.

❦ ❦ ❦

Her touch sparked something deep inside him and he didn't know if it angered him or pleased him, but either way the raw sense to her touch excited him.

Of all the serryns he'd encountered, ironically this fledgling was the most lethal. Those fingers tracing uncertain paths were enrapturing. Her unpredictability enticing. The desire to show her how to please him was overwhelming, but he revelled in her finding her own way. She wasn't just touching him; she was exploring him. And instead of feeling impatience, he simply watched her – her downturned eyes, the tremble in those long, delicate fingers he could imagine wrapping tightly around his already straining erection; those sensual lips wrapped around the tip, her tongue working him to climax before he thrust deep into the wet warmth of her mouth.

Unbuttoning his jeans would tell him just how far she was willing to go, just how deep into the game. Besides, the strain was uncomfortable, and he'd have to release himself no matter what.

As her fingers trailed along the top of his jeans, he lowered one of his hands from beside her head to unfasten them.

She still couldn't look at him – that step in the level of intimacy too much.

Or she feared him seeing her deceit.

Right then, he didn't care which it was. He was going to get her to hold him. He wanted, needed, to see what she'd do.

But the quiver in her breathing as he pulled his shorts down a little to half expose himself told him minor panic was setting in despite her arousal.

Taking her hand he guided it to him, and for a moment he saw she had closed her eyes. This wasn't playing, she was genuinely nervous. He guided her fingers to wrap them around his length, placing his hand over the top to guide her pressure, nudged her thumb to the tip, guiding her to circle his circumcised head.

She kept her eyes shut, and from the tension in her free hand clenched at her side, he had absorbed her in the moment, could hear her breathing escalating in the silence of the room.

He gripped her hand tighter, guiding her to slide her hand along his length and she didn't fight, she didn't protest.

He released her hand to place his back beside her head, wanting her to go it alone.

He expected her to drop her hand away but she didn't. Her grip loosened, she moved her thumb from his already seeping tip, but she didn't withdraw. A second later, she tightened her grip again, ran her thumb under the ridge, sliding it up to the tip again and back down in a slow, sensual and exploratory act that made him scrape his fingers against the books. He lowered his head to hers, breathing in her scent mingling with that of his own building arousal.

❊ ❊ ❊

She couldn't look at him. Couldn't bring herself to look into those beautiful green eyes. She couldn't afford to feel more of the stirring deep inside her. And she couldn't handle the deception.

As the silence enveloped them, as she explored him in the most intimate way, she almost forgot what she was trying to do. It was about lowering his guard. It was about calling the shots. Instead she wasn't sure who she was anymore. And certainly not when he lowered his lips enough to almost kiss her.

She turned her head away. She couldn't allow that. She couldn't allow herself to feel like that. But she did force herself to look at him, to see the thickness of desire in his eyes. And the fact that she had that effect stunned her.

'A little close to the edge, don't you think?' she asked softly.

'You're the one who can't reciprocate; you tell me.'

She squeezed him a little tighter, stupidly taunting him, his arousal inciting hers.

His eyes flared slightly but brimmed with something between amusement and a dangerously dark craving. 'Don't push your luck,' he whispered in her ear.

She needed to get her head straight. She needed to focus. But instead the low and enticing challenge in his words had her struggling to keep her thoughts on track, plunging her deeper into the moment.

Because right then, she wanted to push it. She wanted to see what he'd do. She wanted to get him to that point. Damn it, she wanted to see and feel him come in her hand.

She leaned forward and kissed his chest, so invitingly laid bare to her. Kissed along the length of the scorpion's tail that curled up around his neck as she picked up the pace and pressure of her hand. He tasted so cool, so refreshing beneath her lips. The temptation to lick him was overwhelming.

'Maybe I want to,' she whispered in his ear before nipping his lobe like he had with hers on more than one occasion. 'Maybe I'm liking things near the edge.'

She kissed gently down his chest, lowering down the bookcase in an easy and surprisingly graceful slide considering how much her thighs trembled.

She had no idea where the courage came from but knew, in part, it was fuelled not only by a need for survival but by sheer unadulterated desire as she lowered her lips down onto him. The taste of him was divine, the silkiness of his skin beneath her tongue as enticing as the sheer masculine scent of him. It had never felt so easy or so natural as she swept her tongue slowly full circle around him as she simultaneously squeezed a little tighter.

She thought she heard him curse under his breath as he tensed. In turn, she opened her hand to lick down then back up the full length of his erection before tentatively taking him more fully in her mouth.

But as he entwined his fingers in the hair at the nape of her neck, as he tugged slightly to cause her a tiny amount of pain, she wondered if she had indeed taken that one step too far.

❋ ❋ ❋

It took everything not to force himself fully into the wet heat of her mouth. Those trembling lips encompassed him so provocatively, her slow, steady tongue dangerously lingering. She may have been anxious but her indulgence was painfully arousing. Tightening his grip on her hair, he clawed the books, pressed his forehead against them.

He could so easily make her take more of him, push deeper, stop holding back.

She was working him with perfection. Or the serryn in her was. The clearly deadly serryn based on that sensuality. He needed to stop her. He needed to retract. He needed to withdraw, leave her there on her knees.

But he kept wanting more. Just like the static that had held him to her wrists the first time, his body wouldn't listen to him. His body needed release and relief. His body wanted her.

He needed to leave her and get down to the club. Take a female into the VIP area. Have his pleasure, be it as hard, fast and cruel as he liked, but he didn't want some other female. He knew he couldn't get the satisfaction he needed right then screwing some stranger. He needed Leila. She was the one he needed to dominate and consume, but right now she was the one playing the upper hand.

He withdrew himself from her mouth. Taking her by the upper arms, he pulled her to her feet, pinned her back against the wall as he stared deep into her eyes.

She looked at him bewildered but he also knew he saw a glimmer of disappointment. She'd wanted to keep going. She almost looked panicked he'd stopped her.

❋ ❋ ❋

She wasn't any good. It was the first thought that crossed her mind. He'd stopped her because she wasn't good enough.

Or she was too good and he wanted to reclaim control again.

She was back where she started, staring into eyes that had almost seemed to harden slightly.

'As enticing as your mouth is, I need deeper.'

Her stomach flipped at his bluntness, a stirring deep in her abdomen telling her she wasn't as unnerved by it as she thought she should be. 'Once was a mistake,' she said. 'Twice is unforgiveable.'

He slid his hands up under her dress and tugged down her knickers, making her stomach somersault as he leaned into her neck. 'Then don't forgive me,' he said, his kiss hard and hungry against her sensitive flesh, his hand coiling tight around the nape of her neck.

She swallowed hard. 'I don't intend to.'

And she wouldn't. And if she didn't act now it would be unforgiveable. Because she knew she was on the brink of succumbing to him again – despite all her promises to herself, all her vehement denial, whatever it was that Caleb did her, her reaction to him was instinctive.

She had to overcome the agonising sinking feeling in her heart, screaming at her not to do it. She had to let her head win. She had to believe there was no other way.

After fumbling behind her as discreetly as she could, she slipped the syringe from the book, grasping it as steadily as her trembling hands would allow.

As soon as it saw air, she knew she needed to act. She pressed her thumb on the plunger, drew back her hand ready to stab him with it when, despite his seeming distraction, he grabbed her wrist with precision.

She flinched but froze.

He pulled back, his eyes a mixture of annoyance and amusement – anything but surprise.

Eyes that screamed of more entrapment.

Her heart pounded.

He stretched out her arm to expose the developing bruising as he stared deep into her eyes. 'One tip, serryn. If you're going to extract your own blood, try not to leave a bruise to give it away.'

Chapter Seventeen

Caleb squeezed her wrist. 'Drop it.'

She glowered back at him and clenched the syringe tighter. She had not come that far to give up. Not now.

'I said, drop it,' he repeated, his tone unnervingly calm.

Still Leila wouldn't.

He tugged her away from the bookcase, turned her away from him, pinned her against him, her syringe-holding hand held away from them both as he all but carried her across the room to the fireplace. He kicked the fireguard aside and forced her to her knees, his chest forming a solid wall behind her as he stretched her hand out towards the dying flames, his vice-like grip unrelenting on the wrist of her syringe-holding hand.

'Defy me all you want,' he warned in her ear as he edged her hand closer to the flames. 'You will drop it.'

The heat immediately encompassed her, but despite clutching on to the syringe for sheer belligerence, her brain forced her reflexes to respond to the heat. She dropped it into the flames, the syringe, her blood contents, simmering and crackling in protest.

He pulled her back from the heat, Leila almost in tears from the anger, the fear.

'Just when I started to believe you might be different,' he said as he held her back against him, 'you go and prove yourself to be just as devious as the rest of your kind.'

'I had no choice.'

He rose to his feet, pulling her up with him. He wrapped her arms around her waist, holding her back against him as he carried her across to the threshold.

Leila kicked at his shins to no avail. 'Let me go!' she warned. But with both her arms trapped, struggling was futile.

Crossing the bedroom, he carried her over to the chair by the en-suite door. He cast the shirt on it aside and opened the syringe wrap.

He turned her around to face him and pinned her against the wall, her wrists either side of her head. 'Tell me where the other one is.'

'Scared I'll catch you off guard?'

'Tell me.'

'Or what? You'll torture me like the others? That's so your style, isn't it?'

'Don't tempt me.'

'No, because you're not quite as good at avoiding temptation as you thought you were, are you?'

'Neither are you apparently,' he said, his eyes sparkling darkly. 'So that could be a problem for us both if this escalates. Especially if I've decided it's time I unleash that serryn in you once and for all.'

'No,' she said, trying to buck against him to no avail.

He pinned her harder against the wall, his body holding her there with ease. 'Then tell me where the other syringe is.'

'You like games,' she said with a glower. 'You go find it.'

❋ ❋ ❋

Leila stared at him with such defiance in her eyes that he felt something snap.

He released her wrists to lift her with ease, parting her thighs around him, pressing her against the wall. 'Tell me,' he hissed.

She gasped, but kept her glare locked on his, her lips sealed.

Pulling her from the wall, he carried her to the bed and slammed her down onto it as he braced himself over her.

He pinned her wrists to the bed and looked deep into her hazel eyes. The lethal combination of anxiety and yearning stunned him, incited him, her nubile body pinned beneath him vulnerably exposed to his desires and needs, igniting the vampire inside him.

'Don't push me,' he warned.

'Why?' she asked, her tone laced with belligerence. 'What are you going to do?'

He looked at the soft, upward mounds of her breasts still contained in their clothing, up to her exposed collarbone, to the soft, warm flesh of her penetrable neck.

He'd find out just how hot and sweet and delicious her blood was; that was what he'd do. He'd push deep inside her whilst his incisors pierced deep into her exposed throat. And he'd come as he drank, as she spilled into him, he'd spill into her.

He tightened his grip on her wrists, lowered his head to calm himself. But all he could hear was her pulse racing, the thump of her heart, her shallow breaths, her arousal clearly pressing her own self-destruct button as well as his.

Retract.

He had to retract.

She wasn't serryn enough – nowhere near serryn enough to take that kind of onslaught.

'You're skirting too close to the edge, serryn,' he warned, his lust-filled gaze snapping back to hers.

She almost smiled. Behind the anger and indignation in her eyes, she was goading him. She was daring to goad *him*. 'I'm not the one who's at risk of falling, vampire.'

He exhaled curtly. Damn her potential. Damn that she had saved Jake's life. If not he might have been tempted to end hers then before he ended his own. No serryn had forced him to that point. No serryn had unleashed that suicidal darkness.

He couldn't bite her. Fuck her, but not bite. Take her. Consume her. But keep the most instinctive part of him deep inside, just like she kept the serryn deep inside herself. If she could do it, then so could he. She was not stronger than him. She was not in more control than him. *He* was in charge, not her.

He knew only too well that with how he was feeling then, the only way he could contain his need to feed and sate himself in the sexual act alone was by upping the force, the pace, the intensity.

He released her wrists for fear of breaking them, ripped open the buttons on her dress to expose the soft flesh of the upward curves of her firm breasts that he could so easily pierce. He slid his hand down to grab her hip, to press his thumb into her hip bone, to keep her firmly in place.

He looked back into her eyes. 'Tell me to stop,' he said.

'You stop *yourself*,' she said.

But the look in her eyes, her swollen lips, her flushed cheeks were telling him anything but.

She didn't know what she was asking, he was convinced of it. But those eyes echoed a different message. Eyes that locked squarely on his.

'Is this how you want it?' he asked.

'Is it how *you* want it?'

She was messing with his head. Daring to toy with him. He couldn't look at her. He couldn't risk her hypnotising him with those fatal eyes.

He couldn't face the feelings she was stirring inside him.

He flipped her onto her front and kneed her legs apart before yanking down his trousers and shorts. He didn't hesitate as he found the heat of her sex, pushed his way deep inside her, wrapping himself in liquid fire he knew could so easily drown him.

He snarled under his breath and dug his nails into the duvet at the sensation that enveloped him.

She gasped, clutched the duvet too, her body rising against his.

He felt her shudder, clearly feeling the sensation of the new position as much as he did. As soon as her body relented, he picked up the pace in his penetration, her short, sharp gasps only inciting him further.

He interlaced his fingers with hers as he clutched the back of her right hand. He slid his free hand through her hair to expose the side of her face, tightening his grip on her hair as he maintained his weight on his elbow.

'You're toxic, you know that?' he said in her ear. 'What you do to me.'

He closed his eyes and thrust harder, losing himself in the sensation, in the heat of her body. He felt his excitement peak, his whole body aching.

He was feeling pleasure. He was actually feeling pleasure. But not from the force of the act – from the intimacy. Because in those moments, it was as if they'd shared an understanding.

For one moment, it felt like she'd actually let him in.

He opened his eyes to look at her. Was stunned to see a tear trickle from the corner of her eye. His heart inexplicably hitched.

He stopped.

He waited a moment, composing himself before gently withdrawing, turning her over to face him.

She rubbed her tear away in irritation, but she avoided looking at him until he forced her to do so with the pressure and direction of his thumb under her chin.

He wiped the tears from her cheek with his thumb, placing it in his mouth to taste their saltiness.

'You're the one that's toxic,' she said, her eyes brimming with resentment.

He'd been right. She wasn't serryn enough for this. The fact her tears were real proved that.

He'd never seen a serryn cry, even during their dying breath, no matter what he put them through, they'd never shed a tear.

But those weren't tears of fear or pain. He knew the difference. Those were tears of confusion. Frustration.

And he did the last thing he knew he should have. He should have been just sex. He knew that. He also knew he had slipped too deep for it to be that simple.

'As toxic as they come,' he said, lowering his mouth to hers.

She fought at first, her hands slamming to his chest, but as he pushed them aside, she eventually relented. Reciprocated. Those same hands that had tried to forge some distance between them now sliding up his chest to his neck, one clutching his arm, her nails digging deep as she accepted his kiss, her warm mouth absorbing his tongue with the ease of familiar lovers.

❀ ❀ ❀

The hatred she felt towards herself at goading him the way she had, encouraging him the way she had, overwhelmed her. She'd wanted to punish herself for the feelings stirring inside. She'd wanted to punish him for making her feel that way.

But he'd stopped.

And the fact he'd stopped only confused those feelings more.

Every muscle in her body tensed as his cool, soft lips met hers, his moist mouth joining with hers with perfect pressure as he teased her lips apart. His kiss felt fresh, his tongue sliding to meet hers with an instinctive ease.

She felt a stirring in her lower abdomen, a cold heat rushing through her body. The intimacy of the act consumed her, the absence of aggression stunning her. Instinctively she closed her eyes, subjecting herself to him in the passing moments, her anxiety suppressed.

It was nothing like she expected. Not that she really knew what to expect. But tenderness was by far the least she had anticipated.

But that's just what his kiss was. Despite being cold, those lips were warm in a whole other way as he used them to smoothly and expertly part hers further, his strong hand subtly sliding around to the nape of her neck, her skin instantly breaking out in goosebumps.

A kiss that showed her something more, just like she'd seen in the way he'd pulled her between his legs out on the terrace. In the way he'd slid the sword down her body in the dungeon. How he'd held her against the winged-back chair in that very room. Caleb was capable of something other than brutality. And if he was capable of that kind of passion tempered with sensitivity, he was even more lethal. Lethal to her heart at least.

She was a fool to her heart not to keep fighting. But she was sick of fighting. The syringe lay too far away for to her reach and even if she could, she could no more plunge it deep into the vampire who now pushed his way back inside her than she could drive a stake through his heart.

Because he could have so easily kept going – that was what she realised. He could have left that stinging tear on her face and kept pushing inside her until the pain got intolerable, until she couldn't take any more.

And what little she knew about him, she knew he had stopped out of concern. She had felt it in the way he had turned her over – not out of impatience or sadistic amusement. She knew that from the way he had assessed her eyes pensively. He'd almost seemed perplexed by her tears – by the confused turmoil that had instigated them.

And something in her didn't want any of it – anything that would add to his already intoxicating appeal. She could ignore his good looks to see beyond that to the cruel heart beneath, but a heart equally capable of affection was a poisonous combination. Cruel, single-minded, powerful Caleb was tempting enough with those shocking green eyes and entrancing smile, but gentle, attentive and sensual Caleb was even more dangerous.

He *was* toxic. The worst kind of toxic.

'I hate you,' she whispered against his lips as he broke from their kiss.

'No, you don't,' he whispered back.

He lay her hands either side of her before sliding down her body, his mouth trailing down her cleavage, down her stomach before pushing up her dress to find her sex.

She snatched back a breath, her nails digging into the duvet as his cool tongue slid slowly and coaxingly inside her, easing the throb, the ache that was already on the verge of release.

He held her hips tight, locked her into position as she instinctively arched her back, inviting him to delve deeper, to explore further. His tongue was excruciatingly taunting and purposeful compared with the onslaught of his previous thrusts, the full focus on pleasuring only her almost too much to bear.

She turned her head away, the sensation too intense, the ache in her stomach, the rush of blood, the tingling beneath his persistence making her light-headed and disorientated.

Leila closed her eyes tight as he licked and probed, tried to relax as his tongue pressed at her clitoris, encircling it before sliding inside her, pushing her to an oncoming climax, her whole mind shutting down, her body giving in to the sensations, losing her inhibitions.

And as his hunger increased, as he unashamedly consumed her without restraint, she bit deep into her bottom lip, pushed onto him further, the orgasm that was coiling its way through her the only thing she could focus on.

As it erupted, pulsated fiercely through her body, she grabbed the sheets. Feeling him pull away, she wanted to reach out to him. But he was instantly back on top of her, inside her. This time it was slower, more controlled, as if it would only take a little to bring him to his own climax.

She let him take her hands in his, let him interlace their fingers as he lowered his head to her throat.

And as she closed her eyes again, she prayed that he wouldn't bite, that he wouldn't be tempted.

The thought of losing him was just too painful.

And as she felt another orgasm ricochet through her, she dug her nails deep into his arm.

She was falling. She knew she was falling. Because even if she could get to the syringe, she knew she wouldn't use it. Not then. Not there. Not when she was convinced this was more than just sex to him, those last few moments fracturing her resolve.

And as she felt him come inside her, heard his muted growl against her throat, she knew it had been a struggle for him not to bite. A lethal struggle.

He had to see it now. She had proven enough.

He was going to have to let her go.

But for the first time, she didn't want him to.

And it was all she could think as he gently withdrew, as he lay on his back beside her, between her and the pillows.

She turned away from him to face the door, safeguarding her heart in some way by avoiding the intimacy that could forge more of what she was feeling. Because she was feeling something. Something deep, something undeniable, something unforgiveable.

She felt herself panic at having to acknowledge it. Something was happening and it wasn't to do with the serryn. Something she hadn't felt for a long time – if she'd ever really felt it at all. Whatever feelings were stirring inside her, they were more raw, alive and intense than she'd ever felt.

But she couldn't feel them – she wouldn't allow herself to feel them. Because if she did, the risk of her being there had just multiplied. If she was going to fall for him, the consequences could be dire.

He had to let her go. She couldn't tell him why, but he had to.

And that was the last thing she could think as sleep finally consumed her, sleep that came too easy considering a vampire lay behind her.

A vampire who had opted not to leave her side this time.

A vampire who she inexplicably felt safe beside.

❄ ❄ ❄

Leila had drifted to sleep quickly. She slept almost silently, her body falling lax beside him. She'd fought it, but the exhaustion had won in the end. She'd been through too much in the past few hours for it not to.

He'd never known a serryn let their guard down. Not like that. But then he'd never had a serryn in his bed. He'd never found himself caring what one felt during sex, how much pain he caused them, or, more to the point, whether they were getting equal pleasure.

And he sure as hell had never kissed one like that.

Everything about her was as uncontrived as that kiss – a kiss that had been exquisitely soft, alluringly hesitant, lips that had trembled in anticipation. Those lips that had reciprocated not with lust, but something more.

Countless emotions could be masked by the sexual act, but a kiss, the most intimate and passionate of exchanges, concealed nothing. And Leila didn't kiss like the other serryns – the few serryns who would dare indulge that level of contact with their prey. Leila had kissed like she was feeling something for the last vampire she should feel anything towards. Because she had felt something.

Just as he had.

He'd almost tasted what it was like to be himself again, before the serryn who had set him on the path to destruction. So many experiences since had left him hollow, but nothing with Leila felt hollow.

Even with Feinith he'd never felt it so intensely.

Feinith only brought the darkness out in him. Feinith had seen his pain at the loss of Seth, and had thrived on it, fed on it, encouraged it to grow until he'd become nothing but a shell. A shell that Leila had breathed the life back into. Leila, with her honest emotions and convictions, who had every opportunity to become what he hated, but refused. Leila, who intrigued and excited him and made him question what he'd become – had made his gut wrench at the thought of what he'd done in his past.

And it made him uncomfortable, as if he had been numb for a long time, the pins and needles cutting through him reminding him that it was still there.

He sat up and eased himself back against the headboard, moved the pillows behind him to get into a comfortable position. His hand touched something hard, something cylindrical.

He instantly knew what it was even before he looked at it. He held the syringe up in front of him.

She'd clearly expected to end up in his bed at some point. An opportunity when he would be distracted. When she could tuck her hand beneath the pillows almost undetected. And if he hadn't seen the bruising, if he hadn't always paid so much attention to every inch of her body, if he hadn't noticed it when she stretched out her arm to collect the books on the floor, she may even have succeeded.

He twirled the syringe in his fingers.

She'd already worked out there was no way out of this and she was going to go out fighting. Naïve, but commendable.

He guessed it hadn't turned out how either of them intended.

He was surprised she didn't flinch at the knock on the door, at the turn of the handle, but she was clearly too exhausted for either.

Jake hovered in the open doorway at the foot of the bed, a book in his hand. He looked down at Leila, then up at his brother, disapproval but no great surprise clear in his eyes at realising how his big brother had spent the past couple of hours.

Caleb looked at Leila's purification book he was holding; looked back up at the perturbed look in Jake's eyes.

'I need to talk to you,' Jake said. 'Now.'

Caleb glanced back down at Leila. The whisper hadn't disturbed her either. It looked like nothing was going to wake her.

He reluctantly eased off the bed, crossed the room to Jake, and rested his hand on the doorjamb. 'What's up?'

Jake sent a wary glance in Leila's direction then cocked his head to the library. 'Out here.'

'It's fine. She's asleep.'

Jake cocked his head out the room again and stepped back into the library.

Caleb threw the other syringe on the fire before following Jake down to the table at the far end of the room. 'What's the problem?'

Opening the book on the page he'd been marking with his finger, Jake rested it on the table and slid it towards his brother. He took a step back, his arms folded. 'You want to tell me what that's doing in a serryn's spell book?'

Caleb stepped up to the table and swiftly scanned the pages. 'What?'

Jake slammed his finger down on the lower right-hand corner of the page. 'That,' he said.

Caleb stared down at the symbol. Then he snatched his gaze back to his brother.

Jake's eyes narrowed in suspicion and concern. 'What's going on, Caleb?'

Chapter Eighteen

Caleb locked his bedroom door and slipped the key into his back pocket.

'You stay away from that room, you understand me?'

Jake nodded.

Caleb crossed the room, behind the table and to the bookcases that lined the back wall. He pulled out two of the books, and reached inside the gap. Immediately the whole bookcase slid back to reveal the dark recess behind.

'How long will you be?' Jake asked.

'A couple of hours, maybe three,' he said as he stepped into the darkness. He glanced over his shoulder. 'You stay in the penthouse, okay? I'll come and see you as soon as I'm back.'

Jake nodded. 'I'll wait in the lounge.'

Caleb crossed the tiny recess and opened the door that led into the depths of the building. He descended the rusted spiral staircase into the lengthy corridor below. The way ahead was lit only by weak sunlight breaking through cracks in the boarded-up windows, igniting the dust, flashing neon lights splintering onto the concrete.

The weaving corridor led him through several cellars, each hanging heavy with an unearthly silence – a silence Caleb had always found comforting until then. Some of buildings he owned, some he rented, some were derelict. But in total they covered just under a mile before he pulled back the exit doors and emerged into the back alley.

The storm had passed, but fortunately the dense sky still muted the sun. He pulled up his hood, tucked his hands deep into the front pocket of his hoodie, and marched on ahead through the washed-out alleys.

It was forty-five minutes to her place. Most of the journey he could navigate by the back alleys, a suicide mission for most, but no concern for him other than the prospect of being temporarily slowed down by a couple of chancers looking for trouble.

The journey felt like a trudge because of the urgency to get there. The urgency to know the truth.

He should have been relieved at the prospect of proving himself right, but it left him unsettled. Because, even though resentment seared through his veins, he knew hurting her wasn't going to be as easy as it would have been a few hours before – before he knew she had saved Jake.

She'd got to him. She'd got further inside him than anyone had in a long time. And that only added to his anger at her potential deceit.

He turned down a row of terraced Victorian houses, keeping to the shade of the trees as much as possible as he made his way along the windswept street. Arriving at her house, he stopped and pushed the creaking cast-iron gate open. He made his way up the short winding path and strode up the familiar stone steps to the porch. He stepped inside and knocked on the heavy green door. He took a couple of steps back down, checked the cellar window, and then scanned the other three floors before ducking back under the safety of the porch as he stared back out at the street.

It didn't take her long to answer. She pulled back the door with a wary glance before her wrinkled, sharp eyes gleamed.

'Well, well, well,' she said, staring up at him with a broad smile. 'Caleb Dehain. It's been a long time.'

'Hi, Niras,' he said, towering above her stooped frame. 'I'm hoping you have some time to spare me.'

'Always,' Niras said, stepping back, letting him in.

Caleb stepped into the cool, dark house as Niras closed the door behind them.

She led the way down the long, poorly lit corridor, guiding Caleb into the second door on the left. 'From the troubled look on your face and the fact it's daylight, can I assume this isn't just a social call?'

'I'm afraid not. Not this time, Niras.'

Niras took her seat in the large chair by the open fire and indicated for Caleb to take the one opposite. 'It must be at least ten years.'

He sat back into the heavily woven seat. 'I guess it must be. Time goes so quick.'

'Days become weeks, weeks become months then suddenly years become a decade.' She frowned slightly, her expression grave. 'You have an urgency about you. So uncharacteristic, Caleb.'

He reached into his jeans pocket and took out the piece of paper he had drawn the symbol on. He held it across to her. 'Does that mean anything to you?'

Niras accepted it off him. She lifted her eyebrows, her brown eyes widening before she stared back at him, her soft brown eyes struck with consternation. 'Where did you get this?'

'You know it?'

Niras frowned. 'Yes, I know it. But you shouldn't.'

'What does it mean?'

'Caleb, where did you see this?'

'I need to know what it is.'

Niras's frown deepened. 'And I need to know how you came across this. Caleb, this symbol is known only to the Higher Order. It shouldn't be knowledge to you. If you have been sifting in places you shouldn't—'

'I haven't.' He leaned forward, his hands between his parted legs as he held his gaze steadily on hers. 'Niras. Please. Tell me.'

Niras nestled back in her chair. 'Still as demanding as ever, Caleb. Still as painfully handsome.' She smiled. 'If I was a century and a half younger…'

Caleb smiled back. 'Stop flirting with me, Niras. Diversion won't work.'

'I have told you too much over the years, Caleb,' she said, looking back at the symbol. 'Shared too many texts. Too many secrets.' She looked back at him. 'Those green eyes will be the downfall of me.'

'But I've never betrayed you,' he said. 'And you know I never will.'

'I know. I'm no fool, Caleb. And I have never known one so devoid of betrayal as you.' She handed the piece of paper back across to him. 'But I can't discuss this with you. I'm sorry. You've had a wasted journey this time.'

'Niras…'

'My young friend. There is only one who could have told you of this and she had no right. Her infatuation with you has overstepped the mark. Whatever she has told you, don't trust her motivation.'

'And what would she have told me?'

'Caleb, I will always retain my respect for you, you know that, but I have to speak my mind. As belligerent and wilful, and as opposed and disrespectful as you are to the Higher Order, your fervent defence of those you care about will always remain a trait I most admire.' She paused. 'But as pure-bred as she is, Caleb, as beautiful and as tempting as she is, Feinith is not worthy of your time nor your devotion. And her coupling will only bring the severest consequences to you and Jacob if you continue your relations with her.'

'Feinith and I are no more, Niras. She broke my heart and with it any affection I ever held for her.'

Niras held her gaze steadily on his. 'I wish—' she began, but stopped herself abruptly, taking a moment to rethink her wording. 'I wish that she hadn't spoiled you so. The female who finally won your heart should have been more deserving.'

'You flatter me again, Niras.'

'No, but I hope you will flatter me by at least admitting Feinith was the source of this information.'

'I have seen it but she has said nothing to me. Please, Niras. I have to know what I've got myself into.'

Niras pressed her lips together, lowered her gaze as she seemed to be pondering. She looked back up at him. 'I tell you only because I trust you, but this must not escape from your lips, do you understand me?'

'I understand.'

She wavered only a moment longer, her eyes burning into his. 'It is reserved for the chosen one.'

'The chosen one?'

'The symbol is the Armun. It is a gift to the one who will lead our race to pre-eminence.'

Discomfort stirred in his chest. 'Over the humans?'

'Over humans. Over other vampires.'

'The prophecy. It's true then?'

'We may have come a long way in these past decades but there's still so much further to go. Acceptance is blinkered. The very way they say we must live is indicative of that. We need to move beyond that.'

'But is that not what the Higher Order are attempting? To converse with the human leaders to secure a place on the Global Council?'

'We both know it will never happen. Vampires will never be allowed political control. It was the disclaimer the humans put in to retain the segregation. They've known our kind long enough to know we wouldn't stay in the shadows forever. They knew what we would want, what any species wants: control. And they protected themselves against it.'

'So what is the point of this leader?'

'I've already said too much.'

'Nothing I don't already know.'

Her eyes flared. 'Tell me if you haven't seen it on Feinith.'

'Niras, tell me what the point of the leader is.'

Niras held his gaze for a moment, then, with a sigh, leaned back. 'What you cannot win by negotiation, you have to win by other means. All disclaimers have loopholes. And that symbol is our loophole. A symbol as archaic as our being.'

'What kind of loophole?'

'Those without a soul cannot serve on the Global Council. No shadows are permitted to make judgements on any decisions that will impact on humankind – that was the disclaimer. But a vampire with a soul, that's a whole other matter. The vampire who wears that symbol can steal one. They can replace the shadow inside them, yet remain vampire. The Global Council cannot omit those with a soul, whatever form it takes. After proven by a shadow reader, there would be uproar if they refused to co-operate. It is our first step to freedom.'

'How does the chosen one replace it?'

'The soul can only be transferred through blood-drinking. The chosen one must drink the soul-giver to the point of death and re-main there at the Brink long enough for the soul to transfer. Then the metamorphosis from vampire to the Tryan – our leader – will be complete.'

Caleb frowned. 'But a vampire can't drink dying blood.'

'The Armun protects them – but from only one type of blood. Very special blood. The same as the soul can't be that of just any human. It needs to be a soul that is strong enough to survive long enough for the transference to complete.'

'And such a human exists?'

'Oh, indeed they do. In small numbers. Ever smaller numbers.'

Caleb tensed. His heart that usually beat so slowly began to race.

'Why do you think the Higher Order is so protective over them, Caleb? Why do you think they carry such a weighty price on their heads when slaughtering them is the obvious option?'

'Serryns,' he said, his heart splintering.

'Yes, my sweet Caleb, serryns. More lethal to the vampire than sunlight or hemlock.' She paused. 'The Tryan, the chosen one, must take the life of a serryn, drink her, even her very last drop of dying blood, especially her last drop, abandoning her at the Brink for eternity as they return victorious. Then the prophecy will come into fruition.'

'That's why they changed the rules. That's why they stopped me killing them.'

'If there's no serryn, there's no Tryan. They couldn't risk them becoming extinct.'

'But surely the Higher Order would have known this all along. Why let us hunt them at all?'

'We've always known what the symbol meant, but not how to bring the prophecy into fulfilment. The serryns saw to that. It was their most closely guarded secret – so integral to the very prophecy that they would relinquish their lives to ensure it isn't fulfilled. But when the truth was finally uncovered by one of our own eighty years ago, the Higher Order had no choice but to change the law from hunting serryns to death to salvaging them. They'd been hunted into endangerment and into hiding. We'd put our own future under threat.'

'More reason why we should have been told.'

'And have every mercenary out there demand whatever they wanted for the capture of one? And as the symbol is destined to appear only on a member of the Higher Order, anyone outside had no need to know. Besides, we couldn't let the serryns know we knew their secret. It was the one way we retained the upper hand. They still don't know. The Higher Order make their demands and the ranks follow without question – that's how it works. But there were always the few hunters that didn't heed our advice.' She held his gaze knowingly. 'One in particular. Caleb: the bane of the Higher Order. What were we to do with you?'

'When is this great rising expected?'

'The prophecies give us no clue. Only that the symbol will appear when the time has come.'

'Which is why the Higher Order needs a serryn on standby at all times.'

'Unfortunately the last died twenty years ago. As yet no replacement has been found. But I've said enough. More than enough. And I urge you, Caleb, you must keep this secret. Our future depends on word not getting out.'

'Is the serryn that is needed special in any way? Is there anything recognisable?'

Niras smiled. 'Are you missing the hunt, Caleb?'

'I'd like to know what I was looking for. Is there anything to look for, like the symbol on the chosen one?'

'No. There is nothing that we know of. But if the prophecy is right, the serryn will find the Tryan. It's their fate.'

'If the chosen one is immune to her blood, does she have the ability to kill them? Can she prevent the prophecy happening?'

Niras nodded. 'Yes. And believe me; she will try everything to do just that. It will be her main objective.'

'Will she know of the chosen one? Will she be able to sense it?'

'She will sense it. As they will her.' Her eyes were unnervingly sullen. 'Faced with the chosen one, the serryn is more powerful than even you can imagine, Caleb. And more dangerous. I can assure you, she will stop at nothing. She will do whatever is necessary to prevent the prophecy coming into being – in any way possible. Even forsaking herself, if that's what it takes.'

Chapter Nineteen

Feinith entered Caleb's office alone.

'Well,' she said as she sauntered towards his desk. 'I can't say I appreciate being summoned, let alone during daylight hours.' She leaned back against the sofa to face him and folded her arms. 'But as long as this is a sign you've seen sense, I'll let you off.'

'I want Seth's name taken off the dishonoured list.'

She stared at him as if he had slapped her across the face. 'No.'

'No?'

'Caleb, we have discussed this before—'

'And this time you're not going to turn it down.' He pushed back his chair and moved around to the far side of the desk. He leaned back, folded his arms, mirroring her. 'You want the serryn, I want Seth's name off the list. In fact, I want him redeemed. I want that sniffling excuse for a betrothed of yours to admit that he put Seth's name on there falsely.'

Feinith glared at him. 'That won't happen.'

'We all know Seth was doing his job that night. It was Jarin who sneaked into that house unprotected without him – him and his taste for innocent blood. Jarin lied. Seth would not have run and he would not have hid no matter how many of them were in waiting. It was Jarin who went against the rules of the Higher Order, not my brother. And if he hadn't been dismissed for failure to protect, he would never have been where he was that night the serryn killed him. I want my brother's name cleared.'

'He will never agree.'

'You'll make him agree.'

'And what reasons am I to give him? How will I explain my request?'

'That's your problem. But no pardon, no serryn.'

'You ask the impossible.'

'Do I? I know how much you want her. Or should I say *need* her.' He stepped over to stop squarely in front of her. 'I know about the prophecy.'

She twitched anxiously. 'You'll have to enlighten me,' she said, despite her eyes telling him she knew exactly what he meant. 'There are so many prophecies.'

'Oh, I'm sure this one is at the forefront of your mind. Or at least it would have rebounded back to the forefront when you suspected there was a much-needed serryn on the loose.'

Her eyes narrowed slightly as she held her gaze warily on his. 'I don't know what you mean.'

'Don't play games with me. You know exactly what I mean. The whole Higher Order knows. Not that you want us runts to know what a little pot of gold that serryn is. Or her blood is, at least. Alive, of course. She's no use to the Tryan dead.'

Her eyes flared. 'Where did you get this information?'

He smiled, albeit briefly.

She'd never looked so uneasy, so unsure. 'Never. She would never have told you.'

'You made me curious, Feinith – all that compromise and wanting her alive. And I can be very persuasive. Particularly with serryns, remember? Particularly when a Higher Order vampire strolls into her presence and threatens to take her. But that's not what's important now, whereas keeping her alive clearly is.'

'Caleb, if you've spilled a drop of her blood—'

'Relax,' he said. 'I haven't and I won't. If you do what I ask.'

'And if Jarin doesn't budge?'

Caleb shrugged.

'Caleb, you slay that serryn and you kiss goodbye to our future. I will have no option but to report you. You will be sentenced to The Pit or even to death, Jake with you. You cannot wish that on your brother.'

'It won't come to that because you're going to do as I ask.'

'Jarin will not move on this.'

'I'm sure you can persuade him. Use some of those moves you use on me.'

Her eyes flared in indignation. 'And you would have that, would you? Me writhing in bed with another?'

'He's *your* betrothed.'

'You want to make me suffer, don't you? For wounding you.'

'I want Jarin to expose himself for the liar he is.' He stepped closer to her, cupped her jaw, his lips close to hers. 'How could you be with him, Feinith, knowing what a coward he is? And not just over Seth. All those spot checks and interference – I know it all comes from him. He won't come here and face me himself; he always sends his army instead. He deserves to be exposed. And my brother deserves redemption for all those years of loyalty to the very Order that turned their back on him.'

'I'm sorry, Caleb, but I can't.'

'You can if you want her. Unless you want to try and find another.'

'There are no others.'

'Exactly.' He stared deep into her eyes. 'Who is it, Feinith? Who's your precious Higher Order chosen one? How long have they been waiting for this opportunity?'

'You don't know what you're messing with or what you're jeopardising if that serryn comes to any harm before her time.'

'I want to hear it come from your lips.'

'You are fucking with things way above your pay grade, Caleb,' she said, her voice dangerously low.

'My brother remained silent during that trial as Jarin disgraced him. He was loyal to the bitter end, and still Jarin did nothing. And here you are, now betrothed to the very one who betrayed my family. You won't ask him to do this because you know that if he tells the truth, he'll be shamed. He'll be knocked a few notches down the ranking and with it, as his betrothed, so will you. And you can't handle that, can you? The only reason you accepted the coupling was because it gave you more power. You wouldn't look twice at him otherwise.'

'I don't need to.' She reached up to touch his face. 'Not when I have you.'

He caught her wrist. 'You want me, you do this.'

'Give me the serryn now and I will give myself to you in ways that I never have,' she said, her body pressing longingly, hungrily, into his.

He clasped her face in both palms. 'Redeem Seth. Come back with the proof, and I will have the serryn here waiting for you.'

She studied his eyes warily. 'You're giving me your word?'

'Come back with it, Feinith, and we'll seal our agreement. But fail, and I won't be accountable for my actions towards the serryn. I'm only going to warn you once.'

❄ ❄ ❄

Caleb sat in the chair, swinging steadily back and forth as he scanned the images of the empty club. The club he had built from nothing but ruins. It was once a shell but now, during night-time hours, it thrived with the heart and life of Blackthorn. As the community drank and writhed on the dance floor, yelled and screamed and laughed, they forgot for a while about the reality they were subjected to. The only alternative was to grow in futile rage, resentment and anger at the tyranny and prejudice of others who had created the world they had no hope of breaking free from.

No hope until now it seemed.

Hope through the death of a serryn.

A serryn who now lay in his bed. A serryn who had found a way in and had weaved her way into getting as close to him as she possibly could with only one intention.

A serryn he was still supposed to believe had been there by fluke.

The rhythmic knock on the door told him it was Hade.

'Come on in,' Caleb called out.

Hade stepped into the office. He closed the door before approaching the desk. 'Feinith's gone.'

But Caleb couldn't pull his attention from the empty screen of the dungeon – to the spot where Leila had lay only a few hours before.

'Is everything all right, Caleb?'

Sensing the consternation in his voice, he looked up at him to see Hade's usually steely eyes hesitant with concern. 'Everything's fine, Hade.'

'Jake's still doing good?'

'Really good.'

He handed Caleb a handful of photos. 'I've got some updates on the other sister. It threw us for a while – the hair colour, the cut. But it's definitely her.'

Caleb flicked through the CCTV images.

'Word is that Marid was the last one to have her. I'm trying to find him to see if he's sold her on yet,' Hade continued. 'But that's not all. And you're not going to like the rest.'

Chapter Twenty

In the depths of her sleep, Leila felt cool fingers brush against her cheek, the envelope of hair that had fallen there moved away to expose her face.

She frowned, opened her eyes then flinched. She sat upright and withdrew against the headboard as she remembered where she was, as she scanned the candlelit bedroom, the wall sconces setting the wall ahead alight.

Caleb had changed. She glanced over the smart black trousers he wore, the fitted black shirt, the first few buttons left unfastened. Coupled with his bare feet, it was enticingly casual.

For a fleeting moment she wondered if their last encounter had been a dream. But the ache in her body told her it had been all too real, as did the still-crumpled sheets she lay amidst, let alone the torn buttons on her dress. She closed the fabric and folded her arms to keep it that way as the flat, rectangular cream box at her feet caught her attention, another squarer one beside it. 'What are they?'

'Presents,' Caleb said, taking his seat against the footboard. 'For you.'

She frowned. 'What's in them?'

He slid them up the bed towards her. 'If you open them, you'll see.'

She reached for the rectangular one and pulled one of the loose ends of the ribbon. The satin strip fell away with ease. She lifted the lid and peeked inside to see matching cream tissue paper. She glanced up at him warily.

'It helps if you open it all the way,' he said.

She hesitated a moment then removed the lid. A delicate floral scent escaped from inside. She eased onto her knees and unfolded the tissue paper. Folded red silk lay within. She held the dress up, matching underwear falling into her lap. The dress was almost weightless in her hands – plain, knee-length, with delicate spaghetti shoulder straps and folds of silk curving at its low-scoop back. It felt luxurious in her hand, light against her skin. The quality was unmistakable – pure silk and expertly cut. She stared back at Caleb.

'Like it?' he asked.

She frowned, dropped the dress back into the box and reached for the second. She removed the lid to see red silk dress-sandals, their three-inch heels slender and feminine. She looked back at him. 'Why have you done this?'

'Considering I appear to have a habit of tearing your clothes, it's the least I can do.' He moved off the bed and stepped over to the door. 'Feel free to take a shower and freshen up. I'll be in the library when you're ready. I've got you something to eat.'

As he closed the door behind him, she stayed rooted to the bed.

He could have changed his mind. He could be willing to help her. The flame that had flickered precariously reignited. Maybe she had finally convinced him that she was nothing like what he believed her to be. Maybe Alisha had been right – maybe underneath he was loyal to his word.

Maybe something had happened between them – something instigated by the kiss.

But something wasn't right. Something deep in her gut told her that. He was too calm, too resolute. She'd seen that look before – seen that look when she'd first arrived in the apartment and when he'd stood over her on the dungeon floor.

Considering she'd attempted to kill him, he was too calm indeed.

She reached under the pillow for the syringe she had left there. Finding it gone, her heart both leapt and sank. But he hadn't challenged her about it or let her know he had found it. She pulled all the pillows aside in case it had slipped somewhere. She moved off the bed and checked underneath it. It was gone. Well and truly.

Standing beside the bed, she looked down at the dress. She wrapped her own across her chest again. She couldn't spend the rest of the day with her arms folded around herself. And the part of her that needed to retain some semblance of dignity wanted to freshen up. Desperately.

She picked up the dress box and stepped into the en-suite bathroom.

She closed the door behind her, used the toilet and washed her hands. Facing the shower cubicle, she unfastened the last three buttons that remained so she could slip her dress off down over her hips. She draped it over the bath before unclasping and removing her bra. The morning she had put them on felt like years ago, another life before Blackthorn. A time when she thought having any feelings towards a vampire was ludicrous. A time before she met Caleb.

She switched the shower on and held her hand under the water until it reached a comfortable temperature. Stepping inside, she let the spray trail over her body, taking some much-needed comfort in the wet heat. She let the water run through her hair and attempted to detangle the kinks whilst she shampooed. Turning to face the tiles, she let the water continue to saturate her hair, her body as she lingered longer than she knew she should have before stepping out of the shower and wrapping herself in a thick, warm towel.

She dried off her hair and then her body. Stepping over to the sink, she reached for the comb on the shelf and worked it through her hair. She thoroughly towel dried it, and then combed it again. Reaching into his cabinet, she found toothpaste and rinsed out her mouth.

She pulled on the strapless bra, the same quality silk as the dress, fastened the ties on her knickers and reached for the dress. It draped over her subtle curves with ease, the fabric smooth against her cleansed skin, fitting her to perfection.

Stepping back into the bedroom, she sat on the edge of the bed and reached for the sandals. She guessed he was looking for the full effect when she walked out there. She removed them from the box and rubbed them mindlessly with her thumb for a few moments before slipping them on.

She stood and composed herself. She couldn't remember the last time she wore anything so elegant. She practiced in them for a few steps before crossing the threshold into the library.

Caleb was sat at the table at the far end of the room, the candles in the centre of the table the only source of light. A plate and bowl sat at the opposite end to him, a filled wine glass, a tumbler and bottle of water beside it.

He stood from his chair, inhaled smoke from the cigarette he held and strolled towards her. Her pulse raced as his gaze glided over her toes, up the length of her legs, lingered a moment at her hips and waist before sliding over her chest to slow at her neck.

He circled her in a painfully predatory stroll, raking his fingers up her back, making her spine tingle.

She flinched as he tucked her hair aside from behind, ran the cool back of his hand down her neck and over her shoulder – a slow, caressing move that caused her to catch her breath in her throat.

'You look beautiful,' he said, stepping back in front of her, her height now only a couple of inches less than his. Lifting the back of her hand to his lips, he kissed it tenderly, making her heart leap, before keeping her hand in his as he led her over to the table.

He pulled out the chair at the far end of the table from his, inviting her to sit.

She did so, easing it further under the table as he stepped away again. She took in the aroma of the pasta coated in sundried tomatoes and garnished with rocket, beautifully presented on its immaculate white plate and bowl.

She looked up at him warily as he resumed his seat at the other end of the table, the distance welcome as her stomach somersaulted.

He leaned back in the chair, pulled the ashtray closer so he could tap off some ash.

'Are you not eating?' she asked.

He shook his head, exhaled a steady stream of smoke, his gaze unreadable.

She looked back down at the bowl. She wanted to ask him outright if he'd drugged it, but like he'd told her before – he wasn't that subtle.

And she needed to eat. The tempting aroma alone told her that much. At the very least she needed to keep her strength up. And for all she knew it could have been a simple, civilised attempt on Caleb's part, and one she knew would be stupid and unreasonable to throw back in his face.

She lifted the weighty cutlery and took her first few small mouthfuls.

Something had happened, his silence only prodding her doubts, the room thick with tension. She needed something to break it.

'How's Alisha?' she asked, lowering her cutlery to pour herself some water rather than opting for wine.

He tapped some more ash off his cigarette. 'She's fine. Suffering from an almighty hangover apparently, but she'll get over it. She's only been awake an hour or so.'

'She must be wondering where I am.'

'Jake told her you spent the night with me.'

'What did she say?'

'Apparently if I've forced you into anything or done anything to hurt you, my life won't be worth living.' He exhaled a steady stream of smoke. 'She seemed to find it hard to believe that her big sister would willingly spend the night fucking a vampire, let alone one like me.'

Leila swallowed hard at his bluntness, at the way he made it sound like that's all it was. And the way he said it made her flush in shame, no more so because for a short while, from the way he had kissed her, she'd dare wonder if it could be something more. 'Jake reassured her I was fine?'

Caleb nodded.

She swallowed hard, needed to lower her fork-holding hand to the table so he wouldn't see it tremble. 'So what happens now?'

'Just concentrate on getting some food in you. I don't want you flaking out on me. Then we'll talk.'

Her heart pounded. 'About what?'

'About what we do from here.'

'You make it sound like we have a choice.'

'There's always a choice.'

She wanted to ask him what the kiss had been about. If it meant he had softened, even if only a small amount, towards her cause.

If maybe, just maybe, he had believed her.

She took a few more mouthfuls, glanced up to see he was still watching her.

'What's this about?' she asked. 'The dress. The food. Candlelight.'

'I told you I can be nice.'

'After I tried to kill you?'

He flicked some ash into the tray beside him, a glimmer of a smile escaping. 'I can hardly blame you for that, can I?'

'Can't you?'

'Let's just say the sex made up for it.'

His gaze was impossible to read. She wanted to believe it, *needed* to believe it, but every survival instinct in her sparked.

She took a few more mouthfuls, each one increasingly hard to swallow. She had the feeling she was going to get nowhere until she cleared her plate. She reached for the jug of water, filled her glass, hoping a few mouthfuls would lubricate her throat enough to continue.

'We just need to think of something Feinith might want more than she wants you.'

She glanced up at him again, unease stirring at the pit of her stomach. If Feinith had even an inkling of the truth, there would be *nothing* she wanted more. 'Like what?'

'Maybe those books of yours.'

'What books?'

'The ones your grandfather left you. All those prophecies.'

Her stomach clenched. She reached for more water.

'Alisha seemed to think you were some kind of expert on them all,' he added.

'Far from it. I haven't read them since our grandfather's death and maybe for years before that.'

'But you do still have them all. And you can still read them.'

She looked up at him, unease ricocheting through her at his steady gaze. 'I'm not trading those books for anything.'

'Not even your life?'

Her heart jolted. 'I was entrusted with them.' She returned to eating, now more as a get-out clause than a need to consume any more, her already weak appetite depleting by the moment.

'You brought one here.'

'I had no choice.'

'So you choose your sister over a book but you won't choose yourself. Or is it just because you don't want the Higher Order in particular to get their hands on them?'

'Those books don't belong here.'

He rested his forearms on the table as he leaned forward, exhaled another stream of smoke. 'Books? Or the secrets they contain? Because I bet they're just full of them, aren't they? Like how to cure a vampire of dying blood. It makes me wonder what other useful information is lingering beneath the covers.'

Discomfort rooted deeper. 'It sounds more like it's you who wants to trade.'

He sent her a fleeting smile before extinguishing his cigarette. He stood and sauntered across to the sofa to return with a book – her book – his finger seemingly marking a page as he held it closed. Her heart pounded painfully as he brought his chair around from his end of the table and placed it adjacent to hers.

He pushed her plate and empty bowl aside to lay the book in front of her as he rested his foot on the rung of her chair. 'I want you to take a look at something.' He opened it to where his finger marked the page and pointed at the symbol. 'What do you know about that?'

Her heart skipped a beat. A cold chill of dread consumed her as she stared down at the all-too-familiar symbol. She snapped her attention back to Caleb, forcing herself to hold his gaze as calmly as possible despite her insides wrenching with terror, her anxiety dissociating her from anything but him and the detached look in his eyes. 'Nothing. Why? Should I?'

'It doesn't mean anything to you?'

'Does it mean something to you?' She already knew that answer. Why would he pick it out from all the others littered through the book if he didn't recognise it? And if he recognised it, he'd seen it somewhere. And if he'd seen it, he knew who owned it. And if he knew who owned it, it was even more important that she said absolutely nothing.

Her tired brain needed to kick in. And quick.

'This is your book,' he said.

'Yes. But it doesn't mean I've read it all.'

'But you *can* read it. That's the whole point.'

'Is that what you want me to do?'

'If you would,' he said, his gaze unflinching.

Leila stared down at the beautifully embossed page and the slanted, cursive writing. She skimmed the overly familiar words, words she hadn't read for years, but that she knew almost by heart. The section had been one of the focal points of her grandfather's teaching – his warning. A warning that had never resonated so loud or so clear.

Parts. She just had to tell him parts.

She glanced back up at Caleb. 'It says it's a symbol of protection.'

'Protection against what?'

'It doesn't say.'

'Then what does it say?'

Under the intensity of his gaze, she looked back down at the page, pretending to scan as her mind ploughed into creative overdrive. 'It protects all who have it. All who are *chosen* to have it. Protection from…' She shrugged. 'There are all sorts of mythological and metaphysical hierarchies and orders mentioned here. I haven't even heard of half of them. They probably don't even exist anymore.' She glanced back up at him. 'It doesn't make a lot of sense, but most of this book is like that.'

'Go on.'

The nausea rose in her throat, worsened by the lingering scrutiny in Caleb's eyes. 'There's nothing else to say. It's just a brief reference.'

'It says something about a prophecy.'

She knew the flare in her eyes had not gone unnoticed.

'You're not the only linguist, Leila. Some vocabulary transcends languages. So tell me more.'

Leila stared into his uncompromising eyes. He couldn't know. He couldn't possibly know. None of the vampires knew. Her thumping heart overrode the silence in the room. But if he did, he'd know she was holding back. She had to tread carefully. 'It says it's reserved for those of a certain lineage. The Higher Order probably – that's what it usually means.'

'You mentioned the word *chosen*. Chosen for what?'

'I don't know.'

Caleb kept perfectly still, his eyes narrowing slightly. 'Why's it in that book?'

'Probably because of the reference to the bloodline. It contains everything to do with blood. I'd need countless other reference sources to connect it all together. All the books link together like a puzzle if you want the whole picture. I haven't read them for years. Some I've never read. You're expecting me to pull out one tiny fragment from a whole tapestry. It doesn't work like that.'

Something was simmering behind his eyes – an icy purposefulness, a look that, in contrast to his earlier gaze that could have been mistaken for affection, was now clearly one of a vampire face-to-face with a serryn. 'You're lying.'

Her stomach flipped. 'I'm not.'

'Yes, you are. You're trying to hide something, which tells me there's more going on here. Something you don't want me to know.' His gaze lingered to the point she felt he wasn't going to look away again. 'What's so special about that symbol?'

Her stomach wrenched, her pulse racing, her mouth arid.

Saving a vampire was one thing. Disclosing a secret as ancient as her race that could put her in the heart of her worst fear was another. She had to protect the secret. She had to. The very reason the book should never have been in Blackthorn in the first place.

The secret could never come out.

She flashed back to Beatrice gazing empathetically at her with those soulful eyes.

'You understand why your grandfather had to bring you here,' Beatrice had said. 'He tells me of your studies, how attentive you are. Your knowledge is already impressive, let alone the fluency of your interpreting, even in such a short space of time.'

'I told you, I like to read.'

'And of the prophecies, you have read of the Tryan?'

Even back then it had made every hair on the back of her neck stand up. Of course she knew of the prophecy, it was every serryn's responsibility to know the prophecy. 'Yes.'

'And your grandfather has spoken to you of it?'

'Yes.'

'And, Leila, more than anything else, you have to understand and accept it. If I can convince you of anything today, it will be that. Because if it is you, if you are the pre-destined, then you have to hone your skills better than any other. The survival of humankind depends on it.'

She'd held her gaze, every part of her utterly resolute. 'All the more reason for me to never go near one.'

'Leila, if it is your destiny, your paths will cross and you have to be prepared. All the training serryns go through, all the studies, yes, it's about destroying our enemy but above all, above all else, it's about being ready. If you are the one, and you are found lacking, then everything, everything we have fought to protect, will be theirs. You have to accept this possibility, Leila. You cannot hide from your fate.'

'What if I don't want to be a serryn? How do I get rid of it?'

'Two options – one impossible and the other unthinkable. But neither of which you want to consider. The consequences are too great. You are what you are. The calling is there, Leila. That much you cannot ignore. And if you are the chosen serryn—'

'I'm not. And I don't think I need any more of these meetings, Beatrice. Thank you for your time, but I think I understand enough now.'

Leila had tried to march away but Beatrice had caught her arm.

'Live in the world, Leila, not locked away from it. Books hold no comparison to life experience. Mix with people and learn from them. Fall in love. Get hurt. Know what real emotion is. Let it scar you. All of that will give you the best defence should your time ever come. Innocence will teach you nothing – only numb your awareness of your true feelings. You need to play them at their own game. You must in order to survive.'

How right Beatrice had been – how painfully right. And the reality was hitting her so hard she was almost breathless.

If Caleb had seen it, it was already in form. The mark of the new era had arrived. And the one secret she had been warned to contain was at risk of being in the hands of a vampire who potentially knew the carrier.

There was only one Higher Order vampire he got up close and personal with.

Feinith.

Feinith was the one. Feinith was the chosen one. That's why she'd wanted her alive.

Dread seized her.

Somehow she had found out. Somehow she had uncovered the secret – the key to activate the Armun.

This was it, this was her worst fear – not just being discovered by a vampire, tortured, abused and slaughtered or captured by those who wanted to mercilessly use her blood to slay them. Her greatest fear was the possibility, the tiny possibility that the Tryan would rise in her lifetime.

And if Feinith did know and, in her desperation to get her hands on her, had given Caleb even an inkling of the truth, her chances of getting out alive had just fallen to zero.

This was no longer about just her and Alisha anymore. Her decision to go there hadn't just been stupid, it had been potentially catastrophic.

And if Caleb *did* know, he was playing a very cruel game indeed.

No. She had to tell herself it was just her paranoia. She *needed* to believe it was just her paranoia.

'I told you; it's a symbol for someone of the Higher Order bloodline, and it offers them protection,' she said. 'As for prophecies, the book is full of them. That's all I can tell you.'

He watched her for a moment, studying her eyes pensively. She stared hesitantly back, anxious that her eyes would betray so much to one who seemed to be able to read her every thought.

'Why's it so important to you?' she asked.

'Why are you so reticent to disclose anything if it doesn't mean anything?'

'I took an oath never to tell the secrets of that book to anyone, let alone a vampire.'

'And that's just it, isn't it, Leila – your dedication to your cause?'

Unease wrenched at her stomach. 'My only cause is, and has only ever been, to get me and Alisha out of here alive.'

'So you keep saying.'

His gaze locked on hers, but only for a moment longer before he closed the book and pushed it aside. She expected him to stand, but he just reclined more in his chair, his foot still on the rung of hers, his silence escalating her panic.

'You've seen that symbol somewhere, haven't you?' she said.

He ran his thumb lightly along his lower lip as his gaze didn't leave hers.

'Or why else would you be so interested in it? Or is it more the case of the wearer you're interested in?' she added.

He almost smiled.

The tightness in her chest was excruciating. She couldn't help but ask him. 'Where were you while I was asleep?'

'You're not going to get all possessive of me now, are you, Leila?'

'I asked you a question.'

'And I asked you one, but I guess we both have something we want to hold back on.'

'I'm not stupid, Caleb. That symbol is reserved for the Higher Order and there's only one Higher Order vampire you get up close and personal with, from what I understand.'

'Is that why you're so reticent?' He reached for her wine glass and took a mouthful. 'I know her wanting you has something to do with that symbol. What I want you to tell me is the link.' He looked back at her. 'Why it's making you panic.'

'Anything to do with her makes me uneasy.'

'Clearly.' He paused. 'But she doesn't have the hold over me you think she does.'

'No?'

'No.'

His steady gaze did little to abate her tension, despite the seeming sincerity in his eyes. Silence lingered as that gaze didn't falter, as he waited for her to speak.

But she had nothing to say. Nothing she *could* say. Not until he revealed more of what he knew.

'But I understand why you're worried,' he said. 'Why you're so reluctant. Hell, if I was the key to a pending vampire uprising, I wouldn't want to be talking about it either.'

Horror gripped her and rendered her speechless as his eyes didn't flinch from hers. Suspect though she did, hearing it slip from his lips made it all too real. The walls pulsated, the darkness seeming to encroach even further physically and mentally as words continued to fail her.

'You're not going to deny it then? That the symbol is the Armun. How the one who carries it has to drain every drop of a serryn's blood and steal her soul? How the chosen one leaves her at the Brink in agony for all eternity, while they rise to power, finally dragging humankind into slavery. That's how it goes, right? The Tryan gets their hands on you and the prophecies begin.'

He took another steady mouthful of wine before pushing the base of the glass away with his fingers.

'No wonder you couldn't wait to get out of here,' he said, looking back at her. 'For every second that passed, you knew you were one more second closer to discovery. That's why you've kept yourself so safely locked away all these years. If no one else knew about you, neither would the Tryan. I thought you were valuable before, but now…' He raked his gaze slowly over her. 'You must be absolutely priceless.'

She didn't dare flinch – couldn't, even if she wanted to. 'How long have you known?'

'A few hours.'

'So how much has she offered you to betray me, Caleb? How much is your word worth?'

He almost smiled. 'Betray you? That's an emotive term, Leila.'

She coiled her fingers into *her* damp palms. 'It doesn't take a genius to work out who would have had to disclose their safely guarded truth in order to prize me away from you.' She kept her gaze as squarely on his as her nerves would allow. 'So what's this about now, Caleb? Are you hoping to up your bargaining power with her? Like you said, I must be absolutely priceless.'

'It's more a case of what you're willing to offer, Leila, in exchange for your life; for thwarting the vampiric road to supremacy.'

An icy chill ran through her. 'Because anything I could offer you would be worth more than that, right?'

'Don't be so defeatist, Leila. It's not like you.'

She couldn't help the resentment leaking into her tone. 'What do you want?'

'I want you to look me in the eye and tell me that's not why you're here. Why you targeted me.'

'Because of Feinith? How was I supposed to know about that? If that's what you think, if you think I used you to get to her, you're insane.'

'Really? I had word about Sophie whilst you were sleeping.'

Her stomach flipped.

'Don't worry – she's alive. Last thing I heard she was, anyway. She's definitely here in Blackthorn somewhere. And I have the pictures to prove it. CCTV images from the bars and clubs she was doing. Who with.'

He met her gaze again, his lingering painfully.

'I know she belongs to some kind of vigilante group,' he continued. 'They call themselves The Alliance apparently. They're targeting certain core vampires – vampires with power or influence in Blackthorn.

They've been working underground a long time with no one having a clue, so they're good. They also have very subtle tactics it seems, including suicide missions, in the name of their cause.'

Unease flooded her.

'What kind of twisted organisation agrees to its members being fed to death just so they can kill a vampire with their dying blood?' he added. 'Not Sophie of course. But she's a part of it.'

She stared at him in horror. Shook her head. 'No.'

'So tell me again just how innocent your arrival here was.'

'You've got this wrong. It's a coincidence. My sister wouldn't be involved in that. She has nothing to do with what happened to Jake.'

'So there is absolutely no chance at all that she came here with the vengeance tirade *you* should have had to redeem your mother's murder? How well do you know either of your sisters, Leila?'

She couldn't pull her gaze from his.

'Only it seems to me you don't know them as well as you think you do,' he said.

'None of this has anything to do with my sisters. This is between you and me.'

'You have to understand my concern though, Leila. The plot just keeps thickening with you, doesn't it?'

'I have proved myself to you twice.'

'And I want you to prove yourself once more.'

'What are you talking about?'

'Like you said, this is between you and me.'

'Me and you and the fate of both our species.'

'If you want to put it so dramatically. And what self-respecting serryn wouldn't take every opportunity to tempt me to bite now and get themselves the hell out of here now they'd been found out? You'd have to be suicidal not to.'

'I don't understand?'

'I want you back in my bed, Leila.'

Her pulse raced as she stared at him in the silence. 'What are you talking about?'

'I'm talking about the predicament I'm in – caught between loyalty to you for saving Jake and, now knowing what I do about you, all these doubts creeping in as to why you did it.'

'And sleeping with you again proves what exactly?'

'Under the circumstances, any serryn would be fighting to get out of here. I want you to prove, once and for all, that you can stand by your convictions and control what you are, despite every survival instinct telling you to unearth that serryn. More to the point, I want you to lead. I want to give that serryn every temptation to surface.'

She frowned. 'And if I succeed, I gain what?'

'I don't give you to Feinith.'

'You expect me to believe that? I know where your loyalty lies, Caleb. Even if not to her then at least to your own.'

'And you think I believe having the Higher Order in charge is best for the future of Blackthorn?'

'If that's true, why the games when you could just kill me?'

'Like I said, I have a dilemma.'

She shook her head. 'You *are* insane.'

'I tell you what,' he said, resting his arm on the table as he leaned forward. 'Let's up the stakes. The code to the penthouse door is 7541. You reverse it for the room Alisha's in. As Jake's in his room, she's totally alone down there. You could walk right in and right back out – no obstacles, no confrontations. He wouldn't even know. Though, of course, with me out of the way, you could get to him too. That's how much temptation I'm willing to lay out for you. That's how confident I am that I won't bite.'

Her pulse raced to a painful rate. 'And if I don't want to play your game?'

'You prove me right all along. And you *really* don't want to do that. It's all down to how confident you are that you know yourself.

How confident you are that you can keep yourself contained. It's still daylight out there, but the clock's ticking.'

He pushed back his chair and stood, sauntered across to the bedroom. He left the door open behind him, candlelight pooling onto the floorboards at the threshold.

Leila gripped the edge of the table, barely able to breathe.

It wasn't just that it was a test; it was the fact she had to lead. Last time it had been easier, caught up in the moment, not anticipating it going that far. And all it had done was reinforce the doubt – the simmering self-doubt at just how much she *could* contain it. She wasn't herself when she was with him. Or she was too *much* herself.

Twice now she'd faltered. If she messed up, it would be over. If it went wrong, she'd have no choice *but* to become what she needed to be to get out of there.

But if she shied away, she unravelled everything she had worked towards. Because there had been something between them that convinced her just enough that he could be giving her a chance – something in his kiss, something in the way he had looked at her as he'd wiped away her tears the previous night. Something that told her if she managed to get him on side, he'd be a hell of a powerful ally.

And something in the way he'd looked at Feinith after she'd cruelly disclosed about Seth told her he wanted this to work as much to his advantage as hers.

She pushed back her chair and rose to her feet. Her heels clicked non-rhythmically on the floor as she headed across the library to push the door to the bedroom all the way open.

He was already sat on the bed, leaning back against the headboard, his relaxed arms draped over it. His casually bent legs were slightly spread, his trousers tightened enough to reveal those hard, strong thighs. Abs taut beneath his shirt, the buttons just pleaded to be unfastened.

She couldn't walk away – not from the opportunity, not from his arrogance, not from whatever it was stirring inside her that pleaded with her to straddle the vampire that lay gazing at her with those darkly lethal eyes.

Warily holding his gaze, she closed the door behind her, adding to the claustrophobia of the room already created by the closed curtains blocking out the outside world.

He coiled his hands around the metal bar of the headboard, revealing the strength in his arms, his shirt straining further against the hard curves of his chest as if to taunt her more.

'You stopped last night. Why?'

'Does it matter?'

'It does if you were you tempted to bite again.'

His eyes glinted coaxingly. 'Worried for my welfare?'

'I think the risk of this is greater than you're willing to admit. For you. Not me.'

'And why does that worry you, Leila? It'll give you a way out of here. Isn't that what you've wanted all along? A chance like this?'

'You're really not worried? Not at all?'

'How many situations like this have you survived, fledgling?'

'It only takes one, Caleb.'

'That's for me to worry about, not you.'

'It is for me to worry about if I look at you the wrong way and you decide I haven't proved myself after all.'

'But you're not going to, are you? That's the whole point.'

She stepped around to the side of the bed, perched side-saddle on the edge. 'Then tell me something – did you ever intend to stand by your word? Did you ever intend to let me go?'

'From the first moment I saw you, I intended to kill you.'

'So you lied to my sister. To me.'

'No. I *intended* to kill you. But I was willing to give you a chance to redeem yourself.'

'Which I've done. Which tells me this is more about proving something to *your*self.'

His eyes flared slightly, then narrowed. 'Like what?'

'That you can hold back. That when every temptation is in front of you, you can still contain yourself.'

He almost smiled. 'You're wasting time, Leila.'

'Then give me your word, Caleb. Look me in the eye and you swear to me that if I do this, and prove myself for the last time, Feinith doesn't get near me or my family.'

'I swear on Jake's life that she won't touch you.'

She warily held his gaze for a few moments longer before coiling her legs under her as she reached to unfasten her sandals.

Once she started it would be easier. It always was.

'Leave the heels on,' he said.

Her gaze snapped to his, his eyes glinting darkly.

She felt herself falter, but she wouldn't back down.

She crawled up the bed towards him, parted her thighs either side of his as Caleb slid his together so she could straddle him.

His hands didn't move from holding the bedstead but if she could have strapped him to it, she would have. The thought of it stirred deep in her abdomen. The thought of containing him, controlling him. She glanced into his green eyes before focusing down on his chest, at the straining buttons on his shirt.

She unfastened the first, her fingers more fumbling than she would have thought. And it only got harder as she unfastened one after the other, as she revealed inch after inch of that perfect chest, the fabric falling away by itself.

All too easily, she lowered her mouth to kiss him, trailing her kisses slowly down the crevice between his pecs, his chest hard and cool beneath her warm lips. Until, sliding down over his taut, flat stomach, she reached the top button on his trousers. With hesitant fingers she unfastened it.

Caleb shifted slightly and she knew it wasn't with discomfort.

She'd been there before, less than a few hours ago. She'd done it then and she could do it again.

She wanted to do it again.

She slid down his zipper, and gently prized down his black shorts to free him. Taking him in her mouth was instinctive. Dangerously so. Wrapping her lips around his head, running her tongue full circle on the underside of the ridge, before taking him deeper had *him* gasping for breath this time.

It was barely audible, but she felt it as much as she heard it.

She pulled his shorts down a little further to lick him slowly and lingeringly from base to tip before taking him fully in her mouth again.

She heard him curse under his breath. She felt his body tense. She released his shorts, letting them slide almost back into place.

'Certain you're in control, Caleb?' she asked, glancing back up at him.

She was sure she saw a glimmer of admiration in his eyes. 'As much as I need to be. What about you?'

She eased back up his body, parted her thighs around his again, looked back into his eyes, hoping it was answer enough. 'Perfectly.'

'Then what are you waiting for?'

'Feeling impatient?' She rested her hands either side of his as she leaned closer. 'Or are those nerves spurning you to take control back already?'

'Or is it your nerves making you stall?'

She shifted herself to his groin, his hardness pressing against the silk of her knickers, making her sex throb. She took a moment to steady herself, her body immediately responding to being that close to him again.

She looked back into his eyes as his fingers flexed then tightened around the bar.

He was enjoying it. He was genuinely enjoying it.

She tugged his shorts down, lowered back onto him. She reached up under her dress, her fingers anxiously meeting the ribbon ties.

Looking into his eyes, she gently tugged the binds, which unravelled with ease, leaving only a thin fragile barrier of loose silk between them. Looked into the hazy eyes she could mistake as losing themselves in the moment.

Breaking from the intimacy, she lifted herself slightly to ease the silk away.

She felt him tense again, but this time she didn't look back at him as she guided his ready erection against her.

But she couldn't bring herself to push.

She felt her nerve go, clutched the bar, her hand next to his, her head still lowered, her eyes tightly shut.

His hand wrapped around the one that held him, guiding himself into her just an inch, his hand then grabbing her thigh, keeping her there.

She just had to lower herself, to ease him inside her little by little.

She held her breath and gently pushed.

Renewed arousal shivered through her as she lowered herself further and further, as she felt him start to fill her again – cool, hard and toxically fulfilling. She grasped the metal bar, gripped the pillow beside him and lowered herself even further.

He tightened his grip on her thigh, freed his other hand from the bar to clutch the nape of her neck.

He was claiming back some control, she knew that much, because he was already starting to move within her, using both hands to keep her steady as he helped get the rest of the way inside her in one slow, steady thrust.

She shuddered, at first the position feeling uncomfortable, but as he started to penetrate her slowly, her body started to adjust again.

She kept her eyes closed, kept her head lowered, locked in the sensation, until he sat more upright. His grip on her neck tightened, the pace of his thrusts quickening.

She looked into his eyes and they startled her. Never had they looked darker. Never had they looked more lethal. But never had she been less fearful. Never had she wanted anything more than she wanted him then.

In an instant he was on his knees, pushing her onto her back, resuming the dominant position.

She caught her breath, slammed her hand to his chest. 'Nerves set in?' she asked, not liking the quiver in her voice.

'No. But I can take it from here,' he said, slipping his shirt from his shoulders.

'What if I don't want you to?'

'Then fight me for it,' he said, pinning her hands to the bed.

Her heart leapt. The feel of him in control again had her reeling, her body arching instinctively into his as he lowered his lips to hers, dangerously close, but not close enough to kiss.

He lowered his head, his thrusts picking up pace more quickly than they had before. There was an edge that she sensed to his penetration, something rawer.

Her heart pounded. A ripple of unease crept through her and she tried to calm her breathing.

'What's the matter, serryn?' he asked, looking back at her, his eyes the most sullen and terrifyingly beautiful in their menace she had seen them. 'Where's that confidence gone?'

He wouldn't bite. He'd claimed back power, but he wouldn't bite. He was in control. He had to be in control. She needed him to be in control. Over and over she said it. But those eyes, as she stared deep into them, made her too uneasy.

'You need to let me go,' she said.

'Why?'

She winced as he thrust a little harder and it almost seemed to turn him on more.

She felt something inside her sparking under the threat, something she couldn't allow out.

Damn it, if this was part of his game, if this was part of his temptation to scare her enough to out the serryn within, it was a vicious play on their unspoken rules.

He was upping the ante, and as he lowered his head to her throat, it was starting to work.

She needed him to bite. She needed to encourage him. She could be out of there, long gone – her and Alisha. She needed to let her instincts take over, not the dread at the thought of him drinking her poison.

He gripped her wrists tighter, his penetration making her tremble with the force.

He was losing it.

Damn it, she was giving off signals. Signals she had no control over. She couldn't let him do it.

She couldn't.

'Caleb, you need to slow down.'

His thrusts became harder, thrusts that were increasingly about self-satiation.

'Caleb—'

He released a wrist to clamp his hand over her mouth, silencing her as he picked up pace again.

She struggled beneath him, pushed her hand against his hard chest, but he restrained her with ease. He lifted himself slightly to look in her eyes.

His pupils were constricted, incisors exposed, his vampiric state having never been so apparent.

As his hungry eyes locked on hers, she froze.

She shook her head, her protests muffled behind his hand.

He was seconds away, seconds away from killing himself. Caleb, her beautiful green-eyed vampire who had pushed himself one step too far.

Beatrice had been right – she was too powerful. More powerful than she'd ever imagined if she was defeating him.

And as he lowered his lips to her throat again, she cried out behind his hand.

He licked in one slow steady motion and she caught her breath, her whole body seizing.

She prepared herself for the horror that was inevitable. Prepared herself with a twinge in her heart and a harsh stab of fear.

And he bit.

Leila cried out, the pain piercing through her. Pain she remembered only too well. She arched against him, but he held her fast as he sucked deeply and slowly.

She couldn't move as she gasped for breath, her whole body in shock.

She closed her eyes, a tear trickling down her cheek.

She should have felt triumphant, relieved at the very least, but her head could only focus on the ache in her neck and the pain in her heart as he fed.

And fed.

She couldn't move, couldn't protest, couldn't say anything to save him.

It was too late.

It was all over.

That much seemed obvious, until he pulled back.

She stared up at him, stunned.

Her blood still masked his lips until he licked it off, his constricted pupils dilating again, the look in his eyes bearing no shock for what he'd done.

Her heart pounded as she waited for the agony, the spasms, her blood already filtering into his system.

But there was nothing.

Nothing as he withdrew and eased off the bed.

Nothing as he strolled over to the bathroom, leaving the door ajar behind him.

She remained on her back, her pulse racing at an uncomfortable rate. Horror crept through every vein. Something had happened. Something had changed.

She'd lost it. She wasn't a serryn anymore.

And there was only one way she'd lose it. She was attracted to him, yes. From the moment she had seen him and yes, it had intensified. But love was a whole other matter.

She didn't love Caleb. She couldn't love Caleb. Love wasn't even possible between a serryn and a vampire.

She forced herself off the bed. She needed to know. In a haze, clutching her throbbing neck, she stumbled across to the door.

Caleb was leaning over the sink, splashing water on his face and neck.

She scanned his taut back, the hard muscles in his arms and shoulders illuminated by the artificial light. He ran his hands back through his hair as he stood up straight.

She was instantly drawn to the cursive design of his tattoo that spanned from shoulder blade to shoulder blade – a back as toned and flawless as his torso.

And then it caught her eye.

Another tattoo, a smaller tattoo, rested between his spine and left shoulder blade – an orb crossed with a sword, twisted black-thorned vines coiled around it in their own intricate design.

Leila caught her breath as she locked gazes with Caleb in the mirror, an ice-cold perspiration washing over her.

Taking an instinctive step back, she cursed silently as she backed into the bedroom. Legs like lead, her behind hit the bedpost and she grabbed the orb behind her for support.

Caleb stopped at the threshold as he nonchalantly towel-dried his neck.

She couldn't move as every faculty shut down in terror.

'You really didn't know, did you?' he said, raking her swiftly before turning to the wardrobe. Opening it up, he draped the towel over the door. 'You're supposed to be able to sense it.' He glanced across at her, pulled a T-shirt down over his head, every muscle in his arms and chest flexing.

She *had* sensed it. Amidst all the heated attraction her guard had always remained up – her instinct constantly warning her. She just didn't know what *it* was that she had sensed. And if she'd had more experience with vampires, she may have even detected the difference. The extremities of her emotions weren't just because he was a vampire, weren't just because of her forbidden attraction to him – he was *the* vampire.

No wonder it felt so right in its wrongness. The draw had been impossible to ignore – the battle lines had been laid out from the moment they had met.

Her fate, her destiny, stood less than six feet away gazing back at her with those beautiful cold green eyes.

A destiny that meant that one of them had to die.

Caleb sauntered over to her. 'You were destined to find me, apparently. Did you know that? It seems our brother and sister meeting was fate.'

Leila's grip on the orb tightened, her eyes fixed tentatively and fearfully on his as he stopped directly in front of her. Stunning green eyes that, from the moment she had looked into them, had told her he was going to be her downfall. And she had been right. In the past few hours she had faced the twilight, dusk and darkness of hope, only to now stare into the blackest void, any tiny glimmer of hope finally extinguished.

'And now here we are,' he said. 'Both knowing what you are, both knowing what I am. And that, my little fledgling sacrifice, must make me your worst fucking nightmare.'

Chapter Twenty-one

Caleb could see Leila's lower lip trembling. Her already pale skin was ashen. She was lost for words, her gaze locked in terror on his.

She had no fight left in her. Not when her body and mind were dealing with that much shock.

He had irrevocably proven what he needed to with his bite – as much to himself as to her. They both knew the situation they were in, but her eyes still emanated disbelief.

'But it's not possible,' she said. 'The chosen one has to be from the Higher Order.'

'Our mother turned her back on her heritage on account of the Higher Order's warped principles and treatment of lower-order vampires. She went into hiding. Our father didn't know anything about her background when they started their secret affair. And she never told him for fear of the consequences of her absconding, especially as she was expecting Seth by him. After two more sons with her, he was coupled to a Higher Order vampire elsewhere. He betrayed her. Abandoned her. But to protect us, our mother swore to always keep the secret. Jake and I never knew what we were until after her death, when Seth told us one drunken night. Seth who extended decades of loyal service to the Higher Order in honour of our mother only to later be betrayed and dishonoured by Jarin's lies. I think this is what they call poetic justice.'

Her eyes flared. He sensed the quickening of her pulse. 'You couldn't have told me this? Or just bitten me to prove you're immune? You had to have sex with me knowing what you are?'

Even as he tried to detach himself, he couldn't bear those accusatory eyes scorching into him, those beautiful absorbent eyes trying to read him. 'I had to be sure. Now I am.'

'You cruel bastard,' she hissed quietly.

Beneath the trauma she looked genuinely dazed, realisation filling her sad hazel eyes.

A sadness that cut him too deep.

The exposure made him uncomfortable. The exposure made him want to cling to what he knew.

'Now, now, Leila, best behaviour – particularly as I don't need to be on mine.'

'Why didn't you see it through? What are you stalling for?'

He looked at her, but didn't answer. He didn't tell her that he hadn't made up his mind about what he was going to do yet. He turned towards the door, glanced back over his shoulder at her to see how tightly she was clutching the orb at the small of her back, her fearful eyes locked on his.

He turned his back on her, crossed the library and stepped out into the hallway. He stood still for a moment, something inside compelling him to go back, but he couldn't allow himself to.

He needed time and space from her. Now he had proof, he needed to get his head straight.

As soon as he reached the lounge, Jake rose from the sofa. His eyes emanated relief but the tension was still clear in his composure.

'I told you to wait in your room,' Caleb said as he grabbed a bottle of whisky and a couple of tumblers from the bar.

'You were taking too long. You said you'd be an hour maximum. What happened in there? Did you confirm it? Was Niras right? Is it you?'

Caleb took the sofa opposite Jake's, his brother resuming his seat. He filled a glass and handed it to him before filling his own. 'Based on the fact I took a bite out of her and I'm still here to tell the tale, I think we can safely assume so.'

Jake clutched his glass. 'So it's real? The prophecies – they're real?'

Caleb took a mouthful. 'Seems that way, little brother.'

'How did Leila react? Did she know about you?'

'She had no idea.'

'You're sure?'

'Oh, yeah,' he said. 'I'm sure.'

'So you're immune. You're definitely immune to them?'

'To Leila at least.'

'Did you ask her about Sophie? *Was* this some kind of assassination attempt?'

'If the other McKay sister was targeting us, it was for our reputation – not because of the prophecies. Leila was as clueless about Sophie as she was about me.'

'So what now?'

'I haven't decided yet.'

Jake pressed his lips together as he looked down the hallway. 'No wonder she didn't want you to know what it meant. Shit. I can't believe the Higher Order kept this to themselves.

So Feinith never said *anything* to you about this? Even after all those years hunting them?'

'And discuss Higher Order business? I guess I know more than ever where I stood with that one.'

'And you've never given Feinith a hint about our ancestry?'

'We took an oath. I wasn't going to break that and dishonour our mother just for Feinith's benefit.'

'But what about now? They're going to know now.'

'They'll know when I'm ready.'

'But what about Niras? This is big stuff, Caleb. What if she says something?'

'She doesn't know it's me.'

'You didn't tell her?'

'She thinks Feinith let stuff slip to me.'

'So you didn't tell her about the dream?'

'I couldn't, not without giving the truth away. I needed to get back here. I needed to be sure.'

'And now you are, you have to ask her about it.'

'It's just a dream, Jake.'

'A dream that scared the shit out of you. *Nothing* scares the shit out of you. A dream that scared you enough that you had the very symbol in it tattooed on you. Now you know what it means, you need to know more about the rest.'

'And I'll find out more. When I'm ready.'

'Have you had that dream since?'

'From time to time.'

'It's only been three months since it started. Less than two months since you had that engrained on you.' Jake's concerned gaze narrowed. 'How *many* times?'

'Jake, ease up.'

'I've just found out my brother's the Tryan. I don't know whether to be elated or terrified. But from what I know of your dream, I'm veering towards the latter.'

'It's just a dream.'

'A recurring dream with significance if that symbol is anything to go by.' He sighed with unease. 'And now Leila knows about you, she's not going to want to let this one lie. Why didn't you drug her or something?'

'She was going to know soon enough.'

'She didn't have to. Not if she didn't sense it about you. We could have done what you did before. Unless you wanted her to know. Unless you're still playing games with her.'

He held his brother's gaze. 'She was going to know because I can't do it without her.'

'Can't do what without her?'

'The transformation isn't complete. The dream was just the start. The tattoo is the protection I needed for the final stage.'

Jake frowned. 'What final stage?'

'The final stage of draining a serryn to death, taking her to the Brink and stealing her soul to merge with my shadow. Only a serryn soul is strong enough to survive. A transient state will mean the Global Council can't turn me down in a position of power.'

Horror emanated from Jake's eyes as his troubled gaze burned into him. 'You're going to kill Leila?'

'We want freedom. I don't have much choice.'

Even saying it made it sound so simple, but the wrench in his gut told him it was anything but.

Caleb stood up and strolled over to the balcony doors. He stared through the blackened glass at the muted glow of the sun.

'That's why they put the ban on killing them, isn't it?' Jake said.

'They've known about the symbol for decades, but not how to activate it. Only the serryns knew that, until one of our own uncovered the truth, then the protection order was put on them. We weren't going to rise to supremacy without one of them alive.'

'Leila knew all this?'

'She sure did.'

'And she still came here.' He stood from the sofa and joined his brother. 'She came here to save my life knowing all this?'

'She came here to save her sister's life, Jake. And don't you forget it.'

'Caleb, there has to be another way around this. If this is our destiny, fate will deal us another hand.'

'Because the serryns are out there in abundance, right?'

Jake frowned. 'You can't really be contemplating this.'

'Why not?'

'Because if all it takes is that, why haven't you done it already? You could have finished this already.'

'I need to come to terms with it, that's all.'

'And not deliberate.'

'Deliberate over what? You said it yourself; I can't let her go now, Jake.'

'You know she doesn't deserve this.'

'And our kind deserves another week in this squalor – left with nothing but unwanted scraps off the ones who destroyed all this? We both know what's going on out there, Jake. I do this and we'll be able to walk through green fields again, see clear blue skies and breathe fresh air. We'll be what we once were. When our kind comes into power, we will spread beyond Blackthorn. We'll no longer be confined to this prison, forced to share our space with the human scum they couldn't be bothered to detain or prosecute.'

'I hear what you're saying and you know no one wants this more than me, but taking Leila's life for it. You really think you can do that?'

'You're seriously asking me that?' Caleb asked, his gaze locked on his brother's, irritation stirring at his protests. He needed him telling him it was the right thing to do, not making him question himself even more than he already was. 'A sacrifice needs to be made, Jake. And Leila's that sacrifice. Now that she knows the Armun has come to fruition, she'll have only one mission and that's to stop it happening.'

'Which is why you let her know. You want her to make this decision easier for you. Because you know this is wrong, don't you?'

'I'll tell you what is wrong. That this already overcrowded district will only increase in its density and pollution – increase to the point where the Global Council decide they need more drastic management to prevent the overspill. Where, deemed no better than the criminals we're forced to reside with, we'll be subject again not only to the powers that be, but our own Higher Order. The Higher Order that take their backhanders to manage the district with injustice, while they keep themselves in luxury. The Higher Order that have no more loyalty to their own than the Global Council itself. I won't let that happen.'

'So you'll spill the blood of an innocent girl. A girl who saved my life. A girl who wouldn't be here if it wasn't for me. I don't want to win that way. And the brother I know and love, the real Caleb, doesn't want that either or you'd already be in there feeding her dry.'

'It doesn't matter what I want, Jake. What matters is doing what I can for our kind beyond those doors. What matters is knocking the Higher Order off their pedestal. And if I've got to kill Leila to do it, so be it. I will not beat myself up over some little witch I've known less than two days.'

'But that's not all she is, is she? And you're lying to yourself if you think she is.'

'It was too late the minute I bit into her. I either lock her up and throw away the key or I end this.'

Jake stepped over to the bar. He braced his arms on the counter and lowered his head. 'This is all my fault.'

'If not this way, I would have met her somewhere else and some other way. You bleeding that girl to death has given us the upper hand, Jake. And this is our chance to make the most of that, to turn things around, to change everything we know.'

Jake shook his head and pulled away from the bar. He sat back on the sofa, his head in his hands.

Caleb followed him over, took the seat opposite. 'You know it makes sense, Jake.'

Jake looked back up at him. 'And that's what you're going to keep telling yourself is it, despite the feeling in your gut?'

'Hundreds, maybe even thousands of lives turned around for the sake of the death of one serryn, Jake. Whatever the feeling in my gut, I can ignore it. I have to.'

❀ ❀ ❀

Lying, devious, manipulative bastard.

Leila tried pacing. She tried burying her head in her lap. She tried rocking. Now she sat clutching the edge of the bed, her foot bouncing in agitation on the floor, her eyes fixed on the melting candles to her right.

She'd been thirteen at the time, when she'd first made the promise to Alisha. She'd been at her desk with her piles of schoolwork pushed aside. Her grandfather's texts had been spread in front of her, pages of scribbled notes and diagrams spilling out onto her bedroom floor.

Sophie had been causing a racket downstairs, pouncing over furniture, slamming doors. Alisha's laugh had resounded up the stairs a couple of times, assuring Leila that everything was all right or, at least, not bad enough that she'd have to intervene. Grandfather had another meeting so he had left her in charge again. Usually she didn't mind, but she'd found some interesting pieces in his books whilst reading into the early hours and with school since having consumed most of the day, she'd been keen to get back to it all that night.

'No!' The protest had been somewhere between a scream and a cry. 'I don't want to I said!'

Leila had listened for a moment to Alisha's aggravated and shrill little voice.

'No!' she'd protested again.

A bang. A clunk.

A scream.

Leila had slammed down her pencil, shoved back her chair and swept down the stairs.

The living room door had been wide-open but there was no sign of them – just the chaos of toys, strewn around cushions, the chenille throw from the sofa in a bundle on the floor.

A cup had smashed in the kitchen beyond.

'Get away from me!' Alisha's cries had been more panicked, sobs beginning and ending the sentence.

Leila had propelled herself through the open door, her heart pounding.

She'd walked in to see Alisha curled up on the floor against the dishwasher, her large tearful eyes wild in panic, her black cape spread around her, flour all over her face, red liquid smeared around her mouth.

Sophie had been stood over her, padded up in a body warmer, a headlight plastered to her skull, a pointy wooden stick in her hand, something else clutched in the other.

They had both looked to Leila at the same time.

Sophie had folded her arms as Alisha scrambled towards Leila for protection, grabbing her leg.

'She's trying to kill me!' Alisha had proclaimed.

Leila had crouched down and rubbed the liquid off Alisha's face to try and work out what it was.

'It's just ketchup,' Sophie had declared. 'She's a vampire.'

'I am not a vampire!'

'Yes you are, and you've just bitten someone.'

'No!' Alisha had protested more viscously now that she had her big sister for protection.

Leila had stared at the stick. 'What are you doing with that?'

'I'm going to stake her,' Sophie had declared, arms still folded as she shrugged. 'It's what vampire hunters do.' She had smirked at Alisha. 'After I've fed her garlic.' Her eyes had flashed wide as she'd opened her hand and held it out towards her little sister tauntingly.

'No!' Alisha had protested again. She had stared up dewy eyed at Leila. 'She tried to make me eat it!'

'For goodness sake, Sophie.' Leila had reached forward and snatched the stake out of her hand. 'You know she hates those games.'

'She said she wanted to play then she got all whiney.'

'You said I could be a vampire princess!'

'Yeah, well even vampire princesses have got to be staked!' She had switched on her light. 'Or burned with sunlight.'

'I'm not playing anymore! I'm never going to play with you ever again!'

'Then I'll get you when you're asleep.'

'No!' Alisha had squeezed Leila's leg tighter.

'Enough!' Leila had snapped. 'If she wets the bed again tonight, you're changing it. Do you understand?'

'What have I done? I'm only playing.'

'She's six years old. And you know how she feels about them.'

'She'll get over it.'

'You shouldn't even be joking about it,' Leila had said, her voice low in warning as she half-covered Alisha's ears. 'You know how Grandfather feels about you making light of it.'

'He also says all vampires have to die,' Sophie had exclaimed. 'And that's what I'm doing. One by one,' she had added, smirking at Alisha.

Alisha had yelped, gripped Leila's leg tighter, burying her face in her jeans.

'Enough! The game's over. Clear all this up before Grandfather gets home. Haven't you got homework to do?'

'Done it,' Sophie had declared with a sneer as she'd sauntered back into the living room.

Leila had crouched down in front of Alisha, pushing her fair hair back from her ketchup-smeared face, wiping away some of the tears. 'Let's get this muck off your face, shall we?'

'She wasn't really going to stake me, was she?'

'No, she wasn't. It was just a game, Alisha.'

'She told me she's killed a real one,' Alisha had whispered back.

Leila had held Alisha's gaze for a moment before standing up. Placing the stick on the worktop, she'd run some kitchen towels under the warm water tap. 'She's telling you fibs, Alisha. It was part of the game.'

'Can you really kill a vampire with a piece of wood?'

'Killing vampires is against the law, Alisha. Sophie would be in a lot of trouble if she had killed one.'

'Not if they tried to kill her first. Sophie told me. Sophie told me it's okay to kill vampires if you're a shellfish fence.'

Leila had managed a smile as she lowered back down in front of Alisha, wiped the ketchup from her delicate pale skin. 'I think you mean self-defence.'

Alisha had gazed at her sister, her brown eyes wide. 'Have you ever killed a vampire?'

Leila's hand had frozen against her sister's face for a moment, before she hurriedly wiped the remains off. She stood and marched back over to the bin. 'I think we've had enough vampire talk for one night.' Facing her again, she'd crouched back down in front of her little sister, catching hold of her hands. 'Where do we live, Alisha?'

'19, High Grove Avenue, Summerton.'

'Good girl. Where do the vampires live?'

'Blackthorn. The nasty place.'

'That's right. And we've got two whole districts between us and lots of very strong people who guard all the people who come in and out of Summerton. So we don't have to be afraid, do we, Alisha?'

'What if some move here? What if some move next door?'

'A vampire isn't going to move next door.'

'But if one did, you'd look after me, right?'

'I will always keep you safe,' Leila had said, rubbing the last of the gunk off her face. She had looked her in the eyes. 'I promise.'

And it was a promise she swore she'd keep. For her parents, for her grandfather, for herself, she would always keep her sisters safe.

In the shadows of the room, Leila frowned at the candles. She looked at the sconce to its left and then the sconce to its right before looking out at the ones on the table.

And, like the flames that burned, a plan ignited.

Chapter Twenty-two

Caleb stepped into the library and stared down at the unbroken circle of wax.

'You've got to be kidding me,' he said as he closed the door behind him, his eyes flashing partly in amusement and partly in irritation.

Leila took a step back so she was exactly in the middle of the ten-foot-diameter circle she'd created – an instinctive reaction despite the impenetrable barrier between them.

'Very clever,' he said, as he approached the circle and strolled around its periphery, his eyes locking in resentment on hers. 'Very resourceful.'

Leila remained silent as she watched him warily.

'I admire your ingenuity,' he said, lifting his hand to touch the protective wall, flinching as the spark shot up his arm. 'And this one is very nicely done. But like I keep saying – you're a powerful girl.' He kept walking, his gaze locked on Leila's as she turned on the spot, refusing to break eye contact with him.

'The advantage of pure beeswax candles,' Leila explained. 'As opposed to the synthetic concoctions.'

'What can I say?' Caleb said, his eyes betraying his annoyance. 'I'm a traditionalist.' He ran his hand an inch away from the invisible barrier, a flash of light igniting his fingertips. 'Does this mean we're breaking up?'

'Don't mock me, Caleb,' she warned, her eyes narrowed. 'I'll stay in here until I die of starvation if that's what it takes.'

'What, you in there and your sister out here with me? I don't think so.'

'Alisha leaves now or I'm not stepping out of here.'

'Which you'll do the moment I let my leverage go? Sorry, but there's something very flawed in that deal somewhere.'

'It's the only deal I'm making,' she said. 'You need me. And you're not having me unless she's gone. Unless I know she got home safe.'

Caleb stepped up to the line, his eyes solemnly on hers. 'You know I'll get you out of there, don't you, Leila? You're not that naïve.'

Something clenched in the pit of her stomach. 'You touch her and I promise you will suffer. Both you and Jake.'

'Come on, fledgling. You don't really want me to let her go – out there into the darkness of Blackthorn all by herself.'

'She's in less danger out there than she is in here. At least out there she's got a fighting chance.'

'And let her go straight to the authorities?' Caleb glanced down at the sconce in the circle then narrowed his eyes on Leila. 'What have you got in your hand?'

She clenched her perspiring hand tighter.

He stepped up to the edge of the circle. 'What have you got?'

Leila pulled her hand from behind her back and opened her palm to reveal the three nails.

'Clever girl,' he said softly to her, his attention unwavering.

She could have sworn she saw a glimmer of concern in his eyes. A glimmer of panic.

'And don't think I won't do it,' she said. 'You let my sister go or I will do this and there is nothing you can do to stop me. I swear I will shed every last millilitre of this precious blood you need all over this floor.'

'You don't mean that.'

'Do you want to try me?' she asked, glaring at him. 'You need me alive. The only thing I need is my sister and if I can't save her, what's the point? For all I know, you're going to kill her anyway.

Why should you get your prophecy fulfilled as well? You let her go and I'll throw these out to you. You refuse me and I promise you, I will end this now.'

'And what's to stop you doing it anyway?'

'I will give you the nails once I know Alisha is free and okay. No more bartering.'

Irritation clouded his eyes as he strolled around the circle again. 'You drive a hard bargain, fledgling.'

'You leave me with no choice.'

Caleb surveyed the height of the barrier. 'Just how far do these things go up?'

'There's no way in.'

He smiled. 'There's always a way in.'

'Don't underestimate me, Caleb.'

'I haven't. From the minute you walked into this place.' Caleb stopped and folded his arms. 'I knew you were going to be trouble as soon as I laid eyes on you.'

'Then you should have let me go sooner and none of this would have had to have happened.'

'But then we never would have discovered your little secret.' He paused, stepping as close to the line as he could. 'I came down here to talk to you.' He scanned the barrier again. 'It's a shame about all of this.'

'I think we've done enough talking, Caleb. Unless, that is, you were coming down here to tell me you'd decided to do the right thing. Only that would mean choosing to do that over Feinith, over the entire freedom of your kind, wouldn't it?'

'And what would you do if you were me? If you had the chance to redeem your kind from oppression – to change the course of their destiny? And all for the sake of draining the life out of some serryn who has so much hatred for your kind that she stands for everything you long to overcome.'

'And what would you do if you were me, on the cusp of losing everything you have left to care about? And all because of the decision a deceitful, double-crossing, paranoid vampire made.'

He placed both hands on the barrier, it sparking fiercely at him, his green eyes square on hers. 'Don't make this harder on yourself than it needs to be, Leila'

'Take your own advice, Caleb. Get Alisha out of here.'

He retracted. 'Maybe I should bring Alisha here. Maybe she can watch you give up on her.'

'I'm not giving up on anything.'

'Do you think she'll see it that way? Will it be so easy to slice through your veins with her watching?'

She narrowed her gaze on him. 'I don't make false threats, Caleb.'

'But I've got a lot riding on this one. As well you know. Be honest, Leila – you're not going to take your own life.' He paused. 'Unless you'd like to tell me it's just a myth that if a serryn takes her own life, her curse passes on to one of her siblings – punishment for serryns looking for the easy way out.'

Leila felt as though she'd been punched in the stomach. Her throat constricted, her chest tightened.

His green eyes were unflinching on hers, sharp, perceptive, attentive to her every reaction.

The triumph behind them, the coaxing of his smile, sent a cold perspiration sweeping over her. 'You die and we're going to need a backup,' he said. 'Sophie or Alisha make very suitable replacements. Especially with them already being in the district. It's all very convenient.'

Leila narrowed her eyes. 'You touch either one of them…'

'And what?' He stepped as close as he could, a couple of sparks flying. 'What are you going to do from in there? How are you going to protect your sisters from your little cage?'

Leila's heart threatened to break free of her ribcage as she glared at him. 'You leave them alone.'

'Then step out of the circle, Leila. You know the only one I really want is you. Stay in there and bleed to death or stay in there and let yourself starve, it's the same outcome – it's still suicide.' The taunt of threat and promise in his tone, the intent in his eyes, made her chest clench. 'Either you let your sisters take your place, or you drop those nails, get yourself out here and face what you are for the first time in your life.'

'Even if I do step out, I have no guarantee you'll leave them be.'

'Fine,' he said, turning away. 'Do it your way.'

'Wait!' She propelled herself to the edge of the circle.

He slowly turned to face her. Lifted his eyebrows slightly, expectantly.

She held her breath, wiped her damp palms on her dress.

She had lost. She had called his bluff and lost. And stalling would only make it worse. She had no choice but to attempt the only other option she had left. And she had to get it right first time. She couldn't mess up.

He raked her swiftly with his gaze before turning his back on her again, disappearing across the threshold out into the hallway.

She squeezed her eyes shut, her jaw tense. Opening her eyes again, she let the nails clink to the floor before stepping over the line. 'I said wait!'

She reached the threshold, recoiled as Caleb stood just outside the door waiting for her, his hand on the wall, his sullen gaze locked on hers.

She backed up across the threshold again with every step he made towards her, her gaze warily unflinching from his.

'Smart choice,' he said.

'You didn't *give* me any choice,' she replied, backing into the circle again. 'You never do.'

'That's not strictly true, Leila. I'm just selective about the options.' He stepped into the circle with her, the spell having been diminished with her exit. 'But I admire you for being so calculated under pressure. It couldn't have been easy trying to stay that one step ahead. Resourceful, calculated and a harsh negotiator. You'd make any serryn out there proud.'

'Maybe that should be my aim from hereon in. Maybe you're right. Maybe I should finally let the serryn out. That is what you want, right?'

'Are you finally drawing the battle lines, Leila?'

'Maybe I'm just stepping up to them,' she said, taking another wary step back. 'It's about time I did, isn't it?'

He smiled, took another step forward, and hit a wall. An invisible wall. His gaze fell instantly to the line his foot was less than a centimetre away from. Then he glared right back at her.

Chapter Twenty-three

His slow-beating heart jolted. Panic and anger hit him like an overpowering wave.

Leila folded her arms and cocked her hip to the side slightly in an evocative way so uncharacteristic of her, her glare intentionally and defiantly locked on his.

He felt his temper soar, the indignation of her tricking him exacerbating his knee-jerk reaction to any threat. 'What the fuck have you done?' he hissed quietly.

Leila crossed to the door, but instead of leaving, she took the key out of the lock on the far side. She closed the door, still in the room, and locked it. 'I'm guessing you don't want your brother walking in on this.'

Jake – the thought of him alone beyond the door just as much a catalyst for his fury.

'I asked you a question,' he said, watching her stroll back towards him.

'You're fine to cross the line as long as I'm in the circle with you,' she declared.

'You set me up?'

She shrugged and folded her arms again as she stood directly in front of him. 'That is the sort of thing my kind does, isn't it? Or so you keep telling me. So why so surprised, Caleb?'

His green eyes narrowed. 'You devious little bitch.'

Despite the alarm in her eyes at the venom in his tone, she didn't flinch. But he could hear her telling breaths – the shallow breaths of panic she refused to show in any other way. She was learning to curb her fear. She was learning to manage it.

In less than two days, she had progressed – growing into the serryn she was destined to be. And he had started that snowball. A part of him, even amidst his anger, felt a pang that he had made her that way. He'd wanted to see the serryn, now he was staring at her – that calculated determination and refusal to be beaten by a vampire at any cost. And it was viciously biting him in the arse.

'It seems the fledgling is ready to fly,' he said.

'And you've got exactly what you wanted,' she said, her eyes brimming with accusation. 'Well done, Caleb.'

But his brother in the penthouse was not what he wanted. Not without any ability to do anything about it. The uncomfortable sting of helplessness pierced his self-control – unravelling the fragile stitches that kept those suppressed feelings contained. He bit back his temper. 'So what now?'

'What do you think? The code out of this penthouse and the one to Alisha's room are no good if I don't know where she is.'

He exhaled tersely, smiled. 'This whole place is on lock-down until dusk. Even if I tell you, you're not going anywhere.'

'You let me worry about that.'

He stepped up to the edge of the circle, as close to her as he could get – inches away through the invisible barrier. 'This is a really bad move, Leila.'

'Maybe from where you're standing. From here, the move feels like checkmate. Especially with your brother just beyond these walls. Remind me again how resilient to temptation he is?'

The cold heat of fury washed through his body. If it hadn't been for her spell he would have already had her pinned to the wall. Or floor. Right then he didn't care which. 'You touch him and I'll kill you.'

'From the way I see it, you're going to kill me anyway. If you manage to get out of your new cage, that is. Oh, and just so you know – that can only happen while I'm still breathing.'

He'd only ever felt that clench in his chest three times – finding Seth, holding Jake in his arms only two nights before and then that first time he'd stared into the eyes of a serryn unleashed.

And unleashed she had been. Ropes and manacles around his wrists and ankles transforming instantly from sexual play to restrictors. The cruelty in her lifeless eyes as she'd tortured, taunted and subjugated him in the days that followed – used him as nothing more than a plaything to sate her sadism as much as her desires.

Never would he be that out of control again. Never would he be helpless at the hands of another serryn.

And he was *not* losing another brother to one of them.

This was not the time to let his fury rage. Not yet. Leila wouldn't be getting out of the building. That was a fact.

This was about saving Jake first and foremost.

Her punishment would follow.

'So?' she asked. 'Are you ready to make the right decision?'

He forced himself to smile. 'I like this side of you. It makes my plans for you so much easier.'

'Shame you'll be putting them on hold then. Where is she, Caleb? Or I go and ask Jake. And I won't be held accountable for his actions.'

He exhaled curtly through gritted teeth. 'Three floors down. Only door on the left.'

'Wasn't hard, was it?' she said. 'And you'd better be telling me the truth.'

'There's only one way you'll find out.'

She raked him slowly with her gaze before turning on her heels. She unlocked the door, but instead of stepping straight out, she looked over her shoulder at him. Her gaze lingered longer than she should have been comfortable with, something behind her eyes he couldn't quite work out. But despite him thinking for a moment that she was going to speak, she turned her back on him and stepped out of the room, leaving him with the painful thud of his slow beating heart.

❋ ❋ ❋

Hands trembling, Leila locked the library door. She didn't have time to think – she had to get out of there and get out of there fast. She looked down the dim corridor towards the lounge. Silence rebounded towards her.

Caleb had said Jake was in the penthouse, but there was no guarantee he was.

Slipping off her heels, she crept stealthily down into the darkness and scanned the empty lounge, the whole place emanating on an eerie, translucent shade of dark grey. The balcony doors were shut, the blackened glass blocking out most of what lay beyond other than an orb in the sky that could have just as easily been mistaken for the moon had Leila not been so sure it was daytime. She glanced at the door out of the penthouse, and then straight ahead towards Jake's room.

She needed her book. Wanted her book. Let alone her Kit Box. But she had no time to risk looking for either. Getting Alisha out of there, herself out of there, was all that mattered.

Or at least be able to warn her. To tell her what she needed to do to save herself – to stop Caleb from using her should the worst happen.

Stepping up to the door, she keyed in the code, the pessimistic part of her not expecting it to open. She heaved a sign of relief as it did, the click reverberating around the silence like a cough mid-prayer in church.

Leila stepped out into the hallway and quietly closed the door behind her. She ran down the hallway as fast as her weak legs would carry her and stepped into the open elevator. As the doors closed, she gripped the handrail, willing the elevator to descend faster.

The doors slid open three floors down to reveal a less plush but still well-maintained hallway. She peered out and checked left and right. Seeing it was clear, she took a left and headed down to the only door.

She keyed in the previous code in reverse and, as the door unlocked, her heart jolted. She warily pushed the door all the way open, and welled up the minute her eyes met her sister's across the room.

Alisha stood immediately from the sofa, her eyes wide with confusion as Leila closed the door behind her.

'Lei?' She looked over her sister's shoulder to check for company and frowned when she saw she was alone. 'What are you doing down here? Is everything okay? What's going on?'

She met Alisha halfway across the room, grabbed her and hugged her tight. 'Are you all right?' Leila asked as she pulled back a few inches so she could gaze into her eyes. She brushed back her hair as she'd used to when Alisha was small, the feel of her close to her again forcing her to fight back the tears accumulating at the back of her throat.

'I'm fine,' Alisha said, her brown eyes bewildered. 'What's happening? I've been worried sick. No you. No Jake. He said you and Caleb spent the night together. I mean properly. What's he talking about?'

'Things have got a little complicated, but we're leaving now. I'll explain on the way,' she said, catching Alisha's arm, tugging her towards the door.

'What do you mean "complicated"? Where's Jake? Who's escorting us?'

'It's still daylight out there.'

'It's still Blackthorn.' Alisha yanked her arm free and took a step back. 'What's the hurry? Does Caleb know you're down here?'

'Yes.'

She frowned again. 'Why don't I believe you?'

'How else would I have got in here?'

'So where is he? Or Jake? What have you done? Where are they?'

'Walk and I'll talk,' she said, grabbing her arm again.

Alisha took a step back. 'You've done something.' Her eyes flared in panic. 'You haven't hurt Jake, have you?'

'I haven't seen Jake.' She caught hold of her sister's arm again and tugged her out into the hallway.

'Caleb?'

'He's trapped in a wax circle in the penthouse. But the barrier only lasts when I'm a certain distance from it. A hundred feet or so.' Leila pulled her into the open elevator. 'So we have to get out of here before Caleb realises that.'

Alisha pulled her arm from her sister's grasp again. 'He's what?'

Leila pressed the button for the door to close. 'I had no choice.'

'So we *are* running. I knew it. Trapping Caleb? He's going to be furious! What were you thinking?'

She stared at the buttons. 'What I've been thinking of ever since I stepped into this godforsaken place – getting out.' She pressed for the lowest floor. She guessed it didn't go to ground level, only to the stone staircase, but at least she knew the way from there.

'But I thought you and Caleb were getting along. With all the stuff Jake said…'

'Seriously?' Leila snapped.

'But Lei, the whole building is on lock down during the day. No one comes in and no one goes out – not without Caleb or Jake's say-so. This place is like a fortress until dusk.'

Her heart thudded, her pulse rate kicking into an uncomfortable pace. 'You must know the codes.'

She shrugged. 'They change every night. I watched Jake earlier in case I needed to come and see you so I know the corridor ones, but that's all.'

'Then we'll work with that. We need to get as far as the fire-exit doors. No one's stupid enough to put those on a code.'

'Lei, you do know Blackthorn's more dangerous by day, don't you? That's when all the cons are out.'

'No more dangerous out there than it is in here.'

Leila stepped out of the elevator, pulled Alisha with her and took the sharp right through the door to the stone stairwell.

Alisha yanked her to a standstill half-way down the steps. 'Leila, stop. Take a breath. You're scaring me. Please. Tell me what's happened.'

'Sophie's here in Blackthorn,' Leila declared, continuing down the steps. 'You want to find her, right?'

Alisha followed behind her with less speed. 'But we already knew she was here.'

'But not what she's involved in. We were right in suspecting she came here to get vengeance for what happened to Mum. She got in with some vigilante group that's killing off key vampire players. It seems like what happened to Jake was no accident.'

Alisha came to a standstill midway down the next flight of steps. 'What are you saying?'

Leila turned to face her. 'The group were on a suicide mission, Alisha.'

'You're telling me whoever Jake was feeding on wanted him to kill her?'

'That's what Caleb believes. Enough to go after her, anyway. Now do you understand?'

Alisha frowned. 'Does Jake know about any of this?'

'If Caleb knows, Jake knows.'

'He hasn't said anything to me.'

'Big surprise there,' Leila said, taking the next few steps down to the next stairwell. 'Now will you keep moving?'

'No, this is about more than Sophie. What are you not telling me, Lei?'

Leila reached the bottom of the stairwell and turned to face her sister rooted half-way up the stairs. 'We'll talk when we're out of here.'

'No.' Alisha stepped back, her voice echoing against the stone chasm. 'You're scaring the shit out of me. I've never seen you like this. You tell me now or I'm not going any further. What the hell has happened?'

❆ ❆ ❆

Caleb paced the circle that bound him, his hands clenching into fists before flexing again. She'd closed and locked the door behind her, blocking out any chance of his yells making it down to Jake. Or hearing Jake's rebounding back to him.

If she'd gone after him, he'd kill her slowly and painfully. He knew that then and there with every sinew of his body that was burning in rage.

He'd lost one brother to a serryn and there was no way he'd lose another. Not even to the beautiful, hazel-eyed serryn he'd created. And his anger sickened him. It was an emotion he used to thrive on; now it felt painfully unfamiliar – like revisiting a house with bad memories.

He slammed his hand against the invisible barrier in fury. It sparked, but weakly. He frowned. He placed his hand up to it again. Pins and needles shot up his arm but its strength seemed to be dwindling.

He didn't know if it was his rage that muted the sensation.

Or if the spell was on a time limit. Or a distance limit.

Leila was moving further away and with it, seemingly, was the strength that bound him there.

❆ ❆ ❆

'Please, Alisha. We don't have time for this.'

'And that's what's scaring me. Something *has* happened. What has he done to you?'

She exhaled with impatience. 'Nothing.'

'Don't give me that. Has he hurt you?'

Leila's gaze lingered on her sister's, Alisha's brown eyes wide and troubled. 'Not yet.'

'What do you mean "not yet"?'

She knew she had no choice. She had to do something to make her move. And she had to tell her in order to explain why she had to do what she needed her to do if they didn't get out of there.

'I'm not what you think I am, Alisha. I'm not just an ordinary interpreter – I'm a serryn.'

Alisha's eyes widened, confusion igniting them.

Leila took a couple of steps back up towards her. 'Caleb used to hunt serryns. He hates them. A serryn killed his brother.'

'Seth?' She narrowed her eyes. 'But Seth was killed in a fight. Jake told me about it once.'

'Jake didn't know the truth. He's only just found out.'

She frowned. 'You? A serryn?'

'Do you remember Sophie talking about them? When she was researching how to kill vampires?'

'I know what a serryn is. I just want to know why the hell I didn't know you were one?'

'I didn't tell either of you because there was no point. I'm inactive. Obviously.'

'Did Grandfather know?'

'He was the one who told me.'

'How did *he* know?'

She couldn't tell her the whole story – not there, not then. 'He just did. Like with a lot of things. Please, Alisha. We have to go. Now.'

Alisha's eyes were heavy with trepidation. 'If Caleb knew all this, that must mean he was never going to let you go.'

'Exactly,' Leila remarked, her impatience lacing her tone with more sarcasm than she intended. 'Why do you think I'm trying to get out?'

'I am going to sort this,' Alisha said turning on her heels.

Leila hurried up the steps and caught hold of her arm again. 'And plead with him to let me go, like I've been doing all night, all day? For once in your life, listen to me, Alisha. He could be on his way already. If we don't get out of here now, we might never get out. Trust me. Please.' Then she said more quietly, 'Please.'

'If I had any idea, I never would have brought you here. You should have told me.'

'Maybe I should have. But none of that matters now. All that matters is getting the hell out of here. Please.'

Alisha studied her eyes pensively for a moment. Then she nodded, following her down the steps.

They burst through the door at the bottom of the stairwell.

Alisha stepped up to the first doors, the first code panel. 'I'm telling you, I only have the internal ones though.'

'We'll get as far as we can,' Leila said, glancing anxiously over her shoulder.

Alisha keyed in the code and the door unlocked. They hurried through and stopped at the next set of doors.

Keying in the next code, Alisha glanced across at her sister. 'You're shaking, Lei.'

'I know.'

Alisha led the way through, her and Leila all but running down to the next set of doors. She keyed in the next code and they burst through the next set of doors.

Leila stepped up to the fire-exit doors and tried to force them open. She rattled the handle before slamming her hand. 'No!' she snapped.

'I warned you,' Alisha said.

Leila looked anxiously over her shoulder in the direction they had come from then ahead again. 'We keep going.'

'To where?'

'That goes into the club, right?'

'And it's all sealed, just like the rest of the place.'

'The same code might work.'

'It might, but...'

'No buts, we have to try.'

Alisha keyed in the next code and yanked open the door.

Leila hurried over to the door that she recognised. 'Do you know the code to the office?'

'It'll be the same as the others – 4328. But it's a dead end in there.'

'There are things we can use though. Get the next door open ready,' she said, keying in the code and stepping into the room.

Leila marched over to the desk, to the sword displayed on the wall behind it. Placing her sandals on the desk, she lifted Caleb's sword from the holder, the weight of the cold metal bringing the tip of the blade thudding to the floor. She caught her breath with the shock of it, her shoulders nearly wrenched from their sockets.

She grabbed her sandals and, conserving her energy, dragged the sword behind her towards the door.

Alisha stood at the open door in the corridor, her eyes widening when she looked down at the weapon. 'What the hell are you expecting to do with that?'

'It's the only bit of defence we've got,' Leila declared, leading the way, metal scratching against stone.

'Defence? Just how bad is this?'

Leila looked over her shoulder. 'Just keep moving, Alisha.'

Alisha got in front of her and keyed the code into the next set of doors. 'You can't use a sword? Are you crazy?' She stopped at the next set of doors and led them out into the main club.

It was eerily silent, its emptiness emphasising their cavernous surroundings, the lighting too dim for Leila to be able to detect the corners of the expanse. She stepped forward onto the hardwood floor and looked over her shoulder at the bar that extended along the length of the back wall. Even empty it still had the lingering scent of smoke, alcohol and sex – all no doubt the very core of the booths that surrounded what she guessed to be the dance floor.

'That's the main door,' Alisha said, hurrying ahead.

Leila took a few steps forward, lifting the sword from its nail-like scrape on the wooden floor.

Alisha slammed her palm against the keypad before trying another, then turned to face her sister, giving her all the right signals that they were trapped.

❄ ❄ ❄

Caleb paced as he counted, just as much about keeping himself calm as the fact he'd worked out the barrier was weakening roughly every minute or so.

She was moving fast, that was for sure.

After another minute, he placed his hand on the barrier again.

The sparks were definitely weakening.

Another minute, two, three, four passed until, thrusting his hand into the force-field again, there was nothing more than the dying momentum of a sparkler consuming its last shred of oxygen.

And he was out.

Without hesitation, he kicked the door full force, once, twice, three times. Despite it being inward opening, it buckled at the fourth kick, even the solid mahogany unable to withstand the force of his fury.

Pulling the splintered door open, he stormed out into the hallway, marched down towards the lounge, his stomach wrenching, his heart aching at the prospect of what he would find.

The lounge was empty but, as he looked up, he saw Jake striding towards him from his end of the penthouse.

'What the fuck's going on?' Jake demanded, his eyes flashing concern. 'What the hell was all that noise?'

Relief soared through him, his brother's bewildered gaze telling him he really was clueless.

It would be her only saving grace.

'Leila's out,' Caleb declared.

'What?'

Caleb marched up the steps towards the door.

'What do you mean she's out?' Jake asked, following behind him. 'How?'

'The clever little witch bound me in a wax circle.'

'She bound you?'

'Yes, Jake – bound me. Tricked me, trapped me, bound me.'

'How did she do that?'

'It doesn't matter,' Caleb said, marching down towards the elevator. He stepped inside, Jake close behind him. 'And she's gone for Alisha.'

'But she can't get out of here. She's got to know that.'

'She will now.'

'What are you going to do?'

Caleb looked back at him and the troubled gaze in his eyes. He stepped out into the corridor and headed to the stairwell.

'Caleb,' Jake said, catching hold of him. He stepped in front of him, blocking his way, his hands to his chest. 'Caleb, take it easy, will you?'

'I'll take it easy when I've got her,' Caleb said, brushing past him.

Jake blocked his way again. 'Not like this, you're not. You need to calm down. You go after her like this and you're going to break her in two. You need to get your head straight.'

'My head is straight.'

'No, it's not,' Jake said, pushing him back again. 'So she tried to escape. You can't blame her for that. But she's going nowhere. Just calm down and then we'll go and get her.'

'And give her time to concoct something else?'

'You're furious she outsmarted you, fine. I know why you're angry but I'm okay, Caleb. She could have come after me, but she didn't. You must be able to see that. If she wanted me dead, I would be.' He cupped his brother's neck. 'I'm okay.'

Caleb broke from his gaze and paced the width of the corridor. 'She should have taken you down, Jake. Any self-respecting serryn would have taken you down.'

'She's not like them. You know it and I know it. And that's just as much what this is about, isn't it? You can't get your head around it, but you're going to have to.'

Caleb brushed past him but Jake caught his arm.

'No,' Jake said. 'Sorry, Caleb. This is not her fault. She doesn't deserve your fury or your vengeance. Don't make her suffer for this, Caleb. Don't make her suffer for how you feel. If you hurt her off the back of your temper, I will lose all respect for you. I mean it.'

❋ ❋ ❋

Leila scanned for other options – windows, other doors – her pulse racing at a painful rate. 'There has to be another way out of here. You know this place. Is there a cellar? A window we can get through? The ladies' toilets?'

'Every window is reinforced, just like the shutters that come down. Unbreakable. Bulletproof,' Alisha declared.

Leila dropped the sword and her sandals to the floor and swept past her sister. She rattled the handles to the front door but they didn't budge. Instead she resorted to kicking the door with so much force that Alisha stepped back.

'Lei!' Alisha said startled. 'You need to calm down. We will sort it. I will talk to Caleb. Jake will be on our side—'

'Oh, how I'd love to live in your world for just ten minutes, Alisha,' she said spinning to face her.

Alisha folded her arms. 'Don't snap at me.'

'Then don't say such bloody ridiculous things!' She marched over to pick up the sword again. 'Not every problem has a solution – not if it doesn't involve hair, make-up or boyfriend troubles.'

'Why are you being like this?'

'Because I'm here because of you! I'm here because of what you got yourself involved in! Because you wouldn't listen to me! And now everything Grandfather taught us about is going to happen. The world we know is going to be over because of us!'

Alisha's startled gaze narrowed in confusion. 'What the hell are you talking about?'

'There's a leader, Alisha. A destined vampire leader. Surely you remember that from Grandfather's teachings?'

'I remember something about it. But that's just a fairytale.'

It came out before she had time to even think of the implications. 'No, Alisha, it's not. And it sure as hell isn't for me. The vampire leader needs to sacrifice a serryn to instigate the prophecy.'

Alisha took a step back, horror merging with confusion.

'Caleb's the leader, Alisha.'

Alisha's eyes flared. She shook her head. She laughed nervously. 'This is some kind of wind-up, right?'

'Do I look like I'm winding you up? He needs to kill me. The freedom of his entire kind depends on it. *Now* do you understand? I can't be near him, Alisha. He triggers things. Things I can't control. And for every moment I spend with him, I become more and more what he wants me to be.'

Alisha heaved a shaky sigh. 'What have I done?'

Regret struck Leila deep. She stared at her sister for a moment then stepped back over to her. She gently brushed Alisha's hair back from her face. 'I'm sorry, Alisha. I didn't mean to go off on you like that. You didn't know. You couldn't possibly. This isn't your fault.'

'It looks like it from where I'm standing. It looks like this is *all* my fault.'

Leila sighed heavily, lowered her head before scanning the room and looking back at her sister. 'Alisha, I need you to listen to me. It's really important.'

Alisha stared at her with her glossy eyes.

'If we don't get out of here, I need you to take every opportunity you can to drink a vampire's blood – Jake's preferably.'

Her eyes widened. 'What?'

'It's more important than you know.'

'Why? What's going on?'

'It's the only way to stop the line jumping.'

Alisha stared at her.

'It doesn't work if you're a serryn already,' Leila explained. 'But if anything happens to me—'

'What do you mean, "if anything happens"? It only jumps if...' She grabbed her sister's hand. 'No. No, you are not going to do anything stupid.'

'You're going to be okay. As soon as this place opens, the first opportunity you get, you're going to be gone.'

'I'm not leaving you.'

'I will find a way through this, but I can only do that without you here. You always go on at me to let you take some responsibility, so here it is. You do everything you can to get yourself out of here.'

'And do what? Go where? With vampire blood in me I'll have nowhere *to* go. I'm not doing this. I can't.'

'You can,' Leila said, grabbing her hand and squeezing. 'And you will. You need to contact the VCU. You need to tell them everything. They have to know what's coming. And you have to find Sophie.'

'Sophie can look after herself. She knows what she's doing.' She heaved a frustrated sigh, pulled away, her hands clenched in her hair. 'I should have told you. Why the hell didn't I tell you? Then none of this would be happening.'

Leila frowned. She knew a guilty look on her sister's face like no one else did. 'Tell me what?'

Alisha shook her head, but Leila could see the panic in her eyes.

'Alisha?' she said again, despite the gut feeling that she didn't want to hear what was to come. 'What should you have told me?'

But the door burst open, two outlines appearing in the dimness across the dance floor. She didn't need to see him clearly – every single hair that stood up on the back of her neck told her Caleb had found her.

Leila caught hold of Alisha and tugged her behind her. With all her strength she lifted the sword off the floor, unable to do anything but let the flat of the blade temporarily fall onto her shoulder, nearly buckling as it did so. She'd swing with all she was worth if he came a step closer. She knew she'd only get one attempt but she'd do whatever small amount of damage she could.

Caleb strolled towards her, each step steady but purposeful, Jake close behind him.

He stopped just a couple of feet away, glanced down at the sword, his eyes glinting with amusement as he looked back up at her again. 'There was a time when handling a male's sword was a crime punishable by death.'

'You stay away from us.'

'Have you any idea how difficult it is to wield a sword? To penetrate anybody with it, let alone a vampire?'

'I'm willing to give it a go.'

He took another step closer. 'Go on then.'

She took an instinctive step back, knocking into Alisha, her grip tightening on the hilt. 'I'm warning you.'

'Still so much to learn, fledgling.'

'And I suppose you know it all.'

His eyes narrowed. 'A hell of a lot more than you.'

'Leave her alone,' Alisha demanded, stepping between them before Leila had a chance to catch her.

She took one hand off the sword only to feel the strain on the wrist left behind. She grabbed it with both hands again. 'Alisha, don't,' Leila warned with a hushed whisper, as her sister blocked Caleb's way.

'No,' Alisha said firmly. 'He can't do this to you.' She looked up at Caleb just as Jake pulled alongside him, his eyes brimming with concern. 'You gave me your word, Caleb.'

'Things change, Alisha.'

'I can't believe you're allowing this,' Alisha said, turning her attention on Jake. 'You promised we'd be okay.'

'Alisha,' Jake said, reaching out to her. He looked genuinely troubled; more than that, he looked worried – a fact that chilled Leila even more.

'Get her out the way, Jake,' Caleb said.

'No,' Leila said, clenching the sword tighter as she tried to sidestep her sister and get between them.

Despite Alisha recoiling, Jake caught hold of her with ease, pulling her to him.

'You leave her alone!' Leila demanded, preparing herself to swing, however futile her effort would be.

But Caleb snatched the sword from her hand in an instant and pulled her back against him. He wrapped a vice-like arm around her, keeping both of hers pinned to her waist, his chest a solid wall against her back as he gripped his sword in his free hand.

'Take Alisha back upstairs,' Caleb said.

'Get off my sister!' Alisha warned, trying to pull Jake's hand away, anger emanating in her eyes amidst the pain of betrayal.

Leila kicked and flayed, but Caleb held her tight against him. 'Temper, temper, serryn,' he said, turning her away from Alisha's equal protests.

'You get your hands off me!' Leila warned through gritted teeth.

'You're so lucky he's still alive,' he uttered softly against her ear.

'If he hurts her…'

'He's not going to. Not if her big sister stops with the escapology stunts.'

She kicked at his shins, tried flaying against him again. But even then, trapped against him, the stirring inside astounded her, irritated her.

She looked across her shoulder to see Alisha disappear back through the doors with Jake.

'No!' she snapped again, as much out of despair as protest.

'We can stay like this until the place opens up in a few hours, if that's what you want,' Caleb said, holding her tighter, managing it with ease despite only having one free hand. 'We could give all the guests a floor show, or you can calm yourself down before I'm tempted to do some really bad things to you. You'd better believe I'm just in the mood.'

After a few more moments, she stopped struggling. As she reluctantly stilled, he let her go.

She turned to face him as she backed away.

Enticing eyes locked on hers, Caleb lifted the sword to her collar bone, forcing her to freeze, the blade poised but not touching her, his hand impressively unwavering.

'You worked out how to get out then,' she said, trying not to let resentment cloud her tone.

As cold metal met her skin, she caught her breath.

He slid the tip of the blade gently from her collar bone down her cleavage. 'Unlike you.' He looked back at her, his eyes glinting.

Her gaze didn't falter from his, her breath held, her body tense as he slid the sword back up her neck to under her chin, knocking it up slightly, the blade caressing her skin with lethal control.

She glowered at the taunting amusement in his eyes.

'Take a seat,' he said. 'We need to talk.'

He stepped over to the bar. Leaving his sword on the counter, he returned with a bottle and a couple of glasses. He carried them to the nearest booth and indicated for her to follow.

Reluctantly she did, taking the seat opposite his.

He looked painfully at ease, worryingly resolute, as he placed a measure of whisky in each tumbler before sliding one to her.

She didn't dare take her eyes off him as he leaned back, placed a foot up on the seat beside her, blocking her exit.

He stretched one arm across the back of the booth and knocked back a mouthful of drink, his stony gaze chilling her as it rested squarely on hers. A stony gaze that lacerated her somewhere deep. Eyes that she had mistaken as being capable of affection now looked back at her as if she was nothing more than a commodity.

This was the real Caleb – not the one who had wiped away her tears and kissed her like he meant it.

This was a serryn hunter pinning down his prey.

She felt so stupid, so humiliated, so rejected. And it wrenched more than she knew it should.

'So much hatred in such beautiful eyes,' he coaxed as he lowered his glass.

'Go fuck yourself, Caleb,' Leila said, surprising herself with the venom in her tone.

'Only you get away with talking to me like that.' He slid the tumbler closer to her. 'Drink. It'll dull what's to come.'

She lifted the glass and poured the contents onto the floor before letting go of it, letting it smash onto the floor, her defiant gaze locked on his.

He had used her. All along he had done nothing but use her.

And *nobody* used *her*.

Especially not someone she had dared to start to feel something for.

He licked his incisor as he smiled, looked at the floor then back at her. 'It's good to know your petulant streak hasn't been suppressed. I've always liked that about you. How you're willing to fight until the bitter end. Such an admirable quality.'

'Thanks for the eulogy, but this isn't over yet.'

'Of course, and let's not forget your optimism. Such an enviable, childlike trait. Or maybe it's just naive denial.'

'Do you really think it's going to be that simple, Caleb? You take a bite out of me, bleed me dry and it's all over?'

'Sounds that way to me.'

'I won't go to the Brink easily. And I won't hand over my soul easily, either. You may have the upper hand here, you may have physical strength on your side in these four walls, but there won't be any of that there. Once we're there, we're equals. That's why only a serryn soul can take you on. And I'll fight you, Caleb. I can't let this happen. I want you to know that. I'm not going down without giving it everything I've got.'

'I wouldn't expect anything less,' he said, finishing the remains of his drink before pushing the glass aside. He leaned forward, resting both arms on the table. 'So does this mean you've stopping running, Leila. Are you ready to face this?'

'Are you?'

'I'm ready to take you when I want, where I want, how I want. I have been from the minute you walked in here. You're already mine. It seems you always have been.' He leaned back in the booth seat. He poured another drink but slid the glass towards her. 'So let's have a toast,' he said, keeping the bottle for himself. He clinked it against her glass. 'One of us is going to save the world. Sounds like game on to me.'

She leaned forward, her palms flat on the table. 'This is far from a game, Caleb. You're talking about evoking civil wars. Devastation.

Segmentation and fragmentation even amongst your own. And it will spread to other locales. Once this starts, there is no going back.'

'That's the whole point.'

'There are other ways.'

'Amidst decades of suffering? Until somebody decides this was never a good idea in the first place? Until some new, less liberal council comes to the forefront and decides that actually they'd rather do away with the new laws and resolve we have no entitlement to anything after all. Or until they decide to cull us altogether? And with these boundaries, what chance would we stand?'

'It would never come to that. Things will improve. It just takes time.'

'You don't believe that any more than I do. Your kind – you so-called first species – don't even trust your own. How are you ever going to trust anything remotely different to you? This will never improve – not as long as you're in charge.'

'And things will be so much better when you are? You don't want things to get better for us all – you just want to swap places.'

'Too right I do.'

'Then you're no better.'

'Or maybe our kinds are more similar than they'd like to admit to and that's what worries them. That's why they have to keep us under lock and key – because you don't like the uncomfortable truth staring back at you of what you can become.'

'Our kinds are nothing alike.'

'And the fact you say that so vehemently only confirms my point – that's how we'll always be perceived: no common ground. And you can't share space without common ground, Leila, or at least a perception of it. We're here while your kind bide their time – nothing more. A backdrop of false promises does nothing to improve it.'

'Then I have no choice but to stop you.'

He exhaled tersely. 'I love the way you say that as if you really believe it possible.'

'And I hate the way you make out like it isn't.'

'So what plans do you have to stop me? Trap me in another circle? I'm hardly likely to fall for that again.'

'But you did fall for it the first time. It's all about what you least expect.'

He broke a hint of a smile, knocked back the remains of the drink. He leaned over to the floor and picked up a fragment of glass. Leaning on the table between them, he twisted the two inch shard deftly in his fingers, his attention focused on the motion, the glass glinting in the dim light.

For a moment he fixated her with the rotating motion to the point she didn't notice him reach out for her hand that rested on the tabletop.

As soon as he gripped her wrist she wanted to recoil, but she refused to let herself. She refused to show him any fear.

She was forced to extend her elbow as he drew her hand closer so it was equidistant between them.

She stared into his eyes, her silence the only defiance she could offer him as he maintained his unrelenting grip on her wrist.

'The only reason you didn't kill Jake when you had the chance was because you knew you weren't getting out of here, wasn't it?' he said. 'You just wanted me to know you could. Just like you wanted to tell Alisha to escape so that's one less backup. You've told her everything. And you know that means I can't let her go now, don't you? Not ever.'

'You weren't letting her go anyway. Ever.'

He spread her thumb and forefinger, exposing the delicate flesh between. She clenched her other hand in her lap out of sight, resolute not to show an ounce of fear.

'You really don't like the fact I could have killed him, do you, Caleb?' she said, unable not to goad him as he dared to try and wield such control over her. 'That I *chose* not to. It's hard to justify what you're planning to do to me when time and time again I prove you wrong, isn't it? I think there's actually a conscience in there. Deeply buried maybe, but there all the same.'

'And time and time again, I'll prove you wrong, Leila.'

'So prove me wrong now.'

His green eyes remained squarely locked on hers as she stared him down. He drew her hand a little closer, placed the tip of the shard of glass against her flesh and raked it lightly, coaxingly over her skin. 'Your resilience has improved these last couple of days.'

'My resilience has always been there. I've just got no reason to hide it anymore. Whatever I do or say will make no difference to you. You only see what you want to see. You'll only ever see what you want to see. Just as you'll do whatever you want to do. Make me bleed, Caleb, if it'll make you feel better.'

'It's not about making you bleed, Leila. I just like the taste of you,' he said, dragging the glass gently through her skin. 'Watching the way you catch your breath,' he said, his eyes glinting darkly.

Before the first droplet of blood could hit the table he lifted her hand to his mouth, parted his lips and took a slow and steady draw, his eyes locked on hers.

And despite fighting it, instinctively she did catch her breath, hypnotised by those green eyes that almost absorbed her soul as easily as he consumed her blood. Heat pooled at the base of her abdomen as she watched him feed on her unashamedly, as his cool, soft lips removed every trace of blood.

'Such sweet nothings,' she quipped.

He licked her blood from his lips. 'I'll take you on a bed of roses, if that's what you want.'

'Thorns intact? Prepared to bleed with me, are you?'

'Maybe a drop or two.'

She stared deep into his eyes that transfixed her with their stare. And she would fight him, with all that was left in her. She couldn't save herself, she might not be able to save her sisters, but somehow she would stop this happening. And he was right about her running – it wouldn't happen until she stopped and turned to face what had terrified her for too long.

This was her fate. And there in that dim, empty room, she finally had no choice but to acknowledge it.

'Then roses it will be,' she said.

'Pain with the pleasure,' he replied.

'Just as you like it, right?'

His smile was fleeting. 'By the time I'm done, you won't care what's happening to you.'

'By the time I'm done, you won't even know what hit you.'

He smiled, lowered her hand again and released it, his attention diverted as in the distance the sound of the glass shutters lifting sent a quiet buzz through the club.

'Dusk,' he said, looking back at her. 'Perfect timing.'

Chapter Twenty-four

Leila didn't know what she expected, but it wasn't to be led back upstairs and certainly not back to the library. She warily glanced at the splintered and battered door on her way through, making it perfectly clear what temper Caleb had left in.

She followed him over to the back wall of bookcases beyond the table.

When he removed a handful of books from one of the shelves and a secret chamber was revealed, a surge of panic hit her chest.

It was only a small space – books and paperwork piled on the floor-to-ceiling shelves. It was the door to the left that caught her attention though – the door that Caleb promptly opened to reveal a dark void beyond.

'Where are you taking me?' she asked.

'Out.'

'Through there?'

'I don't trust that we're still not being watched.'

'And then?'

'There's someone I want you to meet.'

'Why don't I like the sound of that?'

'You will. Trust me. Maybe more than you'd like to admit.'

Her heart pounded. The thought crept into her mind – Sophie. She didn't dare vocalise it, least of all for fear of being disappointed. She watched him warily as he stepped into what her adjusted vision could see was the top of a stairwell.

He braced his arms on the doorframe. 'Do you need to be dragged?'

Knowing it wasn't an idle threat was sufficient to make her step over the threshold.

She descended the dark, dank and cold steps, the lengthy corridor at the foot of them maintaining the same unappealing attributes. Neon lights flashed through gaps in the boarded-up windows that ran along the length of the corridor.

Leila glanced anxiously at the heavy doors they passed along the left. 'What is this place?'

'Storage chambers and archives from when it was a library.'

'What do you use it for now?'

He glanced across at her, the hint of a smirk doing nothing to assure her.

'Forget it,' she said. 'I don't want to know.'

After several twists and turns along further corridors and through abandoned rooms, Caleb keyed in a code at sliding doors.

Night air filled the musty room as Caleb pulled opened the door. She followed him out into the alley.

It was the epitome of what she had come to know of Blackthorn – murky, gloomy, abandoned and rife with threat.

Parts of Blackthorn had been a blur when she'd been driven through them the night before but now, as she walked up onto the main street with him, as he led her through the crowds, the noise and brazen lights, there was nothing to hide the neglect, the squalor, the unpleasantness.

The noise levels rebounded off her eardrums – the music reverberating from bars, from open windows above, laughter and jeers emanating between shouting.

She sidestepped litter – broken bottles, discarded food bags.

As the crowds thickened as they reached a denser part of Blackthorn, once or twice Caleb caught her arm, tugging her out of the way of an approaching crowd, his arm sliding down her waist on one occasion, making her spine ache with the intimacy of it. Then he'd let her go, making her walk alone again.

There were the occasional stares, mainly from females. She wondered at first if it was because they sensed what she was, but realised it was more than likely because of whom she was with. She saw them sizing her up, their frowns telling her they were trying to work out why she was the one walking down the street by his side.

The further they went, the more the crowds started to dispel, until he led her down a couple of cobbled side streets, to a quieter part of the district. Heading down a lane, Caleb led her towards what would have once been a grand Edwardian house.

Caleb slipped his hand into hers; the feel of his cold, strong hand gripping hers sent her spiralling back to their encounters in his penthouse – encounters that now felt like a distant dream. Out there in the starkness of reality, their intimacy almost seemed unreal.

She lowered her gaze from the curious stares as he led her though the front door and into the dim and sordid-looking bar.

A melancholic singing voice echoed his misery over the speakers, the conversation around the room troublingly low. The fact everyone was segregated off in booths told her this wasn't as much a social arena as one where business meetings were conducted – trade-offs, shady deals. This was the kind of arena she'd envisaged she would have ended up in had she not been proved more than just financially lucrative.

He selected a U-shaped booth in a dark recess and indicated for her to slide in first, shifting her around to the centre where they would both have a clear view of the bar.

'Is this where we're meeting whoever we came here to see?' she asked.

'It is,' he said, his attention instantly diverted to the tall and slender waitress heading over.

She raked Caleb with a swift, admiring look, her large brown eyes smiling. 'Caleb Dehain. It's been a while.'

'You're looking good, Flick.'

Leila glanced across at him, his reciprocating smile prompting a tight coil in the pit of her stomach.

Her painted red lips, a stunning contrast to her glossy, black bobbed hair, parted briefly. 'What can I get you?'

'House whisky will be fine.'

'And your friend? Shall I get her a milkshake?'

Caleb's smile broadened. 'I think she'll need more than that.'

Flick grinned as if they shared some private joke, sending spirals of irritation through Leila. 'I don't doubt it,' she said before strolling away again.

'She's a charmer,' Leila sniped.

'She's a great girl.'

'A conquest I take it?'

He glanced across at her, but said nothing.

Leila scanned the bar. Her skin crawled just being there. 'If she's such a great girl, why's she working here?'

'We're in Blackthorn, honey – home of the free. We've got an abundance of choices here.'

'Is that why I'm here? You want to show me what life is like? You want to justify what you're planning to do to me? Do you think for one minute that your kind wouldn't do exactly the same if fortunes were reversed? And you call me sanctimonious.'

Flick came back over and placed two whiskies in front of them, her raised eyebrows telling them that she'd picked up on the tension at the table before sauntering away.

'Just tell me why you've brought me here?'

Caleb stretched his arm across the back of the seat behind her, rested one leg out along the seat as if he was settling in for the night. 'Not worried, are you?' he asked as he turned his head towards her, his eyes glinting in the shadows.

'This isn't exactly my kind of place.'

'This is where you'd be spending your time,' Caleb said, 'if you'd already embraced who you were. These are the kind of places you'd target, the people you'd rub shoulders with. You'd slink in here, wait for your target and lead them into some dark recess. This is how your life could have been if you'd come to avenge your mother like you should have.'

'If that isn't an advocate for how right I was not to, I don't know what is. What's your point?'

'You and I could have met in a place like this. If fate hadn't dealt us the hand she has.' He looked across at her as he lifted his glass to his lips. 'You might even have succeeded under different circumstances.'

'Don't play the king until you've got your crown, Caleb.'

He leaned into her ear. 'Of course, the alternative is more likely that I would have been a hell of a lot less restrained. I might not even have bothered to ask your name before I pinned you to the wall in some dark, private corner.'

She looked back at him, the turning of her head almost bringing her lips into contact with his. 'Are you flirting with me?' she asked, refusing to be intimidated.

He smiled. But his eyes narrowed as he watched someone stroll past. Man or vampire, Leila couldn't be sure. He lifted himself onto one of the bar stools directly ahead, his hunched body making him look much older than he was, which she guessed to be around late-thirties. It gave him a shifty look, someone who was used to ducking and diving, trying to keep himself out of the trouble he was clearly immersed in.

He raised his fingers from the bar, catching the attention of the barman who in turn nodded in acknowledgement. He prepared a drink before taking it over to place in front of him. Clearly a regular. And seemingly being a regular there was no good thing.

'See that guy at the bar?' Caleb asked.

'Man or vampire?'

'Oh, very much vampire.' Caleb lifted the tumbler to his lips. 'A very bad vampire.'

Leila glanced nervously back at the focus of Caleb's attention. He looked across both shoulders as if sensing he was being watched, but he didn't look in their direction.

Unease clenched the pit of her stomach. Something told her that's who they were there for, and the chill that swept through her told her things were about to get a whole lot worse because of it.

'From the tension in your body, I'm assuming the possibilities of why I've brought you here are already sparking,' Caleb added.

Her attention snapped to him again. Her heart lunged. Her pulse raced. She repressed the dark and sordid thoughts that filled her head before they could properly surface, before she could acknowledge them. 'He's who we're here for?'

'I want you to go and get to know him. I want you to see exactly how it works here.'

Her throat burned. She couldn't even speak through her shock, her horror at what he was suggesting.

'There are plenty of dark spaces around here, if you'd rather not be so public,' he added.

She stared at him, unable to conceal her revulsion at the suggestion. Something in her heart splintered despite the fact she should have known better. 'You can go to hell, Caleb,' she declared firmly, turning away from him to slide out of the booth.

He caught hold of her forearm, yanking her back next to him.

'You're going out there alone?' he asked. 'You really think that's wise?'

'Any less wise than staying here with you? I am not playing your sick games, Caleb. I know what you're trying to do. But I am not going there – not for anything.'

'Even when I'm handing you vengeance on a platter?'

Her pulse thrummed in her ears. 'Vengeance for what?'

'He comes here the same time every Monday and Thursday. That's so his buyers know where to find him. Vampire and human.'

'Buyers of what?'

'Entertainment. Indulgence.'

He reached into his back pocket and placed the photo in front of her. As soon as Leila saw the familiar picture of her sisters again, she almost wretched. 'Why don't you go and show it to him, Leila? Ask him if he recognises Sophie?'

She shook her head, subconsciously trying to force out the possibility. 'You're lying,' she said quietly.

'He'll do well out of a girl as pretty as your sister. Probably why he took her right off the street.'

Leila glowered back up at the vampire at the bar.

'So why don't you go and ask him if he's still got her?' Caleb added. 'He'll want some payment for the information though, so think carefully of what you're willing to give in exchange. I hear he's a harsh negotiator.'

The coldness of his suggestion lacerated her soul as much as the dark intent in his self-assured eyes, the icy stab of betrayal once again fracturing her heart. Leila gripped the seat, his hold on her forearm feeling colder than it ever had. 'You wouldn't risk me, with all I'm worth to you.'

'Oh, I won't be too far away. I might even watch.' He leaned into her ear. 'You let your mother down, Leila, and you let Alisha down by trying to escape tonight. Do you really want to let Sophie down too?'

'Her name is Sophia,' she said curtly. 'Only her loved ones call her Sophie.'

'So*phia*?' He smirked, unnerving her further. 'That makes a lot of sense.'

'What do you mean?'

'Why no one knew of her. Your little sister has given herself a nickname on the street. Phia apparently. Nice little play on words.

Very mature.' He leaned a little closer. 'Show him the photo of *Sophia* – see if there's a flash of recognition, do something about it or walk away a coward.'

She glared into his eyes. 'Just when I thought you couldn't get any lower.'

'I've got sublevels like you wouldn't believe. And so have you. Dig deep, serryn. Go do what you're made to do. Find out where she is and I'll get someone to go get her. Your choice.'

'And that's what this is really about, isn't it? Your last-ditch attempt to make me exactly what you want me to be.'

'And you'll be fine – as long as you're as good as I think you are.'

'My sister could be dead already. If you knew where she was and you did nothing…'

'I have word she's still very much alive. For now. And I have reliable sources.'

She snatched her gaze back up to Marid. She could. That was what grated at her most deeply. She could march over there, smile sweetly and lead him somewhere to find out the truth.

And if he was responsible, if he had done anything to hurt Sophie, she would gladly see him suffer. She would gladly watch him writhe in agony.

For what?

She shook the thoughts out of her head.

Would she even care after that point? Is that how she wanted her sisters to know her?

It was just another manipulative game. The realisation that he felt so little for her – the lack of respect, of understanding, of compassion tore through her.

He was not going to do it to her. He'd used the final hook he had, clearly thinking it would be the clincher. But he needed to learn that his biggest mistake was not in taking her there; it was in assuming he knew how she'd react.

'Do you think that I'm so weak that I don't know my own mind, Caleb?' she asked, snatching her gaze to his. 'Do you think I will let myself be manipulated by you any more than I already have? You've got everything you want by using Alisha as leverage over me and where has it got me? Do you think you can use Sophie too? Do you think it's that easy to mould me into whatever you want me to be? Do you think I can't see right through you?' She yanked her forearm from his. 'You want to ease your conscience before you kill me – find another way. You want to give me to him – you do it. You may possess me but you don't own me, Caleb. And you never will. I am not yours to toy with, to manipulate, to use to your own ends. Do you understand me?'

She slid out of the booth, too overwhelmed to notice at first that he had actually let her go.

She burst back through the door, letting it ricochet against the wall on her way out onto the cobbled street.

She saw the startled and somewhat amused stares of the clusters that stood around, but not one of them approached her.

And it was obvious why.

Some of them even took a backwards step as Leila glanced over her shoulder to see Caleb had followed her out.

She marched away, splashing through puddles, her anger, the pain at what he had suggested, too great to contain. The temptation to run was overwhelming, but she knew her trembling legs, let alone her heels, wouldn't be able to carry her fast or far enough.

He caught hold of her arm, spinning her to face him.

'Don't touch me!' she warned as she glowered up at him, yanking her arm free and stumbling back a step with the force. 'You stay away from me.'

She looked over his shoulder to see the clusters in the distance had stopped chatting to look in their direction. It was clearly a sight they didn't see often, and their morbid silence only confirmed that she was probably making an even bigger mistake challenging him in public than walking away from him in the first place.

But then maybe it wouldn't do him any harm to feel even a snippet of the humiliation he had bestowed on her.

'You might run this place but you don't run me,' she said loud enough for the others to hear. 'I will never, *ever* subjugate myself to you. So you can go and fuck yourself, fuck your prophecies and fuck the whole of Blackthorn for all I care.'

His green eyes narrowed, his composure like the still waters before the tsunami.

'Some great vampire leader you are.' She looked past him at the crowds. 'Did you hear that? That's what I think of your rise to supremacy. That's what I think—'

A split second later, she was in his arms, tight against his chest, his hand slammed over her mouth as he all but carried her to the alley on their left.

She caught her breath, kicked at his shins, digging her heels in, but he only lifted her higher, removed his hand from her mouth to pull the sandals from her feet.

He burst through the ajar door to the left, kicking it shut behind them, threw her sandals aside before slamming her up against the wall of the shaded interior of the abandoned house.

She glared up into his green eyes, now dark in the shadows, as he pinned her to the cold, hard wall with ease.

'What's the matter, Caleb? Is that composure faltering? Are you not getting your own way *again*?' She knew prodding him further was unforgiveable, just as much for her own sake as his, but her anger was too rife. 'What are you going to do this time? Because do you know what? I don't even care anymore. And you hate that, don't you? You've got no hold over me.'

His silence terrified her, his grip on her upper arms reminding her just how stupid she was being.

She could hear nothing but her own curt and shallow breaths in the silence, the dust of the abandoned room filling the air. She glanced nervously past him to the small vacuous room, the wooden, slatted stairs off to her right.

'I'm not scared of you, Caleb,' she added, glowering back at him.

'Yes, you are, because you may be brave but you're not stupid.'

She wasn't stupid and neither was he. And she could see it in his eyes. She knew he'd want to make more of this than taking her to the Brink in some dark, derelict house, against some chipped and stained wall. He'd want to make more of it than just claiming his Tryan status in a moment of anger. But the thrill of the possibility inexplicably soared through her – that she could have wound him up enough to make that composure break. That she had driven him to that knife-edge – that she was the one daring him to act.

The breeze wafted what was left of curtains through the cracked windows, making them appear as though they were breathing – slowly, erratically. A contrast to her rapid pulse.

But she wasn't as scared as she thought she'd be, and that gave her strength. She understood for the first time how the other serryns felt. How in control they felt and how addictive and thrilling that was. The release was intense. She had feared vampires all her life. Feared them since that vampire had tore her mother's life from her in an alley not dissimilar to the one Caleb had forced her down. She had beaten that vampire then and she would beat this one now.

Only her feelings now couldn't have been more different. His hands tight around her arms sent a flush of heat through her body, the heat gathering in her lower abdomen, her lips parted in anticipation of what he would do next. It wasn't just thrilling, it was arousing to the point she couldn't differentiate the two, her apprehension only intensifying it.

And as he let go and stepped away from the wall, she felt a laceration of disappointment. She wanted him to fight more. She needed him to fight more. And something inside her wanted him to retaliate – to punish her for the unforgiveable feelings stirring inside.

'What's wrong, Caleb?' she asked. 'Do you not know what to do now?'

His eyes darkened, but he didn't move.

She took another step towards him, goading him against every sinew of common sense. But something inside her was taking over, wanting to break the vampire who stood in front of her. The vampire who dared to bargain with her over her sisters, who dared to keep her there against her will. And their equal standing added to her arousal. It felt liberating – liberating enough that she didn't care of the consequences. The quiet voice inside her screamed for her to stop, but she couldn't. Like a lovers' argument, she knew she was pushing that one step too far. She knew she'd regret it, but she couldn't control it.

'Are you scared of me, Caleb?' she asked, taking another step towards him. 'After you dared to call me pathetic for being scared of you?'

He looked away, his eyes narrowed.

She should have read the signal. She should have taken notice of the way both his hands clenched; the tightness in his jaw, but the thrill was too much.

'To think how I've spent years in fear of you. Of all your kind. And look at you – you don't even know what to do with *yourself* let alone me. Am I one serryn too many for you? Have you finally lost your edge just when you need it most?'

His gaze snapped back to meet hers – his green eyes darkened enough to send a sweeping chill through her.

❊ ❊ ❊

The challenge in her eyes, let alone the belligerent insults that slipped so easily from those beautiful lips, was already more than enough to ignite the vampire inside as she dared to mock what she thought was weakness.

It was too much of a reminder. The house that they now stood in was not dissimilar to the one that first serryn had led him to. The bed he knew to be upstairs was not a far cry away from the metal contraption she had strapped him to for those agonising weeks – where she had tortured him, revelling in the pain and humiliation she inflicted on him physically, sexually, emotionally. All the time bringing back the hearts of the vampires she had slain – hearts of the young and mature alike – that she had relished in feeding to him.

He felt his temper surge, the need for control overwhelming him.

'I've had enough of your twisted games,' she added. 'You doing everything your way when you want. Let's finish this. Let's finish it now. Bite me. Take me to the Brink.'

'You think I won't?'

'I'm not afraid of facing this, Caleb. Are you?'

'You think you can take me on? You haven't seen a fraction of what I'm capable of.'

'Is that supposed to deter me?'

'Back down, Leila.'

She exhaled curtly. She dared to fold her arms, her eyebrows hitching up defiantly. 'I'm not backing down from anything. Come on, Caleb. You brought me in here. See it through.'

'Is this how you want it to end? In some rundown, backstreet house?'

'What difference does it make? What difference does *any* of it make?' She took another step closer to him, dropped her arms to her side. 'Come on, Caleb. Do it.'

'You don't call the shots here.'

'No? Then prove it.'

One iota of remorse in her eyes and he could have been tempted to change his mind from all the thoughts that had been running through his head, but not now.

'Have you got so complacent that you don't think I'm capable of hurting you?'

Her hazel eyes locked on his. 'I don't think it, I know it. You like playing the big, bad vampire because that's what your reputation dictates, but when it comes down to it, you're scared of facing me at the Brink.'

'You'll beg me to stop before we even get to that point,' he remarked.

'Don't count on it.'

'Five minutes before you're pleading for my mercy.'

'Five minutes before you realise you're not up to the job.'

'Your inexperience will be your downfall.'

'Your arrogance will be yours.'

He grabbed her by her arm, yanked her to him. He felt it as soon as he held her. She wasn't pretending not to be afraid – she genuinely wasn't. That shortness of breath, that pulse racing was nothing to do with fear. Her outburst has been driven by more than anger. It had incited something else as well.

And, damn it, to her detriment, it was as intoxicating as it got, arousing every base urge in him.

'One temptation too many,' he whispered.

It was effortless dragging her over to the stairs.

She didn't dare fight him, wouldn't lose face by struggling. But as they reached the top of the stairs, he felt her involuntarily recoil as she saw the rusted metal bedstead, contraptions hanging from it, its worn and stained mattress.

But she wasn't going to be that lucky.

He yanked her past the battered balustrade to the open door to the bathroom, across the mottled tiled floor.

He scanned the familiar blood- and graffiti-stained walls, torn clothes that lingered in small bundles. He'd only been there a couple of times, a couple of rendezvous, but enough to know it would meet the purpose.

As he pulled her across to the deep and broad cast-iron bath, she pulled away from him slightly.

'What the hell are you doing?' she demanded.

He reached across to the shower mixer, icy cold spray misting towards them. He lifted her with ease into the tub with him, directly under the spray, the ice-cold water startling her, causing her to gasp.

She tried to fight free, but despite the slippery base they stood in, the grip on his boots and his balance was enough to keep them upright despite her fervent struggles.

He'd only ever done it on three occasions – two by request, another, like with Leila, as punishment.

The two by request had had very different reactions. The one he had had to stop halfway through, her tears and sobs leaving her quaking beneath him. The other had been the most proficient masochist he had ever come across. For her it had been the ultimate high, the sex acts they performed during it only adding to her ecstasy.

'Cold water constricts the blood vessels,' he whispered as he dragged her hair back from her neck. 'Slows down the heart rate. It stops you pumping so easily. Makes the feed that much more painful.'

He heard her snap back a breath.

'You think you know me? You think you've got it all worked out? I'm going to do things to you, Leila. Really bad things. Until you beg me to stop. Because you will plead with me.'

He closed his eyes, thought of all the triggers that would increase his anger enough to hurt her – to do whatever it took to make her break. She would not be the one to beat him. She would not.

And he would *not* prove her right. He knew she was assuming he couldn't hurt her. He knew she was counting on that inkling of humanity.

She believed he was the one who would back down.

But he'd show her. She'd beg him and he'd show her he had no mercy. He'd show her why he'd survived that long. He'd show her why fate had chosen him. Why it had shaped him to be the way he was. Because if he faltered now, what chance did his species stand?

If he couldn't even take his own sacrifice – his defiant, infuriating, belligerent little sacrifice – then he had no right to claim that position.

As he felt his fury build, his incisors extended in ready preparation.

He could do it for Seth, for his kind, against the Higher Order, against her kind; he *could* and *would* prove her wrong. He would not show weakness, and compassion was weakness.

And *she* was his weakness. He knew that much although he hated to admit it. And every time he got closer to her, she weakened him more.

But he would not allow it.

He'd done it all his life – made hard choices, detached himself. And he would embrace that darkness again. But this time it would not control him – he would control *it* and he would be all the more powerful because of that.

Fisting her hair at the nape of her neck, he extended his incisors and bit cruelly into her neck, Leila crying out as he plunged his sharpened incisors deep into her flesh.

He drank deep and hard, keeping her arms pinned around her. There was no steady draw, no giving her blood flow time to adjust; he was dragging it away from her heart, her whole body in protest, panicking for its survival as her heart worked against him, trying to cling on to what little control it had against him.

But he would take her to the Brink only when he was ready, not when she drove him to it.

He would show her control. The serryn had nothing on him.

And he would show her just what a cruel and brutal bastard he could be, the sweet taste of her warm blood, her body subjugated to him unleashing the darkness again.

If the defiant little witch wasn't going to cave in before him, he'd punish her even more.

He withdrew his incisors.

He turned her towards the end of the tub, ready to push her onto her knees but she slammed her foot against the side of the bath instead.

And thrust back with all her remaining strength.

❄ ❄ ❄

She didn't know how she did it. She couldn't remember how she did it – only the sudden feeling of loss of balance from both her and Caleb.

They'd plummeted sideways out of the bath, Caleb softening her blow as she fell on top of him. She heard the crack of his head amidst her elbow slamming against the tiled floor.

Rolling onto her back, she lay there stunned for a moment, sickness rising to the back of her throat at the shock of the fall.

She snapped her head across her shoulder to look at him.

He still lay on his back – motionless, his eyes shut, his body lax against the floor. Blood crept along the tiles towards her, seeping, so it seemed, from the back of his head.

Her heart plummeted. Her stomach clenched in inexplicable despair.

She'd killed him.

She rolled onto her side and forced herself up onto her elbow. She pressed her trembling fingers to his neck in frantic hope of a pulse. She could barely feel his flesh through her own numbness, but she searched and searched, desperately waiting for that elusive slow heartbeat.

With the impatience of failure, her shuddering from the cold, the shock, not helping, she eased onto her haunches and gripped his wrist to simultaneously search for a beat there.

She lowered her ear to his mouth, listening, pleading, for an intermittent breath.

She couldn't lose him. Not Caleb.

'Please,' she whispered, tears accumulating in her eyes, the back of her throat tightening until she could barely breathe, her chest aching from an unbearable sense of loss. 'Don't do this to me.'

She'd pushed him too far – resulting in them both losing their tempers in the heat of the moment. She'd taunted him into it – coaxing and goading him. If she hadn't somehow managed to lever herself against the bath and cause the stumble, he could have lost it completely, taken her to the Brink – the prophecies fulfilled.

It could have been her lying dead on the floor, not him.

In that split second, it felt like the better outcome.

It was an unforgiveable thought. She needed to be grateful. If he lay there dead, it was all over – the horrors and nightmares, the fate she had feared all her life. She was free.

She'd won.

But instead of elation, she felt caged by her own grief, the echoes of helplessness flooding back to her as she sat above his unflinching body, panic and pain seizing her chest.

'Don't,' she said more adamantly. 'Don't you *dare* leave me!'

She felt it – just when she'd almost forgotten she was trying to find it. A pulse that was faint, but it was there, and so was the shallow breath on her cheek.

Her heart leapt. A tear trickled across the bridge of her nose as she remained bent over him.

She counted for as long as it would take to feel another pulse, another breath – needing to be sure her willing it to be true hadn't created a phantom heartbeat.

A minute, two minutes, and the pulse came again.

She let him go and dropped back on her haunches. She brushed away her tear and heaved a grateful sigh as she stared up at the ceiling.

She looked back down at him still lying unconscious on the floor. The blood had stopped seeping. Obviously a superficial wound.

Hands trembling beyond control, she stroked the firm but soft skin of his cheek, rubbed her fingers across his slightly parted lips.

The realisation hit her hard and fast, causing her gut to clench, and her heart to pound. She retracted her hand as if she'd touched a scalding surface.

If her most basic instincts were telling her the truth, the thought of it was abhorrent, never more so than after what he'd just proven himself capable of.

But it was there, stirring deep inside and screaming alarm bells at her.

And those alarm bells had a right to scream, because if she was right, if there was even an inkling of truth in the way she felt then, this was the worst possible outcome – feelings that were a get-out clause for her as far as her destiny went, but a death sentence for her sisters.

Because if she was right, if the impossible had happened – the actualisation of an unuttered serryn secret as closely guarded as the prophecies – if she *had* fallen for Caleb, she was guilty of committing the ultimate serryn taboo.

And if she had fallen for him before that moment, if she'd already consummated that love, her serrynity would already be gone, bounced down the line to Sophie in punishment – Sophie who was already in Blackthorn. Or if Sophie hadn't made it, bounced to Alisha who was already trapped.

Panic clenched her chest.

But how was she to know what she really felt amidst the emotional turmoil she'd been subjected to ever since arriving there? If love, the intensity of the real love that would be needed for her to lose it, was even *possible* in such a short space of time.

She struggled to unsteady feet as she stared down at his still-unconscious body.

She had to get out of there. Far away from there. From Blackthorn. From him.

She stumbled across to the door.

Another moment with Caleb could be the death penalty for all of them. She'd be no use to him anymore. Her sisters would be next in line.

She had no choice, no other option.

Reaching the door she looked back across at him. She resentfully wiped away another tear. She could not allow herself these feelings – these insane, unforgiveable feelings.

She stepped across the threshold, hurried past the balustrade and to the stairs, her legs threatening to collapse beneath her.

She'd get to a phone. She'd call the VCU. She'd tell them her sister was being kept hostage. They'd descend on the club within the hour. Alisha would be in trouble when they found out the truth. Her own life would be over if they discovered what she was. But the alternative was unthinkable.

She clutched the banister all the way down, the blood loss making her head throb, a deep sense of loss still consuming her despite her pending freedom.

Freedom out into Blackthorn. Because she still had to get through Blackthorn. She'd already seen what was out there waiting. If one of those crowds saw her leaving without Caleb they were bound to investigate. She'd have to sneak out. She'd have to keep her head down. Maybe only navigate the back alleys.

She stopped and sank onto the bottom step, clutched one of the spindles as she rested her temple against it.

She was kidding herself. She couldn't go. Not yet.

She couldn't walk away from the opportunity. Maybe the only opportunity she'd ever get.

She looked back over her shoulder up at the stairs.

She had to muster up whatever was left of her physical strength, whatever was left of her emotional strength.

She either ran now or finally faced it.

The choice was hers. And hers alone.

Chapter Twenty-five

Caleb woke to stare up at the damp, patchy ceiling.

It took him a moment longer to realise why he couldn't move.

His attention snapped to the cuffs on one wrist, the barbed wire wrapped around the other –his outstretched arms bound to the rusted metal headboard. He had no doubt the same was digging into his ankles, making any movement as painful as the ache at the back of his head.

He snapped a glare to Leila sat to the right of his waist.

Knees drawn to her chest, arms wrapped around them, she stared down at him intensely with sullen hazel eyes.

Anger and frustration swept through him in an icy shiver.

Leila let her legs fall loose into a crossed position, her hands relaxed in her lap, the breeze through the cracked window to her left blowing lightly through her hair. 'Welcome back,' she said.

He couldn't answer her at first, his jaw too clenched for him to speak. He tightened his fists into balls, his glower fixed on her.

'I guess now you know how it feels.' She looked around. 'You've been here before, right?' she said, looking back at him. 'You had to have to know the shower is here and that it works. Just how many liaisons have you had here, Caleb?'

He still couldn't bring himself to speak, defying the acceptance of it being real.

'There's some dodgy stuff tucked away here,' she added. 'I managed to find the handcuffs, obviously. The barbed wire was already part of the bed. Some people clearly don't like to clear up after themselves.' She pulled the kitchen knife from out behind her and twisted it in her hand. 'I even found some self-defence.'

He looked at the blade then back at her.

She wouldn't. Every part of him wanted to believe that. Not Leila.

'You're very quiet,' she said, echoing one of their first conversations. 'I thought you would have had more to say for yourself.'

'Get me the *fuck* out of these restraints,' he said, his glare locked on hers.

She didn't even flinch. 'And that will help me *how*, exactly?'

He inhaled deeply through his nose, his jaw locked again. If he could rip himself out of the restraints, he'd finish what he'd started in the bathroom with no further hesitation. The indignation was infuriating enough, the humiliation worse.

And the fear. That long-suppressed sense of fear now crawling up his spine sickened him.

'You don't look like the big, bad vampire now, Caleb. In fact, you're looking rather helpless there. And ever so slightly afraid.'

He narrowed his eyes. He'd make her pay. She'd pay for this.

'Still,' she said, glancing down at his chest, raking her gaze tauntingly along the length of his body before looking back into his eyes. 'Dare I say it? There's something very sexy about that vulnerability. Or maybe it's just the serryn in me. The serryn you've been instrumental in creating. Poetically ironic, don't you think?'

He looked away for the first time, the fury too painful.

The images flashed in front of his eyes again. The raven-haired beauty who had led him to a bed that was not dissimilar. A location that she had purposefully chosen away from where anyone could hear him scream.

The agony that followed.

Three weeks she'd chosen to keep him alive.

The taunting. The torture. The degrading and debasing acts she had performed on him, to him, and forced him to participate in. The things she made him watch and experience.

Even worse, if it could be, was seeing the little ones sob and being able to do nothing to help them, their pain intensifying if he didn't watch as she demanded him to. The pleasure she took out of torturing them. The helplessness he had felt bound and manacled knowing if he had been free, he could have overpowered her, stopped it, torn her to shreds for her cruelty.

'You're thinking about her, aren't you? That first serryn. What did she do to you, Caleb? What did she do that was so bad that you think all of this is acceptable? The way you've treated me. What did she do to warp your mind and perceptions so badly? Because this is just as much about her, isn't it? Killing me isn't just about the prophecies – it's about redemption for you, for whatever she did to you.'

He feigned a fleeting smile – an instinctive reaction to the ludicrousness of her thinking he would open up to her.

He hadn't even told Seth. Seth hadn't needed to know. Walking in that room had been enough. Looking at what the serryn had done, what she had used on his younger brother and how. The shock and pain in his Seth's eyes had been enough to confirm some things needed to be left unspoken.

Leila lifted the knife to his chest and slid it down to the tops of his low-slung trousers, before looking back up at him. 'Tell me what happened. Help me understand.'

He irritatingly caught his breath as the cold, hard metal touched his skin. 'Imagine the worst things you can conceive, short of leaving me permanently mutilated, and you won't even come close.'

Her eyes flared a little, but he knew better than to believe the glimmer of empathy they could be mistaken for emanating.

'Yet even now,' she said, 'even after what we've done together, shared, you *still* think I'm capable of *anything* like that?'

He opened his hands to divert her attention to his restraints. 'I'm getting the message loud and clear right now.'

'I can't talk to you any other way, Caleb. I've tried.' She swapped the knife to her left hand as she stretched her right arm across his body to lean across his waist.

She gazed down into his eyes, her body enticingly close. The body he couldn't touch, the body he couldn't get his hands on; the body, to his frustration, he couldn't pin down on the bed there and then. Even then she smelt amazing, refreshingly pure against the density of the dense, dark space and, inexplicably, despite his fury and fear, he felt a jolt of arousal.

'Tell me,' she said, placing the knife on the mattress, to free her fingers to explore the buttons on his shirt. 'What would any self-respecting serryn do now?'

He forced a closed-lipped smile. 'A self-respecting serryn would take me on one-on-one. A cowardly serryn would strap me down to a bed as she knew it was her only chance.'

She almost smiled, unfastened his shirt buttons one by one, before running her warm hand down his chest.

Despite the confidence she was trying to portray, she couldn't hide the slight tremor in her hands – undetectable no doubt to the human eye, to the less sensitive human flesh, but he could feel it. He knew her too well not to feel it.

He looked back into her eyes. Eyes that had always betrayed a myriad of emotions to him.

'A cowardly serryn, or a smart serryn?' she asked, those beautiful, dangerously deep hazel eyes meeting his fleetingly before she returned her attention to her fingers tracing the definition in his chest. 'You wanted me in control before, didn't you? To take the lead. To prove myself. But back then you had every intention from the beginning to take the power back. You always take the power back. Only now it's different, isn't it? You have no power, Caleb.

Not over me. Not anymore. You're not the Tryan yet. And I can stop you becoming the Tryan, can't I? I can stop it all. Isn't that what any serryn would do in my place? And as you lie here, all manacled and defenceless and exposed, wouldn't any serryn make the most of it?'

She ran her hand back up his chest to stop over his heart as she locked gazes with him again, enrapturing him even through his indignation and fear.

'Only I'm not her, Caleb. Just like I'm not Feinith. I wish I could have made you see that.' She reached for the knife and slid it slowly down his chest. 'And I might not be active, but I've studied. I know things you don't. *Lots* of things you don't. You asked me if I know how hard it is to drive something into a vampire.' She slid the blade around to his side. 'But it's only hard if you try to go through the sternum, Caleb. Not so much so if you come in from the side,' she traced the blade up along his skin, 'up under the ribcage. The heart's so vulnerable there. It sounds so clinical, doesn't it? But so much more effective.'

She slid the knife back over to his heart.

'What if I told you I did know about Sophie?' she added. 'That I knew she worked for The Alliance. That I knew they were targeting Jake and you. That I came rushing here because I believed you'd found out about us. What if I also told you I knew what you were the moment our eyes met? That I've been waiting ever since for my chance to get you alone, away from Jake, away from the safety of your club, away from where anyone can hear you scream? Would you still believe that?'

No. As his heart lunged, as his stomach clenched into knots, he wouldn't believe it.

As he stared up into her eyes, as he felt a deep stir of betrayal, it was the last thing he could tolerate believing right then.

'Do you?' she asked. 'Believe it?'

'Is that some kind of trick question?'

'I want to know if you really have learned nothing about me. If you think any of that could possibly be true. I want to know if you are still so locked in your preconceived ideas that you'll never see beyond them.'

'The only way I'll see beyond them is if you untie me.'

'And what will my punishment be then, Caleb? How far will you push it this time? What exactly were you going to do if we hadn't toppled out of the bath?'

He feigned a smile. 'I'll leave that one to your imagination.'

She lifted the blade so it was upright over his heart.

He held his breath and tensed.

'Do you deserve this?' she asked, meeting his gaze. 'Do you deserve me to end it?'

He squarely held her gaze. If she wanted to take his life, he sure as hell wasn't pleading for it. She was bluffing. Every instinct in him told her she was bluffing – every defence mechanism that wouldn't accept that she could finally be the one to destroy him.

And, no, he didn't believe she knew anything about the set-up – he knew that somewhere locked deep in his heart. Something he couldn't accept for fear of what it could develop into – those feelings that had been growing ever since she'd stared back at him, clenching the straps of her rucksack and trying to bargain with him.

'What do *you* think?' he asked.

She slipped astride him in an easy, sensual move. Her soft hair brushed his cheek as she leaned over him, the knife still clenched in her hand as she braced her fists either side of his head.

'Do I deserve the way you've treated me?' she asked.

'Based on now? Absolutely.'

Her eyes flared, telling him it wasn't the answer she was expecting.

'And you feel no shame, no regret for your behaviour?' she asked.

'You're really enjoying this, aren't you?' he said, unable to bite back his resentment. 'The power over me? What's running through your head? What possibilities? What deep, dark suppressed fantasies are you longing to fulfil? I can see it in your eyes. I've made you. Why would I feel shame and regret for unearthing what I said was there all along?'

'Because there's a whole world of vampires beyond those doors. Only now without a pending Tryan to protect them. Like you said – you brought me here and that makes me your responsibility. That makes what happens from here your responsibility too.'

She looked over at the window, clearly purposefully to taunt him.

She looked back at him. 'If I were you, I'd be feeling a hell of a lot of regret and shame.' She leaned close enough to kiss him. 'You might be the chosen one, but just remember – so am I. Your sanctuary can be my playground within minutes from now. I'll find Marid again. I'll find my sister. And I will get Alisha once I've finished what The Alliance started with your brother.'

He bucked in his restraints, the fury too much even to curse her.

She sat upright, her eyes flaring in shock at his ferocity, despite her trying to conceal it.

'Because that's what you expect, isn't it?' she said. 'That's what's plausible. That's what's logical. That's what makes sense. That's what's well within my capabilities. So you need to ask yourself why I won't. You need to ask yourself why, right now, I'm going to walk away. Why I'm not going to kill you, Caleb. Just as I'm not going to kill your brother. Just like I didn't last time I had the chance.'

She picked up the knife and eased off him.

As she strode across to the balustrade, his slow-beating heart pounded painfully.

She was walking away. She wasn't bluffing. He knew her well enough to know that look in her eyes.

'Where are you going?' he asked.

'To get Sophie. Then I'll work out how to get Alisha.'

Caleb examined her profile as she reached the top step and started her descent.

There was no way she was stupid enough to go out there without him. Not into Blackthorn. Not that part of Blackthorn.

His chest tightened. 'You're going after Marid? Without me?'

As she stopped three steps down, met his gaze, it was confirmation enough.

'You're not ready,' he said, more concern echoing in his tone than he'd intended. 'You can't go out there on your own.'

'Worried about what will happen to your precious goods?'

He stunned himself with the realisation that hadn't even crossed his mind. The only thing he thought of was Leila, *his* Leila, going out there alone. The prospect of what would be waiting for her.

Even amidst his fury at her, it was nothing compared to the thought of anyone hurting her. And she would get hurt, even with that toxic blood flowing through her. It would only take a group of them...

As she continued her descent, he strained his wrists against the barbed wire until blood seeped.

He had to stop her. Somehow he had to convince her to come back. 'Leila.'

She glanced across at him, but she didn't stop as she disappeared from sight.

Let her do it. Let her learn her lesson. Let her go out there and discover what it's really like on the streets. He'd track her down soon enough. And he'd enjoy it – being on the hunt again.

The thrill of the capture.

He exhaled curtly. 'Leila!' He lifted his head from the pillow. 'Don't you walk away from me!'

After a moment, she retraced her steps enough to be back in his vision. 'We've been here before, haven't we?' she remarked with a mocking frown, a defiant glare that he'd come to love about her. 'I don't remember your orders working then either.'

Love about her.

He gritted his teeth as she disappeared from sight again.

He slammed his head back against the pillow and glared up at the ceiling.

She would not corner him like this. She would not force anything out of him. She would not grate on his pride – humiliate him, expose him that way.

But as her footsteps became more distant, his frustration erupted, his panic erupted – the acknowledgement that he would not, *could* not let her walk away no matter what it took.

It could have been just a game – a final attempt at humiliation before she killed him, before she finally exposed herself for exactly what she was.

But he couldn't be sure enough that she was calling his bluff to risk it.

To risk losing her.

He knew he could have only seconds left to pull it back.

'I know!' he finally called out. 'I know you're not like them!' He sighed with impatience at her silence. 'Leila, get the fuck back up here and stop screwing with my head!'

❊ ❊ ❊

Leila dropped her hand from clutching the handle.

She looked back up the stairs.

He had fallen silent.

He was clearly listening for her as much as she was for him.

The words could have been a lie – anything said to stop him losing his sacrifice. But the sincerity that resounded in them caused her to still, to linger.

It was more logical for her to walk away. To close the door on him. But this had become about more than that.

This had become about more than the vampire and the serryn. This was about *them*. And this moment was about her.

And up there, lying on that bed, was the only way she knew she'd ever find an iota of happiness or fulfilment. If she walked out of there now, she may as well have given herself to the streets of Blackthorn.

But if he felt *anything* anywhere near enough, if she could get him to prove it, it could be the breakthrough she needed, that he needed – that they both needed, to get them *all* out of it intact.

She needed just a few more minutes.

But everything she knew reminded her he was too damaged. He was too far gone. She had fought for his redemption, but she had to accept that some were too far beyond that.

Whatever that serryn had done to him, whatever those since had done to him, whatever he'd seen and experienced and whatever Feinith had inflicted, they had scarred him permanently.

She reached for the handle again, the tears welling up in her eyes.

Her legs felt leaden, an invisible barrier blocking the exit.

He'd *never* care enough.

She reached for the handle and turned it, the door clicking open.

'Leila!' Caleb called again, his commanding voice rasping in the silence.

There was a moment's pause.

'For fuck's sake,' he said, impatience lacing his tone. 'You're going to get yourself killed! Leila – I can't lose you!'

Her head snapped back to the stairs. She froze for a moment, something deep inside stirring.

He had fallen silent again.

Her heart pounded, her hand still gripping the handle.

She owed herself this. A few more minutes to hear what he had to say.

She quietly closed the door and took to the stairs. As she reached the top step, his sullen green eyes were already locked on hers.

'Why not?' she asked.

He frowned, but he didn't answer her.

'Why can't you lose me?' she persisted.

He looked away, frustration exuding from his eyes, pride clearly winning.

She took another step towards him. 'Caleb, you talk to me or I am turning right back around and this time I will not stop.'

His gaze snapped back to hers. 'You want to talk, you get me out of these restraints.'

'I'm not stupid, Caleb.'

'You want to bring this to a head, right? That's what all this is about. That's why you didn't walk away when you could. Why you didn't kill me when you could. What's going on in that head of yours, Leila? What do you want from me?'

Despite opening herself up for the potential humiliation, she said it. 'I want to know how you feel.'

He frowned. But he didn't laugh. There was no disdain in his eyes at the suggestion. 'How I feel?'

She nodded, her heart pounding painfully, the blood in her ears echoing in the silence.

He exhaled curtly. 'What does it matter how I feel? What does it matter how either of us feel?'

'You wouldn't have hurt me in that bathroom. That's the truth. That's what I believe. That's what I've learned.'

'Yet you felt the need to tie me down.'

'Because I needed to show you. Because I needed *you* to believe *me*.'

'And you showed me. So if your belief is so strong, untie me.'

'I don't think you *do* believe me though. Not enough. I believe you don't *want* to hurt me, but I believe you *need* to. I think you're beyond redemption, Caleb. And without you telling me how you feel, that's all I'm left with.'

'So what do you want? For me to declare undying love? Is that what you're looking for? And in your eyes, will that make everything okay?'

'It'll give me something.'

'I feel more than I should. Is that what you so *desperately* need to hear?'

She frowned. 'You're a cold bastard, Caleb.' She turned on her heels, fighting back the tears as she took the first two steps back down.

She was insane to go back up there. To let her resolve waver. To convince herself to give him a chance.

'A cold bastard who feels a *hell* of a lot more than he should,' he declared. 'Who, despite what you have done to me here, still cannot see you walk away. Who cannot bear the thought of anyone else laying their hands on you. Who I would kill if they ever hurt you the way I have. I don't want you to be a serryn, Leila. It's the last thing I want. And you being the one I need to kill tears me apart more than you'll ever know.'

She couldn't take her eyes off him, his eyes glossy, his body taut in aggravation.

'And I hate myself for letting you get to me,' he added. 'But you can't help who you fall for. And unfortunately for us both, I started to fall for you the minute our eyes met.' He scowled, his eyes penetrating deep. 'Is that confession enough?'

He stared back up at the ceiling, heaved a heavy sigh as he flexed his hands in his constraints.

The tense silence consumed her as she remained rooted to the spot, unable to speak.

If he was telling the truth, the words were the most beautiful she'd ever heard, the conviction behind them astounding – even more so because it came from him, direct from his hardened heart.

And if it was a lie, a ploy, they were the cruellest words ever uttered.

He looked back at her, his green eyes calm and resolute, as if some kind of weight had been lifted. 'So what are you going to do now, fledgling? Untie the monster, or leave him here to suffer?'

If he was the monster she had once believed him to be, what he still self-proclaimed to be, she would be a fool to do anything but the latter.

'What are you going to do if I do untie you, vampire? Unleash the monster or contain him?'

'Did you listen to a word I said?'

Every word. She only wished her head could be as readily accepting as her heart. She nodded.

'You proved something to me tonight. Now let me prove something to you,' he said. 'Let's both experience the edge of our fears.'

She stared deep into his eyes, the ache in her chest intensifying.

'You know you want to,' he said with the dark, playful glint she knew only too well.

'And what's the edge of my fear, Caleb?'

'Letting me loose right now, with the way you feel.' He held his gaze steadily on hers. 'I understand you, Leila. And you understand me.'

Master manipulator. Master seducer. She stared deep into those green eyes as she wavered. Arousal stirred deep inside, pooling at the pit of her abdomen. Arousal she couldn't ignore. Arousal that, right then, she didn't want to ignore.

It was the only way she'd know – the only way she'd know for sure. And if he overstepped the mark, she'd make sure he bit.

She had to. For the sake of her sisters, love him or not.

She would either go to the Brink with him or she would kill him with her last dying drop of human blood if, *if*, her serrynity had already gone.

But she could only hope, with every iota of her being, it wouldn't come to that.

She reached across to take the handcuffs key from the top of the top of the newel post, stepped up to the bed and placed the knife on the cover.

With only a moment's more hesitation, she unfastened the cuff around his left hand, her eyes fleetingly meeting his, making her heart and stomach jolt, as she did so.

Grasping the knife again, she backed away, leaving him to uncoil the barbed wire from his other wrist, his ankles.

He moved to the edge of the bed, kept his head lowered for a minute before looking up at her, his eyes dark in the dim light.

Her grip tightened on the knife handle.

'Is that in case I misbehave?' he asked.

She squeezed the handle, but said nothing.

As he stood and sauntered towards her, stretching and flexing his arms and back, she curved away from him, to her foolishness more into the room as he subtly blocked her only exit.

Suddenly it didn't seem such a good idea.

Suddenly the thought crossed her mind that she had made the biggest mistake of her life.

As she assessed that lithe, virile body, she felt a cool perspiration wash over her not only at the reality of the power of the vampire in front of her, but how easily, she had no doubt then, she could succumb to him.

If he overstepped the mark, if he took her there and then in that room, she would have no choice but to keep him feeding. No choice but to feed him her dying blood until they met at the Brink or, if she was right in her feelings, it killed them both.

It was purely down to his self-control. The fate of both of them was down to his self-control – the vampire closing the gap between them with easy, nonchalant steps more predatory than she had ever seen.

'Don't let me down,' she said, wariness not allowing her to break from his penetrating gaze.

'In terms of what?' he asked, his smirk telling her he knew exactly what she meant.

She backed up against the wall, still clenching the knife.

He looked down at the blade then back at her as he placed his hand on the wall beside her head. He leaned closer. 'So what now? Do you want me to tell you I love you? Will that chase those fears away?' He moved his lips inches from hers. 'Or do you want me to demonstrate how I really feel?'

'This is not about sex.'

'No?'

'Not like that. You'll show me by doing anything but.'

He frowned slightly. 'You want me to refrain?'

She nodded.

'You think I can do that? The way I'm feeling right now? Only I've got a lot bubbling inside me after that little stunt. A lot of darkness needing to escape.'

'What you decide to do in the next few minutes will tell me everything I need to know.'

He glanced back down at the blade. 'And are you going to stab me if I step over the line? Like you tried to with the syringe.' He slid his hand down her forearm, pressing her knife-holding wrist against the wall. 'You can't hurt me, Leila. You already proved that. I've skirted to the edge with you too many times now and each time you've thrived on it. That's what I understand about you. And you know I see it and you know I won't hold back from making the most of it, and that only excites you more. Which is why you're rife with tension right now.'

Unease coiled her chest at the truth spilling from his lips. At his perceptiveness. At his understanding of needs not even she had got her head around. Only that they were incited by him. And only him. 'Which only makes it harder for you, right?'

He smiled. 'Most definitely.'

As he pressed his body against her, captured her lips with his, the unexpected intimacy, his gentleness under the circumstances, stunned her. 'You're not going to insist on me keeping my hands off you completely, are you?' he asked, sliding his hand up under her still-damp dress.

She snapped back a breath, her gaze locking with his as his cool fingers found the heat between her legs.

'Are you going to stab me for this?' he asked, sliding his middle finger firmly, slowly and enticingly inside her.

Before she had time to answer, he leaned into her neck, gliding his lips up to her ear lobe, drawing it painfully slowly into his mouth.

She shuddered, bit into her bottom lip, her nails digging into her palm.

'You stepped over the line tonight. You know that, don't you?' he said, his lips sliding back to hers, enticing her with their closeness. He slid his finger deeper, making her snap back a breath. 'And now you want me to refrain from what is so instinctive to me?'

As he slowly slid his finger back out to tease the most sensitive nub of her sex, as he applied perfect and concise pressure, she spoke more breathily than she intended. 'Your choice,' she said.

He almost smiled as he slid his lips down her throat, across her collar bone, withdrew his hand as he kissed down her cleavage, dragged the fabric aside to take her breast in his mouth. She closed her eyes, his saliva, as cool as the air encompassing them, not helping her already obvious arousal.

As he slid his lips back up her neck to then find her mouth, she accepted him willingly, the increase in his hunger only exacerbating hers as he eased down onto his knees.

She stared down at the top of his head, clenched the handle of the knife tighter as he encouraged her to part her feet further before pushing her dress up her thighs.

She rested her head back against the wall, closed her eyes and held her breath as she felt him pull at the ties on her knickers, the coolness of his mouth against her sex.

She almost lost the circulation in her knife-holding hand, her other fist clenched enough to cut off the blood flow too.

He lifted her foot onto his thigh, continuing to lick slowly and painfully lingeringly before finally pushing his tongue inside her.

She lifted a hand to her head to clutch her hair, cursed under her breath, the flexion in his lips telling her he had detected it, her reaction making him smile.

His pace immediately increased as he held her hip tight, his other hand gripping her thigh as he consumed her more hungrily, fuelling her desire for him more.

She dropped the knife, its clatter echoing in the silence, and gripped the shirt at his shoulder as she found herself edging close towards a too-fast climax.

But he pulled away, eased back onto his feet.

As she stared back at him through misty eyes, she could barely breathe, could barely hold herself up had his arm not slipped around her waist.

As he unfastened his trousers, as he pulled down his shorts, a cold shiver swept through her.

In those moments she didn't care about the prophecies – she didn't care about anything beyond those walls.

And she hated herself for those thoughts.

Hated herself in those moments – her addiction to him, how he overruled every conviction, her whole body responding to him in a way she despised. She needed to hate herself for wanting him that much that she no longer cared.

But she couldn't deny it. Her body wouldn't deny it. The fact was she knew he already was burrowed too deep inside her for her ever to get over him.

And as she felt his erection against her sex, she held his gaze.

But he didn't move.

'This, my beautiful serryn, is self-control,' he declared. 'Decades of practice refined enough to pull back from even *you* right now. You nearly made me lose that control once tonight. The only one who ever has. That won't happen again.'

He kissed her lightly, fleetingly on the lips before pulling back, breaking from her gaze.

Without another word, he turned his back on her, refastening his trousers as he crossed the room to the stairs.

Chapter Twenty-six

They walked back to the club in silence.

Leila wrapped her arms around herself, but it did nothing to fight off the breeze.

They got a few stares, but none lingered. Caleb didn't even seem to notice, though she had no doubt he did. His eyes had been distant since they had left the house, but never had she felt more protected from the dark world they walked through. Silent though he was, his eyes pensive, she knew he was more aware of her than he'd ever been, as she was of him.

He didn't hold her hand this time as he led her back to the club. He was forcing himself to distance himself from her, the act revealing more than enough to her.

He hated her for exposing his weakness. Despised her for shattering the illusion he had constructed so perfectly.

They strolled through the hidden passages that led back up to the penthouse, to his quarters.

The library felt cold and empty, the grate now lifeless. She looked out at the darkness beyond the window, the stillness beyond the boundary exacerbating her tension.

He led the way to his bedroom, his continued silence a lingering and unwelcome companion as Leila stood in the centre of the room, watching him disappear into the en suite.

Never had a sense of isolation consumed her more. Never had she had a greater desire to be near someone. Even with him only in the next room, she ached to be close to him. She needed that one last attempt. That one last attempt to make him want her enough to delay his plans, just long enough to give her more time to find a way through it.

But more than anything, she needed to know if she was right – if the hardened shell had splintered. If there was a renewed glimmer of hope that there was something in him she could appeal to.

Hearing the shower run, she stepped up to the threshold.

She faced the frosted glass, his naked body muted beyond, his back to her, his hands braced on the tiled wall.

She slipped off her sandals as she listened to the water beating off his body and onto the shower tray. She closed the door behind her, sealing out the outside world before tentatively stopping at the opening of the walk-in shower.

She raked his naked body slowly with her gaze, taking in every inch of his lithe, masculine perfection, the shower flowing down onto him like a rainstorm, cleansing every inch of his flawless skin.

And as she met his gaze, his eyes said it all – a transparent, unspoken invitation.

She stepped inside but not into the spray, catching the mist of the downpour as he turned to face her. Despite his nakedness, she couldn't take her eyes from the penetrating green-eyed gaze that blinked away droplets from glossy black lashes.

He reached out to turn the power of the spray down to a gentle but effective mist, making her skin tingle from the warmth as she stepped into it.

She tentatively reached out to touch the tattoo on his pec, her fingers tracing over the outline of the coiled tail that stretched up to his neck before sliding across to touch his beautiful lips – lips already bathed in a tempting moistness.

He instantly drew her thumb into his mouth, sucking on it lightly before sliding his fingers tenderly over the wounds he had left on her neck. He thumbed each in turn before gently holding her jaw, his thumb sliding across her wet lips before he lowered his mouth to hers.

She met him midway, the draw to him all-consuming, no will or fight to deny what she wanted.

He parted her lips gently but authoritatively, sliding his tongue gently and exploratorily over hers. She couldn't help but kiss him back as he tasted and caressed every inch of her mouth, his hand sliding around to clasp the nape of her neck as he delved deeper.

Leila pressed her hands to his hard upper arms as he guided her around to pin her against the tiled wall, lifting her wrists to place them either side of her head as he kissed deeper still, his erection pushing against her wet dress.

Arousal flooded her quickly, the need to have him inside her overwhelming her. Gradually everything around them seemed to fade until all she could see was him; beyond the vampire. And she was able to acknowledge the attraction and accept it, the yearning, the craving to have him closer, to have him touch her, hold her, be inside her – the prospect of more gentle sex, more intimate sex, a temptation all to itself. She wanted that part of him. She needed that part of him. She knew if he could bring himself to do that, it was all she needed. Because she knew that the Caleb who used to exist, the Caleb that, in part, still did, was a loyal, devoted and protective Caleb.

Beyond definition and beyond justification, she *had* fallen for him.

As he'd stood there naked, his skin cleansed from the tarnish of Blackthorn, beautiful green eyes as unguarded as she'd ever seen them, the real Caleb had finally come out of that kiss.

His façade had dropped and he'd shown her what lay beneath. And it wasn't dark and it wasn't terrifying. There was something warm, responsive, sensitive. There was something that held her like she was the only thing that mattered in those few moments. And it felt more fulfilling than she ever could have conceived.

And she was falling deep.

He felt for her too. Every inch of her body and heart told her that Caleb Dehain felt something for her.

She would undo the Caleb that first serryn had created. That Feinith had moulded and defined. She would undo that Caleb and with it undo all that had done damage to him.

As he released her wrists to cradle her neck in both his hands, his thumbs on her jaw, she slid her hands down his hard, wet chest, down over his hips before wrapping her hand around his erection, it doing nothing to abate the hunger of his kiss.

She hoped it was signal enough that she could forgive him. That she understood.

And that she believed he wouldn't do anything to hurt her.

But as his kiss waned, as he gently pulled away, her heart plummeted.

As he turned away, she caught his hand, willing him to stay.

But he didn't look back at her as his wet hand slipped so easily from hers, making her chest ache with the loss of him.

He disappeared back out into the bathroom and the bedroom beyond, leaving Leila alone in the mist.

The realisation hit her hard and fast, causing her gut to clench, and her heart to pound. She clamped her hand over her mouth as she slid down the tiled wall to her haunches.

He knew.

She'd lost it – she'd already lost her serrynity, and he knew.

Chapter Twenty-seven

Caleb closed the library door behind him and slammed his clenched fists, knuckles first, against the wall opposite. Keeping his arms braced, he pressed his forehead to the wall and closed his eyes.

He'd been so close, so unforgivably close to taking her in his arms, wiping the fear from her eyes and reassuring her in a way only that level of intimacy could.

He needed to remember who he was. He needed to remember where his loyalty lay. He needed to remember what he had to lose against what he had to gain – not only the future of his kind that deserved more, but his own self-respect, his dignity. If he chose her, he wasn't just turning his back on vengeance for Seth – he was turning his back on all of his kind, which is exactly what she wanted.

He knew the rules. No one survived in Blackthorn by being soft or by making excuses. No one survived in Blackthorn feeling the way he did right then, because that made him vulnerable. And no one, especially not a serryn, was *ever* going to make him feel vulnerable again.

She might have seen a glimpse of how he was – of how he used to be, but Caleb would not allow himself to revert to that.

He had to keep his mind on all the serryns who had come before her – their bright alluring eyes, their goading sexy smiles; their well-crafted words. The malice. The cruelty. Finding Seth. The agony he was in. And even when he'd clutched Caleb's neck, pulled him down so he could whisper through the suffering, he'd told Caleb to let it go.

Just as he'd told him to let go of the pain, the humiliation, the fear that first serryn had inflicted on his seventeen-year-old body. But he couldn't. Physically the wounds had healed but the scars ran deeper than that. The scars that didn't heal. The scars of feeling that helpless, that *used*.

He clenched his fists tighter.

Wounds that had reopened when he'd held his dying brother in his arms.

If there was such a thing as destiny, then it had happened; he had survived for one reason only – to harden him enough to survive at this point.

Because no matter how hard he tried, no matter how much he wanted it, he could never trust Leila. Her loyalty to her kind would come first, her loyalty to her family second, and he would be right at the bottom of the pile.

It was less than forty-eight hours since she'd lay in his dungeon shivering and crying, torn from the heart of everything she knew, those deep, entrancing eyes looking up at him with fear and disdain and confusion – but never hopelessness. Amidst it all, there had always been that glimmer of fight.

And that would always be there – that survival instinct which thrived in her.

A survival instinct that was fuelled by the fact she didn't trust him either. She never would. Not enough. There would always be that doubt. That division. And they could plaster over it for a while, but it would fester and grow and consume them. And a relationship was nothing without trust. Not the relationship he needed. That he craved.

He'd been right about her dedication to her cause. And her cause was to stop the uprising of vampires. To stop the Tryan. And that's all her cause would ever be. She would never see beyond her own doctrine, her own instincts.

They were fated not to work, and he was only torturing them both by prolonging his decision-making. At least this way he could take her privately and with dignity, not with Feinith or the Higher Order lording over them.

And he had to hold on to that. He'd made his decision and he would stick to it. He couldn't waste time on hopeless promises of a future he had not earned nor deserved.

Ten years from then, even five years from then, she'd mean nothing.

Exhaling tersely, he withdrew from the wall and made his way down to the bar. He grabbed himself a whisky and his packet of cigarettes and headed out onto the terrace. He sat up on the table, feet on the seat as he placed a cigarette between his lips, shielding it as he ignited the tip.

He stared back across the district. The mild breeze teasing his hair, the familiar sounds and smells of what had been his home for over eighty years spiralling up towards him – a reminder of the reality out there, of his home and his species. A species that had been shoved into the dregs of society by mistrustful humans who felt they had the precedence. A species that had no idea they were teetering on claiming it all back. Claiming what was rightfully theirs.

All for the sake of him draining the life from some serryn. Because that's how he had to see her – *some* serryn. A serryn he had a right to lay claim to.

This was as much about sacrificing his own dreams as sacrificing Leila.

And he ended it now.

❅ ❅ ❅

Leila wasn't sure how long she sat on the shower floor, but her pruned fingers told her the shock had taken a while to abate.

There was only one time it could have happened – on the bed, after he'd snatched the syringe from her. Something had changed then.

She clutched her head.

Or when they'd had sex before he bit her.

But no – that didn't make sense. Surely he would have known. But he'd never actually tested her serrynity, only whether he was immune. And that would be true whether she was a serryn or not.

Sickness rose at the back of her throat. She had to know if he suspected something. She couldn't sit there doing nothing.

She pulled herself to her feet and stepped out of the shower. She peeled off her sodden dress, grabbed a towel and stepped through to his bedroom.

There was no Caleb waiting for her, but there was a cream negligee laid out instead.

She clenched the cool silk in her hand as she gazed over at the ajar door.

The irrepressible glimmer of hope still burned inside her – that maybe he'd walked away because he needed to think. Because he needed to contemplate. Because he was wavering.

She dropped her damp towel to the floor and slipped on the negligee, the silk sliding over her body with ease.

She could tell him how she felt. If she hadn't made it obvious enough in the shower, she could look him in the eyes and tell him. It could change everything.

It could change his mind.

But she knew she was only fooling herself. Her heart may have been deceitful against her kind, but his was anything but. Even if he did care, Caleb had his eye on the goal. Caleb always had his eye on the goal.

And if he knew of the secret as much as he seemed to know everything else, and she confessed it, she was feeding him his victory and handing him her sisters on a platter.

With leaden legs, she left the bedroom, crossed the library and made her way down to the lounge.

The balcony doors were open, the emptiness of the lounge telling her exactly where he was.

She found him sat on the round table, a glass of whisky beside him as he exhaled a steady stream of smoke into the night air. A sign she now knew was the contemplative Caleb, the accessible Caleb. Something she knew she needed to make the most of.

He broke from the scenery to look across his shoulder at her. He raked her swiftly with his gaze, the hint of a smile that met his eyes and lips telling her he approved of what he saw.

And something inside her melted.

'It suits you,' he remarked.

'*You* chose it.'

'I chose well.' He broke a fleeting smile, heat flooding through her in response. 'I like to make sure you have nowhere to hide anything.'

'Always on the defensive.'

He flicked ash onto the floor, before lifting the cigarette to his lips again. 'Looking like that, are you surprised?'

As he looked back ahead, she hovered anxiously at the threshold. He didn't look like he knew. He didn't look at her any differently at all.

She knew she shouldn't have said anything. Her pride begged her not to. But he had walked away and she needed to know why.

She wrapped her arms around herself – partly against the breeze, partly to protect herself against the pending emotional exposure because, the way she was feeling then, she wasn't sure *what* she was capable of saying. But she had to know if something in Caleb Dehain had changed. He had tried to prove what she was and instead, if what he had said on the bed had been true.

That was the Caleb she had fallen for. That was the Caleb who could justify her feelings, her desire to give him one last chance.

To give them both one last chance.

'Why did you walk away?' she asked.

The seconds ticked by as he exhaled another stream of smoke. 'Because you wanted something I wasn't willing to give.'

'You gave it before. I know what happened last night, on the bed.'

He looked across at her, his gaze unreadable. 'And what happened, Leila?'

Blood pumped in her ears as she teetered on the edge of potential humiliation. In the sobering night breeze, Blackthorn their backdrop, she felt her assurance falter.

She took a step out onto the terrace, something deep inside her urging her to persist. 'It's not me who's been wearing a façade, Caleb – it's you.'

His eyes narrowed slightly. 'Is that what you need to tell yourself to justify the way you're looking at me right now?'

'No, but the way you're looking at me does. And considering you're immune to the serryn in me, explain that.'

He gazed ahead again. 'Like I said before, your inexperience will be your downfall, Leila.'

His coldness felt contrived and that's what she had to cling on to. The vampire who, when not masked by the darkness, could still be redeemed.

She took a few more steps towards him. 'My inexperience makes me unscathed enough to be able to see things as they are. It's your experience that has polluted your perception; mine has always been crystal clear.'

He cast aside his cigarette before easing down off the table. He reached out and took her hand. 'Come with me. I want to show you something.'

She pulled back. 'What?'

'You'll see,' he said, leading her over to the steps. He opened the gate and took the first couple of steps up. 'And then you'll understand.'

Chapter Twenty-eight

Wrapping her arms around herself, Leila headed across to the low gate. She pressed her foot down hard on the first step, just to be sure, despite Caleb leading the way. Seeing it didn't budge, she stepped up onto it. The rain had ceased again, but the air was still thick with the threat of an ongoing storm. The gentle breeze wafted her hair from her face as she ascended slowly, her left hand sliding over stone for reassurance as she tried not to look at the drop below.

Reaching the recess, she expected to come up against a doorway. Instead she faced a narrow, enclosed stone staircase of maybe another fifteen steps that led up onto the roof. She sent an uneasy glance across her shoulder, down at the warm amber glow spilling onto the balcony, the lounge now seeming a mile away.

Ascending the secret stairwell, she finally emerged onto an extensive flat roof. The chunter of extractor fans resounded from a couple of low brick buildings, one billowing steam into the air. The periphery wall was low, maybe as high as mid-thigh, broken up by square turrets, some flat, some topped with a stone animal or crest.

The breeze channelled through her hair, blowing her negligee against her knees as she caught her breath at the 360-degree view of Blackthorn, bright lights igniting dense darkness. Even in all its urban degradation, it was a breathtaking sight.

She looked across to the dome that lay central to the expanse – a glass dome at least forty feet in diameter, the mirrored walls reflecting the scene that surrounded it, amber lights warping on the polished exterior.

'What's that?' Leila asked.

'What I want to show you,' he said, guiding her towards the doors.

He keyed in a code on the door before pulling it open.

He kept hold of her hand as he led her inside.

It was dark but the view beyond was as clear as if they will still outside, the glass dome, aside from the frame, as transparent from the inside as if it wasn't even there. Her eyes not having adjusted to the dimness, she looked up at the Blackthorn sky above as Caleb let her hand go to step back over to the door. Vertical amber strip lights embedded into the dome's black metal frame suddenly ignited, giving the room a subtle candlelight glow.

She looked from the glass ceiling to the room ahead, her attention falling immediately to the large, circular, sunken bed before her – the blood-red sheets and cushions sprinkled with a plethora of stemmed red roses.

Her heart caught in her throat as she instinctively took a step back.

It would have been a beautifully sensual sight had the message behind it not been so cruel.

Caleb strolled away from her, around the circumference of the room, past the black leather curved seats that sat against the glass walls, all facing the bed below. This was just as much an auditorium as anything – a snatch into his past. A snatch into the Caleb she had started to believe might not exist anymore.

It had been less than two days. Two intense days where she had started to believe whatever she had wanted to believe in order to give herself hope. Faced with her ultimate terror, she had started to see things that she had needed to see. She had started to allow herself to believe he would feel enough for a serryn to turn his back on his entire kind.

But Caleb strolled with enough detachment now to remind her of exactly who he was, the glow of the backdrop of his pending kingdom darkening and strengthening his outline, making her see exactly what he wanted her to understand.

'When did you do this?' she asked.

As if it mattered. But it did matter.

'I didn't,' he said. 'Hade did. I set him on the task when we were out.'

The visit to Marid, just as she had suspected, was intended to be the final sealing to prove what she was – to justify his decision before he brought her up here.

Turning to face her, he tucked his hands in his trouser pockets, giving him a business-like persona. And that's what this was – business. This was the serryn hunter in action – no longer wielding a sword, but only because he didn't need it.

'This is quite the setting,' she said, trying to steady her breathing. 'Quite the backdrop.' She couldn't abide the silence when he didn't answer. 'Why have you brought me up here?'

'Why do you think?'

Her fast-beating heart ached at the betrayal.

He frowned. 'You look so shocked. What was *supposed* to happen next in the optimistic world of Leila McKay? I change my mind?'

'You told me you cared. Those things you said. But they were just a get-out clause, weren't they?'

And she'd been a fool to believe him.

'Tell me I'm right – tell me you're no different to all the others,' she added, her throat dry, her hands trembling. 'Tell me the whole reason for this segregation is right – that our species is right not to trust that you'll ever do the right thing, because that would make all this so much easier for me.'

'I am doing the right thing – for my kind. Take a look around, Leila. We're the forgotten species – a trash heap that at some point your kind will decide to bury. I can't let that happen.'

'So you'll kill me instead?'

'As opposed to what? Turn my back on all this and let you go? And then what? Where are you going to go? There's no way you and

Alisha will be allowed to live in Midtown let alone Summerton. It's Lowtown all the way now you're feeders.'

'I'm not a feeder.'

'Those bite marks beg to differ. As will Alisha's. That many won't pass of as just an attack. You're going to leave her behind are you? And how long do you think she'll survive in Lowtown? How long before you start to put those inherent skills to good use? No, I'd have to keep you here. Keep watching you twenty-four/seven. Until one day you kill me. Kill Jake. It would just be a matter of time. Maybe when we're sleeping. Or I could bite you in the depths of my sleep or in a moment of passion. My nature or yours, something would give in the end.'

'You've really thought about this.'

'Even if we moved beyond that, I'd destroy you eventually,' he said. 'My darkness would consume you too. And once the fascination passes, you would despise me for it. You would despise what I would make you become.'

'I haven't become anything, Caleb, except more myself. So don't you dare patronise me. You told me you felt something and I believe you.'

'Yes, because I'm hard-hearted, Leila, not cold-hearted. But this isn't about us. This has never been about us. You're taking this too personally. That's not how it was meant to be.'

'And you made love to all your serryn victims, did you? You couldn't have made it any more personal.'

'I never made you any promises. You know what I am. I'm not responsible for you wanting me to be what I'm not.'

Her heart skipped a beat as he circled around towards her, Leila unable to take her eyes off him.

If only she could numb her feelings as easily as the loss of sensation in her fingers and toes as she stood there. If only she could act with the same coldness that Caleb did – detach herself for her cause.

But she had to try whatever she could. Anything. 'There are other ways.'

'An abundance of ways, right?'

'I told you. I warned you. The Tryan's rise to power won't just be the downfall of humans, Caleb; it'll be the downfall of the vampires too. That's what the prophecies dictate. That's the secret those of the Higher Order keep to themselves. They're arrogant enough to think they can find a way through it, just like you do.'

'Nice tactic.'

'It's not a tactic – it's the truth. I have lots of them stored away in my grandfather's books. But only I can get access to them. Give me time. A week. Two weeks at most. I'll find other ways, better ways. Those prophesies are nothing but destructive. You have to believe me.'

'And why would I believe anything that comes out of that serryn mouth?'

'Because I'm trying to save us all, Caleb,' she said as she took a step closer, the truth cutting her deeper than she ever thought possible. 'I know you can't see it, but I am.'

His eyes narrowed a little. 'Why?'

'Because of you. Because of what I've seen in you. Because I do believe you can do the right thing. I know of the prophecies. I know things – things your kind don't know. I know what a brutal killer the Tryan is. I know how selfish and cruel he is. I know the destruction he will bring. That's not you, Caleb. I know why you pulled away in the shower. I know you're scared of how I make you feel. I know you hate it. I believed you when you said you feel something for me and that's what I'm appealing to now.'

'And what does it matter? I'd still be living with my decision, amongst my decision, when you're long gone. When I no longer have you close enough to remind me *why* I hesitated.'

Her throat burned dry as he closed the gap between them. His closeness made her stomach flip, the aroma of his aftershave mingled with the scent of smoke and alcohol. And she was back that first moment when she saw him – when he backed her against the sofa in the lounge. When she knew, somewhere deep, she wasn't going to walk away from this the same person. 'We'll find a way.'

'There is no way, Leila. Me and you – we're not meant to be. We don't get our happy ending. We're not made that way.' Pulling level, he gently brushed back her hair. 'My mind's made up. I cannot choose you. You've given me every reason to but it's not enough. It'll never be enough. Part of me wishes it was. But this is about doing what's right and to do what's right, sacrifices need to be made. And if I don't do this now, Feinith will walk back in here and take you from me anyway,' he said. 'This is going to end between us my way, not hers. I'm compassionate enough to do that. That's what I owe you.'

'Out of principle or because you care that much?'

He held her gaze for a moment, something behind his pensive eyes softening, but he didn't answer her.

'Has she told you to do it tonight?' Leila persisted.

'She doesn't know about me.'

'You expect me to believe that?'

'It's the truth.'

'She'll know when she finds me dead. Or both of us. That's why you feel under pressure, isn't it? Because of her?'

'There's no point delaying. It's just drawing out the inevitable.'

'Just admit she's still pulling your strings.'

'Once she did. Never again.'

'Really? Well, I just wish you were as immune to her as you clearly are to me.'

'There's that jealousy again,' he said. 'You never quite learned to detach yourself, did you?'

'Forget my humanity, you mean.'

'*Human*ity is such a biased term.'

'Not from where I'm standing.'

It started to rain again, pummelling on the glass roof, smashing against the walls, obscuring the view beyond.

For a fleeting moment she wondered if it would make any difference if she told him how she truly felt. If he would turn his back on it all, let her and her sisters go.

But if he had any intention of changing his mind, he'd be looking for every possible reason already – grappling with every option she had thrown at him.

'You do this and you're beyond redemption.'

His green eyes narrowed, burning deep into hers. 'I've always been beyond redemption, Leila. I thought you would have accepted that by now.'

But he wasn't. There was good in him. Somewhere deeply buried – somewhere that she had just started to uncover. Two days hadn't been enough. The short time ahead of them before he acted might not have been enough, but she had to have one last try.

'One more day, Caleb. You can postpone Feinith again. Give us just one more day.'

He wrapped his cool hand around hers. But instead of pulling her close, he led her down the steps towards the bed.

'Caleb, I know you meant what you said. Don't do this.'

He lifted one of the roses from the step before handing it to her. 'I've always found it ironic that the very flower used most to symbolise love carries with it such a lethal warning. Tiny little teeth all lined up to make you bleed once you've been drawn in by the beauty of it. Not unlike serryns, I guess.'

She frowned as she met his gaze. 'And then there are those roses that are so toxic, nothing can survive near them,' she said. 'Roses that kill anything that gets too close to their patch. Isn't that right, Caleb?'

He almost smiled, cast the rose aside and led her down another step.

She could have fought, no matter how futile. But that's exactly what it was – futile.

Especially when she had other options. An option that, never more than then, seemed inevitable.

This was the destiny she had fought. This was the destiny she had chosen to ignore. But destiny had chased, pursued and caught her with every single one of her claws. It wasn't down to Caleb, it wasn't down to Jake or Alisha; it wasn't even down to Feinith arriving. Destiny would have found her some way or another – dragged her kicking and screaming from that dark corner she was hiding in just like that vampire had done years ago.

It didn't matter if she wasn't a serryn anymore. Destiny didn't care about that. Destiny could cope with detours like losing her serrynity. Destiny might even have intended all along to create that detour along the way. Destiny, it appeared, wanted to prevent the vampire uprising as much as she did. And if destiny wanted that, then surely fate was on her side.

Losing her serrynity was her best chance of winning.

The Armun protected him only from the serryn in her. Gave him strength to combat her at the Brink. Without her serrynity, taking her to the Brink would kill him. He'd be drinking nothing but a regular witch – a witch without a soul strong enough for him to return with.

All she needed to do was consummate her love for him to guarantee her serrynity would be gone.

Fate had somehow given her a get-out clause – to kill him quietly and furtively, sacrificing herself in the process. Maybe that was fate's plan all along.

She had an obligation, a duty: kill Caleb and save them all.

And she had no greater cause than his willingness to do exactly the same to her.

It should have been the easiest decision in the world but as she stared back at the beautiful, green-eyed vampire, her heart ached. But Caleb had been right – this couldn't be personal.

Whether she killed him with her last drop of blood or, if she was wrong about her feelings, fought him at the Brink, one way or another

her life was ending that night on that rose-covered bed under the night sky of Blackthorn.

Her sisters would have to defend themselves, but she could stop thousands more suffering. Stop everything her grandfather and her predecessors had fought to protect against being actualised through her.

She had to do this. She had to be the serryn she'd always fought being. She had to seduce her executioner there and then before he had any more time to act.

Her death was inevitable. But she wasn't going alone.

❋ ❋ ❋

From the sofa, Alisha watched Jake as he stared out of the window of the apartment.

He hadn't settled since they'd got back up there. His playful nonchalance was nowhere to be seen. He'd paced in the silence, his eyes laden with worry.

Her throat constricted. 'When is he going to do it?'

'I don't know.'

'Please,' she said. 'I don't care how many times I have to keep begging. Please. Let me be with her.'

'He won't let you.'

'I deserve to be with her. I am not going to let her be alone.'

Jake rested his arm on the window frame and his forehead against the back of his hand.

She didn't like the look in his eyes any more than she liked his sorrowful composure. 'Jake, please,' she said, finally being able to build up the strength to stand. 'Let me at least talk to him. Someone needs to make him see sense. He has to see he cannot do this.'

'He has no choice.'

'Of course he has a choice. And I am not going to keep sitting here doing nothing as he does goodness knows what to her.'

'And what else is he supposed to do, Alisha? How can he turn his back on this?'

'There will be other ways. Fair ways. Right ways.'

'There is no fair and right when it comes to our kind. They're not all like you, Alisha. They don't see with your eyes. I'm sorry, okay? I wish there was another way. This isn't easy for him, Alisha.' He looked across at her. 'Don't for one minute think it is. It may be quiet, it may be low-key, but there is an epic battle going on inside him. There may not be swords and flames and fights, but it's tearing him apart.'

Her heart throbbed. 'You make it sound like he doesn't want to do this.' She stepped closer. 'Jake, we need to go and talk to him. If he's hesitating just a little—'

'I've tried, okay?'

'Then try again.' She caught hold of his arm. 'Jake,' she said firmly.

He turned to face her. 'This has to be his decision.'

'Then at least let me talk to Leila.'

'And do you think it'll make it easier for her seeing how upset you are?'

'If you care anything for me, if you have even an ounce of gratitude for what my sister has done for you, you will not let her face this on her own. You owe me. You owe us both.'

He held her gaze for a moment. But then he stepped past her. 'I can't.'

She spun to face him. 'Then do it for Caleb. Do you seriously think she'll go down without a fight?'

'There's nothing she can do.'

'Have you learned nothing? Are you really as arrogant as your brother? You have left him alone, wherever he is, with a serryn who is fighting for her life, let alone the life of her sisters. Trust me,' she said, stepping back up to him. 'You haven't seen anything of what my sister is capable of until you corner her.'

Jake's troubled gaze snapped to hers. 'Is she planning something? Did she say something to you?'

It was a way in. An off-the-cuff remark in irritation had finally captured Jake's attention.

Alisha folded her arms. 'I did warn you, Jake. That first night I warned you that the longer you keep her here the more trouble there will be.'

'No, Alisha,' he said firmly. 'No games. What's she up to?'

'Take me to her.'

'Tell me what you meant.'

'Take me to her, or you'll regret it.'

Jake raked her swiftly with his gaze before turning his back on her again. 'No. I'm not going to fall for this.'

'You're a fool to let this go ahead, Jake.'

He braced his arms on the window frame again and stared out, the agitation clear in his face, his stance.

'Please,' Alisha said. She ducked under his arm to slip between him and the window.

Jake pulled away instantly but she caught him by the upper arm, her fingers digging in deep.

'We can stop this, Jake. Or at least delay it. If he's hesitating now after only a couple of days, think of what a few more days will do. Leila might even start to feel something for him, and if she does, none of this will be an issue anyway.'

Jake's gaze snapped across his shoulder to meet hers. 'What do you mean by that?'

It had slipped out without her thinking, but it had seemed to be such an obvious thing to say in her desperation. Implausible but possible. The look in his eyes unsettled her – but whatever she had said had also unsettled him.

He turned to face her fully. 'Alisha? What did you mean?'

'I mean if she's not a serryn anymore, he won't have to kill her.'

Jake's eyes narrowed. 'What are you talking about?'

'You don't know, do you?'

'Know what?'

'It's the ultimate serryn taboo. Falling for a vampire. It means she'll lose it.'

'She told you this?'

'No – Sophie did.'

His eyes flared in confusion. 'Sophie?'

'I know you know what Sophie's involved in.'

'You'd better tell me that's nothing to do with you.'

'Of course not. I tried to talk her out of it, but she was obsessed. She blames all your kind for what happened to Mum. She hates the authorities just as much – convinced they covered it up. She never used to talk to Leila about it but she used to talk to me. Leila would clam up – at least now I know why. But Sophie didn't come here just hunting vampires. What she was really looking for was a serryn. And she guessed the best place to find one was the heart of Blackthorn.'

'What did she want a serryn for?'

'What do you think? She resolved that if she could get one on side, she'd win this war against you. Of course, she never knew about Leila. And Leila never knew what she was up to.'

'You're still not explaining what you meant.'

'In the end there was nothing Sophie didn't know about serryns. She uncovered all sorts. And she used to tell me things. It's one of their biggest secrets apparently. I don't know how she found out, but she did. Committing suicide or committing the sacrilege of falling for their enemy, the punishment is the same – a serryn loses her serrynity and it jumps to the next in line.'

Jake took a step back and raked her warily. 'You're lying. Even suggesting the possibility would put you and Sophie in the firing line.'

'Sophie's not here. She might not even be alive. As for me, what do I care anymore? I'm not saying she's fallen for him, Jake; I'm saying there's the possibility that she *can*. It's only been a couple of days, but—'

'But what?' Jake asked.

Alisha stared back up at him.

'Alisha?'

'In the club,' she said, the recollections seeping back. 'She told me to drink your blood.'

'So?'

'You can't be a serryn with sullied blood. It doesn't make you lose it but it stops it passing to you. I remember Sophie talking about that, too. Families used to do it decades ago – sully the blood of the sisters of a serryn to protect them. It can't be done now, of course – not with all the blood tests, all the stringencies to stop feeders crossing borders. She must have been desperate to tell me to do it. Either she's planning to end her life or…' Her gaze snapped back to Jake. She frowned. 'Jake, if she's got even an inkling, why the hell hasn't she told him?'

'I know why,' he said, his eyes flaring in panic as he pushed past her on the way to the door.

'Jake!' She rushed after him, but he had already slammed the door. 'Jake!' she said again, slamming her fist against the wood.

And kicked the door for good measure.

Chapter Twenty-nine

Leila pulled back on his hand as she reached the bottom step.

'At least do one thing for me,' she said, no longer able to bite back the treacherous words. 'Be with me once more.'

Caleb turned to face her, his eyes locking on hers.

She tried to steady her breathing and ignore the pounding in her ears. 'Not as the Tryan or the serryn, just me and you.'

'And why would you want that?' he asked, his eyes narrowing slightly.

Her pulse raced, but she still closed the gap between them. 'You're not worried you'll fall at the last hurdle, are you?'

'It won't change my mind, Leila.'

'I know.'

He didn't touch her as she dared to inch closer, her eyes almost level with his with the help of the step she stood on. She hesitated millimetres away, until her mouth met his.

She treacherously parted his lips – cool, firm lips that responded easily. She momentarily lingered, tasting him before easing her tongue inside to meet his. She reached up to cup his jaw as she dared to caress his teeth, finding his incisor, feeling its lethality against her tongue.

She slowly pulled back a little, her vision hazy for a moment until she retracted enough to be able to look at him.

But she couldn't afford to let herself think. For once she couldn't stop to think what she was doing.

And she didn't want to.

She needed to focus only on it being her last time with him.

She closed the gap again, her hand sliding up his arm to his shoulder.

Caleb took her hands in his, interlacing their fingers as he held them up either side of her shoulders.

She winced as he bent them back slightly, enough to make her catch her breath but not enough to cause her any serious pain.

'You're playing a dangerous game,' he said against her lips. 'An out-of-character dangerous game. Why would you even contemplate giving yourself to me right now?'

'I don't want to think about why,' she said. 'I don't want to think at all. And you're scared of doing the same, aren't you? You're scared of letting your guard down. That's the real reason you're in a hurry – you're scared you'll change your mind. That's why you walked away in the shower. You're frightened to be yourself with me. But here I am – unafraid of being myself with you. I'm not out of character. I'm just not scared anymore. I've lived most of my life in fear of your kind. I'm not going to live my last moments that way.'

He pushed back a little on her hands, enough to make her catch her breath again as he stared pensively, dangerously deep, into her eyes.

The rain pummelled against the roof, washing down the glass.

'Is it so unbelievable that I would want to be with you, Caleb? Do you think that little of yourself?'

'Maybe it's because I think more of you.'

'Too much to do this?' she asked.

He stared at her for so long that she was sure he was going to pull away. Instead he leaned in to kiss her, applying just enough pressure as he parted her lips to make heat rush to her abdomen.

And she kissed him back – not just because she had to, but because she wanted to. Even that last kiss, as deceitful as it was, was better than the coldness that had formed between them. She needed his closeness. She needed the comfort. She needed the distraction.

And as he let go of her hands, she didn't fight the instinct to run her hands up his shoulders, the back of his neck, through his hair. And she felt confident enough not to panic when his hands slid to her behind, encouraging her tighter against him, hunger sparking in his kiss as he lifted her thighs around him, pulling her around and onto the bed.

He pushed her hair gently back from her shoulder to expose her neck, the coolness of his fingers, the lingering of his touch making her shudder as she gazed up into his eyes, eyes that she could have sworn almost had a glint of sorrow in them.

But, like he'd said, how he felt didn't matter.

It didn't matter how either of them felt.

He kissed her tenderly, breaking her heart more, goosebumps swamping her at the sensuality of his kiss.

She knew she couldn't back down, even as he brushed his thumb over her trembling lips before kissing her softly again, lingeringly, cupping the nape of her neck as he delved in deeper, knowing both their kisses were the worst betrayal of all.

And as he lowered her onto the bed, she kept her legs wrapped around him – around her perfect vampire who ignited feelings beyond logic. But her feelings for Caleb had never been about logic.

She slid her hands to his behind as she pushed her groin against his to entice him further.

Her head buzzed again, like when she'd first arrived in Blackthorn, when she'd sensed, right from the outset, her own doomed fate, just by being there.

Her survival instinct screamed at her to stop, to tell him how she felt in one last-ditch attempt to save them both. To trust him enough that he would owe her for saving his life as well as his brother's, and save her sisters in return.

Or ring the death knoll for them both. For humankind.

She slid her hands between them and unbuttoned his shirt, sliding it down over his smooth, hard shoulders.

He yanked it off the rest of the way for her, meeting her gaze momentarily.

His lips met hers again, tingles shooting down her spine and fingertips as she gripped his hair tighter at his neck – silky to the touch, just like his cool, flawless skin as she traced her hands down, reaching the small of his back, feeling his muscles rippling beneath her hands as he kissed down her neck, her cleavage.

The hunger in his kisses increased as he started to push himself against her, building a rhythm that had become so natural between them.

Sliding her hands to his hips, along the waistband of his trousers, she unfastened the first button, slid his zip down.

He didn't protest as he kissed back up her neck to her ear, taking her lobe in his mouth, sucking gently as he kept working himself against her.

She eased down his shorts, releasing him and taking his hardness in her hand as he gripped her neck, taking her mouth to his again.

And in that moment, she wanted nothing more than to feel him inside her again. She wanted nothing more than to be that close to him. If it was going to end, she wanted it to end with him. And she needed to show him how she felt, even if she couldn't tell him.

She guided his erection toward her sex, tilting herself up to meet him as she tightened her grip around his hips, slid her thighs higher so that she held his waist.

And she slid her mouth to his, kissing him more deeply, more honestly than she had ever dared. And she would keep that kiss as he pushed inside her, her hands on his neck, her thumbs beneath his jaw.

But he pulled his mouth away.

He lifted his head, gazed into her eyes, froze her in the moment, then, with a flash of his incisors, bit deep and hard into her neck.

❀ ❀ ❀

Jake burst into the penthouse, furious that Caleb's phone was switched off. But the balcony doors were open, which meant his brother was definitely around.

'Caleb!'

He knew exactly what Leila was doing. Caleb would be drinking nothing more than a regular witch, a witch whose soul wasn't strong enough for Caleb to consume at the Brink.

It was inspired. It was ingenious. She couldn't kill him one-on-one in combat but she could kill him with a fatal kiss.

And kill herself in the process.

He marched down to his brother's quarters, across the empty library and through the open bedroom door. He stepped into the en suite, saw the red dress sodden on the floor. He turned on his heels and ran back out into the lounge, through to the terrace.

He looked at the open gate and up at the steps ahead. Panic clenched his chest as every instinct told him that if that was where Caleb had taken her, he might already be too late.

❀ ❀ ❀

Leila flinched as the sudden stinging pain stunned her, numbing every other feeling in her body. Instinctively she slammed her hands to his chest, trying to forge some distance, until, knowing it was futile, she clenched her hands until her knuckles were pale. She clutched his arms as he slowly drew her blood, the ache in her neck, the throb of her heart, the pins and needles in her fingers, her toes, overwhelming every other sensation.

This was not supposed to happen. He'd moved too fast, too quick. Leila swallowed hard, her throat dry with pain. She fought back the tears as she braced herself, scrunched her eyes closed.

There was no way she could fight him off. Nothing would make him stop unless she confessed.

But confess and it was all over anyway.

She gritted her teeth as he drew harder and faster, pinning her hip to the bed.

Leila stared up at the bleak Blackthorn sky, trying to distance herself from the vampire who fed mercilessly on her. Trying to distance herself from the feelings tearing at her insides.

But she would not relent. She would not tell him. She would not let her sisters face his fury when he learned the truth. She would not let one of them die in her place.

And if she was wrong about loving him, she would fight him at the Brink, just as she had always been destined to. She could do no more now. No more than accept her fate.

Caleb fed harder, drawing up her blood with ease, his concentration intense as he drew faster.

She breathed heavily. The sickening feeling of her blood being drawn, the physical ache in her heart, the pain in her veins – a pain she thought would make her insides collapse – made her head light as she lost contact with her body. Leila trembled, overwhelmed with pleasure and pain until the two were indistinguishable, a tear escaping the corner of her eye.

The passing days rushed through her mind, interwoven with her grandfather's teachings. The first time she saw Caleb in the lounge. The first time he had held her on the terrace. *"They will deceive you, Leila. Be warned; charm comes easy to them but you must see through the smokescreen."* The look in Caleb's eyes when he gazed down at Jake lying sick on the bed. *"They want to rule us and they will do whatever it takes to make that happen."* Feinith's cold grey eyes. The hope in Caleb's eyes when she began the spell to heal his brother. The first time she saw Caleb being touched by Feinith. *"You have an importance you have yet to understand, but it will become clear."* The first time Caleb had kissed her. The first time he held her gaze long enough for her to detect there was more behind his eyes than what he was willing to show her. *"You are blessed with a gift, Leila, but also a curse. Know it, accept it – and when you have to, use it."* His firm but tender touch when he made love to her. *"If they succeed, the world as we know it shall end."*

Amidst every thought of confusion and doubt, as she hovered near her last breath, it was those recollections that would help her. The moments they had shared. The moments of real intimacy when she'd felt complete for the first time ever.

When, for once, she hadn't felt afraid.

Those were the moments she would take with her.

Along with the agonisingly painful secret Caleb would never know.

She was supposed to kill vampires, not save them. Those were the rules. That was the lore.

Leila fought back her tears as Caleb drew on her harder and faster, dragging her closer and closer to the edge.

Her basic survival instincts pleaded with her to give him one last chance to redeem himself. One last chance to appeal to whatever was left of his humanity. One last chance to prove he could care for her enough.

She parted her lips but the words wouldn't come out.

Love him though she may, she *would* never, *could* never trust him.

Instead she reached for his hand, interlaced her fingers with his and squeezed for all she was worth.

❊ ❊ ❊

Caleb could feel her weakening beneath him. He felt her resistance, but she wouldn't fight. Like a helpless mammal pinned to the floor by its predator, she almost seemed resolute.

Either she had given up hope or she was so confident she could fight him at the Brink, she wanted to get there. Because there they would be equal. At the Brink there would be no question of physical strength or prowess; it would only be the strength of her soul versus his shadow. One would consume the other. Only one would survive. And she must have thought she stood a chance or she would have been fighting him.

He drank harder. He had to. Even amidst the all-consuming taste of her, he could feel something else in him rejecting it – rejecting taking her. Something instinctive was pulling him back and he had a suspicion of what it was. But he couldn't afford to feel that way. He would not let himself feel that way.

In less than two days she was turning him into something he didn't recognise. He was a survivor, always had been, and she was stripping him of it. She had buried deep, seeping her poison into his system, making him see the things she wanted him to see. But not anymore.

He drank harder and faster.

He needed to end it. He needed to end his developing feelings for her. The way she made him feel. He needed to end it there.

He felt the sheen of perspiration in her palm as she grabbed his hand, as she squeezed her fingers between his.

She was fading and she was fading fast.

❋ ❋ ❋

Pain was rife in his chest as Jake bounded up the protruding steps, the rain chilling his face, dampening his shirt.

He'd lost one brother to a serryn – he wouldn't lose another. He couldn't lose another.

It would be all his fault. All of it.

He stumbled up the next set of steps as he took the sharp left up onto the roof. He missed the top step, his knees cracking against concrete, but he was back on his feet a split second later.

He scanned the roof just in case, but he knew where they were.

He lunged at the door, slammed his hand against the glass door in a hope that it would startle his brother into stopping whilst he keyed in the code.

He yanked the door open and burst inside.

He came to an abrupt halt a couple of feet away from the bed.

His attention fell to Leila as she lay on her back, her skin ashen, her limbs limp, her head turned away from him so he couldn't see her face.

Caleb lay next to her, his body lax, one arm above his head as he gazed unflinching up at Blackthorn's sky.

Jake's slow-beating heart pumped hard as his brother remained perfectly still, didn't even look up at him.

His chest ached, only the smattering of the rain disturbing the otherwise deathly silence.

Alisha had been wrong. Over and over he kept saying it in his head. Alisha had been wrong.

It had happened.

Caleb had taken Leila to the Brink and he had won.

His stomach knotted, a sense of fear washing over him. Had his brother even come back the same? Why didn't he look at him? Why didn't he even acknowledge him?

He didn't think he'd do it. Deep down, he didn't think Caleb was capable of doing it. He had seen the way Caleb had looked at Leila. And part of him had hoped Leila would appeal to that part of Caleb he loved so much. That Caleb, more than anyone he knew, who defended those he loved vehemently. A loyalty that couldn't be broken.

'Caleb,' he whispered, almost fearful to say his name.

Maybe he wasn't back yet. Maybe this was how it was whilst they fought at the Brink – suspended animation back in their worlds.

Maybe the battle was still happening.

He crouched down, maintaining a safe distance. 'Caleb?'

And as Caleb's eyes snapped to his, Jake flinched and recoiled.

Chapter Thirty

'You scared the shit out of me, Caleb.' Jake sank onto the steps and rested his head in his hands. 'Fuck,' he hissed. 'My heart's still pounding. I thought it was all over for you. I swear I've never moved so fast in my life. I grazed my knee,' Jake declared, pointing at where his impact with the top of the steps had scuffed his jeans, the blood seeping through. 'When was the last time I grazed anything? When was the last time I fell over?'

Caleb eased up onto his elbows as Jake's attention switched to rolling up his jeans leg to inspect his wound. 'What the hell were you doing tearing up here? I told you to stay away.'

Jake rolled his jeans back down and rested his elbows on his thighs. 'What happened?' he asked, indicating towards Leila, her breathing resounding in the silence.

Caleb sat up more fully and leaned back on his palms. Staring ahead through the glass at the district beyond, he could feel his brother's eyes burning into him. 'I lost focus for a moment. That's all.'

'Lost focus?'

Meeting the scepticism in Jake's eyes, Caleb sighed with impatience and got to his feet.

'You stopped yourself,' Jake said as Caleb turned his back on him to make his way up the steps. 'You pulled back.'

Caleb stopped in front of the glass and gazed out at the darkness.

'You couldn't do it, could you?' Jake added.

He'd been so close – seconds away, where draining just a little more blood would have meant she would have been beyond recovery anyway. Where she would have died in his arms regardless.

But something in the warmth of her body, something in the way she had interlaced her fingers with his had stopped him. Where the prospect of being without her was unbearable enough for him not to care, just for that moment, about the implications.

Something that had warned him losing her would unleash an even greater darkness inside him.

'I had a moment's lapse, that's all. And that's all it's going to be. As soon as she's conscious, I'll finish it.'

'You can't be serious,' Jake said. He hurried around the circumference of the steps to join his brother. 'Caleb, the fact you stopped must tell you something.'

'Yes – that I made a mistake. It was a moment of weakness I will not allow myself again.'

'It was a moment of weakness because you feel something for her.'

'You know me better than that,' he said, looking back ahead.

'Exactly. Better than anyone. So deny it. Deny you feel anything for her.'

Caleb's gaze locked on his brother's, the seconds grating by. 'And what if I do? What am I supposed to do, Jake? Turn my back on everyone out there?' he asked, sweeping his hand towards the window. 'For what? To keep her here? Because I'd have no choice. I can't let her go – not now she knows about me. And I can't keep her in the dungeon or locked in my room for the next fifty years. But that's the life she'd have. I am not losing you to her, Jake. I am not going through with you what I went through with Seth. I will protect you with my last breath. One way or another I am going to lose her. At least this way I get something out of it.' He looked back towards the glass again. 'We all deserve to get something out of it.'

'And what if she feels the same way?' Jake asked. 'What if she feels something for you, Caleb?'

Caleb glanced across at him again. Even hearing it from his lips made him uneasy. 'She's a serryn, Jake.'

'What if she's not?'

The jolt of Caleb's heart was equivalent to being given an electric shock. His gaze snapped back to his brother's.

Jake's eyes fixed on his. For a moment he didn't move. For a moment he didn't say anything. 'It's why I came tearing up here. She might not be a serryn anymore, Caleb. She might have lost it.'

His chest tightened. He stared down at the bed to where she lay before he looked back at Jake. 'What are you talking about?'

'They don't just lose it through suicide, Caleb. It's the ultimate serryn treachery – falling in love with a vampire.'

'Who told you that?'

'Alisha.'

Caleb exhaled curtly, turned back to the windows, his hands low on his hips. 'I've never heard of it. They're stalling.'

But something niggled – something deep and unsettling and uncomfortable.

'Leila wasn't the one who told Alisha, Sophie did,' Jake said. 'She's quite the serryn expert apparently. She isn't just here in Blackthorn to hunt vampires. She wanted a serryn on side and resolved the best place to find one would be the heart of vampire territory. She told Alisha everything she knew, including what happens if serryns commit the ultimate sacrilege.'

Caleb stared at his own reflection. His chest clenched.

Leila had tried to seduce him – first in the shower and then there in that very room. Tried to seduce him once she worked out he wasn't going to back down.

She tried to have sex with him because she *needed* to have sex with him.

Leila loved him.

Or she thought she did. And sex was consummation. The girl had been hedging her bets. She was taking him down whatever it took. She either killed him with her last drop of blood or faced him at the Brink.

And she would have succeeded if the thought of killing her hadn't torn at his heart. The prospect of losing her unthinkable. Of draining the life from her.

Because when he'd felt her slide her fingers through his in those last moments, he knew he couldn't be the one to do it. Whatever the consequences, whatever the fallout, he couldn't forsake her.

And all that time she had prepared to die and had prepared to take him with her.

Her behaviour hadn't been uncharacteristic of her – it had been totally Leila.

'If what you're telling me is true, she just tried to kill me,' Caleb said, dragging his gaze back to his brother.

Jake's eyes widened in shock, then despondency. 'What?'

'She tried to sleep with me, Jake. She wanted to lose it. She wanted to kill me. Does that sound like love to you?'

'You know it's not as simple as that. She had no choice. It was you or her sisters. You or the fate of her entire kind. You put her in an impossible situation without any reason to believe in any other outcome than her dying anyway. You cornered her and she came out fighting the only way she could. Exactly as you would. Don't tell me you don't admire her for that.'

'Clearly *you* do.'

'There's only one thing that would have stopped you doing this and you need to face that. I know what you're thinking, but this is not you letting Seth down, Caleb. This is not you letting me down. If you go ahead, you're never coming back from it and you know it. You kill her, and I will lose you again. And this time it could be for good.'

'She said nothing. She let me bite her and said nothing.'

'You don't believe it, do you? You don't think she's capable of caring for you. You don't believe anyone other than me is capable of caring for you. Get proof. It's too dangerous for you not to now.' He grabbed his brother's arm. 'But Caleb, whatever the outcome of this test, if what you're saying is right, then she *does* feel something for you. And if she has fallen for you despite everything, you need to wake up and see what you've got here. You betray her and you'll never get over it. If there's Leila, there are others. We'll find one. We'll see this through another way.'

'If that test proves she's lost it, the chances are it has jumped to Sophie, or if we're too late, to Alisha. Are you willing to face that?'

'You wouldn't do that to me.'

Caleb held his gaze steadily on his brother. 'And if they're our last chance? Our only chance?'

Jake reached into his pocket as his phone rang. He lifted it to his ear. He looked back at Caleb as he disconnected, his eyes rife with concern. 'It's Hade. Feinith's here. He's bringing her up.'

'Just her?'

'From what he said. You can't let her in here. If she sees Leila like this, your secret's going to be out.'

Caleb looked back down at Leila. 'Maybe not.'

He stepped over to the drinks cabinet and grabbed a tumbler. He stepped back down onto the bed, gazed down at her for a moment as she lay there oblivious, her body open and exposed to him.

He lowered to his knees beside her and reached for one of the roses. He rubbed his thumb back and forth over the thorn as he gazed down at her closed eyes, the slight parting of those delicate lips.

Lifting her wrist with his other hand, he turned it so the soft pale flesh was exposed to him.

He slid the thorn through her skin before reaching for the tumbler, letting the droplets of her warm blood tap silently against the glass base. He sucked the remains from her wrist before sealing the wound.

He handed the tumbler across to his brother. 'Get the test done and let me know as soon as you can,' he said, standing. He stepped away to grab his shirt. He slipped it on and buttoned it up as he made his way up the steps.

'You don't want me to stay?' Jake asked, following behind him.

'We don't have time.'

'Don't make another deal with Feinith, Caleb. Please.'

Caleb adjusted the collar on his shirt. 'You know what you have to do.'

Jake held his gaze for a moment then nodded.

'And Jake,' Caleb said, recapturing his attention as his brother turned to key in the code to the door.

Jake looked across his shoulder. He could almost feel the weight on them.

Caleb said it, against every instinct. 'There's one more thing I want you to do for me.'

Chapter Thirty-one

Caleb stood at the wall, staring out over the district, when he caught a glimpse of Feinith in the corner of his eye.

He looked across his shoulder as she passed the top step, and turned to face her.

'I haven't been up here for a while,' she said, sauntering towards him, giving her hips her usual purposeful sway.

'You're back early.'

She held up a piece of paper. 'There was no point wasting time.'

He hated to admit to himself that he'd almost believed it impossible. 'You got it?'

'Seth's name cleared of both negligence against the Higher Order and cowardice, anything to the contrary eradicated. Signed by Jarin.'

'How did you manage to wangle that one, Feinith?'

She smiled. 'You didn't think I would, did you?' She stepped over towards him. 'But you have no idea how much you owe me, Caleb. The things I had to do for that piece of paper.' She ran her hand down his chest. She indicated the dome. 'What have you got in there?'

'What do you think I've got in there?'

Her smile was slow, broad. 'Well, well. I must admit, I did think it was a bit touch and go for a while. I almost believed she'd worked her charm on you. I guess I should have known better.'

He held out his hand for the paper, but she snatched it back, her grey eyes tauntingly locked on his.

'I want to see her.'

'And you will.' He kept his palm upturned.

She licked her lips before closing the gap between them, held the paper up behind her back. Her large grey eyes were hooded, her full lips curving in a smile as she ran her hand around his neck. 'Say please.'

'Stop playing to an audience, Feinith,' he said. 'You're teasing her.'

Feinith glanced across at the dome then back at him. 'Do you think she's watching?'

'I don't doubt it.'

'Then kiss me.'

'The paper.'

'The kiss.'

As her cool, lifeless lips parted over his with expert precision, he felt nothing.

She pulled back, her lips parted, her eyes hungry. 'You don't need to be jealous of Jarin. It's just the way it has to be. We have so much time to make up for. And it can all start tonight.'

'I'd hold that thought,' he said, turning to the dome. He looked back across his shoulder at her. 'You might want to come with me first.'

❊ ❊ ❊

Leila opened her eyes and stared up at the night sky. The rain had ceased but the residue of the previous downpour still glistened on the glass like a private planetarium.

She lifted her hand to her neck, where it still throbbed and ached from Caleb's bite.

What she was touching was flesh. Warm flesh beneath her cold fingertips.

She sat up abruptly – too abruptly, the blood rush to her head forcing her to lie down for risk of passing out again.

She was alive. She was alive and still in the dome. Her subconscious had recognised it, and now the rest of her was acknowledging it too.

She eased herself onto her elbows more steadily and scanned the room. There was no sign of Caleb. No sign of anything. She moved onto her side, winced as the flexion in her wrist drew her attention to the pain there. She gently eased up into a seated position and examined the wound.

The last thing she remembered was clutching his hand.

Sickness clenched the pit of her stomach.

She'd been wrong about falling for him. He'd bitten and they'd gone to the Brink. They'd gone to the Brink and only she'd made it back. But she'd have a memory of it, surely. Surely there would be something.

She pulled herself onto her knees, taking a moment to gain her balance.

She needed to know where he was. She needed to see him.

Damn it, she needed to know he was okay.

She looked out of the dome, movement on the far side of the roof catching her attention. Three figures.

Caleb. She homed in on him instantly, everyone else fading into insignificance. He was there. Alive.

Alive and with Feinith.

She snapped back a breath, her heart pounding.

He'd taken only enough to make her pass out. She'd made him suspicious. He didn't trust her. He suspected she was up to something. And he'd called Feinith.

She sank back onto her haunches. He'd gathered an audience. He hadn't even started yet. This could still happen.

Caleb walked back towards the dome, his characteristic easy strides unnerving her. Feinith was following behind, her bodyguard behind her.

But Feinith would see the wounds on her neck. Feinith would know Caleb had fed on her. She'd know what he was. Unless he had lied about Feinith knowing. Unless her suspicions had been right.

Her heart pounded harder.

Caleb wanted her to know. And why wouldn't *he*? Why wouldn't he want the power-hungry love of his life to know how much authority he was going to have in his little finger?

And when, if, Leila killed him, Feinith would be stood right by to watch. Feinith would subsequently slaughter her in vengeance.

She recoiled on the bed as the door opened. She froze as Caleb stepped inside, raked her swiftly with his gaze, even a fleeting moment of eye contact sending her pulse racing.

Feinith followed him in, the bodyguard remaining outside.

Her large grey eyes widened as she glowered down at Leila. She took a few steps closer until she was teetering on the top step, looming over her. She narrowed her eyes at the wounds on Leila's neck then her head snapped towards Caleb. 'What's this?'

'What does it look like?'

'You've been feeding her to someone?' She spun to face him. 'I told you she was to be conserved. Not used for your private punishments. Every drop of her blood—'

'I've not fed her to anyone. I did it.'

Feinith stared at him. 'You? That's impossible,' Feinith said. She stared at Leila and back at Caleb. 'You can't.'

'I can if she's not a serryn anymore.'

He knew. Her pulse raced. How the hell did he know? He must have sensed it just like she thought he would. Then what was he playing at?

Feinith's eyes widened then narrowed. 'This is some kind of joke, right? Some kind of game?'

'I'm afraid not. Not this time. She's lost it. Plain and simple. What we have here now is just a regular little witch.'

Feinith's eyes flared. 'Don't be so ridiculous! She can't lose it.'

'Clearly she can.' He folded his arms. 'But that's my fateful charm for you.'

'What are you talking about?'

'You didn't know either? It seems she's committed the ultimate serryn treachery and gone and fallen in love with me.' He shrugged. 'It can happen apparently.'

Leila's blood ran cold.

Feinith frowned. 'But that's ludicrous! She is born to hate our kind just as it is instinctive for us to despise hers. A serryn cannot feel such a way for one of us. Any more than we can feel anything for one of them. It has never been and it never shall be.'

'Maybe you'd like a demonstration?' Caleb asked, glancing across his shoulder at her as he strolled down the steps towards her.

And he winked at Leila. His back to Feinith, he actually winked at her. Her heart skipped a beat.

Caleb lowered onto his knees behind her, took her wrists in his hands, joining them together before holding them in front of her, one hand keeping both her wrists together. 'Is it really so hard to believe, Feinith?' he asked, as he brushed the hair back from Leila's face, tucking it tenderly behind her ear.

He cupped her chin, tilting her head back against his shoulder.

She winced as he scraped his incisors down her throat, just enough to make her bleed so he could lick it away.

'She's delectably sweet,' he said, looking back up at Feinith. 'You should try some.'

Feinith's eyes widened then narrowed in a glare on Leila. 'You stupid little bitch,' she hissed, taking a step towards her.

'Take it easy, Feinith,' he said, standing again and blocking her way. 'You're not going to blame the girl for falling for me, are you? Not you of all people. You should understand it better than most.'

Feinith's glare narrowed. 'You did this on purpose! You made her fall for you to do this to me!'

'It's always about you, isn't it, Feinith?'

She scowled. 'Then tell me, Caleb,' she said, her voice laced with resentment. 'Are the feelings mutual?'

Leila's attention snapped to Caleb as a hint of a smile reached not only his lips but his eyes too.

Feinith exhaled curtly and moved to step past him. 'I'm taking her with me.'

He moved in front of her. 'No, you're not.'

Feinith's glare locked on his. 'Yes, I am. And I want her name, Caleb. Her full name.' She looked across her shoulder, her grey eyes locking on Leila again. 'Have you got sisters, sweetie? Because if you have, I'm going to find them.'

Leila's instinct was to retaliate but she knew she couldn't. She couldn't give any indication of the truth.

'Walk away, Feinith,' Caleb said, his tone mesmerizingly calm, controlled. 'Like this never happened. You never saw her. You know nothing about her. And you're going to stay away. Because if you threaten my brother, my business or me ever again, you utter one word of any of this to anyone, and I will have images of our very intimate, very sordid, very depraved moments that I've filmed over the years on every fifty-foot-high screen this district has to offer. Then your constituents, Jarin, the whole fucking Higher Order can see exactly what they're dealing with. They will know of every last one of your darkest most depraved desires, let alone you handing over Seth's redemption to your lover. I finish you in this locale, Feinith.'

Her scowl deepened. 'You have no such recordings. You're lying.'

'I can give you copies if you want. They make for very interesting viewing. Share them with Jarin. He might learn a thing or two about what makes you *really* tick.'

Her eyes flared in fury. 'You wouldn't dare.'

'Come on now, Feinith.' He smirked. 'All those nights we've spent together, all we have done together and you still don't know me. You've always been too busy noticing yourself, haven't you? Open your eyes and for the first time see what you're up against. And listen to me when I advise you to get yourself as far away from me as possible. Because if you don't, I promise you, I will be the one to bring you down. And you don't want me as an enemy, Feinith. You really don't.'

Her lips trembled with fury as she kept her glare firmly fixed on his. 'You could have it all.'

'I don't want it all.' He raked her dismissively with his gaze. 'And I sure don't want you.'

Her eyes blazed with indignation, her lips pressed tight together. 'You're making a mistake,' she said through gritted teeth.

'No bigger than the one I'm looking at,' Caleb said. He stepped back over to the door, keyed in the code and opened it.

She glowered down at Leila, back at Caleb then spun on her heels, storming out of the room.

Caleb closed the door before turning to face Leila again. His green eyes were troublingly unreadable. And as he loomed on the top step, tension gripped her chest to the point she thought it would snap.

Feinith was one problem he had sorted.

Every instinct told her she was next.

Chapter Thirty-two

Feinith slumped into the back of the car. She dug her nails into the black leather seat, her scowl rebounding off the blackened-glass divide between her and her bodyguard.

She looked at her assistant's reflection, could feel her expectant gaze boring into her.

'I'm assuming it didn't go according to plan?' Hess remarked.

Feinith glowered into Hess's expectant blue eyes before staring back at her own reflection.

'Has he made further demands?' Hess asked.

'No.'

'So what happened?'

'Caleb Dehain fucked with the wrong Higher Order vampire, that's what happened.'

'He's refusing to hand her over?'

'Worse,' Feinith remarked and met Hess's troubled gaze. 'She lost it. The stupid little bitch lost it.'

'Lost it? What do you mean she lost it?'

'What do you think I mean? How many ways would you like me to say it?'

'You're sure?'

Feinith raised her eyebrows, just on the cusp of using Hess as the punchbag she needed right then. And she might have if the woman hadn't been so talented, so effective, so irreplaceable.

'How is that even possible?' Hess asked.

'It doesn't matter. What matters is finding out if there's more of them.'

'We know there isn't.'

'I meant of her. Sisters, Hess. I need to know if she has sisters. Because taken from her reaction when I mentioned it, I'd say she does.'

'Give me her name and I'll hack into the population records.'

'I don't have a name. But she's not from here – that much is obvious, so she's crossed a border somewhere.'

'You want me to check the records?'

'I want her name. I want where she's from. I want to know everything there is to know about her family.'

'Onto it,' Hess said, flipping open her laptop.

Feinith leaned forward and banged on the glass for her bodyguard to pull out of the alley. She sank back in her seat. 'Please tell me we at least have *some* news on Kane Malloy.'

Hess shook her head. 'He's still underground somewhere.'

'Blackthorn is not a big enough place for me to start losing my temper over this, Hess.'

'I've got the best on it. It's just not so easy when we're trying to keep things low-key. And this is Kane we're talking about. But we'll find him. If not him, Caitlin Parish should prove a hell of a lot easier. There are ways and means to everyone, as you well know.'

'Exactly. I want you to book me a pass to the penitentiary.'

Hess's attention snapped back to her. 'I thought you were going to give Carter some space for a few weeks until everything dies down?'

'Needs must, Hess. He's no good to me locked in there.' She ran her nails lightly over the leather seat. 'And get me one to see that Rob as well. There's something about that one,' she declared with a smirk, her mood lifting slightly for a moment. 'Something in his eyes.'

'Are you sure that's wise?'

'It's pointless being a part of the Diplomatic Unity if you can't twist its purposes to your own ends, Hess. Anyway, if Kane won't respond to my summons, he's going to learn the hard way how I expect things to be done.' She looked over her shoulder at the club. 'Besides, there's nothing like a bit of alpha-baiting to ruffle things up, and something tells me the delectable Kane Malloy is going to be of even more use to me than I first thought.'

Chapter Thirty-three

Caleb sat down on the top step, his phone held against his mouth, his green eyes penetrating hers from across the bed.

'At least now I know what the seduction was about,' he said. 'You needed consummation to finalise it, right? Proper little Black Widow, aren't you?'

'How did you find out?'

'Jake told me.'

'How did he know?'

'It sounds like you're not the only librarian in your family. It seems that on Sophia's quest for vengeance, she decided a serryn would be the ultimate tool for The Alliance. Subsequently it appears Sophia knows just as much about serryns as her big sister does – except the fact she was one. Very ironic considering her mission. Alisha knew all about it. Apparently those two used to talk a lot.'

Leila felt a stab in her chest, the consequences of her secrecy slicing through her. She also wondered if that was what Alisha had been on the cusp of confessing to down in the club before they'd been separated. 'How long have you known about me?'

'Not before I bit you obviously. I may be many things, but suicidal isn't one of them. I wouldn't have known at all if Jake hadn't come tearing up here to tell me. Alisha had let it slip whilst pleaing with him.'

'Then it seems you owe Alisha for saving your life as well as saving Jake's,' she said. 'That had better count for something.'

'She didn't save my life.'

'She did. You said she sent Jake up here to stop you.'

'I'd already stopped.'

Her pulse raced. Her heart pounded painfully. She held his gaze, but she didn't dare utter the thoughts in her head. She'd had it thrown back in her face too many times to swallow her pride again.

'It's a shame you didn't try to do the same instead of resorting to underhand tactics,' he added. 'Then maybe the outcome could have been different.'

'I'd already be dead, you mean.'

He almost smiled. 'Could your opinion of me be any lower?'

'So what now?'

'Feinith won't let this lie, despite the warning I gave her. You won't be safe anywhere. Anywhere but with me.'

'So I may as well give up now – is that what you're saying?'

'You don't give up,' he said, a hint of infuriatingly easy nonchalance in his eyes. 'You never do. You could have stopped me, told me how you felt, instead of trying to kill me. All you've done is finally prove that, in the end, I was right all along.'

'That's not fair.'

'No?'

'I know how I feel about you and yet I still couldn't turn my back on what I was supposed to do, so how do you expect me to believe that *you* could?'

'Because you're so much better than me, aren't you?'

'I never said that.'

'So what are you saying?'

'I'm saying I gave you every reason I possibly could to stop this and still it wasn't enough.'

'You could have told me how you felt.'

'Like you said, what difference would it make?'

He lowered his gaze for a moment before looking back at her. 'I had a split second to make the decision before I reached the point where you'd never return. The point where I'd have no choice but to kill you one way or another. So unless you have lost it and I sensed it, my guess is I was feeling something for you that I shouldn't have. But I can assure you that's been fast rectified by the fact you tried to kill me.'

She glanced at the phone. 'So there's no guessing what call you're awaiting. Why this is on my wrist,' she said, exposing the cut.

'We both need to be sure, Leila, and there's only one way to do that.'

'Full circle, right, Caleb? And what then?'

'I guess the most logical option is that, if you're still a serryn, we finish what we started. If you're not, well, I guess I really need to up that search for Sophia. Whilst keeping Alisha on standby, of course.'

Leila's stomach clenched. 'You can't do that.'

'No? And why's that, Leila? You have a very low opinion of me, remember? I've got to do something to live up to it.' He looked down at his phone before placing it aside. 'Unless we can come to some other arrangement.'

Unease coiled its way through her. 'What kind of arrangement?'

'We consummate now. Before the phone rings. Before we know the outcome.'

She frowned. 'Why?'

'Falling in love is easy, Leila. Trusting not so much. Especially not a vampire, right? Especially not me. A blood test is one way of proving how you feel, but putting your life, let alone the lives of your sisters, in my hands is a whole something else.'

'You've got to be kidding me.'

'We consummate it now, and I'll give you those seven days you requested to show me you were right in what you said – that there's another way. I'll give you seven days to save yourself and your sisters. If you do believe you love me, if there's even a chance you've already lost your serrynity, you know it's the only chance they stand.'

'Or if I'm wrong, I'm knowingly passing on a fate intended for me.'

'I never said it was an easy decision, but I'm giving you the best get-out clause I can. It's up to you whether you take it.' He glanced down at his phone then back at her. 'But that phone could ring at any point, so make your decision quickly.'

As rain smashed against the glass, she stared him down. It was a decision she came to all too quickly, despite the ache in her chest. 'No,' she said. 'I've proved myself enough. Now it's your turn. You want me to trust you? Then give me something to trust you for. I can and I *will* find another way. The question is whether you want to take a punt on me, whether you care about me enough to give me a chance, to give both of us a chance. Or whether you want to take the easy option. *You* make the decision, Caleb.'

After his gaze lingered on hers for a painful few moments, he stood from the steps. He almost smiled, but she couldn't tell if it was out of amusement or irritation. He stepped over to the door, his outline almost a shadow against the amber glow of the distant backdrop.

Leila got unsteadily to her feet. She crossed the bed, avoiding the lethal thorns of the roses. Scooping one up in her hand, she made her way up the steps behind him.

She stopped a few feet away.

'I know you don't trust a word I say,' she said, as she thumbed one of the thorns. 'But I *did* nearly stop you, Caleb. I did nearly tell you the truth. But I couldn't. You once asked me, if I was in your place, what I'd do, and I guess I answered it. Despite how I feel, I was doing exactly the same for my kind as you were for yours. And underneath it all, it's because, no matter how I feel about you, it doesn't make any difference. You've won anyway. One way or another, you'll get what you want and I'll have nothing.'

She looked down at the rose and picked at the thorns on the stem, breaking them off one by one.

'And yet I still love you, you irredeemable, impossible, arrogant bastard. And I hate you for it, but not half as much as I hate myself.

I hate myself for understanding you.' She picked off another. 'I hate myself for seeing something I don't want to see.' And another, casting the thorn aside. 'Something that makes this harder. Because I know what's inside you, Caleb. And you can deny it all you want, but I know the real reason you despise me is because I've made you question yourself. And in that respect, *I've* won.' She picked off the last. 'So do what you want.' She took the steps up towards him. 'Turn your back on me or give us a fighting chance. It all comes down to how much you want to be with me.'

She stopped alongside him, held out the rose for him, the stem now free of all its threat.

'But I will not plead anymore,' she said, as she looked up into his sullen green eyes – eyes that could so easily break her. 'I will not bargain. And I will not give you any more reason than I already have.'

She let the rose go, dropping it to his feet before walking away.

Walked away so he wouldn't see the distress in her eyes, or the way her hands trembled. Instead she strode across the room, gazed out over Blackthorn, her back to him.

It had felt like a lifetime since she had arrived there. The life she led before then now felt like some vague memory – a life before Caleb. Caleb, now tangled in her every waking thought.

She rubbed away a tear of frustration as she waited for the call that would tell her whether she died at his hand or one of her sisters did. She could only hope the blood that pumped through her was serryn blood – the first time ever in her life that she wanted and needed to be one of them.

She felt him approach even before she saw his reflection in the glass, his scent reminding her of intimacies she desperately needed to forget. Goosebumps pooled over her skin, her spine tingling at his proximity.

'That was quite a proclamation,' he said.

She kept her gaze ahead. 'It's the truth. And you know it.'

He stepped alongside her, pushed a few loose strands of hair behind her ear.

She kept her hands clenched by her sides, her bare toes curling against the wooden floor at the gentleness of his touch. She tried to calm her breathing, her heart pounding as he slid the back of his fingers down over her neck.

She dared to look across her shoulder to meet his gaze – eyes that drew her in just as easily as they had the first time she'd looked into them.

He rubbed her tear away. Stepped in front of her. Held up the rose. 'You're supposed to tear the petals off to find out if someone loves you, not the thorns.'

'You're supposed to tell me it's all going to be okay.'

Her heart jolted as he gently ran the back of his hand down her cheek, over her shoulder. 'This is Blackthorn, Leila. Nothing is ever going to be okay here.'

'I think it can be. And you can make that happen, Caleb. We both can. You can make that happen by trusting me.'

He dragged the petals of the rose slowly across her collar bone. 'The ever optimistic world of Leila McKay,' he said.

'Whom you know not to underestimate.'

He dropped the rose onto the sofa behind him, before sliding his hands to her hips, pulling her to him. 'You want me to prove you can trust me? Then don't fight me. Let me do this.'

She frowned with unease as he slid his cool hand around the back of her neck.

But she'd challenged him. She'd demanded it and he had risen to it.

'You're asking too much,' she said.

'And you're not? I will grant you seven days, Leila. I give you my word. If that proclamation was the truth, you'd be a fool not to take this chance – and you know it.'

'So why not just wait for the results? Why do this?'

'You know why.'

And as he pulled her close, right then all she wanted was that moment. If it was all going to end, she needed just that one moment with him: her beautiful green-eyed vampire; her intense, sullen, powerful Caleb. Caleb: the vampire who held her body, heart and soul right in his hands.

He kissed her gently on the neck before tracing his lips back up to hers, slipping both hands into hers to interlace his cool fingers with hers.

She'd pull back, she told herself. If one inkling of doubt took over, she'd pull back. But for that moment, it felt too right.

❋ ❋ ❋

Caleb caressed Leila's lips with his as he pulled her closer. Her warmth was enrapturing. The softness of her body, the ease with which it melded against his own, only made him crave her more.

And this time he'd allow himself to crave her. He slid his mouth down to her slender neck, her pulse beneath his lips bringing the most tortured part of him out. But he would enjoy her. He would make her forget everything. For those moments, it would be only about them. He'd grant them both that.

He lifted her with ease, wrapped her legs around him, and carried her back down onto the bed.

Pulling down his trousers and shorts, he eased into her, just enough to feel the tension ricochet through her body again. It felt just as thrilling – her every reaction playing out on each held or shallow breath.

She had to know how vulnerable she'd made herself and in those moments she didn't seem to care. Something inexplicable had happened between them and he had never felt it more. Something forbidden. Something they fought in equal measure. But more than ever, neither of them could do anything to hide it.

She tensed again as he eased his way inside her completely.

Arousal shot through him, her acceptance pushing him to the edge hard and fast. He instinctively thrust, her nails digging into his neck, her tremor inciting him further.

His need for her was too great to take it steady. Her responses telling him she was aroused enough for him to turn up the momentum.

And at that moment, it was as if every part of him and every part of her was seeping out, intermingling, entwining irrevocably as she instinctively started to relax, allowing him in deeper.

Caleb thrust harder, wanting her to think of nothing but him, of him inside her, being a part of her in an act that was sacrilegious to them both in its intimacy.

Because that's what she was – intensely and intimately his.

He slid his arm beneath the small of her back, encircling her waist as he kept her tight against him, tilting her up slightly to allow himself in deeper, pressing one hand above her head, interlacing their fingers again.

As he felt her hand clench his, he thrust again, her shallow, curt breaths almost too much for him to bear, her nails digging deep into his hand as he lowered his head to her neck again.

He thrust deeper and deeper, her body trembling, a sensual perspiration coating her thighs, her neck, her hips. He tilted her further up to him and thrust again, finally filling her to the hilt, Leila gasping with the force.

He gazed down at her neck, her heart pounding at a powerful rate, her pulse impossible to ignore.

He had to bite her. Never had the desire been greater. Feeding as he sated himself. Sated her. Making her his totally and utterly.

He felt the tension flood his body, every nerve ending burning. He was on the cusp and he knew so was she.

He quickened his pace, escalating in time with the surge through his body.

Leila cried out and shuddered, her muscles tightening around him, her pulsating enough to finally tip him over the edge.

Chapter Thirty-four

Leila lay gazing up at Blackthorn's sky.

The rain beat heavily against the glass again, the droplets glistening against the dark backdrop, an occasional gust of wind smashing a collection against the panes.

Caleb was characteristically silent as he lay beside her. But this time he didn't leave her side. This time he gazed up at Blackthorn's sky with her.

She turned her head to look across at him, his green eyes fixed above, the occasional blink of those dark lashes the only thing that told her he was conscious. Distant sounds of the pending dawn invaded the room, their cocoon, carried on the breeze that now caressed her through the open window above.

She looked back up at the sky. 'How long do you think it'll be before he calls?'

He looked across at her. 'Does it matter now?'

She met his gaze. 'I need to know.'

He pulled himself into a seated position. Leila scanned his taunt, lithe back as he sat there for a moment. Her gaze lingered on the Armun – the first time she'd been able to examine it properly. The symbol that foretold the destruction of everything they knew. The symbol which, unless she could persuade Caleb to find another way, would destroy him too.

He got to his feet and strolled across to the step, flexing his arms and shoulders as he did so.

Leila sat up. Pulled her knees to her chest, wrapped her arms around them as she watched him pick up his phone, his continued silence igniting a stir of unease as he gazed down at the screen.

Her heart pounded. 'Has something come through?'

He strolled back over to meet her. Sitting beside her, facing her, their bent knees side by side, he handed her the phone.

She took it in her hand. Stared down at the screen at the text message from Jake.

She's still a serryn, Caleb.

Her heart thudded as reality of what she had done struck her.

A message from half an hour before.

Her gaze snapped back to his. 'Tell me you didn't know,' she said. 'Tell me you hadn't read this before.'

The unapologetic look in his eyes confirmed her suspicions.

Guilt coiled through her at her stupidity. The fact he could have taken her in place of her sisters seemed a worse betrayal than encouraging her to trust him.

'You tricked me. Why?' she asked. 'Why didn't you just kill me? Why didn't you end this? Why make this harder for us both? Or is it easier killing one of my sisters instead of me?'

'I asked Jake to give Alisha his blood. She's of no use to me.'

'And Sophie?'

'I'll find her. Preferably before Feinith does.'

'And then what?' she asked, trying to suppress her dread. 'You told me I could trust you.'

'And you can. I gave you my word. Seven days, Leila. And I'd say you've got more motivation than you'll ever need to make sure you succeed if I'm still the serryn hunter I once was.'

Seven days that she had pleaded for in the desperation of the moment. Seven days were nowhere near enough time.

'You asked me to give you a chance to find another way,' he said. 'I'm doing exactly what you asked.'

'At a price.'

'You're going to have to go back to Summerton to get what you need. I have to be sure you'll come back to me.'

'So you put a bounty on my sister's head? That puts us right back where we started, Caleb.'

'No,' he said. 'I would have ended your life tonight if we were right back where we started rather than searching for any other way.' He reached out and pushed her hair back behind her ear before tenderly cupping her face. 'I don't know if letting you live is the most selfish or selfless act I've ever committed. I don't know if you'll be my salvation or my damnation, but I can't be without you, Leila.'

As he transfixed her with the solemnity of his gaze, never had she seen him more vulnerable in his sincerity.

'Just don't let me down. This love comes with a risk,' he added 'A risk for both of us. The way I feel about you. You understand that, right?'

Her stomach knotted. She nodded. 'I understand. And don't let me down,' she said. 'You find my sister alive and well and I'll find the alternative.'

A darker, harder, more terrifying alternative if her vague recollections were correct. But he didn't need to know that yet. No one needed to know that yet.

Her chest tightened, her stomach flipping as his eyes narrowed slightly, pensively, as if sensing her unease.

'I'm trusting you, Leila,' he said, sliding his hand around to gently clasp the nape of her neck.

'And I'm trusting you,' she said, holding his gaze

More than she'd ever needed to trust anyone. More than she'd ever dared trust anyone. A common thread they shared that she knew would be the very salvation or damnation that he spoke of.

Because she knew better than anyone there were consequences for breaking the rules. For breaking the lore.

Dire consequences she needed to find her way around.

For all their sakes.

Chapter Thirty-five

Jask descended the narrow, worn, warped slabs into the depths of the derelict ruins. Even over the damp and the mildew, the place reeked of vampires. But he could also smell his own.

His boot steps resounded down the low-ceilinged corridor as he marched ahead. 'They'd better have a damned good reason for being here,' he said, refusing to conceal the annoyance in his tone. If he was close enough to smell the other lycans so clearly, they were close enough to hear him. 'Let alone dragging *me* over to this part of the district.'

'If what they told me is true, I get the feeling it's going to be worth the inconvenience,' Corbin said, keeping up with his strides.

Jask turned the corner.

The two younger lycans stood outside an open doorway, their backs to the wall, their gazes straight ahead like privates in a drill.

As Corbin stepped into the room, Jask stopped square-on in front of them, his glare burning into Samson's grey eyes before searing into Rone's.

Neither dared look up at him. Neither dared speak.

Rone nervously blew his fair hair back from his eyes and spread his feet slightly further apart as he plastered his hands back behind his back.

'You *especially* know better,' he said to him, the youth still unable to meet his gaze.

Rone gave a single nod.

'Jask, you're going to want to see this!' Corbin called out.

Jask crossed the threshold into the dank, stone chamber. The only source of light emanated from the two candles on the cusp of burning out on the wooden table in the centre, hardened wax having rippled down the wine bottles that held them.

He stepped past the table so he could get a clearer view of the figure sat manacled in the far left-hand corner of the room.

Head lowered, her mop of dark hair concealed her face. Her arms were outstretched, her slender wrists roped to rusted hoops on each adjacent wall.

Two vampire bodies lay on the floor in front of her, their contorted faces oozing coagulated blood from their mouths, eyes and ears, their bodies twisted, their limbs stiff and contorted from dying in agony.

He looked back at the female, partially concealed by the shadows.

'Rone said they walked in just as the vampires went in for the feed. The spasms started instantly,' Corbin explained.

Jask stepped up to her, stopping just a foot away. He expected startled eyes at least, but she didn't flinch. She didn't even lift her head.

He lowered to his haunches in front of her.

Still she didn't flinch.

He pushed back her unwashed bobbed hair and gently cupped her jaw to tilt her head so she had to look at him.

Far from the fear and trauma that should have been indicative of her predicament, angry, spirited brown eyes glowered back at him through smudged, smoky-grey eye shadow. Her mask of heavy eye make-up made her look hard, but her pretty features were soft, youthful – mid- to late-twenties at most. And from the way she yanked her jaw from his grip, she was used to looking after herself, or at least prepared to. The cuts and grazes on her cheek and eyebrow, let alone the hint of bruising on her jaw, told him she didn't go down without a fight. But from the ill-fitting black sweatshirt and combat trousers she wore, she certainly hadn't been dressed for the hunt that night. Not for a seductive hunt at least.

He caught hold of her jaw again and pushed her hair back to examine her neck. The bite there was smeared in dry blood. So was her inner arm. 'Most definitely a feast gone wrong,' Jask said. 'For them at least.'

Her bold glare remained locked on his.

'Well, well,' he said. 'Aren't you the interesting one? But I'm no vampire, sweetheart, so that toxic stare doesn't work on me.'

'I know what you are,' she said, her tone laced with as much affront as her glower. 'And I know *who* you are. You're Kane Malloy's pet lycan, right, Jask?'

He couldn't help but smile at her nerve, at the purposeful goad in her tone, despite her insolence instantly grating on his nerves. 'And what's your name, sweetness?'

She raised her eyebrows slightly, her glare unwavering.

'Looks like we've got ourselves a handful,' Corbin said, folding his arms.

'Looks like we've got ourselves a serryn,' Jask remarked. He coaxingly held her gaze. 'But nothing that can't be tamed.'

She snatched back a breath that would have been undetectable to the human ear, her eyes flaring in indignation.

'Oh yes, witch,' he said. 'I know exactly what *you* are, too.' He tilted his head to the side slightly as he tightened the grip on her jaw just enough to let her know who was in charge. 'And you couldn't have turned up at a better time.'

LETTER FROM
LINDSAY J. PRYOR

Dear Reader,

Blood Roses is the second instalment in my Blackthorn series but, for some of you, this may have been your first visit. Whether you're here for the first time or back for more, I really hope you enjoyed Caleb and Leila's story and their revelations about the world of Blackthorn.

I love hearing from readers and can be contacted through my website www.lindsayjpryor.com, or you can follow me on Twitter @lindsayjpryor and Facebook. I can also be found on Goodreads where I am always grateful to read reader reviews.

Blackthorn is a journey into a world fighting for survival but, above all else, it is a love story. Whether for right or wrong, salvation or damnation, the love between each of the couples you meet will play a pivotal role in all their futures.

In *Blood Shadows*, book one in the series, I gave you some insight into the human control behind Blackthorn. Here, in *Blood Roses*, I plunged you a little deeper in the vampire world that exists within its guarded walls. Next, I'll be introducing you to the clandestine lycans.

Jask was first introduced in *Blood Shadows*. He always deserved a story of his own. *Blood Torn* is that story. I hope you look forwards to sharing it with me as much as I am with you. I can guarantee he's going to be a force to be reckoned with.

Lindsay

PS. Read on to get a glimpse of the opening scene from *Blood Torn* - I hope you'll be intrigued!

BLOOD TORN

Chapter One

This was not good. This was not good at all.

Just when she thought the night couldn't have got any worse, Jask Tao walked into the equation.

Sophia glowered into the lycan leader's exquisite azure-blue eyes, his dark lashes a sharp contrast to the untamed fair hair that fell around his defined, stubbled jaw.

'You need to let me go,' she said, as he remained crouched in front of her at eye level, his firm grip on her jaw as unrelenting as his gaze.

'And why would I want to do that?'

It undoubtedly sounded like a ludicrous suggestion, surrounded as she was by four lycans, her outstretched wrists roped to the rusted rings embedded in the dank, subterranean walls. But she said it anyway. 'I'm warning you – you're making a mistake.'

He examined her pensively – those uncompromising eyes betraying his angelic, albeit rugged, appearance. He let go of her jaw and stood up, his candlelit shadow looming on the moss-encased walls of the ruins.

It had been three days since Marid had abducted her – ambushed her. The sleazy vampire knew about The Alliance. And if word was out there about the covert operation, the others were at risk too. She'd already wasted the time Marid had held her hostage, let alone the past three hours she'd been trapped down there since he'd sold her on. She needed to get back to the rest of the group. She needed to warn them.

But more than that, more than anything, she needed to find out what the hell was going on with her two sisters.

She glanced at the two dead vampires lying on the stone-slabbed floor ahead – the vampires that had bartered with Marid over her like she was nothing. Her skin crawled as she thought back to the way they'd grinned conspiratorially at each other as they'd tied her to the wall. And she'd known from the malicious look in their eyes, let alone the conversation they'd had whilst drinking and laughing at the table, they'd planned far more than just a feed.

But they'd seen it coming less than she had.

She'd realised what had happened the minute the shock had subsided. There was only one explanation – only one type of blood that killed a vampire that quickly and that painfully: serryn blood.

She sure hadn't been a serryn before she'd entered that chamber – the leech, Marid, had proven that point. But the evidence spoke for itself – the vampires' bodies now twisted and contorted from biting into her, her blood having imploded every one of their veins. It had taken only seconds for her toxic blood to penetrate their systems.

She knew only too well from her research that only serryns caused that reaction – a rare bloodline of witch long thought extinct. Just as she knew there was only one way anyone not born a serryn would become one – the so-called curse jumping from an older sibling to a younger if one if the former committed either of the two serryn taboos: suicide by their own hand, or falling in love with and consummating it with a vampire. Right then, both seemed as implausible as her big sister Leila being a serryn in the first place.

If the indisputable proof hadn't been plain in front of her, she would have laughed any of the possibilities off. Now she needed to know *exactly* what was going on. Forget The Alliance's rules about no outside contact – this was family. Not only was her little sister, Alisha, in trouble, but now seemingly so was Leila.

Which meant, even more so, that she had no time to waste on lycans.

She glowered back up at Jask.

Feet braced apart, hands low on his lithe hips, she had no doubt his stature was imposing enough when stood eye-to-eye with him. The last thing she needed was her forced submissive position on the floor exacerbating it.

It wasn't helped by the fact she knew more about the uncomfortably good-looking lycan than just his zero-tolerance leadership – he was bad-tempered, temperamental, and fiercely protective of his pack. And – though it was irrelevant it slipped into her mind anyway – rumoured to be proficient in bed. He was certainly well-equipped enough to live up to his reputation – his jeans temptingly fitting those solid thighs, his biceps distractingly taut through his shirt, those rolled-up sleeves exposing well-toned forearms. She lingered over the brown leather straps wrapped around his wrists, matching the ones around his neck, a small platinum pendant nestled in the hollow of his throat.

She glanced at the other lycan beside him: Corbin Saylen – Jask's second in command, with a reputation equally uncompromising. He had a presence all of his own, stood there, arms folded, his grey eyes locked on hers.

But then, when you were one of the minority third species in Blackthorn, you had to have a reputation to survive.

'Get in here and tell me what happened,' Jask demanded, summoning the two lycans from beyond the doorway.

The one she knew to be Rone entered first. On appearance they had to be twenty years younger than Jask – but it was as impossible to tell with lycans as it was with vampires. He and his comrade, Samson, had deliberated over what to do with her for the best part of an hour after gatecrashing the vampire feast gone wrong. They'd paced the room, arguing over whether to just leave her there. Despite having tried to barter with them, she'd seen their faces and that was finally enough for them to relent into calling for backup. Backup being Corbin and, from what she had picked up from overhearing their panicked phone call, and despite their protests, Corbin deciding to inform Jask.

'We were across at the warehouse,' Rone stated. 'We heard the noise she was creating so came out to look. She was putting up a hell of a fight.'

'And then?' Jask asked.

'We saw them bring her down here.'

'And knowing you never interfere in vampire business, you walked away,' Jask added, the disapproval emanating in his eyes.

'We were going to,' Samson said.

'But it was two on one,' Rone interjected. 'They were getting violent with her.'

Jask looked back at Sophia, but she knew he wasn't looking at her – he was examining the evidence of the cuts and grazes on her face. 'The vampires do their thing, we do ours,' he said, looking back at Rone and Samson.

Sophia raised her eyebrows at the indifference in his words. Seemingly his reputation as a heartless bastard was equally justified.

'That's the only way the segregation works and you know it,' he added. 'We have enough to do in protecting our own, without trying to save every helpless victim in this district.'

She nearly protested at the victim remark, but resolved to keep her mouth shut. All that mattered was getting loose.

'We thought she was just a girl,' Rone explained. 'What did she do to them? I've never seen vampires go down that fast. It was all over within minutes.'

'Just be grateful your discovery is sufficient enough to save me ripping into you right now. What were you were doing on this side of the district?'

The two youths glanced nervously at each other.

'We had a deal going,' Rone declared, instantly dropping his gaze to the floor in response to Jask's thunderous glare.

'A deal? With vampires?' he asked, distaste exuding from his tone.

After a moment's hesitation, Rone gave a single nod.

Jask exhaled with exasperation. 'So there's someone who knew you were here?'

'What if they think this was something to do with us?' Samson asked, echoing the line of thought that had no doubt provoked Jask's further irritation with them.

He took two steps towards them. '*This* is why you don't come here. *This* is why you stay in Northern territory. *This* is why we're going to clear up this mess and get you back to the compound so I can deal with you properly.'

He removed something from his back pocket, flicked open a switchblade that glinted in the candlelight as he turned to face her.

Sophia braced herself as he expertly sliced through the ropes that bound her arms to the wall. She barely had time to rub her throbbing wrists or rotate her aching shoulders before he'd grabbed her by the upper arm and tugged her to her feet as if she was weightless.

'Corbin, get her up to the bikes,' he said, shoving her towards him. 'We've spent too long here already.'

She was a little unsteady for a moment, but quickly regained her balance as Corbin wrapped a firm hand around her upper arm.

She refrained from struggling, knowing she stood a hell of a better chance one-on-one against Corbin if Jask and the other two remained distracted for long enough.

As Corbin led her towards the door, Jask stepped over to the table to pick up what was left of a bottle of whisky and the remains of one of the burning candles. It took no imagination to work out *how* he planned to get rid of the bodies, especially all traces of serryn blood.

Corbin tugged her out into the corridor before she could see any more.

His eyes were fixed ahead, his grip on her arm unrelenting as she tried to match her strides to his. His shoulder-length hair blew in the mild breeze as they turned the corner. Tall, broad and with the lithe strength of all lycans, they may have been no match on appearance, but she'd taken down bigger than him.

Just as she'd take Marid down when she caught up with him again. Because she would. And the sharper the object she used to say what she had to say, the better.

The stone corridor seemed endless. She hadn't seen much of it on the way there – she'd spent too long slamming her heels or fists into every available inch of soft flesh on the two vampires who had dared to drag her down there.

The stairwell, when they eventually reached it, was as narrow as she remembered, her knees having scraped against stone as one had held her legs, the other restraining her arms around her as they'd carried her bucking and protesting down there.

Now Corbin pushed her up ahead of him, his size forcing him to be more behind her than next to her, but he didn't let go of her arm.

As soon as she saw moonlight on the steps, she tried to yank her arm from his. 'You're hurting me.'

'Then keep moving.'

'Seriously,' she said, stopping abruptly. 'Just give me a second, okay?' She wrenched her arm from his as she feigned weakness. 'I don't feel too good.' She slid down the wall to collapse onto the steps.

He let go of her just for a second.

It was what she needed.

She snapped her head towards the top of the stairwell and faked a look of shock. As she'd hoped, it was enough to evoke his curiosity – a luxury of a split second when his eyes were averted from her.

With both hands she grabbed his lower leg and yanked with every ounce of strength she had left.

Corbin's startled gaze met hers as he slammed his hands onto either side of the wall to brace himself.

It granted her another split second to slide along to the middle of the step, to pull back her leg before slamming her foot hard into his groin.

He instinctively bent over double and lost balance. He tumbled backwards, but she didn't stop to watch.

She turned and clambered up the remaining steps, her thighs heavy as she struggled to her feet to take the last few steps two at a time.

She heard Corbin's voice echo up the steps behind her – one single call: 'Jask!'

She fell up the last step, her palms scuffing concrete. The dark and barren wasteland loomed ahead – nowhere to hide for at least seventy feet to where the outline of some old factory buildings lay in the distance against the overcast night sky. She had to get to them. Hiding was no use with the lycans' proficient sense of smell, but something would be there that she could use to defend herself. Damn it, the outskirts of the east side of Blackthorn were renowned for their reclusiveness.

Like a runner at the start of a race, she lunged forward, taking off with as much speed as her aching body would allow. She kept her attention firmly on the closest building, the vision in front of her the equivalent of being on the deck of a ship in a storm, her eyes blurring against the cold night air, the terrain rough and uneven beneath her boots.

She told herself not to look over her shoulder, not to dare lose her pace for one moment, but instinct overwhelmed her.

She turned to see an outline closing in on her from maybe only forty feet behind.

Her heart lunged and she ran faster, her throat parched and constricted. She ignored the shooting pains in her chest, the laceration of agony in her side that under any other circumstances would have forced her to stop.

But common sense screamed in her head – she couldn't outrun a lycan even on the best of days. She had to conserve what little energy she had left. She had to take the only chance she could of getting away.

She forced herself to stop despite her instincts urging her to keep running.

She struggled to catch her breath in the few seconds she had as she turned to face Jask coming to a standstill a few feet away.

He clearly hadn't expected her to stop. And, if she had her way, in the last few minutes they were going to have together, he was about to learn a hell of a lot more.

Not least that her refined defence mechanisms evoked only one response to a threat of *any* kind: retaliation.

The dance of amusement in his eyes almost masked the irritation, had the latter not exuded from him so intensely. 'Don't you think you've had enough fights for one night?'

'I'm not going with you,' she said, despite annoyingly ragged breaths.

He raked her swiftly with his gaze. 'So you seem to think.'

'Walk away, Jask, and save yourself the trouble.'

She could have sworn she saw another glint of amusement in his eyes.

'Walk to the shed over there with dignity,' he said, cocking his head over his shoulder. 'And we can forget you tried to run on me.'

'I have a better idea. Go join your puppies and bike it back to your Northern pound. You've got no business being here. And you've got *no* business with me.'

He took a few steps closer. 'I'll let that first comment go, on account of it being a stressful night for you. But as I'm *making* what's in those veins my business, you either be a good girl and do as you're told or I'll be a bad lycan. Your choice.'

The sincerity in his tone, the slight darkening in his eyes, made her stomach jolt and, to her distaste, not just with apprehension. She rolled back her shoulders, preparing herself for battle. 'You've got to get to it first.'

He raised his eyebrows slightly, only this time a smile escaped – a stunning, fleeting smile that ignited those azure eyes and annoyingly only enhanced his handsome face further. He rested his hands back on his hips. 'Seriously?'

It was one mocking look too much.

She closed the gap just enough to lift her leg with lightning speed, less than an inch from making impact with his chest before he moved his foot just as swiftly, swiping her other leg from under her, causing her to hit the floor.

Leaning back on braced arms, she stared up at him; not so much as a hint of a glitch in his composure.

It was a move she'd developed to perfection, and he'd kicked it from her as if it was nothing. His self-assurance riled her as she looked squarely into his unperturbed eyes.

Feeling an alien flush in her cheeks, she moved back slightly to forge some distance before getting to her feet.

She was going to wipe the smug look off his face.

But as she lifted her leg again, he knocked it aside, as he did her right fist and then her left as she tried twice to strike him.

Zach had taught her everything she needed to know about one-on-one combat – if not to take an opponent down completely, then at least long enough to get away.

She paused for only a split second before increasing the on-slaught, hitting out at him with clean and precise moves, only to have him fend them off swiftly and accurately before knocking her leg from under her again.

She fell back down, brushed her hair from her eyes in irritation before glowering up at him.

'You've spent too long fighting vampires, honey,' he said.

The playful challenge in his eyes incensed her. The mocking in his tone, the derision in his eyes, triggered her indignation more.

She knew better than to fight unless she was in complete control of her temper but this was now just as much about pride as escaping. Instead of taking the moment she needed, she got back to her feet.

She picked up pace, using every move she had been taught in quick succession, catching him several times but never with enough force or at the right angle to make any impact.

'Are you scared to fight me?' she demanded, frustrated by his purely defensive moves.

'You want to exhaust yourself, you go ahead.'

She sped up, increasing the speed of her moves, adrenaline pumping as she went at him harder. He missed a couple of her shots, allowing her to make impact with his chest and knee, but it was nowhere near enough to take him down. She knew she was being less precise, fuelled by her anger rather than tactics.

And this time, when he kicked her legs from under her, he purposefully went down on top of her.

She lifted her knees nimbly against her chest ready to use the remaining strength in her thighs as leverage to force him off her, but he instantly closed the gap. He forced her thighs to part either side of his hips, spreading her legs further with the power of his, locking her ankles down to the ground with his own at the same time as pinning her arms to the ground either side of her head.

Despite the futility, she tried to writhe and buck beneath him, but not one inch of his hard, tensed body was moveable.

Gasping, she let the back of her head hit the ground, panting as she looked up into his eyes, every inch of her resounding in umbrage at her helplessness.

'Done?' he asked, the calm in his eyes infuriating her as much as the effortlessness with which he held her to the floor.

She tightened her hands into fists. 'Get off me,' she all but growled.

'Are you *done?*' he repeated, his tone taking on an impatient edge that escalated her agitation.

She defiantly held his gaze, feeling every inch of the power behind his body, the heat emanating between them. As he watched her a little too intently for comfort, mesmerising her with his quiet confidence, she felt another unfamiliar stirring. 'If it means you'll get those feral hands off me, yes, I'm done.'

She grudgingly stilled as she awaited his response; gazed at the masculine lips that hovered inches from hers before looking back into his eyes.

He lowered himself a few inches, his biceps straining distractedly against his shirt. 'Vampires might bite, honey, but lycans tear. You might want to bear that in mind next time you try and take me on.'

With only another moment's linger on her gaze, he released her wrists, eased off her, grabbing her arm to pull her to her feet along with him.

'You don't know what you've got yourself into,' she declared, unable to suppress her indignation.

'You can tell me all about it back at the compound,' he said, only to hoist her up over his shoulder.

Her cheeks flushed from the blood rushing to her head, let alone the humiliation. 'Put me down!' she demanded, slamming a fist into his back as she tried to kick at his groin.

Her retaliation only evoked him to hold her tighter though, her clenched fist barely having any impact on his solid back.

She glowered down at the ground that swayed beneath her, forced her elbows into his back to regain some kind of control, but they reached the shed in no time.

He slid her down onto her feet, catching her forearm as she stumbled with the motion.

Rone and Samson were already helmeted up and astride their motorbikes in the far corner.

Corbin stood in front of the two nearer by, his arms folded as he smirked in amusement at Jask. 'She's going to be a lot of trouble. Are you sure she's worth the effort?'

'You know me – I love a challenge,' Jask said, tugging her over to the nearest motorbike. He unhooked something from the seat, and turned to clasp one cuff of the handcuffs over her right wrist.

He lifted the helmet off the seat and shoved it on her head, before guiding her astride his motorbike. Sitting in front of her, he pulled her other wrist around his taut waist, cuffing both of hers together at his lap, the position forcing her intimately against his back.

She clenched her hands and fought against leaning against him. But she was given no other option as Jask revved the engine.

Sophia quickly found somewhere to rest her feet and braced herself just as they sped off, kicking up dust behind them.

Printed in Great Britain
by Amazon